Black Beauty
and
Thirteen Other
Horse Stories

Black Beauty
and
Thirteen Other
Horse Stories

Edited by
Paul J. Horowitz
and
Lily Owens

AVENEL BOOKS

New York

This 1980 edition is published by Avenel Books,
distributed by Crown Publishers, Inc.,
225 Park Avenue South,
New York, New York 10003

Printed and Bound in the United States of America

Library of Congress Cataloging in Publication Data
Main entry under title:

Black Beauty and thirteen other horse stories.

    SUMMARY: Fourteen horse stories, including the complete novel *Black Beauty,* a selection from "The Red Pony," and many short stories by famous authors.
    1. Horses—Legends and stories. 2. Children's stories. [1. Horses—Fiction. 2. Short stories]
I. Horowitz, Paul J. II. Owens, Lily.
PZ10.3.B5625   [Fic]   80-19112
ISBN 0-517-32104-1

n   m   l   k   j   i   h   g

Contents

INTRODUCTION

EVER since man domesticated the wild but gentle ancestors of modern-day horses, the horse has been his faithful companion and helpmate. If some have not received this gift with the gratitude due it, others have, throughout the centuries, honored the horse in folklore and mythology, painting, poem, and song. Praised for his intelligence, strength, and beauty, the horse is the most valuable and enchanting animal that humans have tamed.

Anyone who has lived with horses knows their sensitivity and intelligence. Yet it would be as mistaken to endow a horse with human characteristics as it would be to stingily restrict the qualities of character and subtle personality to human beings. In the stories presented here, horses are depicted in their full variety and color. Yet horses remain horses, although Anna Sewell has ventured to express a horse's thoughts and emotions. To have Black Beauty narrate his own tale was a persuasive way of generating empathy and sympathy for the horse, and the grace with which she did it still charms readers a near-century later. As the editor of the 1898 edition remarked: "Somebody must write a book which shall be as widely read as *Uncle Tom's Cabin*, and shall have as widespread and powerful influence in abolishing cruelty to horses, as *Uncle Tom's Cabin* had on the abolition of human slavery." That book, he concluded, was *Black*

Beauty, and it is this story that sets the tone for our collection. Whether wild horses are tamed, or tamed horses run free, all desire to be treated with the respect and consideration due them, and this theme runs throughout all the stories here.

Whether the story is of the hunt or the racetrack, the Western ranch or the farm, the quiet life of small towns, or the high life of cities, the horse enlivens the tale; he is the true hero. Rather than group the stories by theme or setting, these are intermingled throughout the book—a raucous cowboy yarn follows an ancient Greek myth and precedes the tale of a beloved streetcar horse. This allows the reader to find his own pace in the stories, and the change of mood may be refreshing.

The text of *Black Beauty* is a reproduction of the 1898 edition, complete with its charming graphic decorations, and has been chosen because it is the finest Victorian edition currently available.

Among the authors, Nathaniel Hawthorne, Arthur Conan Doyle, Mark Twain, and John Steinbeck need no introduction. Others may be well known in other fields or literary genres, but as yet unknown to the fiction reader of today. For instance, Richard Harding Davis, a popular novelist, playwright, and journalist at the turn of the century, was a handsome and successful man-about-town, much like the amused young hero of "Mr. Travers's First Hunt." In fact, he became Charles D. Gibson's model for the dashing escort of his famous "Gibson girl."

Ernest Thompson Seton—a famous children's writer who illustrated his own books—reported that the story of "The Pacing Mustang" was true, except the ending; for, although he knew the mustang died soon after his capture, the manner of his death was unknown. Seton lived most of his life on the plains of Western Canada and the United States; thus his knowledge of horses and horse people comes firsthand. He was also a founder of the Boy Scouts of America.

George Grinnel, author of "The Dun Horse" and many other short stories and novels, was a naturalist and conservationist who founded The Audubon Society. The American author David Gray, best known as a playwright and diplomat, was Minister to Ireland in the 1940s.

Lively, witty, or lovingly detailed, the illustrations also show us the spirit and individuality of the horse. A number of the book's illustrations are by Frederic Remington, the American artist renowned for his dramatic, skillful renderings of the Old West. Sidney Paget, who illustrated "Silver Blaze," had been mistakenly commissioned by the *Strand* magazine to portray the Holmes adventures; the *Strand* had, in fact, originally meant to contact his brother, Walter, who was already a well-known illustrator. Nevertheless, Sidney Paget's characterizations of Holmes and Watson—over 350 of them were published—became the standard for all subsequent Holmes illustrators. Other illustrations you will find here are by artists known and unknown. Together they reveal the horse in all his moods and forms; most of all, they delight and entertain us.

LILY OWENS

BLACK BEAUTY

by Anna Sewell

BLACK BEAUTY

PART I

CHAPTER I

MY EARLY HOME

THE first place that I can well remember was a large pleasant meadow with a pond of clear water in it. Some shady trees leaned over it, and rushes and water-lilies grew at the deep end. Over the hedge on one side we looked into a ploughed field, and on the other we looked over a gate at our master's house, which stood by the road-side; at the top of the meadow was a grove of fir trees, and at the bottom a running brook overhung by a steep bank.

Whilst I was young, I lived upon my mother's milk, as I could not eat grass. In the daytime I ran by her side, and at night I lay down close by her. When it was hot, we used to stand by the pond in the shade of the trees, and when it was cold, we had a nice warm shed near the grove.

As soon as I was old enough to eat grass, my mother used to go out to work in the daytime, and come back in the evening.

There were six young colts in the meadow besides me; they were older than I was; some were
nearly as large as grown-up horses. I used to run
with them, and had great fun; we used to gallop all
together round and round the field as hard as we
could go. Sometimes we had rather rough play,
for they would frequently bite and kick as well as
gallop.

One day, when there was a good deal of kicking,
my mother whinnied to me to come to her, and then
she said, —

"I wish you to pay attention to what I am going
to say to you. The colts who live here are very
good colts, but they are cart-horse colts, and of
course they have not learned manners. You have
been well-bred and well-born; your father has a
great name in these parts, and your grandfather
won the cup two years at the Newmarket races;
your grandmother had the sweetest temper of any
horse I ever knew, and I think you have never seen
me kick or bite. I hope you will grow up gentle
and good, and never learn bad ways; do your work
with a good will, lift your feet up well when you
trot, and never bite or kick even in play."

I have never forgotten my mother's advice; I
knew she was a wise old horse, and our master
thought a great deal of her. Her name was Duchess,
but he often called her Pet.

Our master was a good, kind man. He gave us
good food, good lodging, and kind words; he spoke
as kindly to us as he did to his little children. We
were all fond of him, and my mother loved him very

"In the daytime I ran by her side." (page 9)

We would greet our master at the gate. (page 11)

much. When she saw him at the gate, she would neigh with joy, and trot up to him. He would pat and stroke her and say, "Well, old Pet, and how is your little Darkie?" I was a dull black, so he called me Darkie; then he would give me a piece of bread, which was very good, and sometimes he brought a carrot for my mother. All the horses would come to him, but I think we were his favorites. My mother always took him to the town on a market day in a light gig.

There was a ploughboy, Dick, who sometimes came into our field to pluck blackberries from the hedge. When he had eaten all he wanted, he would have, what he called, fun with the colts, throwing stones and sticks at them to make them gallop. We did not much mind him, for we could gallop off; but sometimes a stone would hit and hurt us.

One day he was at this game, and did not know that the master was in the next field; but he was there, watching what was going on; over the hedge he jumped in a snap, and catching Dick by the arm, he gave him such a box on the ear as made him roar with the pain and surprise. As soon as we saw the master, we trotted up nearer to see what went on.

"Bad boy!" he said, "bad boy! to chase the colts. This is not the first time, nor the second, but it shall be the last. There — take your money and go home; I shall not want you on my farm again." So we never saw Dick any more. Old Daniel, the man who looked after the horses, was just as gentle as our master, so we were well off.

CHAPTER II

THE HUNT

BEFORE I was two years old, a circumstance happened which I have never forgotten. It was early in the spring; there had been a little frost in the night, and a light mist still hung over the woods and meadows. I and the other colts were feeding at the lower part of the field when we heard, quite in the distance, what sounded like the cry of dogs. The oldest of the colts raised his head, pricked his ears, and said, "There are the hounds!" and immediately cantered off, followed by the rest of us to the upper part of the field, where we could look over the hedge and see several fields beyond. My mother and an old riding horse of our master's were also standing near, and seemed to know all about it.

"They have found a hare," said my mother, "and if they come this way we shall see the hunt."

And soon the dogs were all tearing down the field of young wheat next to ours. I never heard such a noise as they made. They did not bark, nor howl, nor whine, but kept on a "yo! yo, o, o! yo! yo, o, o!" at the top of their voices. After them came a number of men on horseback, some of them in green coats, all galloping as fast as they could. The old horse snorted and looked eagerly after them, and we young colts wanted to be galloping with them, but they were soon away into the fields lower down; here it seemed as if they had come to a stand; the dogs left off barking, and ran about every way with their noses to the ground.

" They have lost the scent," said the old horse; " perhaps the hare will get off."

" What hare ? " I said.

" Oh! I don't know *what* hare; likely enough it may be one of our own hares out of the woods; any hare they can find will do for the dogs and men to run after ; " and before long the dogs began their " yo! yo, o, o!" again, and back they came altogether at full speed, making straight for our meadow at the part where the high bank and hedge overhang the brook.

" Now we shall see the hare," said my mother; and just then a hare wild with fright rushed by, and made for the woods. On came the dogs; they burst over the bank, leapt the stream, and came dashing across the field, followed by the huntsmen. Six or eight men leaped their horses clean over, close upon the dogs. The hare tried to get through the fence; it was too thick, and she turned sharp round to make for the road, but it was too late; the dogs were upon her with their wild cries; we heard one shriek, and that was the end of her. One of the huntsmen rode up and whipped off the dogs, who would soon have torn her to pieces. He held her up by the leg torn and bleeding, *and all the gentlemen seemed well pleased.*

As for me, I was so astonished that I did not at first see what was going on by the brook; but when I did look, there was a sad sight; two fine horses were down, one was struggling in the stream, and the other was groaning on the grass. One of the riders was getting out of the water covered with mud, the other lay quite still.

"His neck is broke," said my mother.

"And serve him right, too," said one of the colts.

I thought the same, but my mother did not join with us.

"Well, no," she said, "you must not say that; but though I am an old horse, and have seen and heard a great deal, I never yet could make out why men are so fond of this sport; they often hurt themselves, often spoil good horses, and tear up the fields, and all for a hare, or a fox, or a stag, that they could get more easily some other way; but we are only horses, and don't know."

Whilst my mother was saying this, we stood and looked on. Many of the riders had gone to the young man; but my master, who had been watching what was going on, was the first to raise him. His head fell back and his arms hung down, and every one looked very serious. *There was no noise now; even the dogs were quiet, and seemed to know that something was wrong. They carried him to our master's house.* I heard afterwards that it was young George Gordon, the Squire's only son, a fine, tall young man, and the pride of his family.

There was now riding off in all directions to the doctor's, to the farrier's, and no doubt to Squire

Gordon's, to let him know about his son. When Mr. Bond, the farrier, came to look at the black horse that lay groaning on the grass, he felt him all over, and shook his head; one of his legs was broken. Then some one ran to our master's house and came back with a gun; presently there was a loud bang and a dreadful shriek, and then all was still; the black horse moved no more.

My mother seemed much troubled; she said she had known that horse for years, and that his name was "Rob Roy;" he was a good horse, and there was no vice in him. She never would go to that part of the field afterwards.

Not many days after, we heard the church-bell tolling for a long time; and looking over the gate we saw a long strange black coach that was covered with black cloth and was drawn by black horses; after that came another and another and another, and all were black, while the bell kept tolling, tolling. *They were carrying young Gordon to the churchyard to bury him. He would never ride again. What they did with Rob Roy I never knew; but 'twas all for one little hare.*

CHAPTER III

MY BREAKING IN

I WAS now beginning to grow handsome; my coat had grown fine and soft, and was bright black. I had one white foot, and a pretty white star on my forehead. I was thought very handsome; my master would not sell me till I was four years old; he said lads ought not to work like men, and colts ought not to work like horses till they were quite grown up.

When I was four years old, Squire Gordon came to look at me. He examined my eyes, my mouth, and my legs; he felt them all down; and then I had to walk and trot and gallop before him; he seemed to like me, and said, "When he has been well broken in, he will do very well." My master said he would break me in himself, as he should not like me to be frightened or hurt, and he lost no time about it, for the next day he began.

Every one may not know what breaking in is, therefore I will describe it. It means to teach a horse to wear a saddle and bridle, and to carry on his back a man, woman, or child; to go just the way they wish, and to go quietly. Besides this, he has to learn to wear a collar, a crupper, and a breeching, and to stand still whilst they are put on; then to have a cart or a chaise fixed behind, so that he cannot walk or trot without dragging it after him; and he must go fast or slow, just as his driver wishes. He must never start at what he sees, nor speak to other horses, nor bite, nor kick, nor have any will of his own; but always do his master's will, even though he may be very tired or hungry; but the worst of all is, when his harness is once on, he may neither jump for joy nor lie down for weariness. So you see this breaking in is a great thing.

I had of course long been used to a halter and a headstall, and to be led about in the field and lanes quietly, but now I was to have a bit and bridle; my master gave me some oats as usual, and after a good deal of coaxing he got the bit into my mouth, and the bridle fixed, but it was a nasty thing! Those who have never had a bit in their mouths cannot think how bad it feels; a great piece of cold hard steel as thick as a man's finger to be pushed into one's mouth, between one's teeth, and over one's tongue, with the ends coming out at the corner of your mouth, and held fast there by straps over your head, under your throat, round your nose, and under your chin; so that no way in the world can you get rid of the nasty hard thing; it is very bad! yes, very bad! at least I thought so; but I knew my mother always wore one when she went out, and all horses did when they were grown up; and so, what with the nice oats, and what with my master's pats, kind words, and gentle ways, I got to wear my bit and bridle.

Next came the saddle, but that was not half so bad; my master put it on my back very gently, whilst old Daniel held my head; he then made the girths fast under my body, patting and talking to me all the time; then I had a few oats, then a little leading about; and this he did every day till I began to look for the oats and the saddle. At length, one morning, my master got on my back and rode me round the meadow on the soft grass. It certainly did feel queer; but I must say I felt rather proud to carry my master, and as he continued to ride me a little every day, I soon became accustomed to it.

The next unpleasant business was putting on the iron shoes; that too was very hard at first. My master went with me to the smith's forge, to see that I was not hurt or got any fright. The blacksmith took my feet in his hand, one after the other, and cut away some of the hoof. It did not pain me, so I stood still on three legs till he had done them all. Then he took a piece of iron the shape of my foot, and clapped it on, and drove some nails through the shoe quite into my hoof, so that the shoe was firmly on. My feet felt very stiff and heavy, but in time I got used to it.

And now having got so far, my master went on to break me to harness; there were more new things to wear. First, a stiff heavy collar just on my neck, and a bridle with great side-pieces against my eyes called blinkers, and blinkers indeed they were, for I could not see on either side, but only straight in front of me; next, there was a small saddle with a nasty stiff strap that went right under my tail; that

The hunt. (page 12)

"Master went with me to the smith's forge." (page 18)

was the crupper. I hated the crupper, — to have my long tail doubled up and poked through that strap was almost as bad as the bit. I never felt more like kicking, but of course I could not kick such a good master, and so in time I got used to everything, and could do my work as well as my mother.

I must not forget to mention one part of my training, which I have always considered a very great advantage. My master sent me for a fortnight to a neighboring farmer's, who had a meadow which was skirted on one side by the railway. Here were some sheep and cows, and I was turned in amongst them.

I shall never forget the first train that ran by. I was feeding quietly near the pales which separated the meadow from the railway, when I heard a strange sound at a distance, and before I knew whence it came, — with a rush and a clatter, and a puffing out of smoke, — a long black train of something flew by, and was gone almost before I could draw my breath. I turned and galloped to the further side of the meadow as fast as I could go, and there I stood snorting with astonishment and fear. In the course of the day many other trains went by, some more slowly; these drew up at the station close by, and sometimes made an awful shriek and groan before they stopped. I thought it very dreadful, but the cows went on eating very quietly, and hardly raised their heads as the black frightful thing came puffing and grinding past.

For the first few days I could not feed in peace; but as I found that this terrible creature never came into the field, or did me any harm, I began to disregard it, and very soon I cared as little about the passing of a train as the cows and sheep did.

Since then I have seen many horses much alarmed and restive at the sight or sound of a steam engine; but thanks to my good master's care, I am as fearless at railway stations as in my own stable.

Now if any one wants to break in a young horse well, that is the way.

My master often drove me in double harness with my mother, because she was steady and could teach me how to go better than a strange horse. She told me the better I behaved the better I should be treated, and that it was wisest always to do my best to please my master; "but," said she, "there are a great many kinds of men; there are good, thoughtful men like our master, that any horse may be proud to serve; and there are bad, cruel men, who never ought to have a horse or dog to call their own. Beside, there are a great many foolish men, vain, ignorant, and careless, who never trouble themselves to think; these spoil more horses than all, just for want of sense; they don't mean it, but they do it for all that. I hope you will fall into good hands; but a horse never knows who may buy him, or who may drive him; it is all a chance for us; but still I say, do your best wherever it is, and keep up your good name."

CHAPTER IV

BIRTWICK PARK

AT this time I used to stand in the stable, and my coat was brushed every day till it shone like a rook's wing. It was early in May, when there came a man from Squire Gordon's, who took me away to the Hall. My master said, "Goodby, Darkie; be a good horse, and always do your best." I could not say "good-by," so I put my nose into his hand; he patted me kindly, and I left my first home. As I lived some years with Squire Gordon, I may as well tell something about the place.

Squire Gordon's park skirted the village of Birtwick. It was entered by a large iron gate, at which stood the first lodge, and then you trotted along on a smooth road between clumps of large old trees; then another lodge and another gate, which brought you to the house and the gardens. Beyond this lay the home paddock, the old orchard, and the stables. There was accommodation for many horses and carriages; but I need only describe the stable into which I was taken; this was very roomy, with four good stalls; a large swinging window opened into the yard, which made it pleasant and airy.

The first stall was a large square one, shut in

behind with a wooden gate; the others were common stalls, good stalls, but not nearly so large; it had a low rack for hay and a low manger for corn; it was called a loose box, because the horse that was put into it was not tied up, but left loose, to do as he liked. It is a great thing to have a loose box.

Into this fine box the groom put me; it was clean, sweet, and airy. I never was in a better box than that, and the sides were not so high but that I could see all that went on through the iron rails that were at the top.

He gave me some very nice oats, he patted me, spoke kindly, and then went away.

When I had eaten my corn, I looked round. In the stall next to mine stood a little fat gray pony, with a thick mane and tail, a very pretty head, and a pert little nose.

I put my head up to the iron rails at the top of my box, and said, "How do you do? what is your name?"

He turned round as far as his halter would allow, held up his head, and said, "My name is Merrylegs. I am very handsome, I carry the young ladies on my back, and sometimes I take our mistress out in the low chair. They think a great deal of me, and so does James. Are you going to live next door to me in the box?"

I said, "Yes."

"Well, then," he said, "I hope you are good-tempered; I do not like any one next door who bites."

Just then a horse's head looked over from the stall beyond; the ears were laid back, and the eye looked rather ill-tempered. This was a tall chestnut mare, with a long handsome neck; she looked across to me and said, —

"So it is you who have turned me out of my box; it is a very strange thing for a colt like you to come and turn a lady out of her own home."

"I beg your pardon," I said, "I have turned no one out; the man who brought me put me here, and I had nothing to do with it; and as to my being a colt, I am turned four years old, and am a grown-up horse. I never had words yet with horse or mare, and it is my wish to live at peace."

"Well," she said, "we shall see; of course I do not want to have words with a young thing like you." I said no more.

In the afternoon, when she went out, Merrylegs told me all about it.

"The thing is this," said Merrylegs. "Ginger has a bad habit of biting and snapping; that is why they call her Ginger, and when she was in the loose box, she used to snap very much. One day she bit James in the arm and made it bleed, and so Miss Flora and Miss Jessie, who are very fond of me, were afraid to come into the stable. They used to bring me nice things to eat, an apple or a carrot, or a piece of bread, but after Ginger stood in that box, they dared not come, and I missed them very much. I hope they will now come again, if you do not bite or snap."

I told him I never bit anything but grass, hay, and corn, and could not think what pleasure Ginger found it.

" Well, I don't think she does find pleasure," says Merrylegs; " it is just a bad habit; she says no one was ever kind to her, and why should she not bite? Of course it is a very bad habit; but I am sure, if all she says be true, she must have been very ill-used before she came here. John does all he can to please her, and James does all he can, and our master never uses a whip if a horse acts right; so I think she might be good-tempered here; you see," he said with a wise look, " I am twelve years old; I know a great deal, and I can tell you there is not a better place for a horse all round the country than this. John is the best groom that ever was, he has been here fourteen years; and you never saw such a kind boy as James is, so that it is all Ginger's own fault that she did not stay in that box."

CHAPTER V

A FAIR START

THE name of the coachman was John Manly; he had a wife and one little child, and they lived in the coachman's cottage, very near the stables.

The next morning he took me into the yard and gave me a good grooming, and just as I was going into my box, with my coat soft and bright, the Squire came in to look at me, and seemed pleased. "John," he said, "I meant to have tried the new horse this morning, but I have other business. You may as well take him around after breakfast; go by the common and the Highwood, and back by the watermill and the river; that will show his paces."

"I will, sir," said John. After breakfast he came and fitted me with a bridle. He was very particular in letting out and taking in the straps, to fit my head comfortably; then he brought a saddle, but it was not broad enough for my back; he saw it in a minute and went for another, which fitted nicely. He rode me first slowly, then a trot, then a canter, and when we were on the common he gave me a light touch with his whip, and we had a splendid gallop.

"Ho, ho! my boy," he said, as he pulled me up, "you would like to follow the hounds, I think."

As we came back through the park we met the Squire and Mrs. Gordon walking; they stopped, and John jumped off.

"Well, John, how does he go?"

"First-rate, sir," answered John; "he is as fleet as a deer, and has a fine spirit too; but the lightest touch of the rein will guide him. Down at the end of the common we met one of those traveling carts hung all over with baskets, rugs, and such like; you know, sir, many horses will not pass those carts quietly; he just took a good look at it, and then went on as quiet and pleasant as could be. They were shooting rabbits near the Highwood, and a gun went off close by; he pulled up a little and looked, but did not stir a step to right or left. I just held the rein steady and did not hurry him, and it's my opinion he has not been frightened or ill-used while he was young."

"That's well," said the Squire, "I will try him myself to-morrow."

The next day I was brought up for my master. I remembered my mother's counsel and my good old master's, and I tried to do exactly what he wanted me to do. I found he was a very good rider, and thoughtful for his horse too. When he came home, the lady was at the hall door as he rode up.

"Well, my dear," she said, "how do you like him?"

"He is exactly what John said," he replied; "a pleasanter creature I never wish to mount. What shall we call him?"

"Would you like Ebony?" said she; "he is as black as ebony."

"No, not Ebony."

"Will you call him 'Blackbird,' like your uncle's old horse?"

"No, he is far handsomer than old Blackbird ever was."

"Yes," she said, "he is really quite a beauty, and he has such a sweet good-tempered face and such a fine intelligent eye — what do you say to calling him *Black Beauty*?"

"Black Beauty — why, yes, I think that is a very good name. If you like, it shall be his name;" and so it was.

When John went into the stable, he told James that master and mistress had chosen a good sensible English name for me, that meant something; not like Marengo, or Pegasus, or Abdallah. They both laughed, and James said, "If it was not for bringing back the past, I should have named him 'Rob Roy,' for I never saw two horses more alike."

"That's no wonder," said John; "didn't you know that farmer Grey's old Duchess was the mother of them both?"

I had never heard that before; and *so poor Rob Roy who was killed at that hunt was my brother!* I did not wonder that my mother was so troubled. It seems that horses have no relations; at least they never know each other after they are sold.

John seemed very proud of me; he used to make my mane and tail almost as smooth as a lady's hair, and he would talk to me a great deal; of course I did not understand all he said, but I learned more and more to know what he *meant*, and what he wanted me to do. *I grew very fond of him, he was so gentle and kind; he seemed to know just how a horse feels, and when he cleaned me he knew the tender places and the ticklish places; when he brushed my head, he went as carefully over my eyes as if they were his own, and never stirred up any ill-temper.*

James Howard, the stable boy, was just as gentle and pleasant in his way, so I thought myself well off. There was another man who helped in the yard, but he had very little to do with Ginger and me.

A few days after this I had to go out with Ginger in the carriage. I wondered how we should get on together; but except laying her ears back when I was led up to her, she behaved very well. She did her work honestly, and did her full share, and I never wish to have a better partner in double harness. When we came to a hill, instead of slackening her pace, she would throw her weight right into the collar, and pull away straight up. We had both the same sort of courage at our work, and John had oftener to hold us in than to urge us forward; he never had to use the whip with either of us; then our paces were much the same, and I found it very easy to keep step with her when trotting, which made it pleasant, and master always liked it when we kept step well, and so did John. After we had been out two or three times together we grew quite friendly and sociable, which made me feel very much at home.

As for Merrylegs, he and I soon became great

friends; he was such a cheerful, plucky, good-tempered little fellow, that he was a favorite with every one, and especially with Miss Jessie and Flora, who used to ride him about in the orchard, and have fine games with him and their little dog Frisky.

Our master had two other horses that stood in another stable. One was Justice, a roan cob, used for riding, or for the luggage cart; the other was an old brown hunter, named Sir Oliver; he was past work now, but was a great favorite with the master, who gave him the run of the park; he sometimes did a little light carting on the estate, or carried one of the young ladies when they rode out with their father; for he was very gentle, and could be trusted with a child as well as Merrylegs. The cob was a strong, well-made, good-tempered horse, and we sometimes had a little chat in the paddock, but of course I could not be so intimate with him as with Ginger, who stood in the same stable.

CHAPTER VI

LIBERTY

 WAS quite happy in my new place, and if there was one thing that I missed, it must not be thought I was discontented; all who had to do with me were good, and I had a light airy stable and the best of food. What more could I want? Why, liberty! For three years and a half of my life I had had all the liberty I could wish for; but now, week after week, month after month, and no doubt year after year, I must stand up in a stable night and day except when I am wanted, and then I must be just as steady and quiet as any old horse who has worked twenty years. Straps here and straps there, a bit in my mouth, and blinkers over my eyes. Now, I am not complaining, for I know it must be so. I only mean to say that for a young horse full of strength and spirits, who has been used to some large field or plain, where he can fling up his head, and toss up his tail and gallop away at full speed, then round and back again with a snort to his companions, — I say it is hard never to have a bit more liberty to do as you like. Sometimes, when I have had less exercise than usual, I have felt so full of life and spring, that when John has taken me out to exercise I really could not keep quiet; do what

"Snorting with astonishment and fear." (page 19)

"I was quite happy in my new place." (page 30)

I would, it seemed as if I must jump, or dance, or prance, and many a good shake I know I must have given him, specially at the first; but he was always good and patient.

"Steady, steady, my boy," he would say; "wait a bit, and we'll have a good swing, and soon get the tickle out of your feet." Then as soon as we were out of the village, he would give me a few miles at a spanking trot, and then bring me back as fresh as before, only clear of the fidgets, as he called them. *Spirited horses, when not enough exercised, are often called skittish,* when it is only play; and some grooms will punish them, but our John did not; he knew it was only high spirits. Still, he had his own ways of making me understand by the tone of his voice or the touch of the rein. If he was very serious and quite determined, I always knew it by his voice, and that had more power with me than anything else, for I was very fond of him.

I ought to say that sometimes we had our liberty for a few hours; this used to be on fine Sundays in the summer-time. The carriage never went out on Sundays, because the church was not far off.

It was a great treat to us to be turned out into the home paddock or the old orchard; the grass was so cool and soft to our feet, the air so sweet, and the freedom to do as we liked was so pleasant — to gallop, to lie down, and roll over on our backs, or to nibble the sweet grass. Then it was a very good time for talking, as we stood together under the shade of the large chestnut tree.

CHAPTER VII

GINGER

NE day when Ginger and I were standing alone in the shade, we had a great deal of talk; she wanted to know all about my bringing up and breaking in, and I told her.

"Well," said she, "*if I had had your bringing up, I might have had as good a temper as you*, but now I don't believe I ever shall."

"Why not?" I said.

"Because it has been all so different with me," she replied. "*I never had any one, horse or man, that was kind to me*, or that I cared to please, for in the first place I was taken from my mother as soon as I was weaned, and put with a lot of other young colts; none of them cared for me, and I cared for none of them. There was no kind master like yours to look after me, and talk to me, and bring me nice things to eat. *The man that had the care of us never gave me a kind word in my life.* I do not mean that he ill-used me, but he did not care for us one bit further than to see that we had plenty to eat, and shelter in the winter. A footpath ran through our field, and very often the great boys passing through would fling stones to make us gallop. I was never hit, but one fine young colt was badly cut in the

Ginger. (page 32)

"The grass was so cool and soft to our feet." (page 31)

face, and I should think it would be a scar for life. We did not care for them, but of course it made us more wild, and we settled it in our minds that boys were our enemies. We had very good fun in the free meadows, galloping up and down and chasing each other round and round the field; then standing still under the shade of the trees. But when it came to breaking in, that was a bad time for me; several men came to catch me, and when at last they closed me in at one corner of the field, one caught me by the forelock, another caught me by the nose and held it so tight I could hardly draw my breath; then another took my under jaw in his hard hand and wrenched my mouth open, and so by force they got on the halter and the bar into my mouth; then one dragged me along by the halter, another flogging behind, and this was the first experience I had of men's kindness; it was all force. They did not give me a chance to know what they wanted. I was high bred and had a great deal of spirit, and was very wild, no doubt, and gave them, I dare say, plenty of trouble, but then it was dreadful to be shut up in a stall day after day instead of having my liberty, and I fretted and pined and wanted to get loose. You know yourself it's bad enough when you have a kind master and plenty of coaxing, but there was nothing of that sort for me.

"There was one — the old master, Mr. Ryder — who, I think, could soon have brought me round, and could have done anything with me; but he had given up all the hard part of the trade to his son and to another experienced man, and he only came at times

to oversee. His son was a strong, tall, bold man ;
they called him Samson, and he used to boast that
he had never found a horse that could throw him.
There was no gentleness in him, as there was in his
father, but only hardness, a hard voice, a hard eye,
a hard hand; and I felt from the first that what
he wanted was to wear all the spirit out of me, and
just make me into a quiet, humble, obedient piece of
horse-flesh. ' Horse-flesh !' Yes, that is all that he
thought about," and Ginger stamped her foot as if
the very thought of him made her angry. Then she
went on : —

"If I did not do exactly what he wanted, he would
get put out, and make me run round with that long
rein in the training field till he had tired me out. I
think he drank a good deal, and I am quite sure that
the oftener he drank the worse it was for me. One
day he had worked me hard in every way he could,
and when I laid down I was tired, and miserable,
and angry ; it all seemed so hard. The next morning he came for me early, and ran me round again
for a long time. I had scarcely had an hour's rest,
when he came again for me with a saddle and bridle
and a new kind of bit. I could never quite tell how
it came about ; he had only just mounted me on the
training ground, when something I did put him out
of temper, and he chucked me hard with the rein.
The new bit was very painful, and I reared up suddenly, which angered him still more, and he began
to flog me. I felt my whole spirit set against
him, and I began to kick, and plunge, and rear as I
had never done before, and we had a regular fight ;

for a long time he stuck to the saddle and punished me cruelly with his whip and spurs, but my blood was thoroughly up, and I cared for nothing he could do if only I could get him off. At last after a terrible struggle, I threw him off backwards. I heard him fall heavily on the turf, and without looking behind me, I galloped off to the other end of the field; there I turned round and saw my persecutor slowly rising from the ground and going into the stable. I stood under an oak tree and watched, but no one came to catch me. The time went on, and the sun was very hot; the flies swarmed round me and settled on my bleeding flanks where the spurs had dug in. I felt hungry, for I had not eaten since the early morning, but there was not enough grass in that meadow for a goose to live on. I wanted to lie down and rest, but with the saddle strapped tightly on, there was no comfort, and there was not a drop of water to drink. The afternoon wore on, and the sun got low. I saw the other colts led in, and I knew they were having a good feed.

"At last, just as the sun went down, I saw the old master come out with a sieve in his hand. He was a very fine old gentleman with quite white hair, but his voice was what I should know him by amongst a thousand. It was not high, nor yet low, but full, and clear, and kind, and when he gave orders it was so steady and decided, that every one knew, both horses and men, that he expected to be obeyed. He came quietly along, now and then shaking the oats about that he had in the sieve, and speaking cheerfully and gently to me: 'Come along,

lassie, come along, lassie ; come along, come along.'
I stood still and let him come up ; he held the oats
to me, and I began to eat without fear ; his voice
took all my fear away. He stood by, patting and
stroking me whilst I was eating, and seeing the
clots of blood on my side he seemed very vexed.
' Poor lassie ! it was a bad business, a bad business ! '
then he quietly took the rein and led me to the
stable ; just at the door stood Samson. I laid my
ears back and snapped at him. ' Stand back,' said
the master, ' and keep out of her way ; you 've done
a bad day's work for this filly.' He growled out
something about a vicious brute. ' Hark ye,' said
the father, ' a bad-tempered man will never make a
good-tempered horse. You 've not learned your
trade yet, Samson.' Then he led me into my box,
took off the saddle and bridle with his own hands,
and tied me up ; then he called for a pail of warm
water and a sponge, took off his coat, and while the
stable-man held the pail, he sponged my sides a
good while, so tenderly that I was sure he knew how
sore and bruised they were. ' Whoa ! my pretty
one,' he said, ' stand still, stand still.' *His very
voice did me good*, and the bathing was very comfortable. The skin was so broken at the corners of my
mouth that I could not eat the hay, the stalks hurt
me. He looked closely at it, shook his head, and
told the man to fetch a good bran mash and put
some meal into it. How good that mash was ! and
so soft and healing to my mouth. He stood by all
the time I was eating, stroking me and talking to
the man. ' If a high-mettled creature like this,'

said he, 'can't be broken in by fair means, she will never be good for anything.'

"After that he often came to see me, and when my mouth was healed, the other breaker, Job, they called him, went on training me ; he was steady and thoughtful, and I soon learned what he wanted."

CHAPTER VIII

GINGER'S STORY CONTINUED

HE next time that Ginger and I were together in the paddock, she told me about her first place.

"After my breaking in," she said, "I was bought by a dealer to match another chestnut horse. For some weeks he drove us together, and then we were sold to a fashionable gentleman, and were sent up to London. I had been driven with a check-rein by the dealer, and I hated it worse than anything else; but in this place we were reined far tighter; the coachman and his master thinking we looked more stylish so. We were often driven about in the Park and other fashionable places. You who never had a check-rein on don't know what it is, but I can tell you it is dreadful.

"I like to toss my head about, and hold it as high as any horse; but fancy now yourself, if you tossed your head up high *and were obliged to hold it there, and that for hours together, not able to move it at all, except with a jerk still higher, your neck aching till you did not know how to bear it.* Besides that, to have two bits instead of one; and mine was a sharp one; it hurt my tongue and my jaw, and the blood from my tongue colored the froth that kept flying from my lips, as I chafed and fretted at the bits and rein. *It was worst when we had to stand by the hour waiting for our mistress at some grand party or entertainment ;* and if I fretted or stamped with impatience, the whip was laid on. It was enough to drive one mad."

"We had to stand by the hour waiting for our mistress."

"Did not your master take any thought for you?" I said.

"No," said she, "he only cared to have a stylish turn-out, as they call it; I think he knew very little about horses; he left that to his coachman, who told him I had an irritable temper; that I had not been well broken to the check-rein, but I should soon get used to it; but *he* was not the man to do it, for when I was in the stable, miserable and angry, instead of being soothed and quieted by kindness,

I got only a surly word or a blow. If he had been
civil, I would have tried to bear it. I was willing
to work, and ready to work hard too ; but to be tor-
mented for nothing but their fancies angered me.

Comfortable, without the check-rein.

What right had they to make me suffer like that?
Besides the soreness in my mouth, and the pain in
my neck, *it always made my windpipe feel bad,* and
if I had stopped there long, I know it would have
spoiled my breathing ; but I grew more and more

restless and irritable, I could not help it; and I began to snap and kick when any one came to harness me; for this the groom beat me, and one day, as they had just buckled us into the carriage, and were straining my head up with that rein, I began to plunge and kick with all my might. I soon broke a lot of harness, and kicked myself clear; so that was an end of that place.

" After this, I was sent to Tattersall's to be sold; of course I could not be warranted free from vice, so nothing was said about that. My handsome appearance and good paces soon brought a gentleman to bid for me, and I was bought by another dealer; he tried me in all kinds of ways and with different bits, and he soon found out what I could not bear. At least he drove me quite without a check-rein, and then sold me as a perfectly quiet horse to a gentleman in the country; he was a good master, and I was getting on very well, but his old groom left him and a new one came. This man was as hard-tempered and hard-handed as Samson; *he always spoke in a rough, impatient voice*, and if I did not move in the stall the moment he wanted me, he would hit me above the hocks with his stable broom or the fork, whichever he might have in his hand. Everything he did was rough, and I began to hate him; he wanted to make me afraid of him, but I was too high-mettled for that, and one day when he had aggravated me more than usual, I bit him, which of course put him in a great rage, and he began to hit me about the head with a riding whip. After that, he never dared to come into my stall again; either my heels or my teeth were ready for him, and he knew it. I was quite quiet with my master, but of course he listened to what the man said, and so I was sold again.

"The same dealer heard of me, and said he thought he knew one place where I should do well. ' 'T was a pity,' he said, 'that such a fine horse should go to the bad, for want of a real good chance,' and the end of it was that I came here not long before you did; but I had then made up my mind that men were my natural enemies, and that I must defend myself. Of course it is very different here, but who knows how long it will last? I wish I could think about things as you do; but I can't, after all I have gone through."

"Well," I said, "I think it would be a real shame if you were to bite or kick John or James."

"I don't mean to," she said, "while they are good to me. I did bite James once pretty sharp, but John said, 'Try her with kindness,' and instead of punishing me as I expected, James came to me with his arm bound up, and brought me a bran mash and stroked me; and I have never snapped at him since, and I won't, either."

I was sorry for Ginger, but of course I knew very little then, and I thought most likely she made the worst of it; however, I found that as the weeks went on, she grew much more gentle and cheerful, and had lost the watchful, defiant look that she used to turn on any strange person who came near her; and one day James said, "I do believe that mare is getting fond of me, she quite whinnied after me this morning when I had been rubbing her fore-head."

"Aye, aye, Jim, 't is '*the Birtwick balls*,'" said John, "she'll be as good as Black Beauty by and by; kindness is all the physic she wants, poor thing!" Master noticed the change, too, and one day when he got out of the carriage and came to speak to us, as he often did, he stroked her beauti-ful neck. "Well, my pretty one, well, how do things go with you now? you are a good bit happier than when you came to us, I think."

She put her nose up to him in a friendly, trustful way, while he rubbed it gently.

"We shall make a cure of her, John," he said.

"Yes, sir, she's wonderfully improved; she's not the same creature that she was; it's '*the Birtwick balls*,' sir," said John, laughing.

This was a little joke of John's; he used to say that a regular course of "*the Birtwick horse-balls*" would cure almost any vicious horse; these balls, he said, were made up *of patience and gentleness, firmness and petting, one pound of each to be mixed up with half a pint of common sense, and given to the horse every day.*

CHAPTER IX

MERRYLEGS

MR. BLOMEFIELD, the Vicar, had a large family of boys and girls; sometimes they used to come and play with Miss Jessie and Flora. One of the girls was as old as Miss Jessie; two of the boys were older, and there were several little ones. When they came, there was plenty of work for Merrylegs, for nothing pleased them so much as getting on him by turns and riding him all about the orchard and the home paddock, and this they would do by the hour together.

One afternoon he had been out with them a long time, and when James brought him in and put on his halter, he said, —

"There, you rogue, mind how you behave yourself, or we shall get into trouble."

"What have you been doing, Merrylegs?" I asked.

"Oh!" said he, tossing his little head, "I have only been giving those young people a lesson; they did not know when they had had enough, nor when I had had enough, so I just pitched them off backwards; that was the only thing they could understand."

"What?" said I, "you threw the children off? I

thought you did know better than that! Did you throw Miss Jessie or Miss Flora?"

He looked very much offended, and said, —

"Of course not; I would not do such a thing for the best oats that ever came into the stable; why, I am as careful of our young ladies as the master could be, and as for the little ones, it is I who teach them to ride. When they seem frightened or a little unsteady on my back, I go as smooth and as quiet as old pussy when she is after a bird; and when they are all right I go on again faster, you see, just to use them to it; so don't you trouble yourself preaching to me; I am the best friend and the best riding master those children have. It is not them, it is the boys; boys," said he, shaking his mane, "are quite different; they must be broken in, as we were broken in when we were colts, and just be taught what's what. The other children had ridden me about for nearly two hours, and then the boys thought it was their turn, and so it was, and I was quite agreeable. They rode me by turns, and I galloped them about, up and down the fields and all about the orchard, for a good hour. They had each cut a great hazel stick for a riding whip, and laid it on a little too hard; but I took it in good part, till at last I thought we had had enough, so I stopped two or three times by way of a hint. *Boys, you see, think a horse or pony is like a steam engine or a thrashing machine,* and can go on as long and as fast as they please; they never think that a pony can get tired, or have any feelings; so as the one who was whipping me could not understand, I just rose up on my hind legs and let him slip off behind, — that was all; he mounted me again, and I did the same. Then the other boy got up, and as soon as he began to use his stick I laid him on the grass, and so on, till they were able to understand, that was all. They are not bad boys; they don't wish to be cruel. I like them very well; but you see I had to give them a lesson. When they brought me to James and told him, I think he was very angry to see such big sticks. He said they were only fit for drovers or gypsies, and not for young gentlemen."

"If I had been you," said Ginger, "I would have given those boys a good kick, and that would have given them a lesson."

"No doubt you would," said Merrylegs; "but then I am not quite such a fool (begging your pardon) as to anger our master or make James ashamed of me; besides, those children are under my charge when they are riding; I tell you they are entrusted to me. Why, only the other day I heard our master say to Mrs. Blomefield, 'My dear madam, you need not be anxious about the children, my old Merrylegs will take as much care of them as you or I could; I assure you I would not sell that pony for any money, he is so perfectly good-tempered and trustworthy;' and do you think I am such an ungrateful brute as to forget all the kind treatment I have had here for five years, and all the trust they place in me, and turn vicious because a couple of ignorant boys used me badly? No, no! you never had a good place where they were kind to you, and so you don't know, and I'm sorry for you; but I can

A ride on Merrylegs. (page 47)

Merrylegs. (page 44)

tell you *good places make good horses.* I would n't vex our people for anything; I love them, I do," said Merrylegs, and he gave a low "ho, ho, ho," through his nose, as he used to do in the morning when he heard James's footstep at the door.

"Besides," he went on, "if I took to kicking, where should I be? Why, sold off in a jiffy, and no character, and I might find myself slaved about under a butcher's boy, or worked to death at some seaside place where no one cared for me, except to find out how fast I could go, or be flogged along in some cart with three or four great men in it going out for a Sunday spree, as I have often seen in the place I lived in before I came here; no," said he, shaking his head, "I hope I shall never come to that."

CHAPTER X

A TALK IN THE ORCHARD

GINGER and I were not of the regular tall carriage horse breed, we had more of the racing blood in us. We stood about fifteen and a half hands high; we were therefore just as good for riding as we were for driving, and our master used to say that he disliked either horse or man that could do but one thing; and as he did not want to show off in London parks, he preferred a more active and useful kind of horse. As for us, our greatest pleasure was when we were saddled for a riding party; the master on Ginger, the mistress on me, and the young ladies on Sir Oliver and Merry-legs. It was so cheerful to be trotting and cantering all together, that it always put us in high spirits. I had the best of it, for I always carried the mistress; her weight was little, her voice was sweet, and her hand was so light on the rein, that I was guided almost without feeling it.

Oh! if people knew what a comfort to horses a light hand is, and how it keeps a good mouth and a good temper, they surely would not chuck, and drag, and pull at the rein as they often do. Our mouths are so tender, that where they have not been spoiled or hardened with bad or ignorant treatment, they

"The master on Ginger, the mistress on me." (page 48)

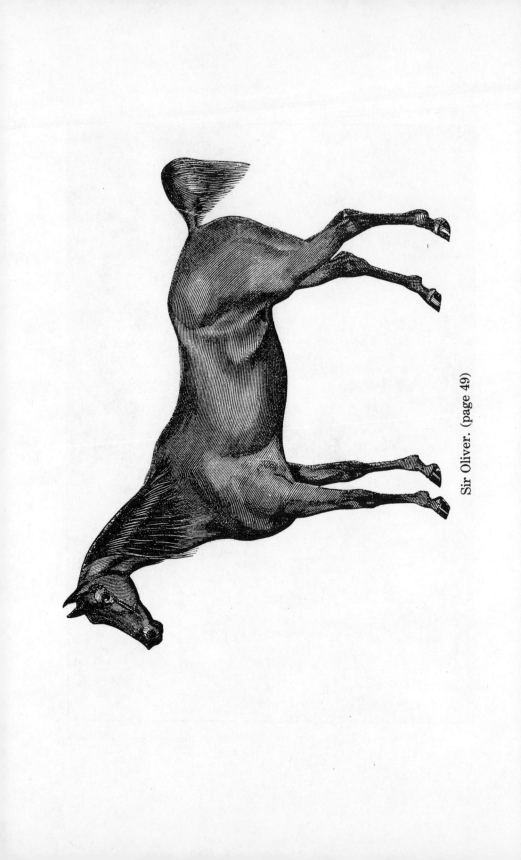

Sir Oliver. (page 49)

feel the slightest movement of the driver's hand, and we know in an instant what is required of us. My mouth had never been spoiled, and I believe that was why the mistress preferred me to Ginger, although her paces were certainly quite as good. She used often to envy me, and said it was all the fault of breaking in, and the gag bit in London, that her mouth was not so perfect as mine; and then old Sir Oliver would say, "There, there! don't vex yourself; you have the greatest honor; a mare that can carry a tall man of our master's weight, with all your spring and sprightly action, does not need to hold her head down because she does not carry the lady; we horses must take things as they come, and always be contented and willing so long as we are kindly used."

I had often wondered how it was that Sir Oliver had such a very short tail; it really was only six or seven inches long, with a tassel of hair hanging from it; and on one of our holidays in the orchard I ventured to ask him by what accident it was that he had lost his tail. "Accident!" he snorted with a fierce look, "it was no accident! *it was a cruel, shameful, cold-blooded act!* When I was young I was taken to a place where these cruel things were done; I was tied up, and made fast so that I could not stir, and then they came and cut off my long beautiful tail, through the flesh and through the bone, and took it away."

"How dreadful!" I exclaimed.

"Dreadful, ah! it was dreadful; but it was not only the pain, though that was terrible and lasted a

long time; it was not only the indignity of having
my best ornament taken from me, though that was
bad; but it was this, *how could I ever brush the flies
off my sides and my hind legs any more?*   You who
have tails just whisk the flies off without thinking
about it, and you can't tell what a torment it is to
have them settle upon you and sting and sting, and
have nothing in the world to lash them off with.   I
tell you it is a life-long wrong, and a life-long loss;
but thank Heaven, they don't do it now."

"What did they do it for then?" said Ginger.

"*For fashion!*" said the old horse with a stamp
of his foot; "*for fashion!* if you know what that
means; there was not a well-bred young horse in my
time that had not his tail docked in that shameful
way, just *as if the good God that made us did not
know what we wanted, and what looked best.*"

"I suppose it is fashion that makes them strap
our heads up with those horrid bits that I was tor-
tured with in London," said Ginger.

"Of course it is," said he; "to my mind, fashion
is one of the wickedest things in the world.   Now
look, for instance, at the way they serve dogs, cutting off their tails to make them look plucky, and
shearing up their pretty little ears to a point to
make them look sharp, forsooth.   I had a dear
friend once, a brown terrier; 'Skye' they called her.
She was so fond of me that she never would sleep
out of my stall; she made her bed under the manger,
and there she had a litter of five as pretty little
puppies as need be; none were drowned, for they
were a valuable kind, and how pleased she was with

them! and when they got their eyes open and crawled about, it was a real pretty sight; but one day the man came and took them all away; I thought he might be afraid I should tread upon them. But it was not so; in the evening poor Skye brought them back again, one by one in her mouth; not the happy little things that they were, but bleeding and crying pitifully; they had all had a piece of their tails cut off, and the soft flap of their pretty little ears was cut quite off. How their mother licked them, and how troubled she was, poor thing! I never forgot it. They healed in time, and they forgot the pain, but the nice soft flap that of course was *intended to protect the delicate part of their ears from dust and injury, was gone forever. Why don't they cut their own children's ears into points to make them look sharp?* why don't they cut the end off their noses to make them look plucky? one would be just as sensible as the other. What right have they to torment and disfigure God's creatures?"

Sir Oliver, though he was so gentle, was a fiery old fellow, and what he said was all so new to me, and so dreadful, that I found a bitter feeling toward men rise up in my mind that I never had before. Of course Ginger was very much excited; she flung up her head with flashing eyes and distended nostrils, declaring that men were both brutes and blockheads.

"Who talks about blockheads?" said Merrylegs, who just came up from the old apple tree, where he had been rubbing himself against the low branch.

"Who talks about blockheads? I believe that is a bad word."

"Bad words were made for bad things," said Ginger, and she told him what Sir Oliver had said.

"It is all true," said Merrylegs sadly, "and I've seen that about the dogs over and over again where I lived first; but we won't talk about it here. You know that master, and John, and James are always good to us, and talking against men in such a place as this does n't seem fair or grateful, and you know there are good masters and good grooms beside ours, though of course ours are the best."

This wise speech of good little Merrylegs, which we knew was quite true, cooled us all down, especially Sir Oliver, who was dearly fond of his master; and to turn the subject I said, "Can any one tell me the use of blinkers?"

"No!" said Sir Oliver shortly, "because they are no use."

"They are supposed," said Justice, the roan cob, in his calm way, "to prevent horses from shying and starting, and getting so frightened as to cause accidents."

"*Then what is the reason they do not put them on riding horses; especially on ladies' horses?*" said I.

"There is no reason at all," said he quietly, "except *the fashion;* they say that a horse would be so frightened to see the wheels of his own cart or carriage coming behind him, that he would be sure to run away, although of course when he is ridden he sees them all about him if the streets are crowded. I admit they do sometimes come too close to be pleasant, but we don't run away; we are used to it, and understand it, and if we never had blinkers put on we should never want them; we should see what was there, and know what was what, and be much less frightened than by only seeing bits of things that we can't understand. Of course there may be some nervous horses who have been hurt or frightened when they were young, who may be the better for them; but as I never was nervous, I can't judge."

"I consider" said Sir Oliver, "*that blinkers are dangerous things in the night;* we horses can see much better in the dark than men can, and many an accident would never have happened if horses might have had the full use of their eyes. Some years ago, I remember, there was a hearse with two horses returning one dark night, and just by farmer Sparrow's house, where the pond is close to the road, the wheels went too near the edge, and the hearse was overturned into the water; both the horses were drowned, and the driver hardly escaped. Of course after this accident a stout white rail was put up that might be easily seen, *but if those horses had not been partly blinded*, they would of themselves have kept farther from the edge, and no accident would have happened. When our master's carriage was overturned, before you came here, it was said, that if the lamp on the left side had not gone out, John would have seen the great hole that the road makers had left; and so he might, *but if old Colin had not had blinkers on,* he would have seen it, lamp or no lamp, for he was far too knowing an old horse to run into danger. As it was, he was very much hurt, the carriage was broken, and how John escaped nobody knew."

"I should say," said Ginger, curling her nostril, "that these men, who are so wise, had better give orders that in future all foals should be born with their eyes set just in the middle of their foreheads, instead of on the side ; they always think they can improve upon nature and mend what God has made."

Things were getting rather sore again, when Merrylegs held up his knowing little face and said, "I'll tell you a secret : I believe John does not approve of blinkers; I heard him talking with master about it one day. The master said, that 'if horses had been used to them, it might be dangerous in some cases to leave them off;' and John said he thought *it would be a good thing if all colts were broken in without blinkers, as was the case in some foreign countries.* So let us cheer up, and have a run to the other end of the orchard; I believe the wind has blown down some apples, and we might just as well eat them as the slugs."

Merrylegs could not be resisted, so we broke off our long conversation, and got up our spirits by munching some very sweet apples which lay scattered on the grass.

CHAPTER XI

PLAIN SPEAKING

THE longer I lived at Birtwick, the more proud and happy I felt at having such a place. Our master and mistress were respected and beloved by all who knew them; they were good and kind to everybody and everything; not only men and women, but horses and donkeys, dogs and cats, cattle and birds; there was no oppressed or ill-used creature that had not a friend in them, and their servants took the same tone. If any of the village children were known to treat any creature cruelly, they soon heard about it from the Hall.

The Squire and farmer Grey had worked together, as they said, for more than twenty years, to get check-reins on the cart horses done away with, and in our parts you seldom saw them; and sometimes if mistress met a heavily laden horse, with his head strained up, she would stop the carriage and get out, and reason with the driver in her sweet serious voice, and try to show him how foolish and cruel it was.

I don't think any man could withstand our mistress. I wish all ladies were like her. Our master, too, used to come down very heavy sometimes. I remember he was riding me towards home one morning, when we saw a powerful man driving towards us in a light pony chaise, with a beautiful little bay pony, with slender legs, and a high-bred sensitive head and face. Just as he came to the park gates, the little thing turned towards them; the man, without word or warning, wrenched the creature's head round with such a force and suddenness, that he nearly threw it on its haunches; recovering itself, it was going on, when he began to lash it furiously; the pony plunged forward, but the strong heavy hand held the pretty creature back with force almost enough to break its jaw, whilst the whip still cut into him. It was a dreadful sight to me, for I knew what fearful pain it gave that delicate little mouth; but master gave me the word, and we were up with him in a second.

"Sawyer," he cried in a stern voice, "is that pony made of flesh and blood?"

"Flesh and blood and temper," he said; "he's too fond of his own will, and that won't suit me." He spoke as if he was in a strong passion; he was a builder, who had often been to the park on business.

"And do you think," said master sternly, "that treatment like this will make him fond of your will?"

"He had no business to make that turn; his road was straight on!" said the man roughly.

"You have often driven that pony up to my place," said master; "it only shows the creature's memory and intelligence; how did he know that you were not going there again? but that has little to do with it. I must say, Mr. Sawyer, that more unmanly, brutal treatment of a little pony, it was never my painful lot to witness; and by giving way to such passion, you injure your own character as much, nay more, than you injure your horse; and remember, we shall all have to be judged according to our works, whether they be towards man or towards beast."

Master rode me home slowly, and I could tell by his voice how the thing had grieved him. He was just as free to speak to gentlemen of his own rank as to those below him; for another day, when we were out, we met a Captain Langley, a friend of our master's; he was driving a splendid pair of grays in a kind of break. After a little conversation the Captain said, —

"What do you think of my new team, Mr. Douglas? You know, you are the judge of horses in these parts, and I should like your opinion."

The master backed me a little, so as to get a good view of them. "They are an uncommonly handsome pair," he said, "and if they are as good as they look, I am sure you need not wish for anything better; but I see you still hold that pet scheme of yours for worrying your horses and lessening their power."

"What do you mean," said the other, "the check-reins? Oh, ah! I know that's a hobby of yours; well, the fact is, I like to see my horses hold their heads up."

"So do I," said master, "as well as any man, but I don't like to see them *held up*; that takes all the shine out of it. Now you are a military man, Langley, and no doubt like to see your regiment look well on parade, 'heads up,' and all that ; but you would not take much credit for your drill, if all your men had their heads tied to a backboard ! It might not be much harm on parade, except to worry and fatigue them ; *but how would it be in a bayonet charge against the enemy,* when they want the free use of every muscle, and all their strength thrown forward ? I would not give much for their chance of victory. And it is just the same with horses : *you fret and worry their tempers, and decrease their power ;* you will not let them throw their weight against their work, and so they have to do too much with their joints and muscles, and of course it wears them up faster. You may depend upon it, horses were intended to have their heads free, as free as men's are ; and if we could act a little more according to common sense, and a good deal less according to fashion, we should find many things work easier ; besides, you know as well as I, that if a horse makes a false step, he has *much less chance of recovering himself if his head and neck are fastened back.* And now," said the master, laughing, "I have given my hobby a good trot out, can't you make up your mind to mount him too, Captain ? Your example would go a long way."

"I believe you are right in theory," said the other, " and that's rather a hard hit about the soldiers; but — well — I'll think about it," and so they parted.

"An uncommonly handsome pair." (page 57)

"Is that pony made of flesh and blood?" (page 56)

CHAPTER XII

A STORMY DAY

ONE day late in the autumn my master had a long journey to go on business. I was put into the dog-cart, and John went with his master. I always liked to go in the dog-cart, it was so light and the high wheels ran along so pleasantly. There had been a great deal of rain, and now the wind was very high and blew the dry leaves across the road in a shower. We went along merrily till we came to the toll-bar and the low wooden bridge. The river banks were rather high, and the bridge, instead of rising, went across just level, so that in the middle, if the river was full, the water would be nearly up to the woodwork and planks; but as there were good substantial rails on each side, people did not mind it.

The man at the gate said the river was rising fast, and he feared it would be a bad night. Many of the meadows were under water, and in one low part of the road, the water was halfway up to my knees; the bottom was good, and master drove gently, so it was no matter.

When we got to the town, of course I had a good bait, but as the master's business engaged him a long time, we did not start for home till rather late in the afternoon. The wind was then much higher, and I heard the master say to John, he had never been out in such a storm; and so I thought, as we went along the skirts of a wood, where the great branches were swaying about like twigs, and the rushing sound was terrible.

"I wish we were well out of this wood," said my master.

"Yes, sir," said John, "it would be rather awkward if one of these branches came down upon us."

The words were scarcely out of his mouth when there was a groan, and a crack, and a splitting sound, and tearing, crashing down amongst the other trees came an oak, torn up by the roots, and it fell right across the road just before us. I will never say I was not frightened, for I was. I stopped still, and I believe I trembled; of course I did not turn round or run away; I was not brought up to that. John jumped out and was in a moment at my head.

"That was a very near touch," said my master. "What's to be done now?"

"Well, sir, we can't drive over that tree, nor yet get round it; there will be nothing for it, but to go back to the four cross ways, and that will be a good six miles before we get round to the wooden bridge again; it will make us late, but the horse is fresh."

So back we went and round by the cross roads, but by the time we got to the bridge it was very nearly dark; we could just see that the water was over the middle of it; but as that happened sometimes when the floods were out, master did not stop. We were going along at a good pace, but the moment my feet touched the first part of the bridge, I felt sure there was something wrong. I dare not go forward, and I made a dead stop. " Go on, Beauty," said my master, and he gave me a touch with the whip, but I dare not stir; he gave me a sharp cut; I jumped, but I dare not go forward.

" There 's something wrong, sir," said John, and he sprang out of the dog-cart and came to my head and looked all about. He tried to lead me forward. " Come on, Beauty, what 's the matter ? " Of course I could not tell him, but I knew very well that the bridge was not safe.

Just then the man at the toll-gate on the other side ran out of the house, tossing a torch about like one mad.

" Hoy, hoy, hoy ! halloo ! stop ! " he cried.

" What 's the matter ? " shouted my master.

" The bridge is broken in the middle, and part of it is carried away ; if you come on you 'll be into the river."

" Thank God ! " said my master. " You Beauty ! " said John, and took the bridle and gently turned me round to the right-hand road by the river side. The sun had set some time ; the wind seemed to have lulled off after that furious blast which tore up the tree. It grew darker and darker, stiller and stiller. I trotted quietly along, the wheels hardly making a sound on the soft road. For a good while neither master nor John spoke, and then master began in a serious voice. I could not understand much of what they said, but I found they thought, if I had gone on as the master wanted me, most likely the bridge would have given way under us, and horse, chaise, master, and man would have fallen into the river; and as the current was flowing very strongly, and there was no light and no help at hand, it was more than likely we should all have been drowned. *Master said, God had given men reason, by which they could find out things for themselves ; but he had given animals knowledge which did not depend on reason, and which was much more prompt and perfect in its way, and by which they had often saved the lives of men.* John had many stories to tell of dogs and horses, and the wonderful things they had done ; he thought people did not value their animals half enough, nor make friends of them as they ought to do. I am sure he makes friends of them if ever a man did.

At last we came to the park gates, and found the gardener looking out for us. He said that mistress had been in a dreadful way ever since dark, fearing some accident had happened, and that she had sent James off on Justice, the roan cob, towards the wooden bridge to make inquiry after us.

We saw a light at the hall door and at the upper windows, and as we came up, mistress ran out, saying, "Are you really safe, my dear? Oh! I have been so anxious, fancying all sorts of things. Have you had no accident ? "

" No, my dear ; but if your Black Beauty had not been wiser than we were, we should all have been carried down the river at the wooden bridge." I heard no more, as they went into the house, and John took me to the stable. Oh, what a good supper he gave me that night, a good bran mash and some crushed beans with my oats, and such a thick bed of straw! and I was glad of it, for I was tired.

CHAPTER XIII

THE DEVIL'S TRADE MARK

ONE day when John and I had been out on some business of our master's, and were returning gently on a long straight road, at some distance we saw a boy trying to leap a pony over a gate; the pony would not take the leap, and the boy cut him with the whip, but he only turned off on one side. He whipped him again, but the pony turned off on the other side. Then the boy got off and gave him a hard thrashing, and knocked him about the head; then he got up again and tried to make him leap the gate, kicking him all the time shamefully, but still the pony refused. When we were nearly at the spot, the pony put down his head and threw up his heels and sent the boy neatly over into a broad quickset hedge, and with the rein dangling from his head he set off home at a full gallop. John laughed out quite loud. "Served him right," he said.

"Oh, oh, oh!" cried the boy as he struggled about amongst the thorns; "I say, come and help me out."

"Thank ye," said John, "I think you are quite in the right place, and may be a little scratching will teach you not to leap a pony over a gate that is too high for him," and so with that John rode off. "It may be," said he to himself, "that young fellow is a liar as well as a cruel one; we'll just go home by farmer Bushby's, Beauty, and then if anybody wants to know, you and I can tell 'em, ye see." So we turned off to the right, and soon came up to the stack yard, and within sight of the house. The farmer was hurrying out into the road, and his wife was standing at the gate, looking very frightened.

"Have you seen my boy?" said Mr. Bushby, as we came up; "he went out an hour ago on my black pony, and the creature is just come back without a rider."

"I should think, sir," said John, "he had better be without a rider, unless he can be ridden properly."

"What do you mean?" said the farmer.

"Well, sir, I saw your son whipping, and kicking, and knocking that good little pony about shamefully, because he would not leap a gate that was too high for him. The pony behaved well, sir, and showed no vice; but at last he just threw up his heels, and tipped the young gentleman into the thorn hedge: he wanted me to help him out; but I hope you will excuse me, sir, I did not feel inclined to do so. There's no bones broken, sir, he'll only get a few scratches. I love horses, and it riles me to see them badly used; it is a bad plan to aggravate an animal till he uses his heels; the first time is not always the last."

During this time the mother began to cry, "Oh, my poor Bill, I must go and meet him, he must be hurt."

"You had better go into the house, wife," said the farmer; "Bill wants a lesson about this, and I must see that he gets it; this is not the first time, nor the second, that he has ill used that pony, and I shall stop it. I am much obliged to you, Manly. Good-evening."

So we went on, John chuckling all the way home; then he told James about it, who laughed and said, "Serve him right. I knew that boy at school; he took great airs on himself because he was a farmer's son; he used to swagger about and bully the little boys; of course we elder ones would not have any of that nonsense, and let him know that in the school and the playground, farmers' sons and laborers' sons were all alike. I well remember one day, just before afternoon school, I found him at the large window catching flies and pulling off their wings. He did not see me, and I gave him a box on the ears that laid him sprawling on the floor. Well, angry as I was, I was almost frightened, he roared and bellowed in such a style. The boys rushed in from the playground, and the master ran in from the road to see who was being murdered. Of course I said fair and square at once what I had done, and why; then I showed the master the flies, some crushed and some crawling about helpless, and I showed him the wings on the window sill. I never saw him so angry before; but as Bill was still howling and whining, like the coward that he was, he did not give him any more punishment of that kind, but set him up on a stool for the rest of the afternoon, and said that he should not go out to

play for that week.   Then he talked to all the boys
very seriously about cruelty, and said how hard-
hearted and cowardly it was to hurt the weak and
the helpless ; but what stuck in my mind was this,
he said that *cruelty was the Devil's own trade mark,*
and if we saw any one who took pleasure in cruelty,
we might know who he belonged to, for the devil
was a murderer from the beginning, and a tormentor
to the end.   On the other hand, where we saw people who loved their neighbors, and were kind to man
and beast, we might know that was God's mark, for
'God is Love.' "

"Your master never taught you a truer thing,"
said John ; "there is no religion without love, and
people may talk as much as they like about their religion, but *if it does not teach them to be good and
kind to man and beast, it is all a sham,* — all a
sham, James, and it won't stand when things come
to be turned inside out, and put down for what they
are."

CHAPTER XIV

JAMES HOWARD

ONE morning early in December, John had just led me into my box after my daily exercise, and was strapping my cloth on, and James was coming in from the corn chamber with some oats, when the master came into the stable; he looked rather serious, and held an open letter in his hand. John fastened the door of my box, touched his cap, and waited for orders.

"Good-morning, John," said the master; "I want to know if you have any complaint to make of James."

"Complaint, sir? No, sir."

"Is he industrious at his work and respectful to you?"

"Yes, sir, always."

"You never find he slights his work when your back is turned?"

"Never, sir."

"That's well; but I must put another question: have you no reason to suspect when he goes out with the horses to exercise them, or to take a message, that he stops about talking to his acquaintances, or goes into houses where he has no business, leaving the horses outside?"

"No, sir, certainly not; and if anybody has been saying that about James, I don't believe it, and I don't mean to believe it unless I have it fairly proved before witnesses; it's not for me to say who has been trying to take away James's character, but I will say this, sir, that a steadier, pleasanter, honester, smarter young fellow I never had in this stable. I can trust his word and I can trust his work; he is gentle and clever with the horses, and I would rather have them in charge with him than with half the young fellows I know of in laced hats and liveries; and whoever wants a character of James Howard," said John, with a decided jerk of his head, "let them come to John Manly."

The master stood all this time grave and attentive, but as John finished his speech, a broad smile spread over his face, and looking kindly across at James, who, all this time had stood still at the door, he said, "James, my lad, set down the oats and come here; I am very glad to find that John's opinion of your character agrees so exactly with my own. John is a cautious man," he said, with a droll smile, "and it is not always easy to get his opinion about people, so I thought if I beat the bush on this side the birds would fly out, and I should learn what I wanted to know quickly; so now we will come to business. I have a letter from my brother-in-law, Sir Clifford Williams, of Clifford Hall. He wants me to find him a trustworthy young groom, about twenty or twenty-one, who knows his business. His old coachman, who has lived with him thirty years, is getting feeble, and he wants a man to work with him and get into his ways, who would be able, when the old man was pensioned off, to step into his place. He would have eighteen shillings a week at first, a stable suit, a driving suit, a bedroom over the coach-house, and a boy under him. Sir Clifford is a good master, and if you could get the place it would be a good start for you. I don't want to part with you, and if you left us I know John would lose his right hand."

"That I should, sir," said John, "but I would not stand in his light for the world."

"How old are you, James?" said master.

"Nineteen next May, sir."

"That's young; what do you think, John?"

"Well, sir, it is young; but he is as steady as a man, and is strong, and well grown, and though he has not had much experience in driving, he has a light firm hand and a quick eye, and he is very care-ful, and I am quite sure no horse of his will be ruined for want of having his feet and shoes looked after."

"Your word will go the furthest, John," said the master, "for Sir Clifford adds in a postscript, 'If I could find a man trained by your John, I should like him better than any other;' so James, lad, think it over, talk to your mother at dinner time, and then let me know what you wish."

In a few days after this conversation, it was fully settled that James should go to Clifford Hall, in a month or six weeks, as it suited his master, and in the meantime he was to get all the practice in driv-ing that could be given to him. I never knew the carriage go out so often before; when the mistress did not go out, the master drove himself in the two-wheeled chaise; but now, whether it was master or the young ladies, or only an errand, Ginger and I were put in the carriage and James drove us. At the first, John rode with him on the box, telling him this and that, and after that James drove alone.

Then it was wonderful what a number of places the master would go to in the city on Saturday, and what queer streets we were driven through. He was sure to go to the railway station just as the train was coming in, and cabs and carriages, carts and omnibuses were all trying to get over the bridge together; that bridge wanted good horses and good drivers when the railway bell was ringing, for it was narrow, and there was a very sharp turn up to the station, where it would not have been at all difficult for people to run into each other, if they did not look sharp and keep their wits about them.

CHAPTER XV

THE OLD OSTLER

AFTER this, it was decided by my master and mistress to pay a visit to some friends who lived about forty-six miles from our home, and James was to drive them. The first day we traveled thirty-two miles. There were some long heavy hills, but James drove so carefully and thoughtfully that we were not at all harassed. He never forgot to put on the brake as we went downhill, nor to take it off at the right place. He kept our feet on the smoothest part of the road, and if the uphill was very long, he set the carriage wheels a little across the road, so as not to run back, and gave us a breathing. All these little things help a horse very much, *particularly if he gets kind words into the bargain.*

We stopped once or twice on the road, and just as the sun was going down, we reached the town where we were to spend the night. We stopped at the principal hotel, which was in the Market Place; it was a very large one; we drove under an archway into a long yard, at the further end of which were the stables and coach-houses. Two ostlers came to take us out. The head ostler was a pleasant, active little man, with a crooked leg, and a yellow striped waistcoat. I never saw a man unbuckle harness so quickly as he did, and with a pat and a good word he led me to a long stable, with six or eight stalls in it, and two or three horses. The other man brought Ginger; James stood by whilst we were rubbed down and cleaned.

I never was cleaned so lightly and quickly as by that little old man. When he had done, James stepped up and felt me over, as if he thought I could not be thoroughly done, but he found my coat as clean and smooth as silk.

" Well," he said, " I thought I was pretty quick, and our John quicker still, but you do beat all I ever saw for being quick and thorough at the same time."

" Practice makes perfect," said the crooked little ostler, " and 't would be a pity if it did n't; forty years' practice, and not perfect! ha, ha! that would be a pity; and as to being quick, why, bless you! that is only a matter of habit; if you get into the habit of being quick, it is just as easy as being slow; easier, I should say; in fact, it don't agree with my health to be hulking about over a job twice as long as it need take. Bless you! I could n't whistle if I crawled over my work as some folks do! You see, I have been about horses ever since I was twelve years old, in hunting stables, and racing stables; and being small, ye see, I was jockey for several years; but at the Goodwood, ye see, the turf was very slippery and my poor Larkspur got a fall, and I broke my knee, and so of course I was of no more use there. But I could not live without

horses, of course I could n't, so I took to the hotels.
And I can tell ye it is a downright pleasure to
handle an animal like this, well-bred, well-mannered,
well-cared for; bless ye! *I can tell how a horse is
treated. Give me the handling of a horse for twenty
minutes, and I 'll tell you what sort of a groom he
has had.* Look at this one, pleasant, quiet, turns
about just as you want him, holds up his feet to be
cleaned out, or anything else you please to wish;
then you 'll find another fidgety, fretty, won't
move the right way, or starts across the stall, tosses
up his head as soon as you come near him, lays his
ears, and seems afraid of you; or else squares about
at you with his heels. Poor things! I know what
sort of treatment they have had. If they are timid,
it makes them start or shy; if they are high-mettled, it makes them vicious or dangerous; their
tempers are mostly made when they are young.
Bless you! *they are like children, train 'em up in
the way they should go, as the good book says, and
when they are old they will not depart from it,* if
they have a chance, that is."

"I like to hear you talk," said James, "that 's
the way we lay it down at home, at our master's."

"Who is your master, young man? if it be a
proper question. I should judge he is a good one,
from what I see."

"He is Squire Gordon, of Birtwick Park, the
other side the Beacon hills," said James.

"Ah! so, so, I have heard tell of him: fine judge
of horses, ain't he? the best rider in the county?"

"I believe he is," said James, "but he rides

very little now, since the poor young master was killed."

"Ah! poor gentleman; I read all about it in the paper at the time; a fine horse killed too, was n't there?"

"Yes," said James, "he was a splendid creature, brother to this one, and just like him."

"Pity! pity!" said the old man, "'t was a bad place to leap, if I remember; a thin fence at top, a steep bank down to the stream, was n't it? no chance for a horse to see where he is going. Now, I am for bold riding as much as any man, but still there are some leaps that only a very knowing old huntsman has any right to take; *a man's life and a horse's life are worth more than a fox's tail*, at least I should say they ought to be."

During this time the other man had finished Ginger, and had brought our corn, and James and the old man left the stable together.

CHAPTER XVI

THE FIRE

LATER on in the evening, a traveler's horse was brought in by the second ostler, and whilst he was cleaning him, a young man with a pipe in his mouth lounged into the stable to gossip.

"I say, Towler," said the ostler, "just run up the ladder into the loft and put some hay down into this horse's rack, will you? *only lay down your pipe.*"

"All right," said the other, and went up through the trap door; and I heard him step across the floor overhead and put down the hay. James came in to look at us the last thing, and then the door was locked.

I cannot say how long I had slept, nor what time in the night it was, but I woke up very uncomfortable, though I hardly knew why. I got up; the air seemed all thick and choking. I heard Ginger coughing, and one of the other horses seemed very restless; it was quite dark, and I could see nothing, but the stable seemed full of smoke, and I hardly knew how to breathe.

The trap door had been left open, and I thought that was the place it came through. I listened, and heard a soft rushing sort of noise, and a low crackling and snapping. I did not know what it was, but there was something in the sound so strange, that it made me tremble all over. The other horses were now all awake ; some were pulling at their halters, others were stamping.

At last I heard steps outside, and the ostler who had put up the traveler's horse burst into the stable with a lantern, and began to untie the horses, and try to lead them out ; but he seemed in such a hurry and so frightened himself that he frightened me still more. The first horse would not go with him ; he tried the second and third, and they too would not stir. He came to me next and tried to drag me out of the stall by force ; of course that was no use. He tried us all by turns and then left the stable.

No doubt we were very foolish, but danger seemed to be all round, and there was nobody we knew to trust in, and all was strange and uncertain. The fresh air that had come in through the open door made it easier to breathe, but the rushing sound overhead grew louder, and as I looked upward, through the bars of my empty rack, I saw a red light flickering on the wall. Then I heard a cry of "Fire!" outside, and the old ostler quietly and quickly came in : he got one horse out, and went to another, but the flames were playing round the trap door, and the roaring overhead was dreadful.

The next thing I heard was James's voice, quiet and cheery, as it always was.

"Come, my beauties, it is time for us to be off, so wake up and come along." I stood nearest the door, so he came to me first, patting me as he came in.

"Come, Beauty, on with your bridle, my boy, we'll soon be out of this smother." It was on in no time; then he took the scarf off his neck, and tied it lightly over my eyes, and patting and coaxing he led me out of the stable. Safe in the yard, he slipped the scarf off my eyes, and shouted, "Here somebody! take this horse while I go back for the other."

A tall broad man stepped forward and took me, and James darted back into the stable. I set up a shrill whinny as I saw him go. Ginger told me afterwards, that whinny was the best thing I could have done for her, for had she not heard me outside, she would never have had courage to come out.

There was much confusion in the yard; the horses being got out of other stables, and the carriages and gigs being pulled out of houses and sheds, lest the flames should spread further. On the other side the yard, windows were thrown up, and people were shouting all sorts of things; but I kept my eye fixed on the stable door, where the smoke poured out thicker than ever, and I could see flashes of red light; presently I heard above all the stir and din a loud clear voice, which I knew was master's, —

"James Howard! James Howard! Are you there?" There was no answer, but I heard a crash of something falling in the stable, and the next moment I gave a loud joyful neigh, for I saw James coming through the smoke leading Ginger with him; she was coughing violently, and he was not able to speak.

"My brave lad!" said master, laying his hand on his shoulder, "are you hurt?"

James shook his head, for he could not yet speak.

"Aye," said the big man who held me; "he is a brave lad, and no mistake."

"And now," said master, "when you have got your breath, James, we 'll get out of this place as quickly as we can," and we were moving towards the entry, when from the Market Place there came a sound of galloping feet and loud rumbling wheels.

"'Tis the fire engine! the fire engine!" shouted two or three voices, "stand back, make way!" and clattering and thundering over the stones two horses dashed into the yard with the heavy engine behind them. The firemen leaped to the ground; there was no need to ask where the fire was — it was rolling up in a great blaze from the roof.

We got out as fast as we could into the broad quiet Market Place; the stars were shining, and except the noise behind us, all was still. Master led the way to a large hotel on the other side, and as soon as the ostler came, he said, "James, I must now hasten to your mistress; I trust the horses entirely to you, order whatever you think is needed," and with that he was gone. The master did not run, but I never saw mortal man walk so fast as he did that night.

There was a dreadful sound before we got into our stalls; the shrieks of those poor horses that were left burning to death in the stable — it was very terrible! and made both Ginger and me feel very bad. We, however, were taken in and well done by.

The next morning the master came to see how we

were and to speak to James. I did not hear much, for the ostler was rubbing me down, but I could see that James looked very happy, and I thought the master was proud of him. Our mistress had been so much alarmed in the night, that the journey was put off till the afternoon, so James had the morning on hand, and went first to the inn to see about our harness and the carriage, and then to hear more about the fire. When he came back, we heard him tell the ostler about it. At first no one could guess how the fire had been caused, but at last a man said he *saw Dick Towler go into the stable with a pipe in his mouth,* and when he came out he had not one, and went to the tap for another. Then the under ostler said he had asked Dick to go up the ladder to put down some hay, but told him to lay down his pipe first. Dick denied taking the pipe with him, but no one believed him. I remember our John Manly's rule, *never to allow a pipe in the stable,* and thought it ought to be the rule everywhere.

James said the roof and floor had all fallen in, and that only the black walls were standing; the two poor horses that could not be got out were buried under the burnt rafters and tiles.

Kindness. (page 67)

In the pasture.

CHAPTER XVII

JOHN MANLY'S TALK

THE rest of our journey was very easy, and a little after sunset we reached the house of my master's friend. We were taken into a clean snug stable; there was a kind coachman, who made us very comfortable, and who seemed to think a good deal of James when he heard about the fire.

"There is one thing quite clear, young man," he said, "your horses know who they can trust; it is one of the hardest things in the world to get horses out of a stable when there is either fire or flood. I don't know why they won't come out, but they won't — not one in twenty."

We stopped two or three days at this place and then returned home. All went well on the journey; we were glad to be in our own stable again, and John was equally glad to see us.

Before he and James left us for the night, James said, "I wonder who is coming in my place."

"Little Joe Green at the Lodge," said John.

"Little Joe Green! why, he's a child!"

"He is fourteen and a half," said John.

"But he is such a little chap!"

"Yes, he is small, but he is quick, and willing, and kind-hearted too, and then he wishes very much

to come, and his father would like it; and I know
the master would like to give him the chance. He
said if I thought he would not do, he would look
out for a bigger boy; but I said I was quite agreeable to try him for six weeks."

"Six weeks!" said James; "why, it will be six
months before he can be of much use! It will make
you a deal of work, John."

"Well," said John with a laugh, "work and I are
very good friends; I never was afraid of work yet."

"You are a very good man," said James. "I wish
I may ever be like you."

"I don't often speak of myself," said John, "but
as you are going away from us out into the world,
to shift for yourself, I'll just tell you how I look on
these things. I was just as old as Joseph when my
father and mother died of the fever, within ten days
of each other, and left me and my crippled sister
Nelly alone in the world, without a relation that
we could look to for help. I was a farmer's boy,
not earning enough to keep myself, much less both
of us, and she must have gone to the workhouse
but for our mistress (Nelly calls her her angel, and
she has good right to do so). She went and hired a
room for her with old widow Mallet, and she gave
her knitting and needlework when she was able to
do it; and when she was ill she sent her dinners
and many nice, comfortable things, and was like a
mother to her. Then the master, he took me into
the stable under old Norman, the coachman that
was then. I had my food at the house and my bed
in the loft, and a suit of clothes, and three shillings

a week, so that I could help Nelly. Then there was Norman; he might have turned round and said at his age he could not be troubled with a raw boy from the plough-tail, but he was like a father to me, and took no end of pains with me. When the old man died some years after, I stepped into his place, and now of course I have top wages, and can lay by for a rainy day or a sunny day, as it may happen, and Nelly is as happy as a bird. So you see, James, I am not the man that should turn up his nose at a little boy, and vex a good, kind master. No, no! I shall miss you very much, James, but we shall pull through, and *there's nothing like doing a kindness when 't is put in your way, and I am glad I can do it.*"

"Then," said James, "you don't hold with that saying, 'Everybody look after himself, and take care of number one.'"

"No, indeed," said John; "where should I and Nelly have been if master and mistress and old Norman had only taken care of number one? Why, she in the workhouse and I hoeing turnips! Where would Black Beauty and Ginger have been if you had only thought of number one? Why, roasted to death! No, Jim, no! that is a selfish, heathenish saying, whoever uses it; and any man who thinks he has nothing to do but take care of number one, why, it's a pity but what he had been drowned like a puppy or a kitten, before he got his eyes open, — that's what I think," said John, with a very decided jerk of his head.

James laughed at this; but there was a thickness

in his voice when he said, "You have been my best friend except my mother; I hope you won't forget me."

"No, lad, no!" said John, "and if ever I can do you a good turn, I hope you won't forget me."

The next day Joe came to the stables to learn all he could before James left. He learned to sweep the stable, to bring in the straw and hay; he began to clean the harness, and helped to wash the carriage. As he was quite too short to do anything in the way of grooming Ginger and me, James taught him upon Merrylegs, for he was to have full charge of him, under John. He was a nice little bright fellow, and always came whistling to his work.

Merrylegs was a good deal put out at being "mauled about," as he said, "by a boy who knew nothing;" but towards the end of the second week he told me confidentially that he thought the boy would turn out well.

At last the day came when James had to leave us; cheerful as he always was, he looked quite down-hearted that morning.

"You see," he said to John, "I am leaving a great deal behind; my mother and Betsy, and you, and a good master and mistress, and then the horses, and my old Merrylegs. At the new place there will not be a soul that I shall know. If it were not that I shall get a higher place, and be able to help my mother better, I don't think I should have made up my mind to it; it is a real pinch, John."

"Ay, James, lad, so it is; but I should not think much of you, if you could leave your home for the first time and not feel it. Cheer up, you'll make friends there; and if you get on well, as I am sure you will, it will be a fine thing for your mother, and she will be proud enough that you have got into such a good place as that."

So John cheered him up, but every one was sorry to lose James; as for Merrylegs, he pined after him for several days, and went quite off his appetite. So John took him out several mornings with a leading rein, when he exercised me, and, trotting and galloping by my side, got up the little fellow's spirits again, and he was soon all right.

Joe's father would often come in and give a little help, as he understood the work; and Joe took a great deal of pains to learn, and John was quite encouraged about him.

CHAPTER XVIII

GOING FOR THE DOCTOR

ONE night, a few days after James had left, I had eaten my hay and was lying down in my straw fast asleep, when I was suddenly roused by the stable bell ringing very loud. I heard the door of John's house open, and his feet running up to the Hall. He was back again in no time; he unlocked the stable door, and came in, calling out, "Wake up, Beauty! You must go well now, if ever you did;" and almost before I could think, he had got the saddle on my back and the bridle on my head. He just ran round for his coat, and then took me at a quick trot up to the Hall door. The Squire stood there, with a lamp in his hand.

"Now, John," he said, "ride for your life, — that is, for your mistress' life; there is not a moment to lose. Give this note to Doctor White; give your horse a rest at the inn, and be back as soon as you can."

John said, "Yes, sir," and was on my back in a minute. The gardener who lived at the lodge had heard the bell ring, and was ready with the gate open, and away we went through the park, and through the village, and down the hill till we came to the toll-gate. John called very loud and thumped upon the door; the man was soon out and flung open the gate.

"Now," said John, " do you keep the gate open for the Doctor; here 's the money," and off we went again.

There was before us a long piece of level road by the river side; John said to me, " Now, Beauty, do your best," and so I did; I wanted no whip nor spur, and for two miles I galloped as fast as I could lay my feet to the ground; I don't believe that my old grandfather, who won the race at Newmarket, could have gone faster. When we came to the bridge, John pulled me up a little and patted my neck. " Well done, Beauty! good old fellow," he said. He would have let me go slower, but my spirit was up, and I was off again as fast as before. The air was frosty, the moon was bright; it was very pleasant. We came through a village, then through a dark wood, then uphill, then downhill, till after an eight miles' run we came to the town, through the streets and into the Market Place. It was all quite still except the clatter of my feet on the stones, — everybody was asleep. The church clock struck three as we drew up at Doctor White's door. John rang the bell twice, and then knocked at the door like thunder. A window was thrown up, and Doctor White, in his nightcap, put his head out and said, " What do you want ? "

" Mrs. Gordon is very ill, sir: master wants you to go at once; he thinks she will die if you cannot get there. Here is a note."

" Wait," he said, " I will come."

He shut the window, and was soon at the door.

"The worst of it is," he said, "that my horse has been out all day and is quite done up; my son has just been sent for, and he has taken the other. What is to be done? Can I have your horse?"

"He has come at a gallop nearly all the way, sir, and I was to give him a rest here; but I think my master would not be against it, if you think fit, sir."

"All right," he said; "I will soon be ready."

John stood by me and stroked my neck; I was very hot. The Doctor came out with his riding-whip.

"You need not take that, sir," said John; "Black Beauty will go till he drops. Take care of him, sir, if you can; I should not like any harm to come to him."

"No, no, John," said the Doctor, "I hope not," and in a minute we had left John far behind.

I will not tell about our way back. The Doctor was a heavier man than John, and not so good a rider; however, I did my very best. The man at the toll-gate had it open. When we came to the hill, the Doctor drew me up. "Now, my good fellow," he said, "take some breath." I was glad he did, for I was nearly spent, but that breathing helped me on, and soon we were in the park. Joe was at the lodge gate; my master was at the Hall door, for he had heard us coming. He spoke not a word; the Doctor went into the house with him, and Joe led me to the stable. I was glad to get home; my legs shook under me, and I could only stand and pant. I had not a dry hair on my body, the water ran down my legs, and I steamed all over, — Joe used to say, like a pot on the fire. Poor Joe! he was young and small, and as yet he knew very little, and his father, who would have helped him, had been sent to the next village; but I am sure he did the very best he knew. He rubbed my legs and my chest, but he did not put my warm cloth on me; he thought I was so hot I should not like it. Then he gave me a pailful of water to drink; it was cold and very good, and I drank it all; then he gave me some hay and some corn, and, thinking he had done right, he went away. Soon I began to shake and tremble, and turned deadly cold; my legs ached, my loins ached, and my chest ached, and I felt sore all over. Oh! how I wished for my warm thick cloth as I stood and trembled. I wished for John, but he had eight miles to walk, so I lay down in my straw and tried to go to sleep. After a long while I heard John at the door; I gave a low moan, for I was in great pain. He was at my side in a moment, stooping down by me. I could not tell him how I felt, but he seemed to know it all; he covered me up with two or three warm cloths, and then ran to the house for some hot water; he made me some warm gruel, which I drank, and then I think I went to sleep.

John seemed to be very much put out. I heard him say to himself over and over again, "Stupid boy! stupid boy! no cloth put on, and I dare say the water was cold, too; boys are no good;" but Joe was a good boy, after all.

I was now very ill; a strong inflammation had attacked my lungs, and I could not draw my breath without pain. John nursed me night and day; he would get up two or three times in the night to come to me. My master, too, often came to see me. "My poor Beauty," he said one day, "my good horse, you saved your mistress' life, Beauty; yes, you saved her life." I was very glad to hear that, for it seems the Doctor had said if we had been a little longer it would have been too late. John told my master he never saw a horse go so fast in his life. It seemed as if the horse knew what was the matter. Of course I did, though John thought not; at least I knew as much as this, — that John and I must go at the top of our speed, and that it was for the sake of the mistress.

CHAPTER XIX

ONLY IGNORANCE

I DO not know how long I was ill. Mr. Bond, the horse-doctor, came every day. One day he bled me; John held a pail for the blood. I felt very faint after it, and thought I should die, and I believe they all thought so, too.

Ginger and Merrylegs had been moved into the other stable, so that I might be quiet, for the fever made me very quick of hearing; any little noise seemed quite loud, and I could tell every one's footstep going to and from the house. I knew all that was going on. One night John had to give me a draught; Thomas Green came in to help him. After I had taken it and John had made me as comfortable as he could, he said he should stay half an hour to see how the medicine settled. Thomas said he would stay with him, so they went and sat down on a bench that had been brought into Merrylegs' stall, and put down the lantern at their feet, that I might not be disturbed with the light.

For a while both men sat silent, and then Tom Green said in a low voice, —

"I wish, John, you'd say a bit of a kind word to Joe. The boy is quite broken-hearted; he can't eat his meals, and he can't smile. He says he knows it was all his fault, though he is sure he did the best he knew, and he says, if Beauty dies, no one will ever speak to him again. It goes to my heart to hear him. I think you might give him just a word; he is not a bad boy."

After a short pause, John said slowly, "You must not be too hard upon me, Tom. I know he meant no harm, I never said he did; I know he is not a bad boy. But you see I am sore myself; that horse is the pride of my heart, to say nothing of his being such a favorite with the master and mistress; and to think that his life may be flung away in this manner is more than I can bear. But if you think I am hard on the boy, I will try to give him a good word to-morrow, — that is, I mean if Beauty is better."

"Well, John, thank you. I knew you did not wish to be too hard, and I am glad you see it was only ignorance."

John's voice almost startled me as he answered, " *Only* ignorance! only *ignorance!* how can you talk about *only* ignorance? *Don't you know that it is the worst thing in the world, next to wickedness?* — and which does the most mischief Heaven only knows. If people can say, ' Oh! I did not know, I did not mean any harm,' they think it is all right. I suppose Martha Mulwash did not mean to kill that baby, when she dosed it with Dalby and soothing-syrups; but she did kill it, and was tried for manslaughter."

" And serve her right, too," said Tom. " A woman should not undertake to nurse a tender little child without knowing what is good and what is bad for it."

"Bill Starkey," continued John, "did not mean to frighten his brother into fits, when he dressed up like a ghost, and ran after him in the moonlight; but he did; and that bright, handsome little fellow, that might have been the pride of any mother's heart, is just no better than an idiot, and never will be, if he live to be eighty years old. You were a good deal cut up yourself, Tom, two weeks ago, when those young ladies left your hothouse door open, with a frosty east wind blowing right in; you said it killed a good many of your plants."

"A good many!" said Tom; "there was not one of the tender cuttings that was not nipped off. I shall have to strike all over again, and the worst of it is that I don't know where to go to get fresh ones. I was nearly mad when I came in and saw what was done."

"And yet," said John, "I am sure the young ladies did not mean it; it was only ignorance."

I heard no more of this conversation, for the medicine did well and sent me to sleep, and in the morning I felt much better; but I often thought of John's words when I came to know more of the world.

CHAPTER XX

JOE GREEN

JOE GREEN went on very well; he learned quickly, and was so attentive and careful that John began to trust him in many things; but, as I have said, he was small of his age, and it was seldom that he was allowed to exercise either Ginger or me; but it so happened one morning that John was out with Justice in the luggage cart, and the master wanted a note to be taken immediately to a gentleman's house, about three miles distant, and sent his orders for Joe to saddle me and take it; adding the caution that he was to ride steadily.

The note was delivered, and we were quietly returning when we came to the brickfield. Here we saw a cart heavily laden with bricks; the wheels had stuck fast in the stiff mud of some deep ruts, and the carter was shouting and flogging the two horses unmercifully. Joe pulled up. It was a sad sight. There were the two horses straining and struggling with all their might to drag the cart out, but they could not move it; the sweat streamed from their legs and flanks, their sides heaved, and every muscle was strained, whilst the man, fiercely pulling at the head of the fore horse, swore and lashed most brutally.

"Hold hard," said Joe; "don't go on flogging the horses like that; the wheels are so stuck that they cannot move the cart."

The man took no heed, but went on lashing.

"Stop! pray stop!" said Joe. "I'll help you to lighten the cart; they can't move it now."

"Mind your own business, you impudent young rascal, and I'll mind mine!" The man was in a towering passion and the worse for drink, and laid on the whip again. Joe turned my head, and the next moment we were going at a round gallop towards the house of the master brickmaker. I cannot say if John would have approved of our pace, but Joe and I were both of one mind, and so angry that we could not have gone slower.

The house stood close by the roadside. Joe knocked at the door, and shouted, "Hallo! Is Mr. Clay at home?" The door was opened, and Mr. Clay himself came out.

"Hallo, young man! You seem in a hurry; any orders from the Squire this morning?"

"No, Mr. Clay, but there's a fellow in your brick-yard flogging two horses to death. I told him to stop, and he wouldn't; I said I'd help him to lighten the cart, and he wouldn't; so I have come to tell you. Pray, sir, go." Joe's voice shook with excitement.

"Thank ye, my lad," said the man, running in for his hat; then pausing for a moment, "Will you give evidence of what you saw if I should bring the fellow up before a magistrate?"

"That I will," said Joe, "and glad too." The

man was gone, and we were on our way home at a smart trot.

"Why, what's the matter with you, Joe? You look angry all over," said John, as the boy flung himself from the saddle.

"I am angry all over, I can tell you," said the boy, and then in hurried, excited words he told all that had happened. Joe was usually such a quiet, gentle little fellow that it was wonderful to see him so roused.

"Right, Joe! you did right, my boy, whether the fellow gets a summons or not. Many folks would have ridden by and said 't was not their business to interfere. *Now I say that with cruelty and oppression it is everybody's business to interfere when they see it; you did right, my boy.*"

Joe was quite calm by this time, and proud that John approved of him, and he cleaned out my feet, and rubbed me down with a firmer hand than usual.

They were just going home to dinner when the footman came down to the stable to say that Joe was wanted directly in master's private room; there was a man brought up for ill-using horses, and Joe's evidence was wanted. The boy flushed up to his forehead, and his eyes sparkled. "They shall have it," said he.

"Put yourself a bit straight," said John. Joe gave a pull at his necktie and a twitch at his jacket, and was off in a moment. Our master being one of the county magistrates, cases were often brought to him to settle, or say what should be done. In the stable we heard no more for some time, as it was the men's dinner hour, but when Joe came next into the stable I saw he was in high spirits; he gave me a good-natured slap, and said, "We won't see such things done, will we, old fellow?" We heard afterwards that he had given his evidence so clearly, and the horses were in such an exhausted state, bearing marks of such brutal usage, that the carter was committed to take his trial, and might possibly be sentenced to two or three months in prison.

It was wonderful what a change had come over Joe. John laughed, and said he had grown an inch taller in that week, and I believe he had. He was just as kind and gentle as before, but there was more purpose and determination in all that he did, — as if he had jumped at once from a boy into a man.

CHAPTER XXI

THE PARTING

I HAD now lived in this happy place three years, but sad changes were about to come over us. We heard from time to time that our mistress was ill. The Doctor was often at the house, and the master looked grave and anxious. Then we heard that she must leave her home at once, and go to a warm country for two or three years. The news fell upon the household like the tolling of a death-bell. Everybody was sorry; but the master began directly to make arrangements for breaking up his establishment and leaving England. We used to hear it talked about in our stable; indeed, nothing else was talked about.

John went about his work silent and sad, and Joe scarcely whistled. There was a great deal of coming and going; Ginger and I had full work.

The first of the party who went were Miss Jessie and Flora with their governess. They came to bid us good-by. They hugged poor Merrylegs like an old friend, and so indeed he was. Then we heard what had been arranged for us. Master had sold Ginger and me to his old friend, the Earl of W——, for he thought we should have a good place there. Merrylegs he had given to the Vicar, who was wanting a pony for Mrs. Blomefield, but it was *on the condition that he should never be sold, and that when he was past work he should be shot and buried.*

Joe was engaged to take care of him and to help in the house, so I thought that Merrylegs was well off. John had the offer of several good places, but he said he should wait a little and look round.

The evening before they left, the master came into the stable to give some directions, and to give his horses the last pat. He seemed very low-spirited; I knew that by his voice. I believe we horses can tell more by the voice than many men can.

"Have you decided what to do, John?" he said. "I find you have not accepted either of those offers."

"No, sir; I have made up my mind that if I could get a situation with some first-rate colt-breaker and horse-trainer, it would be the right thing for me. Many young animals are frightened and spoiled by wrong treatment, which need not be if the right man took them in hand. I always get on well with horses, and if I could help some of them to a fair start I should feel as if I was doing some good. What do you think of it, sir?"

"I don't know a man anywhere," said master, "that I should think so suitable for it as yourself. You understand horses, and somehow they understand you, and in time you might set up for yourself; I think you could not do better. If in any way I can help you, write to me. I shall speak to my agent in London, and leave your character with him."

Master gave John the name and address, and then he thanked him for his long and faithful service; but that was too much for John. "Pray, don't, sir, I can't bear it; you and my dear mistress have done so much for me that I could never repay it. But we shall never forget you, sir, and please God, we may some day see mistress back again like herself; we must keep up hope, sir." Master gave John his hand, but he did not speak, and they both left the stable.

The last sad day had come; the footman and the heavy luggage had gone off the day before, and there were only master and mistress and her maid. Ginger and I brought the carriage up to the Hall door for the last time. The servants brought out cushions and rugs and many other things; and when all were arranged, master came down the steps carrying the mistress in his arms (I was on the side next the house, and could see all that went on); he placed her carefully in the carriage, while the house servants stood round crying.

"Good-by, again," he said; "we shall not forget any of you," and he got in. "Drive on, John."

Joe jumped up, and we trotted slowly through the park and through the village, where the people were standing at their doors to have a last look and to say, "God bless them."

When we reached the railway station, I think mistress walked from the carriage to the waiting-room. I heard her say in her own sweet voice, "Good-by, John. God bless you." I felt the rein twitch, but John made no answer; perhaps he could

"Now, John," he said, "ride for your life." (page 86)

We trotted slowly through the park and village. (page 100)

not speak. As soon as Joe had taken the things out of the carriage, John called him to stand by the horses, while he went on the platform. Poor Joe! he stood close up to our heads to hide his tears. Very soon the train came puffing up into the station; then two or three minutes, and the doors were slammed to; the guard whistled and the train glided away, leaving behind it only clouds of white smoke and some very heavy hearts.

When it was quite out of sight, John came back.

"We shall never see her again," he said, — "never." He took the reins, mounted the box, and with Joe drove slowly home; but it was not our home now.

PART II

CHAPTER XXII

EARLSHALL

HE next morning after breakfast, Joe put Merrylegs into the mistress' low chaise to take him to the vicarage; he came first and said good-by to us, and Merrylegs neighed to us from the yard. Then John put the saddle on Ginger and the leading rein on me, and rode us across the country about fifteen miles to Earlshall Park, where the Earl of W—— lived. There was a very fine house and a great deal of stabling. We went into the yard through a stone gateway, and John asked for Mr. York. It was some time before he came. He was a fine-looking, middle-aged man, and his voice said at once that he expected to be obeyed. He was very friendly and polite to John, and after giving us a slight look he called a groom to take us to our boxes, and invited John to take some refreshment.

We were taken to a light, airy stable, and placed in boxes adjoining each other, where we were rubbed down and fed. In about half an hour John and Mr.

York, who was to be our new coachman, came in to see us.

"Now, Mr. Manly," he said, after carefully looking at us both, "I can see no fault in these horses; but we all know that horses have their peculiarities as well as men, and that sometimes they need different treatment. I should like to know if there is anything particular in either of these that you would like to mention."

"Well," said John, "I don't believe there is a better pair of horses in the country, and right grieved I am to part with them, but they are not alike. The black one is the most perfect temper I ever knew; I suppose he has never known a hard word or a blow since he was foaled, and all his pleasure seems to be to do what you wish; but the chestnut, I fancy, must have had bad treatment; we heard as much from the dealer. She came to us snappish and suspicious, but when she found what sort of place ours was, it all went off by degrees; for three years I have never seen the smallest sign of temper, and if she is well treated there is not a better, more willing animal than she is. But she is naturally a more irritable constitution than the black horse; flies tease her more; anything wrong in the harness frets her more; and if she were ill-used or unfairly treated she would not be unlikely to give tit for tat. You know that many high-mettled horses will do so."

"Of course," said York, "I quite understand; but you know it is not easy in stables like these to have all the grooms just what they should be. I do my best, and there I must leave it. I'll remember what you have said about the mare."

They were going out of the stable, when John stopped, and said, " I had better mention that we have never used the check-rein with either of them ; the black horse never had one on, and the dealer said it was the gag-bit that spoiled the other's temper."

" Well," said York, " if they come here, they must wear the check-rein. *I prefer a loose rein myself, and his lordship is always very reasonable about horses ; but my lady — that's another thing ;* she will have style, and if her carriage horses are not reined up tight she would n't look at them. I always stand out against the gag-bit, and shall do so, but *it must be tight up when my lady rides!* "

" I am sorry for it, very sorry," said John ; " but I must go now, or I shall lose the train."

He came round to each of us to pat and speak to us for the last time ; his voice sounded very sad.

I held my face close to him ; that was all I could do to say good-by ; and then he was gone, and I have never seen him since.

The next day Lord W —— came to look at us ; he seemed pleased with our appearance.

" I have great confidence in these horses," he said, " from the character my friend Mr. Gordon has given me of them. Of course they are not a match in color, but my idea is that they will do very well for the carriage whilst we are in the country. Before we go to London I must try to match Baron ; the black horse, I believe, is perfect for riding."

York then told him what John had said about us.

" Well," said he, " you must keep an eye to the

mare, and put the check-rein easy ; I dare say they
will do very well with a little humoring at first. I 'll
mention it to your lady."

In the afternoon we were harnessed and put in
the carriage, and as the stable clock struck three we
were led round to the front of the house. It was all
very grand, and three or four times as large as the
old house at Birtwick, but not half so pleasant, if
a horse may have an opinion. Two footmen were
standing ready, dressed in drab livery, with scarlet
breeches and white stockings. Presently we heard
the rustling sound of silk as my lady came down the
flight of stone steps. She stepped round to look at
us ; she was a tall, proud-looking woman, and did
not seem pleased about something, but she said nothing, and got into the carriage. This was the first
time of wearing a check-rein, and I must say, though
it certainly was a nuisance not to be able to get my
head down now and then, it did not pull my head
higher than I was accustomed to carry it. I felt
anxious about Ginger, but she seemed to be quiet
and content.

The next day at three o'clock we were again at
the door, and the footmen as before ; we heard the
silk dress rustle, and the lady came down the steps,
and in an imperious voice she said, " *York, you must
put those horses' heads higher ; they are not fit to be
seen.*"

York got down, and said very respectfully, " I
beg your pardon, my lady, but these horses have not
been reined up for three years, and my lord said it
would be safer to bring them to it by degrees ; but

if your ladyship pleases, I can take them up a little more."

"Do so," she said.

York came round to our heads and shortened the rein himself, one hole, I think; every little makes a difference, be it for better or worse, and that day we had a steep hill to go up. Then I began to understand what I had heard of. Of course I wanted to put my head forward and take the carriage up with a will, as we had been used to do; but no, I had to pull with my head up now, and *that took all the spirit out of me, and the strain came on my back and legs.* When we came in, Ginger said, "Now you see what it is like; but this is not bad, and if it does not get much worse than this I shall say nothing about it, for we are very well treated here; but if they strain me up tight, why, let 'em look out! I can't bear it, and I won't."

Day by day, hole by hole our bearing reins were shortened, and instead of looking forward with pleasure to having my harness put on, as I used to do, I began to dread it. Ginger too seemed restless, though she said very little. At last I thought the worst was over; for several days there was no more shortening, and I determined to make the best of it and do my duty, though it was now a constant harass instead of a pleasure; but the worst was not come.

CHAPTER XXIII

A STRIKE FOR LIBERTY

ONE day my lady came down later than usual, and the silk rustled more than ever.

"Drive to the Duchess of B——'s," she said and then after a pause, "Are you never going to get those horses' heads up, York? Raise them at once, and let us have no more of this humoring and nonsense."

York came to me first, whilst the groom stood at Ginger's head. *He drew my head back and fixed the rein so tight that it was almost intolerable;* then he went to Ginger, who was impatiently jerking her head up and down against the bit, as was her way now. She had a good idea of what was coming, and the moment York took the rein off the terret in order to shorten it, she took her opportunity, and reared up so suddenly that York had his nose roughly hit and his hat knocked off; the groom was nearly thrown off his legs. At once they both flew to her head, but she was a match for them, and went on plunging, rearing, and kicking in a most desperate manner; at last she kicked right over the carriage pole and fell down, after giving me a severe blow on my near quarter. There is no knowing what further mischief she might have done, had not

York promptly sat himself down flat on her head to prevent her struggling, at the same time calling out, "Unbuckle the black horse! Run for the winch and unscrew the carriage pole! Cut the trace here, somebody, if you can't unhitch it!" One of the footmen ran for the winch, and another brought a knife from the house. The groom soon set me free from Ginger and the carriage, and led me to my box. He just turned me in as I was, and ran back to York. I was much excited by what had happened, and if I had ever been used to kick or rear I am sure I should have done it then; but I never had, and there I stood, angry, sore in my leg, my head still strained up to the terret on the saddle, and no power to get it down. I was very miserable, and felt much inclined to kick the first person who came near me.

Before long, however, Ginger was led in by two grooms, a good deal knocked about and bruised. York came with her and gave his orders, and then came to look at me. In a moment he let down my head.

"Confound these check-reins!" he said to himself; "I thought we should have some mischief soon. Master will be sorely vexed. But there, if a woman's husband can't rule her, of course a servant can't; so I wash my hands of it, and if she can't get to the Duchess' garden party I can't help it."

York did not say this before the men; he always spoke respectfully when they were by. Now he felt me all over, and soon found the place above my hock where I had been kicked. It was swelled and painful; he ordered it to be sponged with hot water, and then some lotion was put on.

Lord W—— was much put out when he learned what had happened; he blamed York for giving way to his mistress, to which he replied that in future he would much prefer to receive his orders only from his lordship; but I think nothing came of it, for things went on the same as before. I thought York might have stood up better for his horses, but perhaps I am no judge.

Ginger was never put into the carriage again, but when she was well of her bruises one of Lord W——'s younger sons said he should like to have her; he was sure she would make a good hunter. As for me, I was obliged still to go in the carriage, and had a fresh partner called Max; he had always been used to the tight rein. I asked him how it was he bore it.

"Well," he said, "I bear it because I must; but it is shortening my life, and it will shorten yours too if you have to stick to it."

"Do you think," I said, "that our masters know how bad it is for us?"

"I can't say," he replied, "but the dealers and the horse-doctors know it very well. I was at a dealer's once, who was training me and another horse to go as a pair; he was getting our heads up, as he said, a little higher and a little higher every day. A gentleman who was there asked him why he did so. 'Because,' said he, 'people won't buy them unless we do. The London people always

want their horses to carry their heads high and to
step high. Of course it is very bad for the horses,
but then it is good for trade. The horses soon wear
up, or get diseased, and they come for another pair.'
That," said Max, " is what he said in my hearing,
and you can judge for yourself."

What I suffered with that rein for four long
months in my lady's carriage it would be hard to
describe; but I am quite sure that, had it lasted
much longer, either my health or my temper would
have given way. Before that, I never knew what it
was to foam at the mouth, but now the action of the
sharp bit on my tongue and jaw, and the constrained
position of my head and throat, always caused me
to froth at the mouth more or less. Some people
think it very fine to see this, and say, "What fine,
spirited creatures !" *But it is just as unnatural for*
horses as for men to foam at the mouth ; it is a sure
sign of some discomfort, and should be attended to.
Besides this, there was a pressure on my windpipe,
which often made my breathing very uncomfortable ;
when I returned from my work, my neck and chest
were strained and painful, my mouth and tongue
tender, and I felt worn and depressed.

In my old home I always knew that John and my
master were my friends ; but here, although in many
ways I was well treated, I had no friend. York
might have known, and very likely did know, how
that rein harassed me ; but I suppose he took it as
a matter of course that could not be helped ; at any
rate, nothing was done to relieve me.

CHAPTER XXIV

THE LADY ANNE, OR A RUNAWAY HORSE

EARLY in the spring, Lord W—— and part of his family went up to London, and took York with them. I and Ginger and some other horses were left at home for use, and the head groom was left in charge.

The Lady Harriet, who remained at the Hall, was a great invalid, and never went out in the carriage, and the Lady Anne preferred riding on horseback with her brother or cousins. She was a perfect horsewoman, and as gay and gentle as she was beautiful. She chose me for her horse, and named me " Black Auster." I enjoyed these rides very much in the clear cold air, sometimes with Ginger, sometimes with Lizzie. This Lizzie was a bright bay mare, almost thoroughbred, and a great favorite with the gentlemen, on account of her fine action and lively spirit; but Ginger, who knew more of her than I did, told me she was rather nervous.

There was a gentleman of the name of Blantyre staying at the Hall; he always rode Lizzie, and praised her so much that one day Lady Anne ordered the side-saddle to be put on her, and the other saddle on me. When we came to the door, the gentleman seemed very uneasy.

"How is this?" he said. "Are you tired of your good Black Auster?"

"Oh, no, not at all," she replied, "but I am amiable enough to let you ride him for once, and I will try your charming Lizzie. You must confess that in size and appearance she is far more like a lady's horse than my own favorite."

"Do let me advise you not to mount her," he said; "she is a charming creature, but she is too nervous for a lady. I assure you, she is not perfectly safe; let me beg you to have the saddles changed."

"My dear cousin," said Lady Anne, laughing, "pray do not trouble your good careful head about me. I have been a horsewoman ever since I was a baby, and I have followed the hounds a great many times, though I know you do not approve of ladies hunting; but still that is the fact, and I intend to try this Lizzie that you gentlemen are all so fond of; so please help me to mount, like a good friend as you are."

There was no more to be said; he placed her carefully on the saddle, looked to the bit and curb, gave the reins gently into her hand, and then mounted me. Just as we were moving off, a footman came out with a slip of paper and message from the Lady Harriet. "Would they ask this question for her at Doctor Ashley's, and bring the answer?"

The village was about a mile off, and the Doctor's house was the last in it. We went along gayly enough till we came to his gate. There was a short drive up to the house between tall evergreens. Blantyre alighted at the gate, and was going to open it for Lady Anne, but she said, " I will wait for you here, and you can hang Auster's rein on the gate."

He looked at her doubtfully. " I will not be five minutes," he said.

" Oh, do not hurry yourself; Lizzie and I shall not run away from you."

He hung my rein on one of the iron spikes, and was soon hidden amongst the trees. Lizzie was standing quietly by the side of the road a few paces off, with her back to me. My young mistress was sitting easily with a loose rein, humming a little song. I listened to my rider's footsteps until they reached the house, and heard him knock at the door. There was a meadow on the opposite side of the road, the gate of which stood open; just then, some cart horses and several young colts came trotting out in a very disorderly manner, whilst a boy behind was cracking a great whip. The colts were wild and frolicsome, and one of them bolted across the road, and blundered up against Lizzie's hind legs; and whether it was the stupid colt, or the loud cracking of the whip, or both together, I cannot say, but she gave a violent kick, and dashed off into a headlong gallop. It was so sudden that Lady Anne was nearly unseated, but she soon recovered herself. I gave a loud, shrill neigh for help; again and again I neighed, pawing the ground impatiently, and tossing my head to get the rein loose. I had not long to wait. Blantyre came running to the gate; he looked anxiously about, and just caught sight of the flying figure, now far away on the road.

In an instant he sprang to the saddle. I needed no whip, no spur, for I was as eager as my rider; he saw it, and giving me a free rein, and leaning a little forward, we dashed after them.

For about a mile and a half the road ran straight, and then bent to the right, after which it divided into two roads. Long before we came to the bend, she was out of sight. Which way had she turned? A woman was standing at her garden gate, shading her eyes with her hand, and looking eagerly up the road. Scarcely drawing the rein, Blantyre shouted, "Which way?" "To the right!" cried the woman, pointing with her hand, and away we went up the right-hand road; then for a moment we caught sight of her; another bend and she was hidden again. Several times we caught glimpses, and then lost them. We scarcely seemed to gain ground upon them at all. An old road-mender was standing near a heap of stones, his shovel dropped and his hands raised. As we came near he made a sign to speak. Blantyre drew the rein a little. "To the common, to the common, sir; she has turned off there." I knew this common very well; it was for the most part very uneven ground, covered with heather and dark green furze bushes, with here and there a scrubby old thorn-tree; there were also open spaces of fine short grass, with ant-hills and mole-turns everywhere; the worst place I ever knew for a headlong gallop.

We had hardly turned on the common, when we caught sight again of the green habit flying on before us. My lady's hat was gone, and her long

The discomfort and strain of high checking. (page 106)

Her hat was gone—her hair streaming behind her. (page 114)

brown hair was streaming behind her. Her head
and body were thrown back, as if she were pulling with all her remaining strength, and as if that
strength were nearly exhausted. It was clear that
the roughness of the ground had very much les-
sened Lizzie's speed, and there seemed a chance that
we might overtake her.

Whilst we were on the highroad, Blantyre had
given me my head; but now, with a light hand and
a practiced eye, he guided me over the ground in
such a masterly manner that my pace was scarcely
slackened, and we were decidedly gaining on them.

About half-way across the heath there had been a
wide dike recently cut, and the earth from the cutting was cast up roughly on the other side. Surely
this would stop them! But no; with scarcely a
pause Lizzie took the leap, stumbled among the
rough clods, and fell. Blantyre groaned, "Now,
Auster, do your best!" He gave me a steady rein.
I gathered myself well together, and with one determined leap cleared both dike and bank.

Motionless among the heather, with her face to
the earth, lay my poor young mistress. Blantyre
kneeled down and called her name: there was no
sound. Gently he turned her face upward: it was
ghastly white, and the eyes were closed. "Annie,
dear Annie, do speak!" But there was no answer.
He unbuttoned her habit, loosened her collar, felt
her hands and wrist, then started up and looked
wildly round him for help.

At no great distance there were two men cutting
turf, who, seeing Lizzie running wild without a rider,
had left their work to catch her.

Blantyre's hallo soon brought them to the spot. The foremost man seemed much troubled at the sight, and asked what he could do.

"Can you ride?"

"Well, sir, I bean't much of a horseman, but I 'd risk my neck for the Lady Anne; she was uncommon good to my wife in the winter."

"Then mount this horse, my friend, — your neck will be quite safe, — and ride to the Doctor's and ask him to come instantly; then on to the Hall; tell them all that you know, and bid them send me the carriage with Lady Anne's maid and help. I shall stay here."

"All right, sir, I 'll do my best, and I pray God the dear young lady may open her eyes soon." Then seeing the other man, he called out, "Here, Joe, run for some water, and tell my missis to come as quick as she can to the Lady Anne."

He then somehow scrambled into the saddle, and with a "Gee up" and a clap on my sides with both his legs, he started on his journey, making a little circuit to avoid the dike. He had no whip, which seemed to trouble him; but my pace soon cured that difficulty, and he found the best thing he could do was to stick to the saddle; and hold me in, which he did manfully. I shook him as little as I could help, but once or twice on the rough ground he called out, "Steady! Woah! Steady!" On the highroad we were all right; and at the Doctor's and the Hall he did his errand like a good man and true. They asked him in to take a drop of something. "No, no," he said; "I 'll be back to 'em again by a short cut through the fields, and be there afore the carriage."

There was a great deal of hurry and excitement after the news became known. I was just turned into my box; the saddle and bridle were taken off, and a cloth thrown over me.

Ginger was saddled and sent off in great haste for Lord George, and I soon heard the carriage roll out of the yard.

It seemed a long time before Ginger came back, and before we were left alone; and then she told me all that she had seen.

"I can't tell much," she said. "We went a gallop nearly all the way, and got there just as the Doctor rode up. There was a woman sitting on the ground with the lady's head in her lap. The Doctor poured something into her mouth, but all that I heard was, 'She is not dead.' Then I was led off by a man to a little distance. After a while she was taken to the carriage, and we came home together. I heard my master say to a gentleman who stopped him to inquire, that he hoped no bones were broken, but that she had not spoken yet."

When Lord George took Ginger for hunting, York shook his head; he said it ought to be a steady hand to train a horse for the first season, and not a random rider like Lord George.

Ginger used to like it very much, but sometimes when she came back I could see that she had been very much strained, and now and then she gave a short cough. She had too much spirit to complain, but I could not help feeling anxious about her.

Two days after the accident, Blantyre paid me a visit : he patted me and praised me very much ; he told Lord George that he was sure the horse knew of Annie's danger as well as he did. "I could not have held him in if I would," said he ; "she ought never to ride any other horse." I found by their conversation that my young mistress was now out of danger, and would soon be able to ride again. This was good news to me, and I looked forward to a happy life.

CHAPTER XXV

REUBEN SMITH

I MUST now say a little about Reuben Smith, who was left in charge of the stables when York went to London. No one more thoroughly understood his business than he did, and when he was all right there could not be a more faithful or valuable man. He was gentle and very clever in his management of horses, and could doctor them almost as well as a farrier, for he had lived two years with a veterinary surgeon. He was a first-rate driver; he could take a four-in-hand or a tandem as easily as a pair. He was a handsome man, a good scholar, and had very pleasant manners. I believe everybody liked him; certainly the horses did. The only wonder was that he should be in an under situation, and not in the place of a head coachman like York; but he had one great fault, and that was the love of drink. He was not like some men, always at it; he used to keep steady for weeks or months together, and then he would break out and have a "bout" of it, as York called it, and be a disgrace to himself, a terror to his wife, and a nuisance to all that had to do with him. He was, however, so useful that two or three times York had hushed the matter up, and kept it from the Earl's knowledge ; but one night, when Reuben had to drive a party home from a ball, he was so drunk that he could not hold the reins, and a gentleman of the party had to mount the box and drive the ladies home. Of course this could not be hidden, and Reuben was at once dismissed ; his poor wife and little children had to turn out of the pretty cottage by the park gate and go where they could. Old Max told me all this, for it happened a good while ago ; but shortly before Ginger and I came, Smith had been taken back again. York had interceded for him with the Earl, who is very kind-hearted, and the man had promised faithfully that he would never taste another drop as long as he lived there. He had kept his promise so well that York thought he might be safely trusted to fill his place whilst he was away, and he was so clever and honest that no one else seemed so well fitted for it.

It was now early in April, and the family was expected home some time in May. The light brougham was to be fresh done up, and as Colonel Blantyre was obliged to return to his regiment, it was arranged that Smith should drive him to the town in it, and ride back ; for this purpose he took the saddle with him, and I was chosen for the journey. At the station the Colonel put some money into Smith's hand and bid him good-by, saying, " Take care of your young mistress, Reuben, and don't let Black Auster be hacked about by any random young prig that wants to ride him, — keep him for the lady."

We left the carriage at the maker's, and Smith rode me to the White Lion, and ordered the ostler to feed me well, and have me ready for him at four o'clock. A nail in one of my front shoes had started as I came along, but the ostler did not notice it till just about four o'clock. Smith did not come into the yard till five, and then he said he should not leave till six, as he had met with some old friends. The man then told him of the nail, and asked if he should have the shoe looked to.

"No," said Smith, "that will be all right till we get home."

He spoke in a very loud, offhand way, and I thought it very unlike him not to see about the shoe, as he was generally wonderfully particular about loose nails in our shoes. He did not come at six, nor seven, nor eight, and it was nearly nine o'clock before he called for me, and then it was with a loud, rough voice. He seemed in a very bad temper, and abused the ostler, though I could not tell what for.

The landlord stood at the door and said, " Have a care, Mr. Smith ! " but he answered angrily with an oath ; and almost before he was out of the town he began to gallop, frequently giving me a sharp cut with his whip, though I was going at full speed. The moon had not yet risen, and it was very dark. The roads were stony, having been recently mended ; going over them at this pace, my shoe became looser, and when we were near the turnpike gate it came off.

If Smith had been in his right senses he would

have been sensible of something wrong in my pace, but he was too madly drunk to notice anything.

Beyond the turnpike was a long piece of road, upon which fresh stones had just been laid, — large sharp stones, over which no horse could be driven quickly without risk of danger. Over this road, with one shoe gone, I was forced to gallop at my utmost speed, my rider meanwhile cutting into me with his whip, and with wild curses urging me to go still faster. Of course my shoeless foot suffered dreadfully; the hoof was broken and split down to the very quick, and the inside was terribly cut by the sharpness of the stones.

This could not go on; no horse could keep his footing under such circumstances; the pain was too great. I stumbled, and fell with violence on both my knees. Smith was flung off by my fall, and, owing to the speed I was going at, he must have fallen with great force. I soon recovered my feet and limped to the side of the road, where it was free from stones. The moon had just risen above the hedge, and by its light I could see Smith lying a few yards beyond me. He did not rise; he made one slight effort to do so, and then there was a heavy groan. I could have groaned, too, for I was suffering intense pain both from my foot and knees; but horses are used to bear their pain in silence. I uttered no sound, but I stood there and listened. One more heavy groan from Smith; but though he now lay in the full moonlight, I could see no motion. I could do nothing for him nor myself, but, oh! how I listened for the sound of horse, or wheels, or footsteps! The road was not much frequented, and at this time of the night we might stay for hours before help came to us. I stood watching and listening. It was a calm, sweet April night; there were no sounds but a few low notes of a nightingale, and nothing moved but the white clouds near the moon and a brown owl that flitted over the hedge. It made me think of the summer nights long ago, when I used to lie beside my mother in the green pleasant meadow at Farmer Grey's.

CHAPTER XXVI

HOW IT ENDED

IT must have been nearly midnight when I heard at a great distance the sound of a horse's feet. Sometimes the sound died away, then it grew clearer again and nearer. The road to Earlshall led through woods that belonged to the Earl; the sound came in that direction, and I hoped it might be some one coming in search of us. As the sound came nearer and nearer, I was almost sure I could distinguish Ginger's step; a little nearer still, and I could tell she was in the dog-cart. I neighed loudly, and was overjoyed to hear an answering neigh from Ginger and men's voices. They came slowly over the stones, and stopped at the dark figure that lay upon the ground.

One of the men jumped out, and stooped down over it. "It is Reuben," he said, "and he does not stir!"

The other man followed, and bent over him. "He's dead," he said; "feel how cold his hands are."

They raised him up, but there was no life, and his hair was soaked with blood. They laid him down again, and came and looked at me. They soon saw my cut knees.

"Why, the horse has been down and thrown him! Who would have thought the black horse would have done that? Nobody thought he could fall. Reuben must have been lying here for hours! Odd, too, that the horse has not moved from the place."

Robert then attempted to lead me forward. I made a step, but almost fell again.

"Hallo! he's bad in his foot as well as his knees. Look here, — his hoof is cut all to pieces; he might well come down, poor fellow! I tell you what, Ned, I'm afraid it hasn't been all right with Reuben. Just think of his riding a horse over these stones without a shoe! Why, if he had been in his right senses, he would just as soon have tried to ride him over the moon. I'm afraid it has been the old thing over again. Poor Susan! she looked awfully pale when she came to my house to ask if he had not come home. She made believe she was not a bit anxious, and talked of a lot of things that might have kept him. But for all that she begged me to go and meet him. But what must we do? There's the horse to get home as well as the body, and that will be no easy matter."

Then followed a conversation between them, till it was agreed that Robert, as the groom, should lead me, and that Ned must take the body. It was a hard job to get it into the dog-cart, for there was no one to hold Ginger; but she knew as well as I did what was going on, and stood as still as a stone. I noticed that, because, if she had a fault, it was that she was impatient in standing.

Ned started off very slowly with his sad load, and

Robert came and looked at my foot again; then he took his handkerchief and bound it closely round, and so he led me home. I shall never forget that night walk; it was more than three miles. Robert led me on very slowly, and I limped and hobbled on as well as I could with great pain. I am sure he was sorry for me, for he often patted and encouraged me, talking to me in a pleasant voice.

At last I reached my own box, and had some corn; and after Robert had wrapped up my knees in wet cloths, he tied up my foot in a bran poultice, to draw out the heat and cleanse it before the horse-doctor saw it in the morning, and I managed to get myself down on the straw, and slept in spite of the pain.

The next day, after the farrier had examined my wounds, he said he hoped the joint was not injured; and if so, I should not be spoiled for work, but I should never lose the blemish. I believe they did the best to make a good cure, but it was a long and painful one. Proud flesh, as they called it, came up in my knees, and was burnt out with caustic; and when at last it was healed, they put a blistering fluid over the front of both knees to bring all the hair off; they had some reason for this, and I suppose it was all right.

As Smith's death had been so sudden, and no one was there to see it, there was an inquest held. The landlord and ostler at the White Lion, with several other people, gave evidence that he was intoxicated when he started from the inn. The keeper of the toll-gate said he rode at a hard gallop through the gate; and my shoe was picked up amongst the stones, so that the case was quite plain to them, and I was cleared of all blame.

Everybody pitied Susan. She was nearly out of her mind; she kept saying over and over again, "Oh! he was so good — so good! It was all that cursed drink; why will they sell that cursed drink? O Reuben, Reuben!" So she went on till after he was buried; and then, as she had no home or relations, she, with her six little children, was obliged once more to leave the pleasant home by the tall oak-trees, and go into that great gloomy Union House.

CHAPTER XXVII

RUINED, AND GOING DOWNHILL

AS soon as my knees were sufficiently healed, I was turned into a small meadow for a month or two; no other creature was there, and though I enjoyed the liberty and the sweet grass, yet I had been so long used to society that I felt very lonely. Ginger and I had become fast friends, and now I missed her company extremely. I often neighed when I heard horses' feet passing in the road, but I seldom got an answer; till one morning the gate was opened, and who should come in but dear old Ginger. The man slipped off her halter and left her there. With a joyful whinny I trotted up to her; we were both glad to meet, but I soon found that it was not for our pleasure that she was brought to be with me. Her story would be too long to tell, but the end of it was that she had been ruined by hard riding, and was now turned off to see what rest would do.

Lord George was young and would take no warning; he was a hard rider, and would hunt whenever he could get the chance, quite careless of his horse. Soon after I left the stable there was a steeplechase, and he determined to ride. Though the groom told him she was a little strained, and was not fit for the race, he did not believe it, and on the day of the race urged Ginger to keep up with the foremost riders. With her high spirit, she strained herself to the utmost; she came in with the first three horses, but her wind was touched, beside which he was too heavy for her, and her back was strained. "And so," she said, "here we are, ruined in the prime of our youth and strength, you by a drunkard, and I by a fool; it is very hard." We both felt in ourselves that we were not what we had been. However, that did not spoil the pleasure we had in each other's company; we did not gallop about as we once did, but we used to feed, and lie down together, and stand for hours under one of the shady lime-trees with our heads close to each other; and so we passed our time till the family returned from town.

One day we saw the Earl come into the meadow, and York was with him. Seeing who it was, we stood still under our lime-tree, and let them come up to us. They examined us carefully. The Earl seemed much annoyed.

"There is three hundred pounds flung away for no earthly use," said he; "but what I care most for is that these horses of my old friend, who thought they would find a good home with me, are ruined. The mare shall have a twelvemonth's run, and we shall see what that will do for her; but the black one, he must be sold; 'tis a great pity, but I could not have knees like these in my stables."

"No, my lord, of course not," said York; "but he might get a place where appearance is not of much consequence, and still be well treated. I know a man in Bath, the master of some livery stables, who often wants a good horse at a low figure; I know he looks well after his horses. The inquest cleared the horse's character, and your lordship's recommendation, or mine, would be sufficient warrant for him."

"You had better write to him, York. I should be more particular about the place than the money he would fetch."

After this they left us.

"They'll soon take you away," said Ginger, "and I shall lose the only friend I have, and most likely we shall never see each other again. 'T is a hard world!"

About a week after this, Robert came into the field with a halter, which he slipped over my head, and led me away. There was no leave-taking of Ginger; we neighed to each other as I was led off, and she trotted anxiously along by the hedge, calling to me as long as she could hear the sound of my feet.

Through the recommendation of York, I was bought by the master of the livery stables. I had to go by train, which was new to me, and required a good deal of courage the first time; but as I found the puffing, rushing, whistling, and, more than all, the trembling of the horse-box in which I stood did me no real harm, I soon took it quietly.

When I reached the end of my journey, I found myself in a tolerably comfortable stable, and well attended to. These stables were not so airy and

"Bought by the master of the livery stables." (page 130)

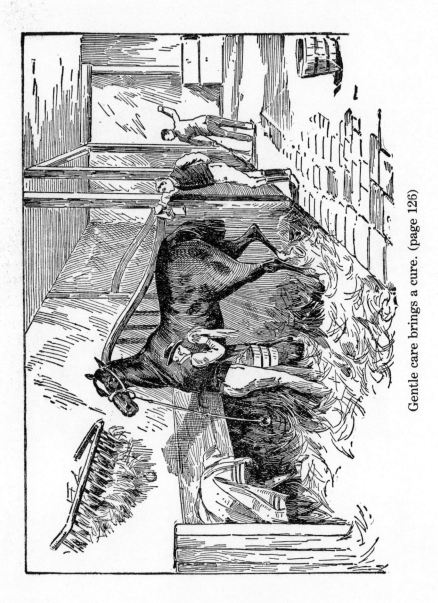

Gentle care brings a cure. (page 126)

pleasant as those I had been used to. The stalls were laid on a slope instead of being level, and as my head was kept tied to the manger, *I was obliged always to stand on the slope, which was very fatiguing.* Men do not seem to know yet that horses can do more work if they can stand comfortably and can turn about; however, I was well fed and well cleaned, and, on the whole, I think our master took as much care of us as he could. He kept a good many horses and carriages of different kinds for hire. Sometimes his own men drove them; at others, the horse and chaise were let to gentlemen or ladies who drove themselves.

CHAPTER XXVIII

A JOB HORSE AND HIS DRIVERS

HITHERTO I had always been driven by people who at least knew how to drive; but in this place I was to get my experience of all the different kinds of bad and ignorant driving to which we horses are subjected; for I was a "job horse," and was let out to all sorts of people who wished to hire me; and as I was good-tempered and gentle, I think I was oftener let out to the ignorant drivers than some of the other horses, because I could be depended upon. It would take a long time to tell of all the different styles in which I was driven, but I will mention a few of them.

First, there were *the tight-rein drivers,*—men who seemed to think that all depended on holding the reins as hard as they could, never relaxing the pull on the horse's mouth, or giving him the least liberty of movement. They are always talking about "keeping the horse well in hand," and "holding a horse up," just as if a horse was not made *to hold himself up.*

Some poor broken-down horses, whose mouths have been made hard and insensible by just such drivers as these, may, perhaps, find some support in it; but for a horse who can depend upon his own legs, and who has a tender mouth and is easily guided, it is not only tormenting, but it is stupid.

Then there are the *loose-rein drivers*, who let the reins lie easily on our backs, and their own hand rest lazily on their knees. Of course such gentlemen have no control over a horse, if anything happens suddenly. If a horse shies, or starts, or stumbles, they are nowhere, and cannot help the horse or themselves, till the mischief is done. Of course for myself I had no objection to it, as I was not in the habit either of starting or stumbling, and had only been used to depend on my driver for guidance and encouragement; still, one likes to feel the rein a little in going downhill, and likes to know that one's driver is not gone to sleep.

Besides, a slovenly way of driving gets a horse into bad and often lazy habits; and when he changes hands he has to be whipped out of them with more or less pain and trouble. Squire Gordon always kept us to our best paces and our best manners. He said that spoiling a horse, and letting him get into bad habits, was just as cruel as spoiling a child, and both had to suffer for it afterwards.

Besides, these drivers are often careless altogether, and will attend to anything else more than their horses. I went out in the phaeton one day with one of them; he had a lady and two children behind. He flopped the reins about as we started, and of course gave me several unmeaning cuts with the whip, though I was fairly off. There had been a good deal of road-mending going on, and even where the stones were not freshly laid down there

were a great many loose ones about. My driver was
laughing and joking with the lady and the children,
and talking about the country to the right and the
left; but he never thought it worth while to keep
an eye on his horse, or *to drive on the smoothest
parts of the road ;* and so it easily happened that I
got a stone in one of my fore feet.

Now if Mr. Gordon or John, or in fact any good
driver, had been there, he would have seen that
something was wrong, before I had gone three
paces. Or even if it had been dark, a practiced
hand would have felt by the rein that there was
something wrong in the step, and they would have
got down and picked out the stone. But this man
went on laughing and talking, whilst at every step
the stone became more firmly wedged between my
shoe and the frog of my foot. The stone was sharp
on the inside and round on the outside, which, as
every one knows, is the most dangerous kind that a
horse can pick up; at the same time cutting his
foot, and making him most liable to stumble and
fall.

Whether the man was partly blind, or only very
careless, I can't say ; but he drove me with that
stone in my foot for a good half mile before he saw
anything. By that time I was going so lame with
the pain that at last he saw it, and called out,
"Well, here's a go! Why, they have sent us out
with a lame horse! What a shame!"

He then chucked the reins and flipped about with
the whip, saying, "Now, then, it's no use playing
the old soldier with me; there's the journey to go,
and it's no use turning lame and lazy."

Just at this time a farmer came riding up on a brown cob; he lifted his hat and pulled up.

"I beg your pardon, sir," he said, "but I think there is something the matter with your horse; he goes very much as if he had a stone in his shoe. If you will allow me, I will look at his feet; these loose scattered stones are confounded dangerous things for the horses."

"He's a hired horse," said my driver. "I don't know what's the matter with him, but it is a great shame to send out a lame beast like this."

The farmer dismounted, and, slipping his rein over his arm, at once took up my near foot.

"Bless me, there's a stone! Lame! I should think so!"

At first he tried to dislodge it with his hand, but as it was now very tightly wedged, he drew a stone-pick out of his pocket, and very carefully, and with some trouble, got it out. Then holding it up, he said, "There, that's the stone your horse had picked up; it is a wonder he did not fall down and break his knees into the bargain!"

"Well, to be sure!" said my driver; "that is a queer thing! I never knew that horses picked up stones before."

"Didn't you?" said the farmer rather contemptuously; "but they do, though, and the best of them will do it, and can't help it sometimes on such roads as these. And if you don't want to lame your horse, you must look sharp and get them out quickly. This foot is very much bruised," he said, setting it gently down and patting me. "If I might advise, sir, you had better drive him gently for a while ; the foot is a good deal hurt, and the lameness will not go off directly."

Then mounting his cob and raising his hat to the lady, he trotted off.

When he was gone, my driver began to flop the reins about and whip the harness, by which I understood that I was to go on, which of course I did, glad that the stone was gone, but still in a good deal of pain.

This was the sort of experience we job horses often came in for.

CHAPTER XXIX

COCKNEYS

HEN there is the steam-engine style of driving; these drivers were mostly people from towns, who never had a horse of their own, and generally traveled by rail.

They always seemed to think that a horse was something like a steam-engine, only smaller. At any rate, they think that if only they pay for it, a horse is bound to go just as far and just as fast and with just as heavy a load as they please. And be the roads heavy and muddy, or dry and good ; be they stony or smooth, uphill or downhill, it is all the same, — on, on, on, one must go, at the same pace, with no relief and no consideration.

These people never think of getting out to walk up a steep hill. Oh, no, they have paid to ride, and ride they will! The horse ? Oh, he 's used to it ! What were horses made for, if not to drag people uphill ? Walk ! A good joke indeed ! And so the whip is plied and the rein is chucked and often a rough, scolding voice cries out, " Go along, you lazy beast ! " And then another slash of the whip, when all the time we are doing our very best to get along, uncomplaining and obedient, though often sorely harassed and down-hearted.

This steam-engine style of driving wears us up faster than any other kind. *I would far rather go twenty miles with a good considerate driver than I would go ten with some of these ; it would take less out of me.*

Another thing, they scarcely ever put on the brake, however steep the downhill may be, and thus bad accidents sometimes happen; or if they do put it on, they often forget to take it off at the bottom of the hill, and more than once I have had to pull half-way up the next hill, with one of the wheels held by the brake, before my driver chose to think about it; and that is a terrible strain on a horse.

Then these cockneys, instead of starting at an easy pace, as a gentleman would do, generally set off at full speed from the very stable yard; and when they want to stop, they first whip us, and then pull up so suddenly that we are nearly thrown on our haunches, and our mouths jagged with the bit, — they call that pulling up with a dash; and when they turn a corner, they do it as sharply as if there were no right side or wrong side of the road.

I well remember one spring evening I and Rory had been out for the day. (Rory was the horse that mostly went with me when a pair was ordered, and a good honest fellow he was.) We had our own driver, and as he was always considerate and gentle with us, we had a very pleasant day. We were coming home at a good smart pace, about twilight. Our road turned sharp to the left; but as we were close to the hedge on our own side, and there was plenty of room to pass, our driver did not pull us in. As we neared the corner I heard a horse and two wheels coming rapidly down the hill towards us. The hedge was high, and I could see nothing, but the next moment we were upon each other. Happily for me, I was on the side next the hedge. Rory was on the left side of the pole, and had not even a shaft to protect him. The man who was driving was making straight for the corner, and when he came in sight of us he had no time to pull over to his own side. The whole shock came upon Rory. The gig shaft ran right into the chest, making him stagger back with a cry that I shall never forget. The other horse was thrown upon his haunches and one shaft broken. It turned out that it was a horse from our own stables, with the high-wheeled gig that the young men were so fond of.

The driver was one of those random, ignorant fellows, who don't even know which is their own side of the road, or, if they know, don't care. And there was poor Rory with his flesh torn open and bleeding, and the blood streaming down. They said if it had been a little more to one side it would have killed him ; and a good thing for him, poor fellow, if it had.

As it was, it was a long time before the wound healed, and then he was sold for coal-carting ; *and what that is, up and down those steep hills, only horses know.* Some of the sights I saw there, where a horse had to come downhill with a heavily loaded two-wheel cart behind him, on which no brake could be placed, make me sad even now to think of.

After Rory was disabled, I often went in the carriage with a mare named Peggy, who stood in the next stall to mine. She was a strong, well-made animal, of a bright dun color, beautifully dappled, and with a dark brown mane and tail. There was no high breeding about her, but she was very pretty and remarkably sweet-tempered and willing. Still, there was an anxious look about her eye, by which I knew that she had some trouble. The first time we went out together I thought she had a very odd pace; she seemed to go partly a trot, partly a canter, three or four paces, and then a little jump forward.

It was very unpleasant for any horse who pulled with her, and made me quite fidgety. When we got home, I asked her what made her go in that odd, awkward way.

"Ah," she said in a troubled manner, " I know my paces are very bad, but what can I do ? It really is not my fault; it is just because my legs are so short. I stand nearly as high as you, *but your legs are a good three inches longer above your knee than mine,* and of course you can take a much longer step and go much faster. You see I did not make myself. I wish I could have done so; I would have had long legs then. All my troubles come from my short legs," said Peggy, in a desponding tone.

"But how is it," I said, " when you are so strong and good-tempered and willing ? "

" Why, you see," said she, " men will go so fast, and if one can't keep up to other horses it is noth-

ing but whip, whip, whip, all the time. And so I
have had to keep up as I could, and have got into
this ugly shuffling pace. It was not always so;
when I lived with my first master I always went
a good regular trot, but then he was not in such
a hurry. He was a young clergyman in the country, and a good, kind master he was. He had two
churches a good way apart, and a great deal· of
work, but he never scolded or whipped me for not
going faster. He was very fond of me. I only wish
I was with him now ; but he had to leave and go to
a large town, and then I was sold to a farmer.

" Some farmers, you know, are capital masters ;
but I think this one was a low sort of man. He
cared nothing about good horses or good driving ;
he only cared for going fast. I went as fast as I
could, but that would not do, and he was always
whipping ; so I got into this way of making a spring
forward to keep up. On market nights he used to
stay very late at the inn, and then drive home at a
gallop.

" One dark night he was galloping home as usual,
when all on a sudden the wheel came against some
great heavy thing in the road, and turned the gig
over in a minute. He was thrown out and his arm
broken, and some of his ribs, I think. At any rate,
it was the end of my living with him, and I was not
sorry. But you see it will be the same everywhere
for me, if men *must* go so fast. I wish my legs
were longer ! "

Poor Peggy ! I was very sorry for her, and I
could not comfort her, for I knew *how hard it was*

*upon slow-paced horses to be put with fast ones ; all
the whipping comes to their share, and they can't
help it.*

She was often used in the phaeton, and was very
much liked by some of the ladies, because she was so
gentle ; and some time after this she was sold to
two ladies who drove themselves, and wanted a safe,
good horse.

I met her several times out in the country, going
a good steady pace, and looking as gay and contented
as a horse could be.   I was very glad to see her, for
she deserved a good place.

After she left us, another horse came in her stead.
He was young, and had a bad name for shying and
starting, by which he had lost a good place.   I asked
him what made him shy.

"Well, I hardly know," he said.   "I was timid
when I was young, and was a good deal frightened
several times, and if I saw anything strange I used
to turn and look at it, — you see, *with our blinkers*
one can't see or understand what a thing is unless
one looks round, — and then my master always gave
me a whipping, which of course made me start on,
and did not make me less afraid.   *I think if he
would have let me just look at things quietly*, and see
that there was nothing to hurt me, it would have
been all right, and I should have got used to them.
One day an old gentleman was riding with him, and
a large piece of white paper or rag blew across just
on one side of me.   I shied and started forward.
My master as usual whipped me smartly, but the old
man cried out, ' You 're wrong ! you 're wrong ! You

should never whip a horse for shying; he shies because he is frightened, and you only frighten him more and make the habit worse.' So I suppose all men don't do so. I am sure I don't want to shy for the sake of it; but how should one know what is dangerous and what is not, if one is never allowed to get used to anything? I am never afraid of what I know. Now I was brought up in a park where there were deer; of course I knew them as well as I did a sheep or a cow, but they are not common, and I know many sensible horses who are frightened at them, and who kick up quite a shindy before they will pass a paddock where there are deer."

I knew what my companion said was true, and I wished that every young horse had as good masters as Farmer Grey and Squire Gordon.

Of course we sometimes came in for good driving here. I remember one morning I was put into the light gig, and taken to a house in Pulteney Street. Two gentlemen came out; the taller of them came round to my head; he looked at the bit and bridle, and just shifted the collar with his hand, to see if it fitted comfortably.

" Do you consider this horse wants a curb ? " he said to the ostler.

" Well," said the man, " I should say he would go just as well without; he has an uncommon good mouth, and though he has a fine spirit he has no vice; but we generally find people like the curb."

" I don't like it," said the gentleman; " be so good as to take it off, and put the rein in at the cheek. An easy mouth is a great thing on a long journey, is it not, old fellow?" he said, patting my neck.

Then he took the reins, and they both got up. I can remember now how quietly he turned me round, and then with a light feel of the rein, and drawing the whip gently across my back, we were off.

I arched my neck and set off at my best pace. I found I had some one behind me who knew how a good horse ought to be driven. It seemed like old times again, and made me feel quite gay.

This gentleman took a great liking to me, and after trying me several times with the saddle he prevailed upon my master to sell me to a friend of his, who wanted a safe, pleasant horse for riding. And so it came to pass that in the summer I was sold to Mr. Barry.

CHAPTER XXX

A THIEF

Y new master was an unmarried man. He lived at Bath, and was much engaged in business. His doctor advised him to take horse exercise, and for this purpose he bought me. He hired a stable a short distance from his lodgings, and engaged a man named Filcher as groom. My master knew very little about horses, but he treated me well, and I should have had a good and easy place but for circumstances of which he was ignorant. He ordered the best hay with plenty of oats, crushed beans, and bran, with vetches, or rye grass, as the man might think needful. I heard the master give the order, so I knew there was plenty of good food, and I thought I was well off.

For a few days all went on well. I found that my groom understood his business. He kept the stable clean and airy, and he groomed me thoroughly; and was never otherwise than gentle. He had been an ostler in one of the great hotels in Bath. He had given that up, and now cultivated fruit and vegetables for the market; and his wife bred and fattened poultry and rabbits for sale. After a while it seemed to me that my oats came very short; I had the beans, *but bran was mixed with them instead of oats,* of which there were very few; certainly not more than a quarter of what there should have been. In two or three weeks this began to tell upon my strength and spirits. The grass food, though very good, was not the thing to keep up my condition without corn. However, I could not complain, nor make known my wants. So it went on for about two months; and I wondered my master did not see that something was the matter. However, one afternoon he rode out into the country to see a friend of his, a gentleman farmer, who lived on the road to Wells.

This gentleman had a very quick eye for horses; and after he had welcomed his friend, he said, casting his eye over me, —

"It seems to me, Barry, that your horse does not look so well as he did when you first had him; has he been well?"

"Yes, I believe so," said my master; "but he is not nearly so lively as he was; my groom tells me that horses are always dull and weak in the autumn, and that I must expect it."

"Autumn, fiddlestick!" said the farmer. "Why, this is only August; and with your light work and good food he ought not to go down like this, even if it was autumn. How do you feed him?"

My master told him. The other shook his head slowly, and began to feel me over.

"*I can't say who eats your corn, my dear fellow, but I am much mistaken if your horse gets it.* Have you ridden very fast?"

"No, very gently."

"Then just put your hand here," said he, passing his hand over my neck and shoulder; "he is as warm and damp as a horse just come up from grass. I advise you to look into your stable a little more. I hate to be suspicious, and, thank Heaven, I have no cause to be, for I can trust my men, present or absent; *but there are mean scoundrels, wicked enough to rob a dumb beast of his food ;* you must look into it." And turning to his man who had come to take me, "Give this horse a right good feed of bruised oats, and don't stint him."

"Dumb beasts !" Yes, we are; but if I could have spoken, I could have told my master where his oats went to. My groom used to come every morning about six o'clock, and with him a little boy, who always had a covered basket with him. He used to go with his father into the harness room, where the corn was kept, and I could see them, when the door stood ajar, fill a little bag with oats out of the bin, and then he used to be off.

Five or six mornings after this, just as the boy had left the stable, the door was pushed open, and a policeman walked in, holding the child tight by the arm; another policeman followed, and locked the door on the inside, saying, "Show me the place where your father keeps his rabbits' food."

The boy looked very frightened and began to cry; but there was no escape, and he led the way to the corn-bin. Here the policeman found another empty bag like that which was found full of oats in the boy's basket.

Filcher was cleaning my feet at the time, but they

soon saw him, and though he blustered a good deal they walked him off to the "lock-up," and his boy with him. I heard afterwards that the boy was not held to be guilty, but the man was sentenced to prison for two months.

CHAPTER XXXI

A HUMBUG

MY master was not immediately suited, but in a few days my new groom came. He was a tall, good-looking fellow enough; but if ever there was a humbug in the shape of a groom, Alfred Smirk was the man. He was very civil to me, and never used me ill; in fact, he did a great deal of stroking and patting, when his master was there to see it. He always brushed my mane and tail with water, and my hoofs with oil, before he brought me to the door, to make me look smart; but as to cleaning my feet, or looking to my shoes, or grooming me thoroughly, he thought no more of that than if I had been a cow. *He left my bit rusty, my saddle damp, and my crupper stiff.*

Alfred Smirk considered himself very handsome; he spent a great deal of time about his hair, whiskers, and necktie before a little looking-glass in the harness room. When his master was speaking to him, it was always, " Yes, sir; yes, sir," — touching his hat at every word; and every one thought he was a very nice young man, and that Mr. Barry was very fortunate to meet with him. I should say he was the laziest, most conceited fellow I ever came near. Of course it was a great thing not to be ill-used, but then a horse wants more than that. I had a loose box, and might have been very comfortable if he had not been too indolent to clean it out. He never took all the straw away, and *the smell from what lay underneath was very bad ;* while the strong vapors that rose made my eyes smart and inflame, and I did not feel the same appetite for my food.

One day his master came in and said, " Alfred, the stable smells rather strong ; should not you give that stall a good scrub, and throw down plenty of water ? "

" Well, sir," he said, touching his cap, " I 'll do so if you please, sir ; but it is rather dangerous, sir, throwing down water in a horse's box ; they are very apt to take cold, sir. I should not like to do him an injury, but I 'll do it if you please, sir."

" Well," said his master, " I should not like him to take cold, but I don't like the smell of this stable. Do you think the drains are all right ? "

" Well, sir, now you mention it, I think the drain does sometimes send back a smell ; there may be something wrong, sir."

" Then send for the bricklayer and have it seen to," said his master.

" Yes, sir, I will."

The bricklayer came, and pulled up a great many bricks, but found nothing amiss ; so he put down some lime and charged the master five shillings, and the smell in my box was as bad as ever. But that was not all : *standing as I did on a quantity of moist straw*, my feet grew unhealthy and tender, and the master used to say, —

"I don't know what is the matter with this horse; he goes very fumble-footed. I am sometimes afraid he will stumble."

"Yes, sir," said Alfred, "I have noticed the same myself, when I have exercised him."

Now the fact was that he hardly ever did exercise me, and when the master was busy I often stood for days together without stretching my legs at all, and yet being fed just as high as if I were at hard work. This often disordered my health, and made me sometimes heavy and dull, but more often restless and feverish. He never even gave me a meal of green food or a bran mash, which would have cooled me, for he was altogether as ignorant as he was conceited; and then, instead of exercise or change of food, I had to take horse balls and draughts; which, beside the nuisance of having them poured down my throat, used to make me feel ill and uncomfortable.

One day my feet were so tender that, trotting over some fresh stones with my master on my back, I made two such serious stumbles that, as he came down Lansdown into the city, he stopped at the farrier's, and asked him to see what was the matter with me. The man took up my feet one by one and examined them; then standing up and dusting his hands one against the other, he said, —

"Your horse has got the 'thrush,' and badly, too; his feet are very tender; it is fortunate that he has not been down. I wonder your groom has not seen to it before. This is the sort of thing we find in foul stables, where the litter is never properly cleaned out. If you will send him here to-morrow I will attend to the hoof, and I will direct your man how to apply the liniment which I will give him."

The next day I had my feet thoroughly cleansed and stuffed with tow soaked in some strong lotion; and a very unpleasant business it was.

The farrier ordered all the litter to be taken out of my box day by day, and the floor kept very clean. Then I was to have bran mashes, a little green food, and not so much corn, till my feet were well again. With this treatment I soon regained my spirits; but Mr. Barry was so much disgusted at being twice deceived by his grooms that he determined to give up keeping a horse, and to hire when he wanted one. I was therefore kept till my feet were quite sound, and was then sold again.

PART III

CHAPTER XXXII

A HORSE FAIR

O doubt a horse fair is a very amusing place to those who have nothing to lose; at any rate, there is plenty to see.

Long strings of young horses out of the country, fresh from the marshes; and droves of shaggy little Welsh ponies, no higher than Merrylegs; and hundreds of cart horses of all sorts, some of them with their long tails braided up and tied with scarlet cord; and a good many like myself, handsome and high-bred, but fallen into the middle class, through some accident or blemish, unsoundness of wind, or some other complaint. There were some splendid animals quite in their prime, and fit for anything; they were throwing out their legs and showing off their paces in high style, as they were trotted out with a leading rein, the groom running by the side. But round in the background there were a number of poor things, sadly broken down with hard work, with their knees knuckling over and their hind legs swinging out at every step; and there were some very dejected-looking old horses, with the under lip hanging down and the ears lying back heavily, as if there was no more pleasure in life, and no more hope; there were some so thin you might see all their ribs, and some with old sores on their backs and hips. These were sad sights for a horse to look upon, who knows not but he may come to the same state.

There was a great deal of bargaining, of running up and beating down; and if a horse may speak his mind so far as he understands, I should say *there were more lies told and more trickery at that horse fair than a clever man could give an account of.* I was put with two or three other strong, useful-looking horses, and a good many people came to look at us. The gentlemen always turned from me when they saw my broken knees; though the man who had me swore it was only a slip in the stall.

The first thing was to pull my mouth open, then to look at my eyes, then feel all the way down my legs and give me a hard feel of the skin and flesh, and then try my paces. It was wonderful what a difference there was in the way these things were done. Some did it in a rough, offhand way, as if one was only a piece of wood; while others would take their hands gently over one's body, with a pat now and then, as much as to say, "By your leave." Of course I judged a good deal of the buyers by their manners to myself.

There was one man, I thought, if he would buy me, I should be happy. He was not a gentleman, nor yet one of the loud, flashy sort that called them-

selves so. He was rather a small man, but well
made, and quick in all his motions. I knew in a
moment, by the way he handled me, that he was
used to horses; he spoke gently, and his gray eye
had a kindly, cheery look in it. It may seem
strange to say — but it is true all the same — that
the clean, fresh smell there was about him made me
take to him; *no smell of old beer and tobacco*, which
I hated, but a fresh smell as if he had come out of
a hayloft. He offered twenty-three pounds for me;
but that was refused, and he walked away. I looked
after him, but he was gone, and a very hard-looking,
loud-voiced man came. I was dreadfully afraid he
would have me; but he walked off. One or two
more came who did not mean business. Then the
hard-faced man came back again and offered twenty-
three pounds. A very close bargain was being
driven, for my salesman began to think he should
not get all he asked, and must come down; but just
then the gray-eyed man came back again. I could
not help reaching out my head towards him. He
stroked my face kindly.

"Well, old chap," he said, "I think we should
suit each other. I 'll give twenty-four for him."

"Say twenty-five, and you shall have him."

"Twenty-four ten," said my friend, in a very decided tone, "and not another sixpence, — yes or
no ? "

"Done," said the salesman; "and you may depend
upon it there 's a monstrous deal of quality in that
horse, and if you want him for cab work, he 's a
bargain."

The money was paid on the spot, and my new master took my halter, and led me out of the fair to an inn, where he had a saddle and bridle ready. He gave me a good feed of oats, and stood by whilst I ate it, talking to himself and talking to me. Half an hour after, we were on our way to London, through pleasant lanes and country roads, until we came into the great London thoroughfare, on which we traveled steadily, till in the twilight we reached the great city. The gas lamps were already lighted; there were streets to the right, and streets to the left, and streets crossing each other, for mile upon mile. I thought we should never come to the end of them. At last, in passing through one, we came to a long cab stand, when my rider called out in a cheery voice, " Good-night, Governor ! "

" Hallo ! " cried a voice. " Have you got a good one ? "

" I think so," replied my owner.

" I wish you luck with him."

" Thank ye, Governor," and he rode on. We soon turned up one of the side-streets, and about half-way up that we turned into a very narrow street, with rather poor-looking houses on one side, and what seemed to be coach-houses and stables on the other.

My owner pulled up at one of the houses and whistled. The door flew open, and a young woman, followed by a little girl and boy, ran out. There was a very lively greeting as my rider dismounted.

" Now, then, Harry, my boy, open the gates, and mother will bring us the lantern."

My new master led me to an inn. (page 156)

The dishonest groom and the boy. (page 148)

The next minute they were all standing round me in a small stable yard.

"Is he gentle, father?"

"Yes, Dolly, as gentle as your own kitten; come and pat him."

At once the little hand was patting about all over my shoulder without fear. How good it felt!

"Let me get him a bran mash while you rub him down," said the mother.

"Do, Polly, it's just what he wants; and I know you've got a beautiful mash ready for me."

"Sausage dumpling and apple turnover!" shouted the boy, which set them all laughing. I was led into a comfortable, clean-smelling stall with plenty of dry straw, and after a capital supper I lay down, thinking I was going to be happy.

CHAPTER XXXIII

A LONDON CAB HORSE

M Y new master's name was Jeremiah Barker, but as every one called him Jerry, I shall do the same. Polly, his wife, was just as good a match as a man could have. She was a plump, trim, tidy little woman, with smooth dark hair, dark eyes, and a merry little mouth. The boy was nearly twelve years old, a tall, frank, good-tempered lad; and little Dorothy (Dolly they called her) was her mother over again, at eight years old. They were all wonderfully fond of each other; I never knew such a happy, merry family before or since. Jerry had a cab of his own, and two horses, which he drove and attended to himself. His other horse was a tall, white, rather large-boned animal, called "Captain." He was old now, but when he was young he must have been splendid; he had still a proud way of holding his head and arching his neck; in fact, he was a high-bred, fine-mannered, noble old horse, every inch of him. He told me that in his early youth he went to the Crimean War; he belonged to an officer in the cavalry, and used to lead the regiment. I will tell more of that hereafter.

The next morning, when I was well groomed,

Polly and Dolly came into the yard to see me and make friends. Harry had been helping his father since the early morning, and had stated his opinion that I should turn out "a regular brick." Polly brought me a slice of apple, and Dolly a piece of bread, and made as much of me as if I had been the "Black Beauty" of olden time. It was a great treat to be petted again and talked to in a gentle voice, and I let them see as well as I could that I wished to be friendly. Polly thought I was very handsome, and a great deal too good for a cab, if it was not for the broken knees.

"Of course there's no one to tell us whose fault that was," said Jerry, "and as long as I don't know I shall give him the benefit of the doubt; for a firmer, neater stepper I never rode. We'll call him 'Jack,' after the old one, — shall we, Polly?"

"Do," she said, "for I like to keep a good name going."

Captain went out in the cab all the morning. Harry came in after school to feed me and give me water. In the afternoon I was put into the cab. Jerry took as much pains to see if the collar and bridle fitted comfortably as if he had been John Manly over again. When the crupper was let out a hole or two, it all fitted well. There was no check-rein, no curb, nothing but a plain ring snaffle. What a blessing that was!

After driving through the side-street we came to the large cab stand where Jerry had said "Good-night." On one side of this wide street were high houses with wonderful shop fronts, and on the other was an old church and churchyard, surrounded by iron palisades. Alongside these iron rails a number of cabs were drawn up, waiting for passengers; bits of hay were lying about on the ground; some of the men were standing together talking; some were sitting on their boxes reading the newspaper; and one or two were feeding their horses with bits of hay, and giving them a drink of water. We pulled up in the rank at the back of the last cab. Two or three men came round and began to look at me and pass their remarks.

"Very good for a funeral," said one.

"Too smart-looking," said another, shaking his head in a very wise way; "you'll find out something wrong one of these fine mornings, or my name is n't Jones."

"Well," said Jerry pleasantly, "I suppose I need not find it out till it finds me out, eh? And if so, I'll keep up my spirits a little longer."

Then there came up a broad-faced man, dressed in a great gray coat with great gray capes and great white buttons, a gray hat, and a blue comforter loosely tied round his neck; his hair was gray, too; but he was a jolly-looking fellow, and the other men made way for him. He looked me all over, as if he had been going to buy me; and then straightening himself up with a grunt, he said, "He's the right sort for you, Jerry; I don't care what you gave for him, he'll be worth it." Thus my character was established on the stand.

This man's name was Grant, but he was called "Gray Grant," or "Governor Grant." He had been the longest on that stand of any of the men, and he took it upon himself to settle matters and stop disputes. He was generally a good-humored, sensible man; but if his temper was a little out, as it was sometimes when he had drunk too much, nobody liked to come too near his fist, for he could deal a very heavy blow.

The first week of my life as a cab horse was very trying. I had never been used to London, and the noise, the hurry, the crowds of horses, carts, and carriages, that I had to make my way through, made me feel anxious and harassed; but I soon found that I could perfectly trust my driver, and then I made myself easy, and got used to it.

Jerry was as good a driver as I had ever known; and what was better, *he took as much thought for his horses as he did for himself.* He soon found out that I was willing to work and do my best; and he never laid the whip on me, unless it was gently drawing the end of it over my back, when I was to go on; but generally I knew this quite well by the way in which he took up the reins; and I believe his whip was more frequently stuck up by his side than in his hand.

In a short time I and my master understood each other, as well as horse and man can do. In the stable, too, he did all that he could for our comfort. The stalls were the old-fashioned style, too much on the slope; but he had two movable bars fixed across the back of our stalls, so that at night, and when we were resting, he just took off our halters and put up the bars, and thus we could turn about and stand whichever way we pleased, which is a great comfort.

Jerry kept us very clean, and gave us as much change of food as he could, and always plenty of it; and not only that, but he always gave us plenty of clean fresh water, which he allowed to stand by us both night and day, *except of course when we came in warm.* Some people say that a horse ought not to drink all he likes; but I know if we are allowed to drink when we want it we drink only a little at a time, and it does us a great deal more good than swallowing down half a bucket full at a time, because we have been left without till we are thirsty and miserable. Some grooms will go home to their beer and leave us for hours with our dry hay and oats and nothing to moisten them; then of course we gulp down too much at once, which helps to spoil our breathing and sometimes chills our stomachs. *But the best thing that we had here was our Sundays for rest;* we worked so hard in the week, that I do not think we could have kept up to it, but for that day; besides, we had then time to enjoy each other's company. It was on these days that I learned my companion's history.

CHAPTER XXXIV

AN OLD WAR HORSE

CAPTAIN had been broken in and trained for an army horse; his first owner was an officer of cavalry going out to the Crimean War. He said he quite enjoyed the training with all the other horses, trotting together, turning together, to the right hand or the left, halting at the word of command, or dashing forward at full speed at the sound of the trumpet or signal of the officer. He was, when young, a dark, dappled iron gray, and considered very handsome. His master, a young, high-spirited gentleman, was very fond of him, and treated him from the first with the greatest care and kindness. He told me he thought the life of an army horse was very pleasant; but when it came to being sent abroad over the sea in a great ship, he almost changed his mind.

"That part of it," said he, "was dreadful! Of course we could not walk off the land into the ship; so they were obliged to put strong straps under our bodies, and then we were lifted off our legs in spite of our struggles, and were swung through the air over the water, to the deck of the great vessel. There we were placed in small close stalls, and never for a long time saw the sky, or were able to stretch our legs. The ship sometimes rolled about in high winds, and we were knocked about, and felt bad enough. However, at last it came to an end, and we were hauled up, and swung over again to the land; we were very glad, and snorted and neighed for joy, when we once more felt firm ground under our feet.

We soon found that the country we had come to was very different from our own, and that we had many hardships to endure besides the fighting; but many of the men were so fond of their horses, that they did everything they could to make them comfortable, in spite of snow, wet, and all things out of order.

"But what about the fighting?" said I; "was not that worse than anything else?"

"Well," said he, "I hardly know; we always liked to hear the trumpet sound, and to be called out, and were impatient to start off, though sometimes we had to stand for hours, waiting for the word of command; and when the word was given, we used to spring forward as gayly and eagerly as if there were no cannon balls, bayonets, or bullets. I believe so long as we felt our rider firm in the saddle, and his hand steady on the bridle, not one of us gave way to fear, not even when the terrible bombshells whirled through the air and burst into a thousand pieces.

" I, with my noble master, went into many actions together without a wound; and though I saw horses shot down with bullets, pierced through with lances, and gashed with fearful sabre-cuts; though we left them dead on the field, or dying in the agony of their wounds, I don't think I feared for myself. My master's cheery voice, as he encouraged his men, made me feel as if he and I could not be killed. I had such perfect trust in him, that whilst he was guiding me, I was ready to charge up to the very cannon's mouth. I saw many brave men cut down, many fall mortally wounded from their saddles. I had heard the cries and groans of the dying, I had cantered over ground slippery with blood, and frequently had to turn aside to avoid trampling on wounded man or horse, but, until one dreadful day, I had never felt terror; that day I shall never forget."

Here old Captain paused for a while and drew a long breath; I waited, and he went on.

"It was one autumn morning, and as usual, an hour before daybreak our cavalry had turned out, ready caparisoned for the day's work, whether it might be fighting or waiting. The men stood by their horses waiting, ready for orders. As the light increased, there seemed to be some excitement among the officers; and before the day was well begun, we heard the firing of the enemy's guns.

"Then one of the officers rode up and gave the word for the men to mount, and in a second, every man was in his saddle, and every horse stood expecting the touch of the rein, or the pressure of his rider's heels, all animated, all eager; but still we had been trained so well, that, except by the champing of our bits, and the restive tossing of our heads from time to time, it could not be said that we stirred.

"My dear master and I were at the head of the line, and as all sat motionless and watchful, he took a little stray lock of my mane which had turned over on the wrong side, laid it over on the right, and smoothed it down with his hand; then patting my neck, he said, 'We shall have a day of it to-day, Bayard, my beauty; but we'll do our duty as we have done.' He stroked my neck that morning more, I think, than he had ever done before; quietly on and on, as if he were thinking of something else. I loved to feel his hand on my neck, and arched my crest proudly and happily; but I stood very still, for I knew all his moods, and when he liked me to be quiet, and when gay.

"I cannot tell all that happened on that day, but I will tell of the last charge that we made together: it was across a valley right in front of the enemy's cannon. By this time we were well used to the roar of heavy guns, the rattle of musket fire, and the flying of shot near us; but never had I been under such a fire as we rode through on that day. From the right, from the left, and from the front, shot and shell poured in upon us. Many a brave man went down, many a horse fell, flinging his rider to the earth; many a horse without a rider ran wildly out of the ranks: then, terrified at being alone, with no hand to guide him, came pressing in amongst his old companions, to gallop with them to the charge.

"Fearful as it was, no one stopped, no one turned back. Every moment the ranks were thinned, but as our comrades fell, we closed in to keep them

The last charge. (page 167)

Two of Black Beauty's friends.

together; and instead of being shaken or staggered in our pace, our gallop became faster and faster as we neared the cannon, all clouded in white smoke, while the red fire flashed through it.

"My master, my dear master was cheering on his comrades with his right arm raised on high, when one of the balls whizzing close to my head, struck him. I felt him stagger with the shock, though he uttered no cry; I tried to check my speed, but the sword dropped from his right hand, the rein fell loose from the left, and sinking backward from the saddle he fell to the earth; the other riders swept past us, and by the force of their charge I was driven from the spot where he fell.

"I wanted to keep my place by his side, and not leave him under that rush of horses' feet, but it was in vain; and now without a master or a friend, I was alone on that great slaughter ground; then fear took hold on me, and I trembled as I had never trembled before; and I too, as I had seen other horses do, tried to join in the ranks and gallop with them; but I was beaten off by the swords of the soldiers. Just then, a soldier whose horse had been killed under him, caught at my bridle and mounted me; and with this new master I was again going forward: but our gallant company was cruelly overpowered, and those who remained alive after the fierce fight for the guns, came galloping back over the same ground. Some of the horses had been so badly wounded that they could scarcely move from the loss of blood; other noble creatures were trying on three legs to drag themselves along, and others were struggling to rise on their fore feet, when their hind legs had been shattered by shot. Their groans were piteous to hear, and the beseeching look in their eyes as those who escaped passed by, and left them to their fate, I shall never forget. After the battle the wounded men were brought in, and the dead were buried."

"And what about the wounded horses?" I said; "were they left to die?"

"No, the army farriers went over the field with their pistols, and shot all that were ruined; some that had only slight wounds were brought back and attended to, but the greater part of the noble, willing creatures that went out that morning never came back! In our stables there was only about one in four that returned.

"I never saw my dear master again. I believe he fell dead from the saddle. I never loved any other master so well. I went into many other engagements, but was only once wounded, and then not seriously; and when the war was over, I came back again to England, as sound and strong as when I went out."

I said, "I have heard people talk about war as if it was a very fine thing."

"Ah!" said he, "I should think they never saw it. No doubt it is very fine when there is no enemy, when it is just exercise and parade, and sham fight. Yes, it is very fine then; but when thousands of good brave men and horses are killed, or crippled for life, it has a very different look."

" *Do you know what they fought about?* " said I.

" No," he said, " that is more than a horse can understand, but the enemy must have been awfully wicked people, if it was right to go all that way over the sea on purpose to kill them."

CHAPTER XXXV

JERRY BARKER

I NEVER knew a better man than my new master. He was kind and good, and as strong for the right as John Manly; and so good-tempered and merry, that very few people could pick a quarrel with him. He was very fond of making little songs, and singing them to himself. One he was very fond of, was this —

"Come, father and mother,
And sister and brother,
Come, all of you, turn to
And help one another."

And so they did; Harry was as clever at stable-work as a much older boy, and always wanted to do what he could. Then Polly and Dolly used to come in the morning to help with the cab — to brush and beat the cushions, and rub the glass, while Jerry was giving us a cleaning in the yard, and Harry was rubbing the harness. There used to be a great deal of laughing and fun between them, and it put Captain and me in much better spirits than if we had heard scolding and hard words. They were always early in the morning, for Jerry would say —

"If you in the morning
Throw minutes away,

> You can't pick them up
>   In the course of the day.
> You may hurry and scurry,
> And flurry and worry,
> You 've lost them for ever,
>   For ever and aye."

He could not bear any careless loitering and waste of time; and nothing was so near making him angry as to find people, who were always late, wanting a cab horse to be driven hard, to make up for their idleness.

One day, two wild-looking young men came out of a tavern close by the stand, and called Jerry.

"Here, cabby! look sharp, we are rather late; put on the steam, will you, and take us to the Victoria in time for the one o'clock train? You shall have a shilling extra."

"*I will take you at the regular pace, gentlemen; shillings don't pay for putting on the steam like that.*"

Larry's cab was standing next to ours; he flung open the door, and said, "I 'm your man, gentlemen! take my cab, my horse will get you there all right;" and as he shut them in, with a wink towards Jerry, said, "It 's against his conscience to go beyond a jogtrot." Then slashing his jaded horse, he set off as hard as he could. Jerry patted me on the neck: "No, Jack, a shilling would not pay for that sort of thing, would it, old boy?"

Although Jerry was determinately set against hard driving, to please careless people, he always went a good fair pace, and was not against putting on the steam, as he said, if only he knew *why*.

I well remember one morning, as we were on the stand waiting for a fare, that a young man, carrying a heavy portmanteau, trod on a piece of orange peel which lay on the pavement, and fell down with great force.

Jerry was the first to run and lift him up. He seemed much stunned, and as they led him into a shop, he walked as if he were in great pain. Jerry of course came back to the stand, but in about ten minutes one of the shopmen called him, so we drew up to the pavement.

"Can you take me to the South-Eastern Railway?" said the young man; "this unlucky fall has made me late, I fear; but it is of great importance that I should not lose the twelve o'clock train. I should be most thankful if you could get me there in time, and will gladly pay you an extra fare."

"I'll do my very best," said Jerry heartily, "if you think you are well enough, sir," for he looked dreadfully white and ill.

"I *must* go," he said, earnestly, "please to open the door, and let us lose no time."

The next minute Jerry was on the box; with a cheery chirrup to me, and a twitch of the rein that I well understood.

"Now then, Jack, my boy," said he, "spin along, we'll show them how we can get over the ground, if we only know why."

It is always difficult to drive fast in the city in the middle of the day, when the streets are full of traffic, but we did what could be done; and when a good driver and a good horse, who understand each other, are of one mind, it is wonderful what they can do. I had a very good mouth, — that is, I could be guided by the slightest touch of the rein; and that is a great thing in London, amongst carriages, omnibuses, carts, vans, trucks, cabs, and great wagons creeping along at a walking pace; some going one way, some another, some going slowly, others wanting to pass them; omnibuses stopping short every few minutes to take up a passenger, obliging the horse that is coming behind to pull up too, or to pass, and get before them : perhaps you try to pass, but just then something else comes dashing in through the narrow opening, and you have to keep in behind the omnibus again; presently you think you see a chance, and manage to get to the front, going so near the wheels on each side, that half-an-inch nearer and they would scrape. Well, — you get along for a bit, but soon find yourself in a long train of carts and carriages all obliged to go at a walk; perhaps you come to a regular block-up, and have to stand still for minutes together, till something clears out into a side street, or the policeman interferes; you have to be ready for any chance, — to dash forward if there be an opening, and be quick as a rat dog to see if there be room and if there be time, lest you get your own wheels locked or smashed, or the shaft of some other vehicle run into your chest or shoulder. All this is what you have to be ready for. If you want to get through London fast in the middle of the day, it wants a deal of practice.

Jerry and I were used to it, and no one could beat us at getting through when we were set upon it.

I was quick and bold, and could always trust my driver; Jerry was quick and patient at the same time, and could trust his horse, which was a great thing, too. He very seldom used the whip; I knew by his voice, and his click click, when he wanted to get on fast, and by the rein where I was to go; so there was no need for whipping; but I must go back to my story.

The streets were very full that day, but we got on pretty well as far as the bottom of Cheapside, where there was a block for three or four minutes. The young man put his head out, and said anxiously, " I think I had better get out and walk, I shall never get there if this goes on."

" I 'll do all that can be done, sir," said Jerry, " I think we shall be in time ; this block-up cannot last much longer, and your luggage is very heavy for you to carry, sir."

Just then the cart in front of us began to move on, and then we had a good turn. In and out, — in and out we went, as fast as horseflesh could do it, and for a wonder had a good clear time on London Bridge, for there was a whole train of cabs and carriages, all going our way at a quick trot, — perhaps wanting to catch that very train ; at any rate, we whirled into the station with many more, just as the great clock pointed to eight minutes to twelve o'clock.

" Thank God ! we are in time," said the young man, " and thank you, too, my friend, and your good horse ; you have saved me more than money can ever pay for ; take this extra half-crown."

" No, sir, no, thank you all the same ; so glad we
hit the time, sir ; but don't stay now, sir, the bell is
ringing. Here, porter! take this gentleman's luggage, — Dover line — twelve o'clock train, — that's
it," and without waiting for another word, Jerry
wheeled me round to make room for other cabs that
were dashing up at the last minute, and drew up on
one side till the crush was past.

" ' So glad!' he said, ' so glad!' poor young fellow! I wonder what it was that made him so anxious!"

Jerry often talked to himself quite loud enough
for me to hear, when we were not moving.

On Jerry's return to the rank, there was a good
deal of laughing and chaffing at him, for driving
hard to the train for an extra fare, as they said, all
against his principles ; and they wanted to know
how much he had pocketed.

" A good deal more than I generally get," said he,
nodding slyly; " what he gave me will keep me in
little comforts for several days."

" Gammon ! " said one.

" He's a humbug," said another, " preaching to
us, and then doing the same himself."

" Look here, mates," said Jerry, " the gentleman
offered me half a crown extra, but I did n't take it ;
't was quite pay enough for me, to see how glad he
was to catch that train ; and if Jack and I choose to
have a quick run now and then, to please ourselves,
that's our business and not yours."

" Well," said Larry, " *you'll* never be a rich man."

" Most likely not," said Jerry, " but I don't know

that I shall be the less happy for that. I have heard the commandments read a great many times, and I never noticed that any of them said, 'Thou shalt be rich;' and there are a good many curious things said in the New Testament about rich men, that I think would make me feel rather queer if I was one of them."

"If you ever do get rich," said Governor Gray, looking over his shoulder across the top of his cab, "you'll deserve it, Jerry, and you won't find a curse come with your wealth. As for you, Larry, you'll die poor, you spend too much in whipcord."

"Well," said Larry, "what is a fellow to do if his horse won't go without it?"

"You never take the trouble to see if he will go without it; your whip is always going as if you had the St. Vitus' dance in your arm; and if it does not wear you out, it wears your horse out; you know you are always changing your horses, and why? because you never give them any peace or encouragement."

"Well, I have not had good luck," said Larry, "that's where it is."

"And you never will," said the Governor. "Good Luck is rather particular who she rides with, and mostly prefers those who have got common sense and a good heart: at least, that is my experience."

Governor Gray turned round again to his newspaper, and the other men went to their cabs.

CHAPTER XXXVI

THE SUNDAY CAB

ONE morning, as Jerry had just put me into the shafts and was fastening the traces, a gentleman walked into the yard. "Your servant, sir," said Jerry.

"Good morning, Mr. Barker," said the gentleman. "I should be glad to make some arrangements with you for taking Mrs. Briggs regularly to church on Sunday mornings. We go to the New Church now, and that is rather further than she can walk."

"Thank you, sir," said Jerry, "but I have only taken out a six-days' license, and therefore I could not take a fare on a Sunday; it would not be legal."

"Oh!" said the other, "I did not know yours was a six-days' cab; but of course it would be very easy to alter your license. I would see that you did not lose by it; the fact is, Mrs. Briggs very much prefers you to drive her."

"I should be glad to oblige the lady, sir, but I had a seven-days' license once, and the work was too hard for me, *and too hard for my horses.* Year in and year out, not a day's rest, and never a Sun-

day with my wife and children; and never able to
go to a place of worship, which I had always been
used to do before I took to the driving box. So for
the last five years I have only taken a six-days'
license, and I find it better all the way round."

"Well, of course," replied Mr. Briggs, "it is very
proper that every person should have rest, and be
able to go to church on Sundays, but I should have
thought you would not have minded such a short
distance for the horse, and only once a day; you
would have all the afternoon and evening for yourself, and we are very good customers, you know."

" Yes, sir, that is true, and I am grateful for all
favors, I am sure; and anything that I could do to
oblige you, or the lady, I should be proud and happy
to do; but I can't give up my Sundays, sir, indeed
I can't. I read that God made man, and *He made
horses* and all the other beasts, and as soon as He
had made them He made a day of rest, and bade
that all should rest one day in seven; and I think,
sir, He must have known what was good for them,
and I am sure it is good for me; I am stronger and
healthier altogether, now that I have a day of rest;
the horses are fresh too, and do not wear up nearly
so fast. The six-day drivers all tell me the same,
and I have laid by more money in the Savings' Bank
than ever I did before; and as for the wife and children, sir, why, heart alive! they would not go back
to the seven days for all they could see."

"Oh, very well," said the gentleman. " Don't
trouble yourself, Mr. Barker, any further. I will
inquire somewhere else," and he walked away.

"Well," says Jerry to me, "we can't help it, Jack, old boy, we must have our Sundays."

"Polly!" he shouted, "Polly! come here."

She was there in a minute.

"What is it all about, Jerry?"

"Why, my dear, Mr. Briggs wants me to take Mrs. Briggs to church every Sunday morning. I say, I have only a six-days' license. He says, 'Get a seven-days' license, and I'll make it worth your while;' and you know, Polly, they are very good customers to us. Mrs. Briggs often goes out shopping for hours, or making calls, and then she pays down fair and honorable like a lady; there's no beating down, or making three hours into two hours and a half, as some folks do; and it is easy work for the horses; not like tearing along to catch trains for people that are always a quarter of an hour too late; and if I don't oblige her in this matter it is very likely we shall lose them altogether. What do you say, little woman?"

"I say, Jerry," says she, speaking very slowly, "I say, if Mrs. Briggs would give you a sovereign every Sunday morning, I would not have you a seven-days' cabman again. We have known what it was to have no Sundays, and now we know what it is to call them our own. Thank God, you earn enough to keep us, though it is sometimes close work to pay for all the oats and hay, the license, and the rent besides; but Harry will soon be earning something, and I would rather struggle on harder than we do than go back to those horrid times, when you hardly had a minute to look at your own children, and we never could go to a place of worship together, or have a happy, quiet day. God forbid that we should ever turn back to those times; that's what I say, Jerry."

"And that is just what I told Mr. Briggs, my dear," said Jerry, "and what I mean to stick to; so don't go and fret yourself, Polly (for she had begun to cry); I would not go back to the old times if I earned twice as much, so that is settled, little woman. Now cheer up, and I'll be off to the stand."

Three weeks had passed away after this conversation, and no order had come from Mrs. Briggs; so there was nothing but taking jobs from the stand. Jerry took it to heart a good deal, for of course the work was harder for horse and man; but Polly would always cheer him up and say, "Never mind, father, never mind.

' Do your best,
And leave the rest,
'T will all come right
Some day or night.' "

It soon became known that Jerry had lost his best customer, and for what reason; most of the men said he was a fool, but two or three took his part.

"If workingmen don't stick to their Sunday," said Truman, "they'll soon have none left; *it is every man's right and every beast's right. By God's law we have a day of rest, and by the law of England we have a day of rest; and I say we ought to hold to the rights these laws give us, and keep them for our children.*"

"All very well for you religious chaps to talk so," said Larry, "but I'll turn a shilling when I can. I don't believe in religion, for I don't see that your religious people are any better than the rest."

"If they are not better," put in Jerry, "it is because they are *not* religious. You might as well say that our country's laws are not good because some people break them. If a man gives way to his temper, and speaks evil of his neighbor, and does not pay his debts, he is *not* religious; I don't care how much he goes to church. If some men are shams and humbugs, that does not make religion untrue. Real religion is the best and the truest thing in the world; and the only thing that can make a man really happy, or make the world any better."

"If religion was good for anything," said Jones, "it would prevent your religious people from making us work on Sundays, as you know many of them do, and that's why I say religion is nothing but a sham; why, if it was not for the church and chapel goers it would be hardly worth while our coming out on a Sunday; but they have their privileges, as they call them, and I go without. I shall expect them to answer for my soul, if I can't get a chance of saving it."

Several of the men applauded this, till Jerry said, —

"That may sound well enough, but it won't do; every man must look after his own soul; you can't lay it down at another man's door like a foundling, and expect him to take care of it; and don't you see, if you are always sitting on your box waiting for a fare, they will say, 'If we don't take him, some one else will, and he does not look for any Sunday.' Of course they don't go to the bottom of it, or they would see if they never came for a cab it would be no use your standing there; but people don't always like to go to the bottom of things; it may not be convenient to do it; but if you Sunday drivers would all strike for a day of rest, the thing would be done."

" And what would all the good people do, if they could not get to their favorite preachers ? " said Larry.

"'T is not for me to lay down plans for other people," said Jerry, " but if they can't walk so far, they can go to what is nearer; and if it should rain they can put on their mackintoshes as they do on a week-day. If a thing is right, it *can* be done, and if it is wrong, it *can be done without;* and a good man will find a way; and that is as true for us cabmen as it is for the churchgoers."

CHAPTER XXXVII

THE GOLDEN RULE

TWO or three weeks after this, as we came into the yard rather late in the evening, Polly came running across the road with the lantern (she always brought it to him if it was not very wet).

"It has all come right, Jerry; Mrs. Briggs sent her servant this afternoon to ask you to take her out to-morrow at eleven o'clock. I said, 'Yes, I thought so, but we supposed she employed some one else now.'"

"'Well,' says he, 'the real fact is, master was put out because Mr. Barker refused to come on Sundays, and he has been trying other cabs, but there 's something wrong with them all; some drive too fast, and some too slow, and the mistress says, there is not one of them so nice and clean as yours, and nothing will suit her but Mr. Barker's cab again.'"

Polly was almost out of breath, and Jerry broke out into a merry laugh.

"'*'T will all come right some day or night:*' you were right, my dear; you generally are. Run in and get the supper, and I 'll have Jack's harness off and make him snug and happy in no time."

After this, Mrs. Briggs wanted Jerry's cab quite as often as before, never, however, on a Sunday; but there came a day when we had Sunday work, and this was how it happened. We had all come home on the Saturday night very tired, and very glad to think that the next day would be all rest, but so it was not to be.

On Sunday morning Jerry was cleaning me in the yard, when Polly stepped up to him, looking very full of something.

"What is it?" said Jerry.

"Well, my dear," she said, "poor Dinah Brown has just had a letter brought to say that her mother is dangerously ill, and that she must go directly if she wishes to see her alive. The place is more than ten miles away from here, out in the country, and she says if she takes the train she should still have four miles to walk; and so weak as she is, and the baby only four weeks old, of course that would be impossible; and she wants to know if you would take her in your cab, and she promises to pay you faithfully, as she can get the money."

"Tut, tut! we'll see about that. It was not the money I was thinking about, but of losing our Sunday; the horses are tired, and I am tired, too,— that's where it pinches."

"It pinches all round, for that matter," said Polly, "for it's only half Sunday without you, but you know we should do to other people as we should like they should do to us; and I know very well what I should like if my mother was dying; and Jerry, dear, I am sure it won't break the Sabbath;

for if pulling a poor beast or donkey out of a pit would not spoil it, I am quite sure taking poor Dinah would not do it."

"Why, Polly, you are as good as the minister, and so, as I've had my Sunday-morning sermon early to-day, you may go and tell Dinah that I'll be ready for her as the clock strikes ten; but stop, — just step round to butcher Braydon's with my compliments, and ask him if he would lend me his light trap; I know he never uses it on the Sunday, *and it would make a wonderful difference to the horse.*"

Away she went, and soon returned, saying that he could have the trap and welcome.

"All right," said he; "now put me up a bit of bread and cheese, and I'll be back in the afternoon as soon as I can."

"And I'll have the meat pie ready for an early tea instead of for dinner," said Polly; and away she went, whilst he made his preparations to the tune of " Polly's the woman and no mistake," of which tune he was very fond.

I was selected for the journey, and at ten o'clock we started, in a light, high-wheeled gig, which ran so easily, that after the four-wheeled cab, it seemed like nothing.

It was a fine May day, and as soon as we were out of the town, the sweet air, the smell of the fresh grass, and the soft country roads were as pleasant as they used to be in the old times, and I soon began to feel quite fresh.

Dinah's family lived in a small farmhouse, up a green lane, close by a meadow with some fine shady trees; there were two cows feeding in it. A young man asked Jerry to bring his trap into the meadow, and he would tie me up in the cowshed; he wished he had a better stable to offer.

" If your cows would not be offended," said Jerry, " there is nothing my horse would like so well as to have an hour or two in your beautiful meadow; he's quiet, and it would be a rare treat for him."

" Do, and welcome," said the young man; "the best we have is at your service for your kindness to my sister; we shall be having some dinner in an hour, and I hope you'll come in, though with mother so ill we are all out of sorts in the house."

Jerry thanked him kindly, but said as he had some dinner with him, there was nothing he should like so well as walking about in the meadow.

When my harness was taken off, I did not know what I should do first, — whether to eat the grass, or roll over on my back, or lie down and rest, or have a gallop across the meadow out of sheer spirits at being free; and I did all by turns. Jerry seemed to be quite as happy as I was; he sat down by a bank under a shady tree, and listened to the birds, then he sang himself, and read out of the little brown book he is so fond of, then wandered round the meadow and down by a little brook, where he picked the flowers and the hawthorn, and tied them up with long sprays of ivy; then he gave me a good feed of the oats which he had brought with him; but the time seemed all too short, — I had not been in a field since I left poor Ginger at Earlshall.

We came home gently, and Jerry's first words

were as we came into the yard, " Well, Polly, I have
not lost my Sunday after all, for the birds were
singing hymns in every bush, and I joined in the
service ; and as for Jack, he was like a young colt."

When he handed Dolly the flowers, she jumped
about for joy.

CHAPTER XXXVIII

DOLLY AND A REAL GENTLEMAN

THE winter came in early, with a great deal of cold and wet. There was snow, or sleet, or rain, almost every day for weeks, changing only for keen driving winds, or sharp frosts. The horses all felt it very much. When it is a dry cold, a couple of good thick rugs will keep the warmth in us; but when it is soaking rain, they soon get wet through and are no good. Some of the drivers had a waterproof cover to throw over, which was a fine thing; but some of the men were so poor that they could not protect either themselves or their horses, and many of them suffered very much that winter. When we horses had worked half the day we went to our dry stables, and could rest; whilst they had to sit on their boxes, sometimes staying out as late as one or two o'clock in the morning, if they had a party to wait for.

When the streets were slippery with frost or snow, that was the worst of all for us horses; one mile of such traveling, with a weight to draw, and no firm footing, would take more out of us than four on a good road; every nerve and muscle of our bodies is on the strain to keep our balance; and

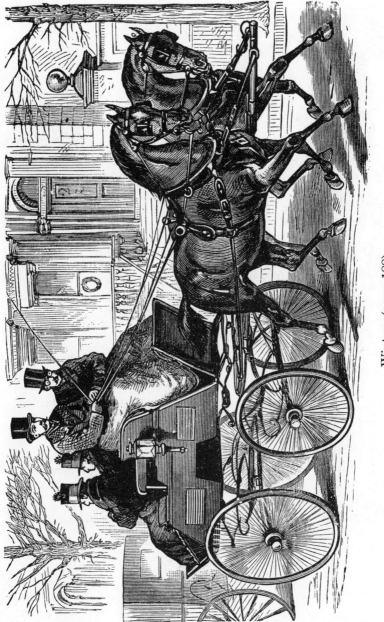

Winter. (page 188)

Back to the stables.

added to this, the fear of falling is more exhausting than anything else. If the roads are very bad indeed, our shoes are roughed, but that makes us feel nervous at first.

When the weather was very bad, many of the men would go and sit in the tavern close by, and get some one to watch for them; but they often lost a fare in that way, and could not, as Jerry said, be there without spending money. He never went to the Rising Sun; there was a coffee-shop near, where he now and then went, or he bought of an old man, who came to our rank with tins of hot coffee and pies. It was his opinion that spirits and beer made a man colder afterwards, and that dry clothes, good food, cheerfulness, and a comfortable wife at home, were the best things to keep a cabman warm. Polly always supplied him with something to eat when he could not get home, and sometimes he would see little Dolly peeping from the corner of the street, to make sure if "father" was on the stand. If she saw him, she would run off at full speed and soon come back with something in a tin or basket, some hot soup or pudding that Polly had ready. It was wonderful how such a little thing could get safely across the street, often thronged with horses and carriages; but she was a brave little maid, and felt it quite an honor to bring "father's first course," as he used to call it. She was a general favorite on the stand, and there was not a man who would not have seen her safely across the street, if Jerry had not been able to do it.

One cold windy day, Dolly had brought Jerry a

basin of something hot, and was standing by him whilst he ate it. He had scarcely begun, when a gentleman, walking towards us very fast, held up his umbrella. Jerry touched his hat in return, gave the basin to Dolly, and was taking off my cloth, when the gentleman, hastening up, cried out, "*No, no, finish your soup, my friend;* I have not much time to spare, but I can wait till you have done, and set your little girl safe on the pavement." So saying, he seated himself in the cab. Jerry thanked him kindly, and came back to Dolly.

"*There, Dolly, that's a gentleman;* that's a real gentleman, Dolly; he has got time and thought for the comfort of a poor cabman and a little girl."

Jerry finished his soup, set the child across, and then took his orders to drive to Clapham Rise. Several times after that, the same gentleman took our cab. I think he was very fond of dogs and horses, for whenever we took him to his own door, two or three dogs would come bounding out to meet him. Sometimes he came round and patted me, saying in his quiet, pleasant way, "This horse has got a good master, and he deserves it." It was a very rare thing for any one to notice the horse that had been working for him. I have known ladies do it now and then, and this gentleman, and one or two others have given me a pat and a kind word; *but ninety-nine out of a hundred would as soon think of patting the steam engine that drew the train.*

This gentleman was not young, and there was a forward stoop in his shoulders as if he was always going at something. His lips were thin and close shut, though they had a very pleasant smile; his eye was keen, and there was something in his jaw and the motion of his head that made one think he was very determined in anything he set about. His voice was pleasant and kind; any horse would trust that voice, though it was just as decided as everything else about him.

One day, he and another gentleman took our cab; they stopped at a shop in R—— Street, and whilst his friend went in, he stood at the door. A little ahead of us on the other side of the street, a cart with two very fine horses was standing before some wine vaults; the carter was not with them, and I cannot tell how long they had been standing, but they seemed to think they had waited long enough, and began to move off. Before they had gone many paces, the carter came running out and caught them. He seemed furious at their having moved, and with whip and rein punished them brutally, even beating them about the head. Our gentleman saw it all, and stepping quickly across the street, said in a decided voice, —

"If you don't stop that directly, I'll have you arrested for leaving your horses, and for brutal conduct."

The man, who had clearly been drinking, poured forth some abusive language, but he left off knocking the horses about, and taking the reins, got into his cart; meantime our friend had quietly taken a notebook from his pocket, and looking at the name and address painted on the cart, he wrote something down.

"What do you want with that?" growled the carter, as he cracked his whip and was moving on. A nod and a grim smile, was the only answer he got.

On returning to the cab, our friend was joined by his companion, who said laughingly, "I should have thought, Wright, you had enough business of your own to look after, without troubling yourself about other people's horses and servants."

Our friend stood still for a moment, and throwing his head a little back, "Do you know why this world is as bad as it is?"

"No," said the other.

"Then I'll tell you. *It is because people think only about their own business, and won't trouble themselves to stand up for the oppressed, nor bring the wrong-doer to light.* I never see a wicked thing like this without doing what I can, and many a master has thanked me for letting him know how his horses have been used."

"I wish there were more gentlemen like you, sir," said Jerry, "for they are wanted badly enough in this city."

After this we continued our journey, and as they got out of the cab, our friend was saying, "My doctrine is this, that *if we see cruelty or wrong that we have the power to stop, and do nothing, we make ourselves sharers in the guilt.*"

CHAPTER XXXIX

SEEDY SAM

I SHOULD say that for a cab-horse I was very well off indeed; my driver was my owner, and it was his interest to treat me well, and not overwork me, even had he not been so good a man as he was; but there were a great many horses which belonged to the large cab-owners, who let them out to their drivers for so much money a day. As the horses did not belong to these men, the only thing they thought of was how to get their money out of them, first, to pay the master, and then to provide for their own living, and a dreadful time some of these horses had of it. Of course I understood but little, but it was often talked over on the stand, and the Governor, who was a kind-hearted man, and fond of horses, would sometimes speak up if one came in very much jaded or ill-used.

One day a shabby, miserable-looking driver, who went by the name of "Seedy Sam," brought in his horse looking dreadfully beat, and the Governor said, —

"You and your horse look more fit for the police station than for this rank."

The man flung his tattered rug over the horse, turned full round upon the Governor, and said in a voice that sounded almost desperate, —

" If the police have any business with the matter, it ought to be with the masters who charge us so much, or with the fares that are fixed so low. If a man has to pay eighteen shillings a day for the use of a cab and two horses, as many of us have to do in the season, and must make that up before we earn a penny for ourselves — I say 't is more than hard work ; nine shillings a day to get out of each horse, before you begin to get your own living ; you know that's true, and if the horses don't work we must starve, and I and my children have known what that is before now. I've six of 'em, and only one earns anything ; I am on the stand fourteen or six-teen hours a day, and I haven't had a Sunday these ten or twelve weeks ; you know Skinner never gives a day if he can help it, and if I don't work hard, tell me who does ! I want a warm coat and a mackin-tosh, but with so many to feed, how can a man get it ? I had to pledge my clock a week ago to pay Skinner, and I shall never see it again."

Some of the other drivers stood round nodding their heads, and saying he was right. The man went on, —

" You that have your own horses and cabs, or drive for good masters, have a chance of getting on, and a chance of doing right ; I haven't. We can't charge more than sixpence a mile after the first, within the four-mile radius. This very morning I had to go a clear six miles and only took three shil-lings. I could not get a return fare, and had to come all the way back ; there's twelve miles for the horse and three shillings for me. After that I had a three-mile fare, and there were bags and boxes enough to have brought in a good many twopences if they had been put outside; but you know how people do, all that could be piled up inside on the front seat were put in, and three heavy boxes went on the top; that was sixpence, and the fare one and sixpence; then I got a return for a shilling; now that makes eighteen miles for the horse and six shillings for me; there's three shillings still for that horse to earn, and nine shillings for the afternoon horse before I touch a penny. Of course it is not always so bad as that, but you know it often is, and I say 't is a mockery to tell a man that he must not overwork his horse, for when a beast is downright tired there's nothing but the whip that will keep his legs agoing; you can't help yourself — you must put your wife and children before the horse; the masters must look to that, we can't. I don't ill-use my horse for the sake of it; none of you can say I do. There's wrong lays somewhere — never a day's rest, never a quiet hour with the wife and children. I often feel like an old man, though I'm only forty-five. You know how quick some of the gentry are to suspect us of cheating and overcharging; why, they stand with their purses in their hands counting it over to a penny, and looking at us as if we were pickpockets. I wish some of 'em had got to sit on my box sixteen hours a day and get a living out of it, and eighteen shillings beside, and that in all weathers; they would not be so uncommon particular never to give us a sixpence over, or to cram all the luggage inside. Of course some of 'em tip us pretty handsome now and then, or else we could not live, but you can't *depend* upon that."

The men who stood round much approved this speech, and one of them said, "It is desperate hard, and if a man sometimes does what is wrong it is no wonder, and if he gets a dram too much, who's to blow him up?"

Jerry had taken no part in this conversation, but I never saw his face look so sad before. The Governor had stood with both his hands in his pockets; now he took his handkerchief out of his hat, and wiped his forehead.

"You've beaten me, Sam," he said, "for it's all true, and I won't cast it up to you any more about the police; it was the look in that horse's eye that came over me. *It is hard lines for man, and it is hard lines for beast,* and who's to mend it I don't know; but anyway you might tell the poor beast that you were sorry to take it out of him in that way. *Sometimes a kind word is all we can give 'em, poor brutes, and 't is wonderful what they do understand.*"

A few mornings after this talk a new man came on the stand with Sam's cab.

"Hallo!" said one, "what's up with Seedy Sam?"

"He's ill in bed," said the man; "he was taken last night in the yard, and could scarcely crawl home. His wife sent a boy this morning to say his father was in a high fever and could not get out; so I'm here instead."

The next morning the same man came again.

"How is Sam?" inquired the Governor.

"He's gone," said the man.

"What, gone? You don't mean to say he's dead?"

"Just snuffed out," said the other; "he died at four o'clock this morning; all yesterday he was raving — raving about Skinner, and having no Sundays. 'I never had a Sunday's rest,' these were his last words."

No one spoke for awhile, and then the Governor said, "I tell you what, mates, this is a warning for us."

CHAPTER XL

POOR GINGER

ONE day, whilst our cab and many others were waiting outside one of the parks where music was playing, a shabby old cab drove up beside ours. The horse was an old worn-out chestnut, with an ill-kept coat, and bones that showed plainly through it, the knees knuckled over, and the fore-legs were very unsteady. I had been eating some hay, and the wind rolled a little lock of it that way, and the poor creature put out her long thin neck and picked it up, and then turned round and looked about for more. There was a hopeless look in the dull eye that I could not help noticing, and then, as I was thinking where I had seen that horse before, she looked full at me and said, "Black Beauty, is that you?"

It was Ginger! but how changed! The beautifully arched and glossy neck was now straight, and lank, and fallen in; the clean straight legs and delicate fetlocks were swelled; the joints were grown out of shape with hard work; the face, that was once so full of spirit and life, was now full of suffering, and I could tell by the heaving of her sides, and her frequent cough, how bad her breath was.

Our drivers were standing together a little way

off, so I sidled up to her a step or two, that we might have a little quiet talk. It was a sad tale that she had to tell.

After a twelvemonth's run off at Earlshall, she was considered to be fit for work again, and was sold to a gentleman. For a little while she got on very well, but after a longer gallop than usual, the old strain returned, and after being rested and doctored she was again sold. In this way she changed hands several times, but always getting lower down.

"And so at last," said she, "I was bought by a man who keeps a number of cabs and horses, and lets them out. You look well off, and I am glad of it, but I could not tell you what my life has been. When they found out my weakness, they said I was not worth what they gave for me, *and that I must go into one of the low cabs, and just be used up ;* that is what they are doing, whipping and working with never one thought of what I suffer — they paid for me, and must get it out of me, they say. The man who hires me now pays a deal of money to the owner every day, and so he has to get it out of me too; and so it's all the week round and round, with never a Sunday rest."

I said, "You used to stand up for yourself if you were ill-used."

"Ah !" she said, "I did once, but it's no use; men are strongest, and if they are cruel and have no feeling, there is nothing that we can do, but just bear it, — bear it on and on to the end. I wish the end was come, I wish I was dead. I have seen dead horses, and I am sure they do not suffer pain; I wish

I may drop down dead at my work, and not be sent off to the knackers."

I was very much troubled, and I put my nose up to hers, but I could say nothing to comfort her. I think she was pleased to see me, for she said, "You are the only friend I ever had."

Just then her driver came up, and with a tug at her mouth, backed her out of the line and drove off, leaving me very sad indeed.

A short time after this, a cart with a dead horse in it passed our cab-stand. The head hung out of the cart tail, the lifeless tongue was slowly dropping with blood; and the sunken eyes! but I can't speak of them, the sight was too dreadful. It was a chestnut horse with a long thin neck. I saw a white streak down the forehead. I believe it was Ginger; I hoped it was, for then her troubles would be over. *Oh! if men were more merciful, they would shoot us before we came to such misery.*

CHAPTER XLI

THE BUTCHER

 SAW a great deal of trouble amongst the horses in London, and much of it that might have been prevented by a little common sense. We horses do not mind hard work if we are treated reasonably; and I am sure there are many driven by quite poor men who have a happier life than I had, when I used to go in the Countess of W——'s carriage, with my silver-mounted harness and high feeding.

It often went to my heart to see how the little ponies were used, straining along with heavy loads, or staggering under heavy blows from some low, cruel boy. Once I saw a little gray pony with a thick mane and a pretty head, and so much like Merrylegs, that if I had not been in harness, I should have neighed to him. He was doing his best to pull a heavy cart, while a strong rough boy was cutting him under the belly with his whip, and chucking cruelly at his little mouth. Could it be Merrylegs? It was just like him; but then Mr. Blomefield was never to sell him, and I think he would not do it; but this might have been quite as good a little fellow, and had as happy a place when he was young.

I often noticed the great speed at which butchers' horses were made to go, though I did not know why it was so, till one day when we had to wait some time in St. John's Wood. There was a butcher's shop next door, and as we were standing, a butcher's cart came dashing up at a great pace. The horse was hot, and much exhausted; he hung his head down, while his heaving sides and trembling legs showed how hard he had been driven. The lad jumped out of the cart and was getting the basket, when the master came out of the shop much displeased. After looking at the horse, he turned angrily to the lad.

"How many times shall I tell you not to drive in this way? You ruined the last horse and broke his wind, and you are going to ruin this in the same way. If you were not my own son, I would dismiss you on the spot; it is a disgrace to have a horse brought to the shop in a condition like that; you are liable to be taken up by the police for such driving, and if you are, you need not look to me for bail, for I have spoken to you till I am tired; you must look out for yourself."

During this speech, the boy had stood by, sullen and dogged, but when his father ceased, he broke out angrily. It wasn't his fault, and he wouldn't take the blame, he was only going by orders all the time.

"You always say, 'Now be quick; now look sharp!' and when I go to the houses, one wants a leg of mutton for an early dinner, and I must be back with it in a quarter of an hour. Another cook has forgotten to order the beef; I must go and fetch it and be back in no time, or the mistress will scold; and the housekeeper says they have company coming unexpectedly, and must have some chops sent up directly; and the lady at No. 4, in the Crescent, *never* orders her dinner till the meat comes in for lunch, and it's nothing but hurry, hurry, all the time. *If the gentry would think of what they want, and order their meat the day before, there need not be this blow up!*"

" I wish to goodness they would," said the butcher; " 't would save me a wonderful deal of harass, and I could suit my customers much better if I knew beforehand — But there! what's the use of talking — who ever thinks of a butcher's convenience, or a butcher's horse ? Now, then, take him in and look to him well; mind, he does not go out again to-day, and if anything else is wanted, you must carry it yourself in the basket." With that he went in, and the horse was led away.

But all boys are not cruel. I have seen some as fond of their pony or donkey as if it had been a favorite dog, and the little creatures have worked away as cheerfully and willingly for their young drivers as I work for Jerry. It may be hard work sometimes, but a friend's hand and voice make it easy.

There was a young coster-boy who came up our street with greens and potatoes; he had an old pony not very handsome, but the cheerfullest and pluckiest little thing I ever saw, and to see how fond those two were of each other was a treat. The pony

followed his master like a dog, and when he got into
his cart, would trot off without a whip or a word,
and rattle down the street as merrily as if he had
come out of the Queen's stables.   Jerry liked the
boy, and called him "Prince Charlie," for he said he
would make a king of drivers some day.

There was an old man, too, who used to come up
our street with a little coal cart; he wore a coal-
heaver's hat, and looked rough and black.   He and
his old horse used to plod together along the street,
like two good partners who understood each other;
the horse would stop of his own accord at the doors
where they took coal of him; he used to keep one
ear bent towards his master.   The old man's cry
could be heard up the street long before he came
near.   I never knew what he said, but the children
called him "Old Ba-a-ar Hoo," for it sounded like
that.   Polly took her coal of him, and was very
friendly, and Jerry said it was a comfort to think
how happy an old horse *might* be in a poor place.

CHAPTER XLII

THE ELECTION

S we came into the yard one afternoon, Polly came out. "Jerry! I've had Mr. B—— here asking about your vote, and he wants to hire your cab for the election; he will call for an answer."

"Well, Polly, you may say that my cab will be otherwise engaged. I should not like to have it pasted over with their great bills, and as to making Jack and Captain race about to the public-houses to bring up half-drunken voters, why, I think 't would be an insult to the horses. No, I sha'n't do it."

"I suppose you 'll vote for the gentleman? He said he was of your politics."

"So he is in some things, but I shall not vote for him, Polly; you know what his trade is?"

"Yes."

"Well, a man who gets rich by that trade may be all very well in some ways, but he is blind as to what workingmen want; I could not in my conscience send him up to make the laws. I dare say they 'll be angry, but every man must do what he thinks to be the best for his country."

On the morning before the election, Jerry was putting me into the shafts, when Dolly came into the yard sobbing and crying, with her little blue frock and white pinafore spattered all over with mud.

" Why, Dolly, what is the matter ? "

" Those naughty boys," she sobbed, " have thrown the dirt all over me, and called me a little raga— raga— "

" They called her a little ' *blue* ' ragamuffin, father," said Harry, who ran in looking very angry; " but I have given it to them ; they won't insult my sister again. I have given them a thrashing they will remember ; a set of cowardly, rascally ' *orange* ' blackguards ! "

Jerry kissed the child and said, " Run in to mother, my pet, and tell her I think you had better stay at home to-day and help her."

Then turning gravely to Harry —

" My boy, I hope you will always defend your sister, and give anybody who insults her a good thrashing — that is as it should be ; but mind, I won't have any election blackguarding on my premises. There are as many ' *blue* ' blackguards as there are ' *orange*,' and as many white as there are purple, or any other color, and I won't have any of my family mixed up with it. Even women and children are ready to quarrel for the sake of a color, and not one in ten of them knows what it is about."

" Why, father, I thought blue was for Liberty."

" My boy, Liberty does not come from colors, they only show party, and all the liberty you can get out of them is, liberty to get drunk at other people's expense, liberty to ride to the poll in a dirty old cab, liberty to abuse any one that does not wear your color, and to shout yourself hoarse at what you only half understand — that's your liberty!"

"Oh, father, you are laughing."

"No, Harry, I am serious, and I am ashamed to see how men go on that ought to know better. An election is a very serious thing; at least it ought to be, and every man ought to vote according to his conscience, and let his neighbor do the same."

CHAPTER XLIII

A FRIEND IN NEED

AT last came the election day; there was no lack of work for Jerry and me. First came a stout puffy gentleman with a carpet bag; he wanted to go to the Bishopsgate Station; then we were called by a party who wished to be taken to the Regent's Park; and next we were wanted in a side street where a timid, anxious old lady was waiting to be taken to the Bank; there we had to stop to take her back again, and just as we had set her down, a red-faced gentleman, with a handful of papers, came running up out of breath, and before Jerry could get down, he had opened the door, popped himself in, and called out "Bow Street Police Station, quick!" so off we went with him, and when after another turn or two we came back, there was no other cab on the stand. Jerry put on my nose-bag, for as he said, "We must eat when we can on such days as these; so munch away, Jack, and make the best of your time, old boy."

I found I had a good feed of crushed oats wetted up with a little bran; this would be a treat any day, but very refreshing then. Jerry was so thoughtful and kind — what horse would not do his best for such a master? Then he took out one of Polly's meat pies, and standing near me, he began to eat it. The streets were very full, and the cabs, with the candidates' colors on them, were dashing about through the crowd as if life and limb were of no consequence; we saw two people knocked down that day, and one was a woman. The horses were having a bad time of it, poor things! but the voters inside thought nothing of that; many of them were half drunk, hurrahing out of the cab windows if their own party came by. It was the first election I had seen, and I don't want to be in another, though I have heard things are better now.

Jerry and I had not eaten many mouthfuls, before a poor young woman, carrying a heavy child, came along the street. She was looking this way, and that way, and seemed quite bewildered. Presently she made her way up to Jerry and asked if he could tell her the way to St. Thomas's Hospital, and how far it was to get there. She had come from the country that morning, she said, in a market cart; she did not know about the election, and was quite a stranger in London. She had got an order for the Hospital for her little boy. The child was crying with a feeble pining cry.

"Poor little fellow!" she said, "he suffers a deal of pain; he is four years old, and can't walk any more than a baby; but the doctor said if I could get him into the Hospital, he might get well; pray, sir, how far is it? and which way is it?"

"Why, missis," said Jerry, "you can't get there walking through crowds like this! why, it is three miles away, and that child is heavy."

"Yes, bless him, he is; but I am strong, thank God, and if I knew the way, I think I should get on somehow; please tell me the way."

"You can't do it," said Jerry, "you might be knocked down and the child be run over. Now look here, just get into this cab, and I'll drive you safe to the Hospital. Don't you see the rain is coming on?"

"No, sir, no; I can't do that, thank you, I have only just money enough to get back with. Please tell me the way."

"Look you here, missis," said Jerry, "I've got a wife and dear children at home, and I know a father's feelings; now get you into that cab, and I'll take you there for nothing. I'd be ashamed of myself to let a woman and a sick child run a risk like that."

"Heaven bless you!" said the woman, and burst into tears.

"There, there, cheer up, my dear, I'll soon take you there; come, let me put you inside."

As Jerry went to open the door, two men, with colors in their hats and button-holes, ran up calling out, "Cab!"

"Engaged," cried Jerry; but one of the men pushing past the woman, sprang into the cab, followed by the other. Jerry looked as stern as a policeman. "This cab is already engaged, gentlemen, by that lady."

"Lady!" said one of them; "oh! she can wait; our business is very important, beside we were in first, it is our right, and we shall stay in."

A droll smile came over Jerry's face as he shut the door upon them. "All right, gentlemen, pray stay in as long as it suits you ; I can wait whilst you rest yourselves ;" and turning his back upon them, he walked up to the young woman, who was standing near me. "They 'll soon be gone," he said, laughing, "don't trouble yourself, my dear."

And they soon were gone, for when they understood Jerry's dodge, they got out, calling him all sorts of bad names, and blustering about his number and getting a summons. After this little stoppage we were soon on our way to the Hospital, going as much as possible through by-streets. Jerry rung the great bell, and helped the young woman out.

"Thank you a thousand times," she said; "I could never have got here alone."

"You 're kindly welcome, and I hope the dear child will soon be better."

He watched her go in at the door, and gently he said to himself, "*Inasmuch as ye have done it to one of the least of these.*" Then he patted my neck, which was always his way when anything pleased him.

The rain was now coming down fast, and just as we were leaving the Hospital, the door opened again, and the porter called out, "Cab!" We stopped, and a lady came down the steps. Jerry seemed to know her at once; she put back her veil and said, "Barker! Jeremiah Barker! is it you? I am very glad to find you here ; you are just the friend I want, for it is very difficult to get a cab in this part of London to-day."

"I shall be proud to serve you, ma'am, I am right glad I happened to be here; where may I take you to, ma'am?"

"To the Paddington Station, and then if we are in good time, as I think we shall be, you shall tell me all about Mary and the children."

We got to the station in good time, and being under shelter, the lady stood a good while talking to Jerry. I found she had been Polly's mistress, and after many inquiries about her, she said, —

"How do you find the cab work suit you in winter? I know Mary was rather anxious about you last year."

"Yes, ma'am, she was; I had a bad cough that followed me up quite into the warm weather, and when I am kept out late she does worry herself a good deal. You see, ma'am, it is all hours and all weathers, and that does try a man's constitution; but I am getting on pretty well, and I should feel quite lost if I had not horses to look after. I was brought up to it, and I am afraid I should not do so well at anything else."

"Well, Barker," she said, "it would be a great pity that you should seriously risk your health in this work, not only for your own but for Mary's and the children's sake; there are many places where good drivers or good grooms are wanted; and if ever you think you ought to give up this cab work, let me know."

Then sending some kind messages to Mary she put something into his hand, saying, "There is five shillings each for the two children; Mary will know how to spend it."

Jerry thanked her and seemed much pleased, and turning out of the station we at last reached home, and I, at least, was tired.

CHAPTER XLIV

OLD CAPTAIN AND HIS SUCCESSOR

CAPTAIN and I were great friends. He was a noble old fellow, and he was very good company. I never thought that he would have to leave his home and go down the hill, but his turn came; and this was how it happened. I was not there, but I heard all about it.

He and Jerry had taken a party to the great railway station over London Bridge, and were coming back, somewhere between the Bridge and the Monument, when Jerry saw a brewer's empty dray coming along, drawn by two powerful horses. The drayman was lashing his horses with his heavy whip; the dray was light, and they started off at a furious rate; the man had no control over them, and the street was full of traffic; one young girl was knocked down and run over, and the next moment they dashed up against our cab; both the wheels were torn off and the cab was thrown over. Captain was dragged down, the shafts splintered, and one of them ran into his side. Jerry, too, was thrown, but was only bruised; nobody could tell how he escaped; he always said 't was a miracle. When poor Captain was got up, he was found to be very much cut and knocked about. Jerry led him home gently, and a sad sight it was to see the blood soaking into his white coat, and dropping from his side and shoulder. *The drayman was proved to be very drunk,* and was fined, and the brewer had to pay damages to our master ; but there was no one to pay damages to poor Captain.

The farrier and Jerry did the best they could to ease his pain and make him comfortable. The fly had to be mended, and for several days I did not go out, and Jerry earned nothing. The first time we went to the stand after the accident, the Governor came up to hear how Captain was.

"He'll never get over it," said Jerry, "at least not for my work, so the farrier said this morning. He says he may do for carting, and that sort of work. It has put me out very much. Carting, indeed! I've seen what horses come to at that work round London. I only wish all the drunkards could be put in a lunatic asylum instead of being allowed to run foul of sober people. If they would break their *own* bones, and smash their *own* carts, and lame their *own* horses, that would be their own affair, and we might let them alone, but it seems to me that the innocent always suffer ; and then they talk about compensation ! You can't make compensation ; there's all the trouble, and vexation, and loss of time, besides losing a good horse that's like an old friend, — it's nonsense talking of compensation ! *If there's one devil that I should like to see in the bottomless pit more than another, it's the drink devil.*"

"I say, Jerry," said the Governor, "you are treading pretty hard on my toes, you know; I'm not so good as you are, more shame for me; I wish I was."

"Well," said Jerry, "why don't you cut with it, Governor? You are too good a man to be the slave of such a thing."

"I'm a great fool, Jerry, but I tried once for two days, and I thought I should have died; how did you do?"

"I had hard work at it for several weeks; you see I never did get drunk, but I found that I was not my own master, and that when the craving came on it was hard work to say 'no.' I saw that one of us must knock under, the drink devil or Jerry Barker, and I said that it should not be Jerry. Barker, God helping me; but it was a struggle, and I wanted all the help I could get, for till I tried to break the habit I did not know how strong it was; but then Polly took such pains that I should have good food, and when the craving came on I used to get a cup of coffee, or some peppermint, or read a bit in my book, and that was a help to me; sometimes I had to say over and over to myself, 'Give up the drink or lose your soul! Give up the drink or break Polly's heart!' But thanks be to God, and my dear wife, my chains were broken, and now for ten years I have not tasted a drop, and never wish for it."

"I've a great mind to try at it," said Grant, "for 't is a poor thing not to be one's own master."

"Do, Governor, do, you'll never repent it, and what a help it would be to some of the poor fellows in our rank if they saw you do without it. I know there's two or three would like to keep out of that tavern if they could."

At first Captain seemed to do well, but he was a very old horse, and it was only his wonderful constitution, and Jerry's care, that had kept him up at the cab work so long; now he broke down very much. The farrier said he might mend up enough to sell for a few pounds, but Jerry said, no! a few pounds got by selling a good old servant into hard work and misery would canker all the rest of his money, and he thought the kindest thing he could do for the fine old fellow would be to put a sure bullet through his head, and then he would never suffer more; for he did not know where to find a kind master for the rest of his days.

The day after this was decided, Harry took me to the forge for some new shoes; when I returned, Captain was gone. I and the family all felt it very much.

Jerry had now to look out for another horse, and he soon heard of one through an acquaintance who was under-groom in a nobleman's stables. He was a valuable young horse, but he had run away, smashed into another carriage, flung his lordship out, and so cut and blemished himself that he was no longer fit for a gentleman's stables, and the coachman had orders to look round, and sell him as well as he could.

"I can do with high spirits," said Jerry, "if a horse is not vicious or hard-mouthed."

"There is not a bit of vice in him," said the man; "his mouth is very tender, and I think myself that was the cause of the accident; you see he had just been clipped, and the weather was bad, and he had not had exercise enough, and when he did go out, he was as full of spring as a balloon. Our governor (the coachman, I mean) had him harnessed in as tight and strong as he could, with the martingale, and the check-rein, a very sharp curb, and the reins put in at the bottom bar. It is my belief that it made the horse mad, being tender in the mouth and so full of spirit."

"Likely enough; I'll come and see him," said Jerry.

The next day, Hotspur, that was his name, came home; he was a fine brown horse, without a white hair in him, as tall as Captain, with a very handsome head, and only five years old. I gave him a friendly greeting by way of good fellowship, but did not ask him any questions. The first night he was very restless. Instead of lying down, he kept jerking his halter rope up and down through the ring, and knocking the block about against the manger till I could not sleep. However, the next day, after five or six hours in the cab, he came in quiet and sensible. Jerry patted and talked to him a good deal, and very soon they understood each other, and Jerry said that with an easy bit and plenty of work he would be as gentle as a lamb; and that it was an ill wind that blew nobody good, for if his lordship had lost a hundred-guinea favorite, the cabman had gained a good horse with all his strength in him.

Hotspur thought it a great come-down to be a

cab-horse, and was disgusted at standing in the rank, but he confessed to me at the end of the week, *that an easy mouth and a free head made up for a great deal, and after all, the work was not so degrading as having one's head and tail fastened to each other at the saddle.* In fact, he settled in well, and Jerry liked him very much.

CHAPTER XLV

JERRY'S NEW YEAR

CHRISTMAS and the New Year are very merry times for some people; but for cabmen and cabmen's horses it is no holiday, though it may be a harvest. There are so many parties, balls, and places of amusement open, that the work is hard and often late. Sometimes driver and horse have to wait for hours in the rain or frost, shivering with cold, whilst the merry people within are dancing away to the music. *I wonder if the beautiful ladies ever think of the weary cabman waiting on his box, and his patient beast standing, till his legs get stiff with cold.*

I had now most of the evening work, as I was well accustomed to standing, and Jerry was also more afraid of Hotspur taking cold. We had a great deal of late work in the Christmas week, and Jerry's cough was bad; but however late we were, Polly sat up for him, and came out with a lantern to meet him, looking anxious and troubled.

On the evening of the New Year, we had to take two gentlemen to a house in one of the West End Squares. We set them down at nine o'clock, and were told to come again at eleven, "but," said one of them, "as it is a card party, you may have to wait a few minutes, but don't be late."

I wonder if the beautiful ladies ever think of the weary cabman. (page 220)

Black Beauty.

As the clock struck eleven we were at the door, for Jerry was always punctual. The clock chimed the quarters, one, two, three, and then struck twelve, but the door did not open.

The wind had been very changeable, with squalls of rain during the day, but now it came on sharp, driving sleet, which seemed to come all the way round; it was very cold, and there was no shelter. Jerry got off his box and came and pulled one of my cloths a little more over my neck; then he took a turn or two up and down, stamping his feet; then he began to beat his arms, but that set him off coughing; so he opened the cab door and sat at the bottom with his feet on the pavement, and was a little sheltered. Still the clock chimed the quarters, and no one came. At half-past twelve, he rang the bell and asked the servant if he would be wanted that night.

"Oh, yes, you 'll be wanted safe enough," said the man; "you must not go, it will soon be over," and again Jerry sat down, but his voice was so hoarse I could hardly hear him.

At a quarter past one the door opened, and the two gentlemen came out; they got into the cab without a word, and told Jerry where to drive, that was nearly two miles. My legs were numb with cold, and I thought I should have stumbled. When the men got out, they never said they were sorry to have kept us waiting so long, but were angry at the charge; however, as Jerry never charged more than was his due, so he never took less, and they had to pay for the two hours and a quarter waiting; but it was hard-earned money to Jerry.

At last we got home; he could hardly speak, and his cough was dreadful. Polly asked no questions, but opened the door and held the lantern for him.

"Can't I do something?" she said.

"Yes; get Jack something warm, and then boil me some gruel."

This was said in a hoarse whisper; he could hardly get his breath, but he gave me a rub down as usual, and even went up into the hayloft for an extra bundle of straw for my bed. Polly brought me a warm mash that made me comfortable, and then they locked the door.

It was late the next morning before any one came, and then it was only Harry. He cleaned us and fed us, and swept out the stalls, then he put the straw back again as if it was Sunday. He was very still, and neither whistled nor sang. At noon he came again and gave us our food and water; this time Dolly came with him; she was crying, and I could gather from what they said, that Jerry was dangerously ill, and the doctor said it was a bad case. So two days passed, and there was great trouble indoors. We only saw Harry, and sometimes Dolly. I think she came for company, for Polly was always with Jerry, and he had to be kept very quiet.

On the third day, whilst Harry was in the stable, a tap came at the door, and Governor Grant came in.

"I would n't go to the house, my boy," he said, "but I want to know how your father is."

"He is very bad," said Harry, "he can't be much worse; they call it 'bronchitis'; the doctor thinks it will turn one way or another to-night."

"That's bad, very bad," said Grant, shaking his head; "I know two men who died of that last week; it takes 'em off in no time; but whilst there's life there's hope, so you must keep up your spirits."

"Yes," said Harry quickly, "and the doctor said that father had a better chance than most men, because he did n't drink. He said yesterday the fever was so high, that if father had been a drinking man, it would have burnt him up like a piece of paper; but I believe he thinks he will get over it; don't you think he will, Mr. Grant?"

The Governor looked puzzled.

"If there's any rule that good men should get over these things, I am sure he will, my boy; he's the best man I know. I'll look in early to-morrow."

Early next morning he was there.

"Well?" said he.

"Father is better," said Harry. "Mother hopes he will get over it."

"Thank God!" said the Governor, "and now you must keep him warm, and keep his mind easy, and that brings me to the horses; you see, Jack will be all the better for the rest of a week or two in a warm stable, and you can easily take him a turn up and down the street to stretch his legs; but this young one, if he does not get work, he will soon be all up on end, as you may say, and will be rather too much for you; and when he does go out, there'll be an accident."

"It is like that now," said Harry, "I have kept him short of corn, but he's so full of spirit I don't know what to do with him."

"Just so," said Grant. "Now look here, will you tell your mother that if she is agreeable, I will come for him every day till something is arranged, and take him for a good spell of work, and whatever he earns, I'll bring your mother half of it, and that will help with the horses' feed. Your father is in a good club, I know, but that won't keep the horses, and they'll be eating their heads off all this time; I'll come at noon and hear what she says," and without waiting for Harry's thanks, he was gone.

At noon I think he went and saw Polly, for he and Harry came to the stable together, harnessed Hotspur, and took him out.

For a week or more he came for Hotspur, and when Harry thanked him or said anything about his kindness, he laughed it off, saying, it was all good luck for him, for his horses were wanting a little rest which they would not otherwise have had.

Jerry grew better steadily, but the doctor said that he must never go back to the cab work again if if he wished to be an old man. The children had many consultations together about what father and mother would do, and how they could help to earn money.

One afternoon Hotspur was brought in very wet and dirty.

"The streets are nothing but slush," said the Governor; "it will give you a good warming, my boy, to get him clean and dry."

"All right, Governor," said Harry, "I shall not leave him till he is; you know I have been trained by my father."

"I wish all the boys had been trained like you," said the Governor.

While Harry was sponging off the mud from Hotspur's body and legs, Dolly came in, looking very full of something.

"Who lives at Fairstowe, Harry? Mother has got a letter from Fairstowe; she seemed so glad, and ran upstairs to father with it."

"Don't you know? Why, it is the name of Mrs. Fowler's place, — mother's old mistress, you know, — the lady that father met last summer, who sent you and me five shillings each."

"Oh! Mrs. Fowler; of course I know all about her; I wonder what she is writing to mother about."

"Mother wrote to her last week," said Harry; "you know she told father if ever he gave up the cab work, she would like to know. I wonder what she says; run in and see, Dolly."

Harry scrubbed away at Hotspur with a huish! huish! like any old ostler. In a few minutes Dolly came dancing into the stable.

"Oh! Harry, there never was anything so beautiful; Mrs. Fowler says we are all to go and live near her. There is a cottage now empty that will just suit us, with a garden, and a hen-house, and apple trees, and everything! and her coachman is going away in the spring, and then she will want father in his place; and there are good families round, where you can get a place in the garden, or the stable, or as a page boy; and there's a good school for me; and mother is laughing and crying by turns, and father does look *so* happy!"

"That's uncommon jolly," said Harry, "and just the right thing, I should say; it will suit father and mother both; but I don't intend to be a page boy with tight clothes and rows of buttons. I'll be a groom or a gardener."

It was quickly settled that as soon as Jerry was well enough, they should remove to the country, and that the cab and horses should be sold as soon as possible.

This was heavy news for me, for I was not young now, and could not look for any improvement in my condition. Since I left Birtwick I had never been so happy as with my dear master Jerry; but three years of cab work, even under the best conditions, will tell on one's strength, and I felt that I was not the horse that I had been.

Grant said at once that he would take Hotspur; and there were men on the stand who would have bought me; but Jerry said I should not go to cab work again with just anybody, and the Governor promised to find a place for me where I should be comfortable.

The day came for going away. Jerry had not been allowed to go out yet, and I never saw him after that New Year's eve. Polly and the children came to bid me good-by. "Poor old Jack! dear old Jack! I wish we could take you with us," she said, and then laying her hand on my mane, she put her face close to my neck and kissed me. Dolly was crying and kissed me too. Harry stroked me a great deal, but said nothing, only he seemed very sad, and so I was led away to my new place.

PART IV

CHAPTER XLVI

JAKES AND THE LADY

 WAS sold to a corn dealer and baker, whom Jerry knew, and with him he thought I should have good food and fair work. In the first he was quite right, and if my master had always been on the premises, I do not think I should have been overloaded, but there was a foreman who was always hurrying and driving every one, and frequently when I had quite a full load, he would order something else to be taken on. My carter, whose name was Jakes, often said it was more than I ought to take, but the other always overruled him. " 'T was no use going twice when once would do, and he chose to get business forward."

Jakes, like the other carters, always *had the check-rein up*, which prevented me from drawing easily, and by the time I had been there three or four months, I found the work telling very much on my strength.

One day, I was loaded more than usual, and part of the road was a steep uphill. I used all my strength, but I could not get on, and was obliged continually to stop. This did not please my driver, and he laid his whip on badly. " Get on, you lazy fellow," he said, " or I 'll make you."

Again I started the heavy load, and struggled on a few yards ; again the whip came down, and again I struggled forward. The pain of that great cart whip was sharp, but my mind was hurt quite as much as my poor sides. To be punished and abused when I was doing my very best was so hard it took the heart out of me. A third time he was flogging me cruelly, when a lady stepped quickly up to him, and said in a sweet, earnest voice, —

" Oh! pray do not whip your good horse any more ; I am sure he is doing all he can, and the road is very steep ; I am sure he is doing his best."

" If doing his best won't get this load up, he must do something more than his best ; that 's all I know, ma'am," said Jakes.

" But is it not a heavy load ? " she said.

" Yes, yes, too heavy," he said ; " but that 's not my fault ; the foreman came just as we were starting, and would have three hundredweight more put on to save him trouble, and I must get on with it as well as I can."

He was raising the whip again, when the lady said, —

" Pray, stop ; I think I can help you if you will let me."

The man laughed.

" You see," she said, " you do not give him a fair chance ; he cannot use all his power with his head held back as it is with that check-rein ; if you would

take it off, I am sure he would do better, — *do* try
it," she said persuasively, "I should be very glad if
you would."

"Well, well," said Jakes, with a short laugh,
"anything to please a lady, of course. How far
would you wish it down, ma'am?"

"Quite down, give him his head altogether."

The rein was taken off, and in a moment I put my
head down to my very knees. What a comfort it
was! Then I tossed it up and down several times
to get the aching stiffness out of my neck.

"Poor fellow! that is what you wanted," said she,
patting and stroking me with her gentle hand; "and
now if you will speak kindly to him and lead him
on, I believe he will be able to do better."

Jakes took the rein. "Come on, Blackie." I put
down my head, and threw my whole weight against
the collar; I spared no strength; the load moved on,
and I pulled it steadily up the hill, and then stopped
to take breath.

The lady had walked along the footpath, and now
came across into the road. She stroked and patted
my neck, as I had not been patted for many a long
day.

"You see he was quite willing when you gave him
the chance; I am sure he is a fine-tempered creature,
and I dare say has known better days. You won't
put that rein on again, will you?" for he was just
going to hitch it up on the old plan.

"Well, ma'am, I can't deny that having his head
has helped him up the hill, and I'll remember it
another time, and thank you, ma'am; but if he went

without a check-rein, I should be the laughing-stock of all the carters ; it is the fashion, you see."

"Is it not better," she said, "to lead a good fashion than to follow a bad one ? A great many gentlemen do not use check-reins now ; our carriage horses have not worn them for fifteen years, and work with much less fatigue than those who have them ; besides," she added in a very serious voice, "we have no right to distress any of God's creatures without a very good reason ; we call them dumb animals, and so they are, for they cannot tell us how they feel, but they do not suffer less because they have no words. But I must not detain you now ; I thank you for trying my plan with your good horse, and I am sure you will find it far better than the whip. Good-day," and with another soft pat on my neck she stepped lightly across the path, and I saw her no more.

"That was a real lady, I 'll be bound for it," said Jakes to himself ; "she spoke just as polite as if I was a gentleman, and I 'll try her plan, uphill, at any rate ; " and I must do him the justice to say, that he let my rein out several holes, and going uphill after that, he always gave me my head ; but the heavy loads went on. Good feed and fair rest will keep up one's strength under full work, *but no horse can stand against overloading ;* and I was getting so thoroughly pulled down from this cause, that a younger horse was bought in my place. I may as well mention here, what I suffered at this time from another cause. I had heard horses speak of it, but had never myself had experience of the evil ; this was *a badly-lighted stable ;* there was only one very small window at the end, and the consequence was that the stalls were almost dark.

Besides the depressing effect this had on my spirits, it very much weakened my sight, and when I was suddenly brought out of the darkness into the glare of daylight, it was very painful to my eyes. Several times I stumbled over the threshold, and could scarcely see where I was going.

I believe, had I stayed there very long, I should have become purblind, and that would have been a great misfortune, for I have heard men say, that a stone-blind horse was safer to drive than one which had imperfect sight, as it generally makes them very timid. However, I escaped without any permanent injury to my sight, and was sold to a large cab owner.

CHAPTER XLVII

HARD TIMES

SHALL never forget my new master; he had black eyes and a hooked nose, his mouth was as full of teeth as a bull-dog's, and his voice was as harsh as the grinding of cart wheels over gravel stones. His name was Nicholas Skinner, and I believe he was the same man that poor Seedy Sam drove for.

I have heard men say, that seeing is believing; but I should say that *feeling* is believing; for much as I had seen before, I never knew till now the utter misery of a cab-horse's life.

Skinner had a low set of cabs and a low set of drivers; he was hard on the men, and the men were hard on the horses. In this place we had no Sunday rest, and it was in the heat of summer.

Sometimes on a Sunday morning, a party of fast men would hire the cab for the day; four of them inside and another with the driver, and I had to take them ten or fifteen miles out into the country, and back again: *never would any of them get down to walk up a hill*, let it be ever so steep, or the day ever so hot, — unless, indeed, when the driver was afraid I should not manage it, and sometimes I was so fevered and worn that I could hardly touch my food. How I used to long for the nice bran mash with nitre in it that Jerry used to give us on Saturday nights in hot weather, that used to cool us down and make us so comfortable. Then we had two nights and a whole day for unbroken rest, and on Monday morning we were as fresh as young horses again; but here there was no rest, and my driver was just as hard as his master. He had a cruel whip with something so sharp at the end that it sometimes drew blood, and he would even whip me under the belly, and flip the lash out at my head. Indignities like these took the heart out of me terribly, but still I did my best and never hung back; for, as poor Ginger said, it was no use; men are the strongest.

My life was now so utterly wretched, that I wished I might, like Ginger, drop down dead at my work, and be out of my misery; and one day my wish very nearly came to pass.

I went on the stand at eight in the morning, and had done a good share of work, when we had to take a fare to the railway. A long train was just expected in, so my driver pulled up at the back of some of the outside cabs, to take the chance of a return fare. It was a very heavy train, and as all the cabs were soon engaged, ours was called for. There was a party of four; a noisy, blustering man with a lady, a little boy, and a young girl, and a great deal of luggage. The lady and the boy got into the cab, and while the man ordered about the luggage, the young girl came and looked at me.

"Papa," she said, "I am sure this poor horse cannot take us and all our luggage so far, he is so very weak and worn up; do look at him."

"Oh ! he 's all right, miss," said my driver, "he 's strong enough."

The porter, who was pulling about some heavy boxes, suggested to the gentleman, as there was so much luggage, whether he would not take a second cab.

"Can your horse do it, or can't he ? " said the blustering man.

"Oh ! he can do it all right, sir ; send up the boxes, porter ; he could take more than that," and he helped to haul up a box so heavy that I could feel the springs go down.

"Papa, papa, do take a second cab," said the young girl in a beseeching tone ; " I am sure we are wrong, I am sure it is very cruel."

" Nonsense, Grace, get in at once, and don't make all this fuss ; a pretty thing it would be if a man of business had to examine every cab-horse before he hired it, — the man knows his own business of course ; there, get in and hold your tongue ! "

My gentle friend had to obey ; and box after box was dragged up and lodged on the top of the cab, or settled by the side of the driver. At last all was ready, and with his usual jerk at the rein, and slash of the whip, he drove out of the station.

The load was very heavy, and I had had neither food nor rest since morning ; but I did my best, as I always had done, in spite of cruelty and injustice.

I got along fairly till we came to Ludgate Hill, but there, the heavy load and my own exhaustion were too much. I was struggling to keep on, goaded by constant chucks of the rein and use of the whip, when, in a single moment — I cannot tell how — my feet slipped from under me, and I fell heavily to the ground on my side; the suddenness and the force with which I fell seemed to beat all the breath out of my body. I lay perfectly still; indeed, I had no power to move, and I thought now I was going to die. I heard a sort of confusion round me, loud angry voices, and the getting down of the luggage, but it was all like a dream. I thought I heard that sweet pitiful voice saying, "Oh! that poor horse! it is all our fault." Some one came and loosened the throat strap of my bridle, and undid the traces which kept the collar so tight upon me. Some one said, "He's dead, he'll never get up again." Then I could hear a policeman giving orders, but I did not even open my eyes; I could only draw a gasping breath now and then. Some cold water was thrown over my head, and some cordial was poured into my mouth, and something was covered over me. I cannot tell how long I lay there, but I found my life coming back, and a kind-voiced man was patting me and encouraging me to rise. After some more cordial had been given me, and after one or two attempts, I staggered to my feet, and was gently led to some stables which were close by. Here I was put into a well-littered stall, and some warm gruel was brought to me, which I drank thankfully.

In the evening I was sufficiently recovered to be led back to Skinner's stables, where I think they did the best for me they could. In the morning Skinner came with a farrier to look at me. He examined me very closely, and said, —

"This is a case of overwork more than disease, and if you could give him a run off for six months, he would be able to work again; but now there is not an ounce of strength in him."

"Then he must just go to the dogs," said Skinner. "I have no meadows to nurse sick horses in, — he might get well or he might not; that sort of thing don't suit my business; *my plan is to work 'em as long as they'll go, and then sell 'em for what they'll fetch, at the knacker's or elsewhere.*"

"If he was broken-winded," said the farrier, "you had better have him killed out of hand, but he is not; there is a sale of horses coming off in about ten days; if you rest him and feed him up, he may pick up, and you may get more than his skin is worth, at any rate."

Upon this advice, Skinner, rather unwillingly, I think, gave orders that I should be well fed and cared for, and the stable man, happily for me, carried out the orders with a much better will than his master had in giving them. Ten days of perfect rest, plenty of good oats, hay, bran mashes, with boiled linseed mixed in them, did more to get up my condition than anything else could have done; those linseed mashes were delicious, and I began to think, after all, it might be better to live than go to the dogs. When the twelfth day after the accident came, I was taken to the sale, a few miles out of London. I felt that any change from my present place must be an improvement, so I held up my head, and hoped for the best.

CHAPTER XLVIII

FARMER THOROUGHGOOD AND HIS GRANDSON WILLIE

T this sale, of course I found myself in company with the old broken-down horses, — some lame, some broken-winded, some old, and some that I am sure it would have been merciful to shoot.

The buyers and sellers too, many of them, looked not much better off than the poor beasts they were bargaining about. There were poor old men, trying to get a horse or pony for a few pounds, that might drag about some little wood or coal cart. There were poor men trying to sell a worn-out beast for two or three pounds, rather than have the greater loss of killing him. Some of them looked as if poverty and hard times had hardened them all over; but there were others that I would have willingly used the last of my strength in serving; poor and shabby, but kind and human, with voices that I could trust. There was one tottering old man that took a great fancy to me, and I to him, but I was not strong enough, — it was an anxious time! Coming from the better part of the fair, I noticed a man who looked like a gentleman farmer, with a young boy by his side; he had a broad back and round shoulders, a kind, ruddy face, and he wore a broad-brimmed hat. When he came up to me and my companions, he stood still, and gave a pitiful look round upon us. I saw his eye rest on me; I had still a good mane and tail, which did something for my appearance. I pricked my ears and looked at him.

"There's a horse, Willie, that has known better days."

"Poor old fellow!" said the boy, "do you think, grandpapa, he was ever a carriage horse?"

"Oh, yes! my boy," said the farmer, coming closer, "he might have been anything when he was young; look at his nostrils and his ears, the shape of his neck and shoulder; there's a deal of breeding about that horse." He put out his hand and gave me a kind pat on the neck. I put out my nose in answer to his kindness; the boy stroked my face.

"Poor old fellow! see, grandpapa, how well he understands kindness. Could not you buy him and make him young again as you did with Lady-bird?"

"My dear boy, I can't make all old horses young; besides, Ladybird was not so very old, as she was run down and badly used."

"Well, grandpapa, I don't believe that this one is old; look at his mane and tail. I wish you would look into his mouth, and then you could tell; though he is so very thin, his eyes are not sunk like some old horses'."

The old gentleman laughed. "Bless the boy! he is as horsey as his old grandfather."

"But do look at his mouth, grandpapa, and ask the price; I am sure he would grow young in our meadows."

The man who had brought me for sale now put in his word.

"The young gentleman's a real knowing one, sir. Now the fact is, this 'ere hoss is just pulled down with overwork in the cabs; he's not an old one, and I heerd as how the vetenary should say, that a six months' run off would set him right up, being as how his wind was not broken. I've had the tending of him these ten days past, and a gratefuller, pleasanter animal I never met with, and 't would be worth a gentleman's while to give a five-pound note for him, and let him have a chance. I 'll be bound he 'd be worth twenty pounds next spring."

The old gentleman laughed, and the little boy looked up eagerly.

"O grandpapa, did you not say, the colt sold for five pounds more than you expected? You would not be poorer if you did buy this one."

The farmer slowly felt my legs, which were much swelled and strained; then he looked at my mouth. "Thirteen or fourteen, I should say; just trot him out, will you?"

I arched my poor thin neck, raised my tail a little, and threw out my legs as well as I could, for they were very stiff.

"What is the lowest you will take for him?" said the farmer as I came back.

"Five pounds, sir; that was the lowest price my master set."

"'T is a speculation," said the old gentleman, shaking his head, but at the same time slowly drawing out his purse, "quite a speculation! Have you any more business here?" he said, counting the sovereigns into his hand.

"No, sir, I can take him for you to the inn, if you please."

"Do so, I am now going there."

They walked forward, and I was led behind. The boy could hardly control his delight, and the old gentleman seemed to enjoy his pleasure. I had a good feed at the inn, and was then gently ridden home by a servant of my new master's, and turned into a large meadow with a shed in one corner of it.

Mr. Thoroughgood, for that was the name of my benefactor, gave orders that I should have hay and oats every night and morning, and the run of the meadow during the day, and, "you, Willie," said he, "must take the oversight of him; I give him in charge to you."

The boy was proud of his charge, and undertook it in all seriousness. There was not a day when he did not pay me a visit; sometimes picking me out from amongst the other horses, and giving me a bit of carrot, or something good, or sometimes standing by me whilst I ate my oats. He always came with kind words and caresses, and of course I grew very fond of him. He called me Old Crony, as I used to come to him in the field and follow him about. Sometimes he brought his grandfather, who always looked closely at my legs.

"This is our point, Willie," he would say; "but he is improving so steadily that I think we shall see a change for the better in the spring."

The perfect rest, the good food, the soft turf, and gentle exercise, soon began to tell on my condition and my spirits. I had a good constitution from my mother, and I was never strained when I was young, so that I had a better chance than many horses, who have been worked before they came to their full strength. During the winter my legs improved so much, that I began to feel quite young again. The spring came round, and one day in March Mr. Thoroughgood determined that he would try me in the phaeton. I was well pleased, and he and Willie drove me a few miles. My legs were not stiff now, and I did the work with perfect ease.

"He's growing young, Willie; we must give him a little gentle work now, and by midsummer he will be as good as Ladybird. He has a beautiful mouth, and good paces, they can't be better."

"O grandpapa, how glad I am you bought him!"

"So am I, my boy; but he has to thank you more than me; we must now be looking out for a quiet, genteel place for him, where he will be valued."

CHAPTER XLIX

MY LAST HOME

ONE day, during this summer, the groom cleaned and dressed me with such extraordinary care that I thought some new change must be at hand; he trimmed my fetlocks and legs, passed the tarbrush over my hoofs, and even parted my forelock. I think the harness had an extra polish. Willie seemed half-anxious, half-merry, as he got into the chaise with his grandfather.

"If the ladies take to him," said the old gentleman, "they 'll be suited, and he 'll be suited; we can but try."

At the distance of a mile or two from the village, we came to a pretty, low house, with a lawn and shrubbery at the front, and a drive up to the door. Willie rang the bell, and asked if Miss Blomefield or Miss Ellen was at home. Yes, they were. So, whilst Willie stayed with me, Mr. Thoroughgood went into the house. In about ten minutes he returned, followed by three ladies; one tall, pale lady, wrapped in a white shawl, leaned on a younger lady, with dark eyes and a merry face; the other, a very stately-looking person, was Miss Blomefield. They all came and looked at me and asked questions. The younger lady — that was Miss Ellen — took to me very much; she said she was sure she should like

me, I had such a good face. The tall, pale lady said
that she should always be nervous in riding behind
a horse that had once been down, as I might come
down again, and if I did, she should never get over
the fright.

"You see, ladies," said Mr. Thoroughgood, "many
first-rate horses have had their knees broken through
the carelessness of their drivers, without any fault
of their own, and from what I see of this horse, I
should say that is his case; but of course I do not
wish to influence you. If you incline, you can have
him on trial, and then your coachman will see what
he thinks of him."

"You have always been such a good adviser to us
about our horses," said the stately lady, "that your
recommendation would go a long way with me, and
if my sister Lavinia sees no objection, we will accept
your offer of a trial, with thanks."

It was then arranged that I should be sent for the
next day.

In the morning a smart-looking young man came
for me; at first, he looked pleased; but when he saw
my knees, he said in a disappointed voice, —

"I did n't think, sir, you would have recommended
my ladies a blemished horse like that."

"'Handsome is that handsome does,'" said my
master; "you are only taking him on trial, and I am
sure you will do fairly by him, young man; if he is
not as safe as any horse you ever drove, send him
back."

I was led home, placed in a comfortable stable,
fed, and left to myself. The next day, when my
groom was cleaning my face, he said, —

"That is just like the star that Black Beauty had, he is much the same height too; I wonder where he is now."

A little further on, he came to the place in my neck where I was bled, and where a little knot was left in the skin. He almost started, and began to look me over carefully, talking to himself.

"White star in the forehead, one white foot on the off side, this little knot just in that place;" then looking at the middle of my back — "and as I am alive, there is that little patch of white hair that John used to call 'Beauty's threepenny bit.' It *must* be Black Beauty! Why, Beauty! Beauty! do you know me? little Joe Green, that almost killed you?" And he began patting and patting me as if he was quite overjoyed.

I could not say that I remembered him, for now he was a fine grown young fellow, with black whiskers and a man's voice, but I was sure he knew me, and that he was Joe Green, and I was very glad. I put my nose up to him, and tried to say that we were friends. I never saw a man so pleased.

"Give you a fair trial! I should think so indeed! I wonder who the rascal was that broke your knees, my old Beauty! you must have been badly served out somewhere; well, well, it won't be my fault if you haven't good times of it now. I wish John Manly was here to see you."

In the afternoon I was put into a low Park chair and brought to the door. Miss Ellen was going to try me, and Green went with her. I soon found that she was a good driver, and she seemed pleased

"I have now lived in this happy place a whole year." (page 245)

Out to graze.

with my paces. I heard Joe telling her about me, and that he was sure I was Squire Gordon's old Black Beauty.

When we returned, the other sisters came out to hear how I had behaved myself. She told them what she had just heard, and said, —

"I shall certainly write to Mrs. Gordon, and tell her that her favorite horse has come to us. How pleased she will be!"

After this I was driven every day for a week or so, and as I appeared to be quite safe, Miss Lavinia at last ventured out in the small close carriage. After this it was quite decided to keep me and call me by my old name of "Black Beauty."

I have now lived in this happy place a whole year. Joe is the best and kindest of grooms. My work is easy and pleasant, and I feel my strength and spirits all coming back again. Mr. Thoroughgood said to Joe the other day, —

"In your place he will last till he is twenty years old, — perhaps more."

Willie always speaks to me when he can, and treats me as his special friend. *My ladies have promised that I shall never be sold,* and so I have nothing to fear; and here my story ends. My troubles are all over, and I am at home; and often before I am quite awake, I fancy I am still in the orchard at Birtwick, standing with my old friends under the apple trees.

THE END

The stable on a summer's day.

OTHER HORSE STORIES

Ponies.

THE GIFT

from *The Red Pony*

by John Steinbeck

AT daybreak Billy Buck emerged from the bunk-house and stood for a moment on the porch looking up at the sky. He was a broad, bandy-legged little man with a walrus mustache, with square hands, puffed and muscled on the palms. His eyes were a contemplative, watery gray and the hair which protruded from under his Stetson hat was spiky and weathered. Billy was still stuffing his shirt into his blue jeans as he stood on the porch. He unbuckled his belt and tightened it again. The belt showed, by the worn shiny places opposite each hole, the gradual increase of Billy's middle over a period of years. When he had seen to the weather, Billy cleared each nostril by holding its mate closed with his forefinger and blowing fiercely. Then he walked down to the barn, rubbing his hands together. He curried and brushed two saddle horses in the stalls, talking quietly to them all the time; and he had hardly finished when the iron triangle started ringing at the ranch house. Billy stuck the brush and currycomb together and laid them on the rail, and went up to breakfast. His action had been so deliberate and yet so wasteless of time that he came to the house while Mrs. Tiflin was still ringing the triangle. She nodded her gray head to him and withdrew into the kitchen. Billy Buck sat down on the steps, because he was a cowhand, and it wouldn't be fitting that he should go first into the dining room. He heard Mr. Tiflin in the house, stamping his feet into his boots.

The high jangling note of the triangle put the boy Jody
in motion. He was only a little boy, ten years old, with hair
like dusty yellow grass and with shy polite gray eyes, and
with a mouth that worked when he thought. The triangle
picked him up out of sleep. It didn't occur to him to
disobey the harsh note. He never had: no one he knew
ever had. He brushed the tangled hair out of his eyes and
skinned his nightgown off. In a moment he was dressed—
blue chambray shirt and overalls. It was late in the
summer, so of course there were no shoes to bother with.
In the kitchen he waited until his mother got from in front
of the sink and went back to the stove. Then he washed
himself and brushed back his wet hair with his fingers. His
mother turned sharply on him as he left the sink. Jody
looked shyly away.

"I've got to cut your hair before long," his mother said.
"Breakfast's on the table. Go on in, so Billy can come."

Jody sat at the long table, which was covered with white
oilcloth washed through to the fabric in some places. The
fried eggs lay in rows on their platter. Jody took three
eggs on his plate and followed with three thick slices of
crisp bacon. He carefully scraped a spot of blood from one
of the egg yolks.

Billy Buck clumped in. "That won't hurt you," Billy
explained. "That's only a sign the rooster leaves."

Jody's tall stern father came in then and Jody knew
from the noise on the floor that he was wearing boots, but
he looked under the table anyway, to make sure. His
father turned off the oil lamp over the table, for plenty of
morning light now came through the windows.

Jody did not ask where his father and Billy Buck were
riding that day, but he wished he might go along. His
father was a disciplinarian. Jody obeyed him in everything
without questions of any kind. Now, Carl Tiflin sat down
and reached for the egg platter.

"Got the cows ready to go, Billy?" he asked.

"In the lower corral," Billy said. "I could just as well take them in alone."

"Sure you could. But a man needs company. Besides, your throat gets pretty dry." Carl Tiflin was jovial this morning.

Jody's mother put her head in the door. "What time do you think to be back, Carl?"

"I can't tell. I've got to see some men in Salinas. Might be gone till dark."

The eggs and coffee and big biscuits disappeared rapidly. Jody followed the two men out of the house. He watched them mount their horses and drive six old milk cows out of the corral and start over the hill toward Salinas. They were going to sell the old cows to the butcher.

When they had disappeared over the crown of the ridge Jody walked up the hill in back of the house. The dogs trotted around the house corner hunching their shoulders and grinning horribly with pleasure. Jody patted their heads—Doubletree Mutt with the big thick tail and yellow eyes, and Smasher, the shepherd, who had killed a coyote and lost an ear in doing it. Smasher's one good ear stood up higher than a collie's ear should. Billy Buck said that always happened. After the frenzied greeting the dogs lowered their noses to the ground in a businesslike way and went ahead, looking back now and then to make sure that the boy was coming. They walked up through the chicken yard and saw the quail eating with the chickens. Smasher chased the chickens a little to keep in practice in case there should ever be sheep to herd. Jody continued on through the large vegetable patch where the green corn was higher than his head. The cowpumpkins were green and small yet. He went on to the sagebrush line where the cold spring ran out of its pipe and fell into a round wooden tub. He leaned over and drank close to the green mossy wood where the water tasted best. Then he turned and looked back on the ranch, on the low, whitewashed house girded with red geraniums, and on the long bunkhouse by the cypress tree where Billy Buck lived alone. Jody could see the great black kettle under the cypress tree. That was where the pigs were scalded. The sun was coming over the ridge now, glaring on the whitewash of the houses and barns, making the wet grass blaze softly. Behind him, in the tall sagebrush, the birds were scampering on the ground, making a great noise among the dry leaves; the squirrels piped shrilly on the side-hills. Jody looked along at the farm buildings. He felt an uncertainty in the air, a feeling of change and of loss and of the gain of new and unfamiliar things. Over the hillside two big black buzzards sailed low to the ground and their shadows slipped smoothly and quickly ahead of them. Some animal had died in the vicinity. Jody knew it. It might be a cow or it might be the remains of a rabbit. The buzzards overlooked nothing. Jody hated them as all decent things hate them, but they could not be hurt because they made away with carrion.

After a while the boy sauntered down hill again. The dogs had long ago given him up and gone into the brush to do things in their own way. Back through the vegetable garden he went, and he paused for a moment to smash a green muskmelon with his heel, but he was not happy about it. It was a bad thing to do, he knew perfectly well. He kicked dirt over the ruined melon to conceal it.

Back at the house his mother bent over his rough hands, inspecting his fingers and nails. It did little good to start him clean to school for too many things could happen on the way. She sighed over the black cracks on his fingers, and then gave him his books and his lunch and started him on the mile walk to school. She noticed that his mouth was working a good deal this morning.

Jody started his journey. He filled his pockets with little pieces of white quartz that lay in the road, and every so often he took a shot at a bird or at some rabbit that had stayed sunning itself in the road too long. At the crossroads over the bridge he met two friends and the three of them walked to school together, making ridiculous strides and being rather silly. School had just opened two weeks before. There was still a spirit of revolt among the pupils.

It was four o'clock in the afternoon when Jody topped the hill and looked down on the ranch again. He looked for the saddle horses, but the corral was empty. His father was not back yet. He went slowly, then, toward the afternoon chores. At the ranch house, he found his mother sitting on the porch, mending socks.

"There's two doughnuts in the kitchen for you," she said. Jody slid to the kitchen, and returned with half of one of the doughnuts already eaten and his mouth full. His mother asked him what he had learned in school that day, but she didn't listen to his doughnut-muffled answer. She interrupted, "Jody, tonight see you fill the woodbox clear full. Last night you crossed the sticks and it wasn't only about half full. Lay the sticks flat tonight. And Jody, some of the hens are hiding eggs, or else the dogs are eating them. Look about in the grass and see if you can find any nests."

Jody, still eating, went out and did his chores. He saw the quail come down to eat with the chickens when he threw out the grain. For some reason his father was proud to have them come. He never allowed any shooting near the house for fear the quail might go away.

When the woodbox was full, Jody took his twenty-two

rifle up to the cold spring at the brush line. He drank again
and then aimed the gun at all manner of things, at rocks,
at birds on the wing, at the big black pig kettle under the
cypress tree, but he didn't shoot for he had no cartridges
and wouldn't have until he was twelve. If his father had
seen him aim the rifle in the direction of the house he
would have put the cartridges off another year. Jody
remembered this and did not point the rifle down the hill
again. Two years was enough to wait for cartridges.
Nearly all of his father's presents were given with reser-
vations which hampered their value somewhat. It was
good discipline.

The supper waited until dark for his father to return.
When at last he came in with Billy Buck, Jody could smell
the delicious brandy on their breaths. Inwardly he rejoiced, for his father sometimes talked to him when he
smelled of brandy, sometimes even told things he had done
in the wild days when he was a boy.

After supper, Jody sat by the fireplace and his shy polite
eyes sought the room corners, and he waited for his father
to tell what it was he contained, for Jody knew he had
news of some sort. But he was disappointed. His father
pointed a stern finger at him.

"You'd better go to bed, Jody. I'm going to need you in
the morning."

That wasn't so bad. Jody liked to do things he had to do
as long as they weren't routine things. He looked at the
floor and his mouth worked out a question before he spoke
it. "What are we going to do in the morning, kill a pig?" he
asked softly.

"Never you mind. You better get to bed."

When the door was closed behind him, Jody heard his
father and Billy Buck chuckling and he knew it was a joke
of some kind. And later, when he lay in bed, trying to
make words out of the murmurs in the other room, he

heard his father protest, "But, Ruth, I didn't give much for him."

Jody heard the hoot owls hunting mice down by the barn, and he heard a fruit tree limb tap-tapping against the house. A cow was lowing when he went to sleep.

When the triangle sounded in the morning, Jody dressed more quickly even than usual. In the kitchen, while he washed his face and combed back his hair, his mother addressed him irritably. "Don't you go out until you get a good breakfast in you."

He went into the dining room and sat at the long white table. He took a steaming hotcake from the platter, arranged two fried eggs on it, covered them with another hotcake and squashed the whole thing with his fork.

His father and Billy Buck came in. Jody knew from the sound of the floor that both of them were wearing flat-heeled shoes, but he peered under the table to make sure. His father turned off the oil lamp, for the day had arrived, and he looked stern and disciplinary, but Billy Buck didn't look at Jody at all. He avoided the shy questioning eyes of the boy and soaked a whole piece of toast in his coffee.

Carl Tiflin said crossly, "You come with us after breakfast!"

Jody had trouble with his food then, for he felt a kind of doom in the air. After Billy had tilted his saucer and drained the coffee which had slopped into it, and had wiped his hands on his jeans, the two men stood up from the table and went out into the morning light together, and Jody respectfully followed a little behind them. He tried to keep his mind from running ahead, tried to keep it absolutely motionless.

His mother called, "Carl! Don't you let it keep him from school."

They marched past the cypress, where a singletree

hung from a limb to butcher the pigs on, and past the black iron kettle, so it was not a pig killing. The sun shone over the hill and threw long, dark shadows of the trees and buildings. They crossed a stubble-field to shortcut to the barn. Jody's father unhooked the door and they went in. They had been walking toward the sun on the way down. The barn was black as night in contrast and warm from the hay and from the beasts. Jody's father moved over toward the one box stall. "Come here!" he ordered. Jody could begin to see things now. He looked into the box stall and then stepped back quickly.

A red pony colt was looking at him out of the stall. Its tense ears were forward and a light of disobedience was in its eyes. Its coat was rough and thick as an airedale's fur and its mane was long and tangled. Jody's throat collapsed in on itself and cut his breath short.

"He needs a good currying," his father said, "and if I ever hear of you not feeding him or leaving his stall dirty, I'll sell him off in a minute."

Jody couldn't bear to look at the pony's eyes any more. He gazed down at his hands for a moment, and he asked very shyly, "Mine?" No one answered him. He put his hand out toward the pony. Its gray nose came close, sniffing loudly, and then the lips drew back and the strong teeth closed on Jody's fingers. The pony shook its head up and down and seemed to laugh with amusement. Jody regarded his bruised fingers. "Well," he said with pride— "Well, I guess he can bite all right." The two men laughed, somewhat in relief. Carl Tiflin went out of the barn and walked up a sidehill to be by himself, for he was embarrassed, but Billy Buck stayed. It was easier to talk to Billy Buck. Jody asked again—"Mine?"

Billy became professional in tone. "Sure! That is, if you look out for him and break him right. I'll show you how. He's just a colt. You can't ride him for some time."

Jody put out his bruised hand again, and this time the red pony let his nose be rubbed. "I ought to have a carrot," Jody said. "Where'd we get him, Billy?"

"Bought him at a sheriff's auction," Billy explained. "A show went broke in Salinas and had debts. The sheriff was selling off their stuff."

The pony stretched out his nose and shook the forelock from his wild eyes. Jody stroked the nose a little. He said softly, "There isn't a—saddle?"

Billy Buck laughed. "I'd forgot. Come along."

In the harness room he lifted down a little saddle of red morocco leather. "It's just a show saddle," Billy Buck said disparagingly. "It isn't practical for the brush, but it was cheap at the sale."

Jody couldn't trust himself to look at the saddle either, and he couldn't speak at all. He brushed the shining red leather with his fingertips, and after a long time he said, "It'll look pretty on him though." He thought of the grandest and prettiest things he knew. "If he hasn't a name already, I think I'll call him Gabilan Mountains," he said.

Billy Buck knew how he felt. "It's a pretty long name. Why don't you just call him Gabilan? That means hawk. That would be a fine name for him." Billy felt glad. "If you will collect tail hair, I might be able to make a hair rope for you sometime. You could use it for a hackamore."

Jody wanted to go back to the box stall. "Could I lead him to school, do you think—to show the kids?"

But Billy shook his head. "He's not even halter-broke yet. We had a time getting him here. Had to almost drag him. You better be starting for school though."

"I'll bring the kids to see him here this afternoon," Jody said.

Six boys came over the hill half an hour early that afternoon, running hard, their heads down, their forearms working, their breath whistling. They swept by the house and cut across the stubble-field to the barn. And then they stood self-consciously before the pony, and then they looked at Jody with eyes in which there was a new admiration and a new respect. Before today Jody had been a boy, dressed in overalls and a blue shirt—quieter than most, even suspected of being a little cowardly. And now he was different. Out of a thousand centuries they drew the ancient admiration of the footman for the horseman. They knew instinctively that a man on a horse is spiritually as well as physically bigger than a man on foot. They knew that Jody had been miraculously lifted out of equality with them, and had been placed over them. Gabilan put his head out of the stall and sniffed them.

"Why'n't you ride him?" the boys cried. "Why'n't you braid his tail with ribbons like in the fair?" "When you going to ride him?"

Jody's courage was up. He too felt the superiority of the horseman."He's not old enough. Nobody can ride him for a long time. I'm going to train him on the long halter. Billy Buck is going to show me how."

"Well, can't we even lead him around a little?"

"He isn't even halter-broke," Jody said. He wanted to be completely alone when he took the pony out the first time. "Come and see the saddle."

They were speechless at the red morocco saddle, completely shocked out of comment. "It isn't much use in the brush," Jody explained. "It'll look pretty on him though. Maybe I'll ride bareback when I go into the brush."

"How you going to rope a cow without a saddle horn?"

"Maybe I'll get another saddle for every day. My father might want me to help him with the stock." He let them feel the red saddle, and showed them the brass chain throat latch on the bridle and the big brass buttons at each temple where the headstall and brow band crossed. The whole thing was too wonderful. They had to go away after a little while, and each boy, in his mind, searched among his possessions for a bribe worthy of offering in return for a ride on the red pony when the time should come.

Jody was glad when they had gone. He took brush and currycomb from the wall, took down the barrier of the box stall and stepped cautiously in. The pony's eyes glittered, and he edged around into kicking position. But Jody touched him on the shoulder and rubbed his high arched neck as he had always seen Billy Buck do, and he crooned, "So-o-o, Boy," in a deep voice. The pony gradually relaxed his tenseness. Jody curried and brushed until a pile of dead hair lay in the stall and until the pony's coat had taken on a deep red shine. Each time he finished he thought it might have been done better. He braided the mane into a dozen little pigtails, and he braided the forelock, and then he undid them and brushed the hair out straight again.

Jody did not hear his mother enter the barn. She was angry when she came, but when she looked in at the pony and at Jody working over him, she felt a curious pride rise up in her. "Have you forgot the woodbox?" she asked gently. "It's not far off from dark and there's not a stick of wood in the house, and the chickens aren't fed."

Jody quickly put up his tools. "I forgot, ma'am."

"Well, after this do your chores first. Then you won't forget. I expect you'll forget lots of things now if I don't keep an eye on you."

"Can I have carrots from the garden for him, ma'am?"

She had to think about that. "Oh—I guess so, if you only take the big tough ones."

"Carrots keep the coat good," he said, and again she felt the curious rush of pride.

Jody never waited for the triangle to get him out of bed after the coming of the pony. It became his habit to creep out of bed even before his mother was awake, to slip into his clothes and to go quietly down to the barn to see Gabilan. In the gray quiet mornings when the land and the brush and the houses and the trees were silver-gray and black like a photograph negative, he stole toward the barn, past the sleeping stones and the sleeping cypress tree. The turkeys, roosting in the tree out of coyotes' reach, clicked drowsily. The fields glowed with a gray frostlike light and in the dew the tracks of rabbits and of field mice stood out sharply. The good dogs came stiffly out of their little houses, hackles up and deep growls in their throats. Then they caught Jody's scent, and their stiff tails rose up and waved a greeting—Doubletree Mutt with the big thick tail, and Smasher, the incipient shepherd—then went lazily back to their warm beds.

It was a strange time and a mysterious journey, to Jody—an extension of a dream. When he first had the pony he liked to torture himself during the trip by thinking Gabilan would not be in his stall, and worse, would never have been there. And he had other delicious self-induced pains. He thought how the rats had gnawed ragged holes in the red saddle, and how the mice had nibbled Gabilan's tail until it was stringy and thin. He usually ran the last little way to the barn. He unlatched the rusty hasp of the barn door and stepped in, and no matter how quietly he opened the door, Gabilan was always looking at him over the barrier of the box stall and Gabilan whinnied softly and stamped his front foot, and his eyes had big sparks of red fire in them like oakwood embers.

Sometimes, if the work horses were to be used that day, Jody found Billy Buck in the barn harnessing and currying. Billy stood with him and looked long at Gabilan and he told Jody a great many things about horses. He explained that they were terribly afraid for their feet, so that one must make a practice of lifting the legs and patting the hoofs and ankles to remove their terror. He told Jody how horses love conversation. He must talk to the pony all the time, and tell him the reasons for everything. Billy wasn't sure a horse could understand everything that was said to him, but it was impossible to say how much was understood. A horse never kicked up a fuss if someone he liked explained things to him. Billy could give examples, too. He had known, for instance, a horse nearly dead beat with fatigue to perk up when told it was only a little farther to his destination. And he had known a horse paralyzed with fright to come out of it when his rider told him what it was that was frightening him. While he talked in the mornings, Billy Buck cut twenty or thirty straws into neat three-inch lengths and stuck them into his hatband. Then during the whole day, if he wanted to pick his teeth or merely to chew on something, he had only to reach up for one of them.

Jody listened carefully, for he knew and the whole country knew that Billy Buck was a fine hand with horses. Billy's own horse was a stringy cayuse with a hammer head, but he nearly always won the first prizes at the stock trials. Billy could rope a steer, take a double half-hitch about the horn with his riata, and dismount, and his horse would play the steer as an angler plays a fish, keeping a tight rope until the steer was down or beaten.

Every morning, after Jody had curried and brushed the pony, he let down the barrier of the stall, and Gabilan thrust past him and raced down the barn and into the corral. Around and around he galloped, and sometimes he jumped forward and landed on stiff legs. He stood quivering, stiff ears forward, eyes rolling so that the whites showed, pretending to be frightened. At last he walked snorting to the water trough and buried his nose in the water up to the nostrils. Jody was proud then, for he knew that was the way to judge a horse. Poor horses only touched their lips to the water, but a fine spirited beast put his whole nose and mouth under, and only left room to breathe.

Then Jody stood and watched the pony, and he saw things he had never noticed about any other horse, the sleek, sliding flank muscles and the cords of the buttocks, which flexed like a closing fist, and the shine the sun put on the red coat. Having seen horses all his life, Jody had never looked at them very closely before. But now he noticed the moving ears which gave expression and even inflection of expression to the face. The pony talked with his ears. You could tell exactly how he felt about everything by the way his ears pointed. Sometimes they were stiff and upright and sometimes lax and sagging. They went back when he was angry or fearful, and forward when he was anxious and curious and pleased; and their exact position indicated which emotion he had.

Billy Buck kept his word. In the early fall the training began. First there was the halter-breaking, and that was the hardest because it was the first thing. Jody held a carrot and coaxed and promised and pulled on the rope. The pony set his feet like a burro when he felt the strain. But before long he learned. Jody walked all over the ranch leading him. Gradually he took to dropping the rope until the pony followed him unled wherever he went.

And then came the training on the long halter. That was slower work. Jody stood in the middle of a circle, holding the long halter. He clucked with his tongue and the pony started to walk in a big circle, held in by the long rope. He clucked again to make the pony trot, and again to make him gallop. Around and around Gabilan went thundering and enjoying it immensely. Then he called, "Whoa," and the pony stopped. It was not long until Gabilan was perfect at it. But in many ways he was a bad pony. He bit Jody in the pants and stomped on Jody's feet. Now and then his ears went back and he aimed a tremendous kick at the boy. Every time he did one of these bad things, Gabilan settled back and seemed to laugh to himself.

Billy Buck worked at the hair rope in the evenings before the fireplace. Jody collected tail hair in a bag, and he sat and watched Billy slowly constructing the rope, twisting a few hairs to make a string and rolling two strings together for a cord, and then braiding a number of cords to make the rope. Billy rolled the finished rope on the floor under his foot to make it round and hard.

The long halter work rapidly approached perfection. Jody's father, watching the pony stop and start and trot and gallop, was a little bothered by it.

"He's getting to be almost a trick pony," he complained. "I don't like trick horses. It takes all the—dignity out of a horse to make him do tricks. Why, a trick horse is kind of like an actor—no dignity, no character of his own." And his father said, "I guess you better be getting him used to the saddle pretty soon."

Jody rushed for the harness room. For some time he had been riding the saddle on a sawhorse. He changed the stirrup length over and over, and could never get it just right. Sometimes, mounted on the sawhorse in the harness room, with collars and hames and tugs hung all about him, Jody rode out beyond the room. He carried his rifle across the pommel. He saw the fields go flying by, and he heard the beat of the galloping hoofs.

It was a ticklish job, saddling the pony the first time. Gabilan hunched and reared and threw the saddle off before the cinch could be tightened. It had to be replaced again and again until at last the pony let it stay. And the cinching was difficult, too. Day by day Jody tightened the girth a little more until at last the pony didn't mind the saddle at all.

Then there was the bridle. Billy explained how to use a

stick of licorice for a bit until Gabilan was used to having something in his mouth. Billy explained, "Of course we could forcebreak him to everything, but he wouldn't be as good a horse if we did. He'd always be a little bit afraid, and he wouldn't mind because he wanted to."

The first time the pony wore the bridle he whipped his head about and worked his tongue against the bit until the blood oozed from the corners of his mouth. He tried to rub the headstall off on the manger. His ears pivoted about and his eyes turned red with fear and with general rambunctiousness. Jody rejoiced, for he knew that only a mean-souled horse does not resent training.

And Jody trembled when he thought of the time when he would first sit in the saddle. The pony would probably throw him off. There was no disgrace in that. The disgrace would come if he did not get right up and mount again. Sometimes he dreamed that he lay in the dirt and cried and couldn't make himself mount again. The shame of the dream lasted until the middle of the day.

Gabilan was growing fast. Already he had lost the long-leggedness of the colt; his mane was getting longer and blacker. Under the constant currying and brushing his coat lay as smooth and gleaming as orange-red lacquer. Jody oiled the hoofs and kept them carefully trimmed so they would not crack.

The hair rope was nearly finished. Jody's father gave him an old pair of spurs and bent in the side bars and cut down the strap and took up the chainlets until they fitted. And then one day Carl Tiflin said:

"The pony's growing faster than I thought. I guess you can ride him by Thanksgiving. Think you can stick on?"

"I don't know," Jody said shyly. Thanksgiving was only three weeks off. He hoped it wouldn't rain, for rain would spot the red saddle.

Gabilan knew and liked Jody by now. He nickered when

Jody came across the stubble field, and in the pasture he came running when his master whistled for him. There was always a carrot for him every time.

Billy Buck gave him riding instructions over and over. "Now when you get up there, just grab tight with your knees and keep your hands away from the saddle, and if you get throwed, don't let that stop you. No matter how good a man is, there's always some horse can pitch him. You just climb up again before he gets to feeling smart about it. Pretty soon, he won't throw you no more, and pretty soon he *can't* throw you no more. That's the way to do it."

"I hope it don't rain before," Jody said.

"Why not? Don't want to get throwed in the mud?"

That was partly it, and also he was afraid that in the flurry of bucking Gabilan might slip and fall on him and break his leg or his hip. He had seen that happen to men before, had seen how they writhed on the ground like squashed bugs, and he was afraid of it.

He practiced on the sawhorse how he would hold the reins in his left hand and a hat in his right hand. If he kept his hands thus busy, he couldn't grab the horn if he felt himself going off. He didn't like to think of what would happen if he did grab the horn. Perhaps his father and Billy Buck would never speak to him again, they would be so ashamed. The news would get about and his mother would be ashamed too. And in the schoolyard—it was too awful to contemplate.

He began putting his weight in a stirrup when Gabilan was saddled, but he didn't throw his leg over the pony's back. That was forbidden until Thanksgiving.

Every afternoon he put the red saddle on the pony and cinched it tight. The pony was learning already to fill his stomach out unnaturally large while the cinching was going on, and then to let it down when the straps were fixed. Sometimes Jody led him up to the brush line and let him drink from the round green tub, and sometime he led him up through the stubble field to the hilltop from which it was possible to see the white town of Salinas and the geometric fields of the great valley, and the oak trees clipped by the sheep. Now and then they broke through the brush and came to little cleared circles so hedged in that the world was gone and only the sky and the circle of brush were left from the old life. Gabilan liked these trips and showed it by keeping his head very high and by quivering his nostrils with interest. When the two came back from an expedition they smelled of the sweet sage they had forced through.

Time dragged on toward Thanksgiving, but winter came fast. The clouds swept down and hung all day over the land and brushed the hilltops, and the winds blew shrilly at night. All day the dry oak leaves drifted down from the trees until they covered the ground, and yet the trees were unchanged.

Jody had wished it might not rain before Thanksgiving, but it did. The brown earth turned dark and the trees glistened. The cut ends of the stubble turned black with mildew; the haystacks grayed from exposure to the damp, and on the roofs the moss, which had been all summer as gray as lizards, turned a brilliant yellow-green. During the week of rain, Jody keep the pony in the box stall out of the dampness, except for a little time after school when he took him out for exercise and to drink at the water-trough in the upper corral. Not once did Gabilan get wet.

The wet weather continued until little new grass appeared. Jody walked to school dressed in a slicker and short rubber boots. At length one morning the sun came out brightly. Jody, at his work in the box stall, said to

Billy Buck, "Maybe I'll leave Gabilan in the corral when I go to school today."

"Be good for him to be out in the sun," Billy assured him. "No animal likes to be cooped up too long. Your father and me are going back on the hill to clean the leaves out of the spring." Billy nodded and picked his teeth with one of his little straws.

"If the rain comes, though—" Jody suggested.

"Not likely to rain today. She's rained herself out." Billy pulled up his sleeves and snapped his arm bands. "If it comes on to rain—why a little rain don't hurt a horse."

"Well, if it comes on to rain, you put him in, will you, Billy? I'm scared he might get cold so I couldn't ride him when the time comes."

"Oh sure! I'll watch out for him if we get back in time. But it won't rain today."

And so Jody, when he went to school, left Gabilan standing out in the corral.

Billly Buck wasn't wrong about many things. He couldn't be. But he was wrong about the weather that day, for a little after noon the clouds pushed over the hills and the rain began to pour down. Jody heard it start on the schoolhouse roof. He considered holding up one finger for permission to go to the outhouse and, once outside, running for home to put the pony in. Punishment would be prompt both at school and at home. He gave it up and took ease from Billy's assurance that rain couldn't hurt a horse. When school was finally out, he hurried home through the dark rain. The banks at the sides of the road spouted little jets of muddy water. The rain slanted and swirled under a cold and gusty wind. Jody dog-trotted home, slopping through the gravelly mud of the road.

From the top of the ridge he could see Gabilan standing miserably in the corral. The red coat was almost black, and streaked with water. He stood head down with his rump to the rain and wind. Jody arrived running and threw open the barn door and led the wet pony in by his forelock. Then he found a gunny sack and rubbed the soaked hair and rubbed the legs and ankles. Gabilan stood patiently, but he trembled in gusts like the wind.

When he had dried the pony as well as he could, Jody went up to the house and brought hot water down to the barn and soaked the grain in it. Gabilan was not very hungry. He nibbled at the hot mash, but he was not very much interested in it, and he still shivered now and then. A little steam rose from his damp back.

It was almost dark when Billy Buck and Carl Tiflin came home. "When the rain started we put up at Ben Herche's place, and the rain never let up all afternoon," Carl Tiflin explained. Jody looked reproachfully at Billy Buck and Billy felt guilty.

"You said it wouldn't rain," Jody accused him.

Billy looked away. "It's hard to tell, this time of year," he said, but his excuse was lame. He had no right to be fallible, and he knew it.

"The pony got wet, got soaked through."

"Did you dry him off?"

"I rubbed him with a sack and I gave him hot grain."

Billy nodded in agreement.

"Do you think he'll take cold, Billy?"

"A little rain never hurt anything," Billy assured him.

Jody's father joined the conversation then and lectured the boy a little. "A horse," he said, "isn't any lap-dog kind of thing." Carl Tiflin hated weakness and sickness, and he held a violent contempt for helplessness.

Jody's mother put a platter of steaks on the table and boiled potatoes and boiled squash, which clouded the room with their steam. They sat down to eat. Carl Tiflin still grumbled about weakness put into animals and men by too much coddling.

Billy Buck felt bad about his mistake. "Did you blanket him?" he asked.

"No. I couldn't find any blanket. I laid some sacks over his back."

"We'll go down and cover him up after we eat, then." Billy felt better about it then. When Jody's father had gone in to the fire and his mother was washing dishes, Billy found and lighted a lantern. He and Jody walked through the mud to the barn. The barn was dark and warm and sweet. The horses still munched their evening hay. "You hold the lantern!" Billy ordered. And he felt the pony's legs and tested the heat of the flanks. He put his cheek against the pony's gray muzzle and then he rolled up the eyelids to look at the eyeballs and he lifted the lips to see the gums, and he put his fingers inside the ears. "He don't seem so chipper," Billy said. "I'll give him a rub-down."

Then Billy found a sack and rubbed the pony's legs violently and he rubbed the chest and the withers. Gabilan was strangely spiritless. He submitted patiently to the rubbing. At last Billy brought an old cotton comforter from the saddle room, and threw it over the pony's back and tied it at neck and chest with string.

"Now he'll be all right in the morning," Billy said.

Jody's mother looked up when he got back to the house. "You're late up from bed," she said. She held his chin in her hard hand and brushed the tangled hair out of his eyes and she said, "Don't worry about the pony. He'll be all right. Billy's as good as any horse doctor in the country."

Jody hadn't known she could see his worry. He pulled gently away from her and knelt down in front of the fireplace until it burned his stomach. He scorched himself through and then went in to bed, but it was a hard thing to go to sleep. He awakened after what seemed a long time. The room was dark but there was a grayness in the window like that which precedes the dawn. He got up and found his overalls and searched for the legs, and then the clock in the other room struck two. He laid his clothes down and got back into bed. It was broad daylight when he awakened again. For the first time he had slept through the ringing of the triangle. He leaped up, flung on his clothes and went out of the door still buttoning his shirt. His mother looked after him for a moment and then went quietly back to her work. Her eyes were brooding and kind. Now and then her mouth smiled a little but without changing her eyes at all.

Jody ran on toward the barn. Halfway there he heard the sound he dreaded, the hollow rasping cough of a horse. He broke into a sprint then. In the barn he found Billy Buck with the pony. Billy was rubbing his legs with his strong thick hands. He looked up and smiled gaily. "He just took a little cold," Billy said. "We'll have him out of it in a couple of days."

Jody looked at the pony's face. The eyes were half closed and the lids thick and dry. In the eye corners a crust of hard mucus stuck. Gabilan's ears hung loosely sideways and his head was low. Jody put out his hand, but the pony did not move close to it. He coughed again and his whole body constricted with the effort. A little stream of thin fluid ran from his nostrils.

Jody looked back at Billy Buck. "He's awful sick, Billy."

"Just a little cold, like I said," Billy insisted. "You go get some breakfast and then go back to school. I'll take care of him."

"But you might have to do something else. You might leave him."

"No, I won't. I won't leave him at all. Tomorrow's

Saturday. Then you can stay with him all day." Billy had failed again, and he felt badly about it. He had to cure the pony now.

Jody walked up to the house and took his place listlessly at the table. The eggs and bacon were cold and greasy, but he didn't notice it. He ate his usual amount. He didn't even ask to stay home from school. His mother pushed his hair back when she took his plate. "Billy'll take care of the pony," she assured him.

He moped through the whole day at school. He couldn't answer any questions nor read any words. He couldn't even tell anyone the pony was sick, for that might make him sicker. And when school was finally out he started home in dread. He walked slowly and let the other boys leave him. He wished he might continue walking and never arrive at the ranch.

Billy was in the barn, as he had promised, and the pony was worse. His eyes were almost closed now, and his breath whistled shrilly past an obstruction in his nose. A film covered that part of the eyes that was visible at all. It was doubtful whether the pony could see any more. Now and then he snorted, to clear his nose, and by the action seemed to plug it tighter. Jody looked dispiritedly at the pony's coat. The hair lay rough and unkempt and seemed to have lost all of its old luster. Billy stood quietly beside the stall. Jody hated to ask, but he had to know.

"Billy, is he—is he going to get well?"

Billy put his fingers between the bars under the pony's jaw and felt about. "Feel here," he said and he guided Jody's fingers to a large lump under the jaw. "When that gets bigger, I'll open it up and then he'll get better."

Jody looked quickly away, for he had heard about that lump. "What is the matter with him?"

Billy didn't want to answer, but he had to. He couldn't be wrong three times. "Strangles," he said shortly, "but don't you worry about that. I'll pull him out of it. I've seen them get well when they were worse than Gabilan is. I'm going to steam him now. You can help."

"Yes," Jody said miserably. He followed Billy into the grain room and watched him make the steaming bag ready. It was a long canvas nose bag with straps to go over a horse's ears. Billy filled it one-third full of bran and then he added a couple of handfuls of dried hops. On the top of the dry substance he poured a little carbolic acid and a little turpentine. "I'll be mixing it all up while you run to the house for a kettle of boiling water," Billy said.

When Jody came back with the steaming kettle, Billy buckled the straps over Gabilan's head and fitted the bag tightly around his nose. Then through a little hole in the side of the bag he poured the boiling water on the mixture. The pony started away as a cloud of strong steam rose up, but then the soothing fumes crept through his nose and into his lungs, and the sharp steam began to clear out the nasal passages. He breathed loudly. His legs trembled in an ague, and his eyes closed against the biting cloud. Billy poured in more water and kept the steam rising for fifteen minutes. At last he set down the kettle and took the bag from Gabilan's nose. The pony looked better. He breathed freely, and his eyes were open wider than they had been.

"See how good it makes him feel," Billy said. "Now we'll wrap him up in the blanket again. Maybe he'll be nearly well by morning."

"I'll stay with him tonight," Jody suggested.

"No. Don't you do it. I'll bring my blankets down here and put them in the hay. You can stay tomorrow and steam him if he needs it."

The evening was falling when they went to the house for their supper. Jody didn't even realize that someone else had fed the chickens and filled the woodbox. He walked up past the house to the dark brush line and took a drink of water from the tub. The spring water was so cold that it stung his mouth and drove a shiver through him. The sky above the hills was still light. He saw a hawk flying so high that it caught the sun on its breast and shone like a spark. Two blackbirds were driving him down the sky, glittering as they attacked their enemy. In the west, the clouds were moving in to rain again.

Jody's father didn't speak at all while the family ate supper, but after Billy Buck had taken his blankets and gone to sleep in the barn, Carl Tiflin built a high fire in the fireplace and told stories. He told about the wild man who ran naked through the country and had a tail and ears like a horse, and he told about the rabbit-cats of Moro Cojo that hopped into the trees for birds. He revived the famous Maxwell brothers who found a vein of gold and hid the traces of it so carefully that they could never find it again.

Jody sat with his chin in his hands; his mouth worked nervously, and his father gradually became aware that he wasn't listening very carefully. "Isn't that funny?" he asked.

Jody laughed politely and said, "Yes, sir." His father was angry and hurt, then. He didn't tell any more stories. After a while, Jody took a lantern and went down to the barn. Billy Buck was asleep in the hay, and, except that his breath rasped a little in his lungs, the pony seemed to be much better. Jody stayed a little while, running his fingers over the red rough coat, and then he took up the lantern and went back to the house. When he was in bed, his mother came into the room.

"Have you enough covers on? It's getting winter."

"Yes, ma'am."

"Well, get some rest tonight." She hesitated to go out, stood uncertainly. "The pony will be all right," she said.

Jody was tired. He went to sleep quickly and didn't awaken until dawn. The triangle sounded, and Billy Buck came up from the barn before Jody could get out of the house.

"How is he?" Jody demanded.

Billy always wolfed his breakfast. "Pretty good. I'm going to open that lump this morning. Then he'll be better maybe."

After breakfast, Billy got out his best knife, one with a needle point. He whetted the shining blade a long time on a little carborundum stone. He tried the point and the blade again and again on his callused thumb ball, and at last he tried it on his upper lip.

On the way to the barn, Jody noticed how the young grass was up and how the stubble was melting day by day into the new green crop of volunteer. It was a cold sunny morning.

As soon as he saw the pony, Jody knew he was worse. His eyes were closed and sealed shut with dried mucus. His head hung so low that his nose almost touched the straw of his bed. There was a little groan in each breath, a deep-seated, patient groan.

Billy lifted the weak head and made a quick slash with the knife. Jody saw the yellow pus run out. He held up the head while Billy swabbed out the wound with weak carbolic acid salve.

"Now he'll feel better," Billy assured him. "That yellow poison is what makes him sick."

Jody looked unbelieving at Billy Buck. "He's awful sick."

Billy thought a long time what to say. He nearly tossed off a careless assurance, but he saved himself in time. "Yes, he's pretty sick," he said at last. "I've seen worse ones get well. If he doesn't get pneumonia, we'll pull him through. You stay with him. If he gets worse, you can come and get me."

For a long time after Billy went away, Jody stood beside

the pony, stroking him behind the ears. The pony didn't flip his head the way he had done when he was well. The groaning in his breathing was becoming more hollow.

Doubletree Mutt looked into the barn, his big tail waving provocatively, and Jody was so incensed at his health that he found a hard black clod on the floor and deliberately threw it. Doubletree Mutt went yelping away to nurse a bruised paw.

In the middle of the morning, Billy Buck came back and made another steam bag. Jody watched to see whether the pony improved this time as he had before. His breathing eased a little, but he did not raise his head.

The Saturday dragged on. Late in the afternoon Jody went to the house and brought his bedding down and made up a place to sleep in the hay. He didn't ask permission. He knew from the way his mother looked at him that she would let him do almost anything. That night he left a lantern burning on a wire over the box stall. Billy had told him to rub the pony's legs every little while.

At nine o'clock the wind sprang up and howled around the barn. And in spite of his worry, Jody grew sleepy. He got into his blankets and went to sleep, but the breathy groans of the pony sounded in his dreams. And in his sleep he heard a crashing noise which went on and on until it awakened him. The wind was rushing through the barn. He sprang up and looked down the lane of stalls. The barn door had blown open, and the pony was gone.

He caught the lantern and ran outside into the gale, and he saw Gabilan weakly shambling away into the darkness, head down, legs working slowly and mechanically. When Jody ran up and caught him by the forelock, he allowed himself to be led back and put into his stall. His groans were louder, and a fierce whistling came from his nose. Jody didn't sleep any more then. The hissing of the pony's breath grew louder and sharper.

He was glad when Billy Buck came in at dawn. Billy looked for a time at the pony as though he had never seen him before. He felt the ears and flanks. "Jody," he said, "I've got to do something you won't want to see. You run up to the house for a while."

Jody grabbed him fiercely by the forearm. "You're not going to shoot him?"

Billy patted his hand. "No. I'm going to open a little hole in his windpipe so he can breathe. His nose is filled up. When he gets well, we'll put a little brass button in the hole for him to breathe through."

Jody couldn't have gone away if he had wanted. It was awful to see the red hide cut, but infinitely more terrible to know it was being cut and not to see it. "I'll stay right here," he said bitterly. "You sure you got to?"

"Yes. I'm sure. If you stay, you can hold his head. If it doesn't make you sick, that is."

The knife came out again and was whetted again just as carefully as it had been the first time. Jody held the pony's head up and the throat taut, while Billy felt up and down for the right place. Jody sobbed once as the bright knife point disappeared into the throat. The pony plunged weakly away and then stood still, trembling violently. The blood ran thickly out and up the knife and across Billy's hand and into his shirtsleeve. The sure square hand sawed out a round hole in the flesh, and the breath came bursting out of the hole, throwing a fine spray of blood. With the rush of oxygen, the pony took a sudden strength. He lashed out with his hind feet and tried to rear, but Jody held his head down while Billy mopped the new wound with carbolic salve. It was a good job. The blood stopped flowing and the air puffed out of the hole and sucked it in regularly with a little bubbling noise.

The rain brought in by the night wind began to fall on the barn roof. Then the triangle rang for breakfast. "You go up and eat while I wait," Billy said. "We've got to keep this hole from plugging up."

Jody walked slowly out of the barn. He was too dispirited to tell Billy how the barn door had blown open and let the pony out. He emerged into the wet gray morning and sloshed up to the house, taking a perverse pleasure in splashing through all the puddles. His mother fed him and put dry clothes on. She didn't question him. She seemed to know he couldn't answer questions. But when he was ready to go back to the barn she brought him a pan of steaming meal. "Give him this," she said.

But Jody did not take the pan. He said, "He won't eat anything," and ran out of the house. At the barn, Billy showed him how to fix a ball of cotton on a stick, with which to swab out the breathing hole when it became clogged with mucus.

Jody's father walked into the barn and stood with them in front of the stall. At length he turned to the boy. "Hadn't you better come with me? I'm going to drive over the hill." Jody shook his head. "You better come on, out of this," his father insisted.

Billy turned on him angrily. "Let him alone. It's his pony, isn't it?"

Carl Tiflin walked away without saying another word. His feelings were badly hurt.

All morning Jody kept the wound open and the air passing in and out freely. At noon the pony lay wearily down on his side and stretched his nose out.

Billy came back. "If you're going to stay with him tonight, you better take a little nap," he said. Jody went absently out of the barn. The sky had cleared to a hard thin blue. Everywhere the birds were busy with worms that had come to the damp surface of the ground.

Jody walked to the brush line and sat on the edge of the mossy tub. He looked down at the house and at the old bunkhouse and at the dark cypress tree. The place was familiar, but curiously changed. It wasn't itself any more, but a frame for things that were happening. A cold wind blew out of the east now, signifying that the rain was over for a little while. At his feet Jody would see the little arms of new weeds spreading out over the ground. In the mud about the spring were thousands of quail tracks.

Doubletree Mutt came sideways and embarrassed up through the vegetable patch, and Jody, remembering how he had thrown the clod, put his arm about the dog's neck and kissed him on his wide black nose. Doubletree Mutt sat still, as though he knew some solemn thing was happening. His big tail slapped the ground gravely. Jody pulled a swollen tick out of Mutt's neck and popped it dead between his thumbnails. It was a nasty thing. He washed his hands in the cold spring water.

Except for the steady swish of the wind, the farm was very quiet. Jody knew his mother wouldn't mind if he didn't go in to eat his lunch. After a little while he went slowly back to the barn. Mutt crept into his own little house and whined softly to himself for a long time.

Billy Buck stood up from the box and surrendered the cotton swab. The pony still lay on his side and the wound in his throat bellowed in and out. When Jody saw how dry and dead the hair looked, he knew at last that there was no hope for the pony. He had seen the dead hair before on dogs and on cows, and it was a sure sign. He sat heavily on the box and let down the barrier of the box stall. For a long time he kept his eyes on the moving wound, and at last he dozed, and the afternoon passed quickly. Just before dark his mother brought a deep dish of stew and left it for him and went away. Jody ate a little of it, and, when it was dark, he set the lantern on the floor by the pony's head so he could watch the wound and keep it open. And he dozed again until the night chill awakened him.

The wind was blowing fiercely, bringing the north cold with it. Jody brought a blanket from his bed in the hay and wrapped himself in it. Gabilan's breathing was quiet at last; the hole in his throat moved gently. The owls flew through the hayloft, shrieking and looking for mice. Jody put his hands down on his head and slept. In his sleep he was aware that the wind had increased. He heard it slamming about the barn.

It was daylight when he awakened. The barn door had swung open. The pony was gone. He sprang up and ran out into the morning light.

The pony's tracks were plain enough, dragging through the frostlike dew on the young grass, tired tracks with little lines between them where the hoofs had dragged. They headed for the brush line halfway up the ridge. Jody broke into a run and followed them. The sun shone on the sharp white quartz that stuck through the ground here and there. As he followed the plain trail, a shadow cut across in front of him. He looked up and saw a high circle of black buzzards, and the slowly revolving circle dropped lower and lower. The solemn birds soon disappeared over the ridge. Jody ran faster then, forced on by panic and rage. The trail entered the brush at last and followed a winding route among the tall sagebrushes.

At the top of the ridge Jody was winded. He paused, puffing noisily. The blood pounded in his ears. Then he saw what he was looking for. Below, in one of the little clearings in the brush, lay the red pony. In the distance, Jody could see the legs moving slowly and convulsively. And in a circle around him stood the buzzards, waiting for the moment of death they know so well.

Jody leaped forward and plunged down the hill. The wet ground muffled his steps and the brush hid him. When he arrived, it was all over. The first buzzard sat on the pony's head and its beak had just risen dripping with dark eye

fluid. Jody plunged into the circle like a cat. The black
brotherhood arose in a cloud, but the big one on the pony's
head was too late. As it hopped along to take off, Jody
caught its wing tip and pulled it down. It was nearly as big
as he was. The free wing crashed into his face with the
force of a club, but he hung on. The claws fastened on his
leg and the wing elbows battered his head on either side.
Jody groped blindly with his free hand. His fingers found
the neck of the struggling bird. The red eyes looked into
his face, calm and fearless and fierce; the naked head
turned from side to side. Then the beak opened and
vomited a stream of putrcfied fluid. Jody brought up his
knee and fell on the great bird. He held the neck to the
ground with one hand while his other found a piece of
sharp white quartz. The first blow broke the beak sideways and black blood spurted from the twisted, leathery
mouth corners. He struck again and missed. The red
fearless eyes still looked at him, impersonal and unafraid
and detached. He struck again and again, until the buzzard
lay dead, until its head was a red pulp. He was still beating
the dead bird when Billy Buck pulled him off, and held him
tightly to calm his shaking.

Carl Tiflin wiped the blood from the boy's face with a
red bandanna. Jody was limp and quiet now. His father
moved the buzzard with his toe. "Jody," he explained, "the
buzzard didn't kill the pony. Don't you know that?"

"I know it," Jody said wearily.

It was Billy Buck who was angry. He had lifted Jody in
his arms, and had turned to carry him home. But he
turned back on Carl Tiflin. "'Course he knows it," Billy
said furiously, "Jesus Christ! man, can't you see how he'd
feel about it?"

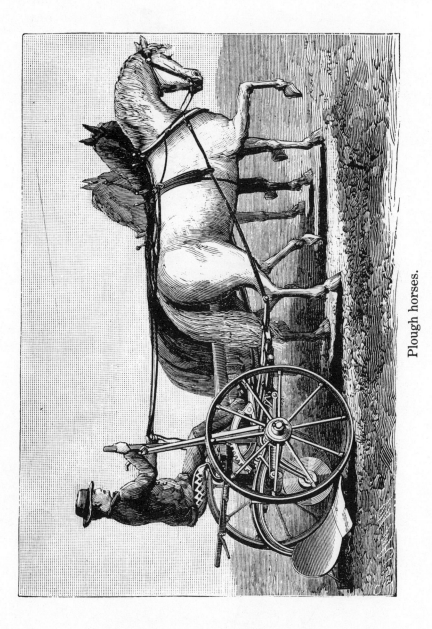

Plough horses.

The defiant stallion.

BLACK EAGLE WHO ONCE RULED
THE RANGES

by Sewell Ford

O F his sire and dam there is no record. All that is known is that he was raised on a Kentucky stock farm. Perhaps he was a son of Hanover, but Hanoverian or no, he was a thoroughbred. In the ordinary course of events he would have been tried out with the other three-year-olds for the big meet on Churchill Downs. In the hands of a good trainer he might have carried to victory the silk of some great stable and had his name printed in the sporting almanacs to this day.

But there was about Black Eagle nothing ordinary, either in his blood or in his career. He was born for the part he played. So at three, instead of being entered in his class at Louisville, it happened that he was shipped West, where his fate waited.

No more comely three-year-old ever took the Santa Fe trail. Although he stood but thirteen hands and tipped the beam at scarcely twelve hundred weight, you might have guessed him to be taller by two hands. The deception lay in the way he carried his shapely head and in the manner in which his arched neck tapered from the well-placed shoulders.

A horseman would have said that he had a "perfect barrel," meaning that his ribs were well rounded. His very gait was an embodied essay on graceful pride. As for his coat, save for a white star just in the middle of his forehead, it was as black and sleek as the nap on a new silk hat. After a good rubbing he was so shiny that at a distance you might have thought him starched and ironed and newly come from the laundry.

His arrival at Bar L Ranch made no great stir, however. They were not connoisseurs of good blood and sleek coats at the Bar L outfit. They were busy folks who most needed tough animals that could lope off fifty miles at a stretch. They wanted horses whose education included the fine art of knowing when to settle back on the rope and dig in toes. It was not a question as to how fast you could do your seven furlongs. It was more important to know if you could make yourself useful at a round-up.

"'Nother bunch o' them green Eastern horses," grumbled the ranch boss as the lot was turned into a corral. "But that black fellow'd make a rustler's mouth water, eh, Lefty?" In answer to which the said Lefty, being a man little given to speech, grunted.

"We'll brand 'em in the mornin'," added the ranch boss.

Now most steers and all horses object to the branding process. Even the spiritless little Indian ponies, accustomed to many ingenious kinds of abuse, rebel at this. A meek-eyed mule, on whom humility rests as an all-covering robe, must be properly roped before submitting.

In branding they first get a rope over your neck and shut off your wind. Then they trip your feet by roping your forelegs while you are on the jump. This brings you down hard and with much abruptness. A cowboy sits on your head while others pin you to the ground from various vantage points. Next someone holds a red-hot iron on your rump until it has sunk deep into your skin. That is branding.

Well, this thing they did to the black thoroughbred, who had up to that time felt not so much as the touch of a whip. They did it, but not before a full dozen cowpunchers had worked themselves into such a fury of exasperation that no shred of picturesque profanity was left unused among them.

Quivering with fear and anger, the black, as soon as the ropes were taken off, dashed madly about the corral looking in vain for a way of escape from his torturers. Corrals, however, are built to resist just such dashes. The burn of a branding iron is supposed to heal almost immediately. Cowboys will tell you that a horse is always more frightened than hurt during the operation, and that the day after he feels none the worse.

All this you need not credit. A burn is a burn, whether made purposely with a branding iron or by accident in any other way. The scorched flesh puckers and smarts. It hurts every time a leg is moved. It seems as if a thousand needles were playing a tattoo on the exposed surface. Neither is this the worst of the business. To a high-strung animal the roping, throwing, and burning is a tremendous nervous shock. For days after branding a horse will jump and start, quivering with expectant agony, at the slightest cause.

It was fully a week before the black thoroughbred was himself again. In that time he had conceived such a deep and lasting hatred for all men, cowboys in particular, as only a high-spirited, blue-blooded horse can acquire. With deep contempt he watched the scrubby little cow ponies as they doggedly carried about those wild, fierce men who threw their circling, whistling, hateful ropes, who wore such big, sharp spurs, and who were viciously handy in using their rawhide quirts.

So when a cowboy put a breaking-bit into the black's mouth there was another lively scene. It was somewhat confused, this scene, but at intervals one could make out that the man, holding stubbornly to mane and forelock, was being slatted and slammed and jerked, now with his feet on the ground, now thrown high in the air and now dangling perilously and at various angles as the stallion raced away.

In the end, of course, came the whistle of the choking foot-tangling ropes, and the black was saddled. For a fierce half hour he took punishment from bit and spur and quirt. Then, although he gave it up, it was not that his spirit was broken, but because his wind was gone. Quite passively he allowed himself to be ridden out on the prairie to where the herds were grazing.

Undeceived by this apparent docility, the cowboy, when the time came for him to bunk down under the chuck wagon for a few hours of sleep, tethered his mount quite securely to a deep-driven stake. Before the cattleman had taken more than a round dozen of winks the black had tested his tether to the limit of his strength. The tether stood the test. A cow pony might have done this much. There he would have stopped. But the black was a Kentucky thoroughbred, blessed with the inherited intelligence of noble sires, some of whom had been household pets. So he investigated the tether at close range.

Feeling the stake with his sensitive upper lip he discovered it to be firm as a rock. Next he backed away and wrenched tentatively at the halter until convinced that the throat strap was thoroughly sound. His last effort must have been an inspiration. Attacking the taut buckskin rope with his teeth he worked diligently until he had severed three of the four strands. Then he gathered himself for another lunge. With a snap the rope parted and the black dashed away into the night, leaving the cowboy snoring confidently by the campfire.

All night he ran, on and on in the darkness, stopping only to listen tremblingly to the echo of his own hoofs and to sniff suspiciously at the crouching shadows of innocent bushes. By morning he had left the Bar L outfit many miles behind, and when the red sun rolled up over the edge of the prairie he saw that he was alone in a field that stretched unbroken to the circling skyline.

Not until noon did the runaway black scent water. Half mad with thirst he dashed to the edge of a muddy little stream and sucked down a great draught. As he raised his head he saw standing poised above him on the opposite bank, with ears laid menacingly flat and nostrils aquiver in nervous palpitation, a buckskin-colored stallion.

Snorting from fright the black wheeled and ran. He heard behind him a shrill neigh of challenge and in a moment the thunder of many hoofs. Looking back he saw fully a score of horses, the buckskin stallion in the van, charging after him. That was enough. Filling his great lungs with air he leaped into such a burst of speed that his pursuers soon tired of the hopeless chase. Finding that he was no longer followed the black grew curious. Galloping in a circle he gradually approached the band. The horses had settled down to the cropping of buffalo grass, only the buckskin stallion, who had taken a position on a little knoll, remaining on guard.

The surprising thing about this band was that each and every member seemed riderless. Not until he had taken long up-wind sniffs was the thoroughbred convinced of this fact. When certain on this point he cantered toward the band, sniffing inquiringly. Again the buckskin stallion charged, ears back, eyes gleaming wickedly and snorting defiantly. This time the black stood his ground until the buckskin's teeth snapped savagely within a few inches of his throat. Just in time did he rear and swerve. Twice more—for the paddock-raised black was slow to understand such behavior—the buckskin charged. Then the black was roused into aggressiveness.

There ensued such a battle as would have brought delight to the brute soul of a Nero. With forefeet and teeth the two stallions engaged, circling madly about on their hind legs, tearing up great clods of turf, biting and striking as opportunity offered. At last, by a quick, desperate rush, the buckskin caught the thoroughbred fairly by the throat. Here the affair would have ended had not the black stallion, rearing suddenly on his muscle-ridged haunches and lifting his opponent's forequarters clear of the ground, showered on his enemy such a rain of blows from his iron-shod feet that the wild buckskin dropped to the ground, dazed and vanquished.

Standing over him, with all the fierce pride of a victorious gladiator showing in every curve of his glisten-ing body, the black thoroughbred trumpeted out a sten-torian call of defiance and command. The band, that had watched the struggle from a discreet distance, now came galloping in, whinnying in friendly fashion.

Black Eagle had won his first fight. He had won the leadership. By right of might he was now chief of this free company of plains rangers. It was for him to lead whither he chose, to pick the place and hour of grazing, the time for watering, and his to guard his companions from all dangers.

As for the buckskin stallion, there remained for him the choice of humbly following the new leader or of limping off alone to try to raise a new band. Being a worthy descendant of the chargers which the men of Cortez rode so fearlessly into the wilds of the New World, he chose the latter course, and having regained his senses, galloped stiffly toward the north, his bruised head lowered in defeat.

Some months later Arizona stockmen began to hear tales of a great band of wild horses, led by a magnificent black stallion which was fleeter than a scared coyote. There came reports of much mischief. Cattle were stam-peded by day, calves trampled to death, and steers scattered far and wide over the prairie. By night bunches

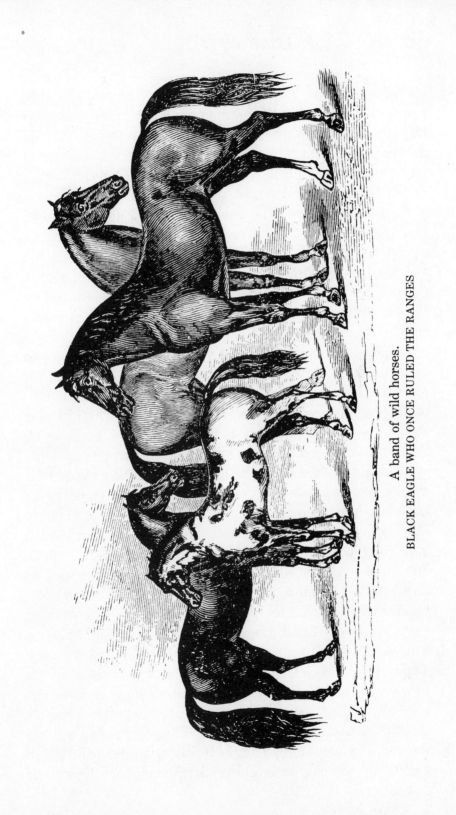

A band of wild horses.
BLACK EAGLE WHO ONCE RULED THE RANGES

of tethered cow ponies disappeared. The exasperated cowboys could only tell that suddenly out of the darkness had swept down on their quiet camps an avalanche of wild horses. And generally they caught glimpses of a great black branded stallion who led the marauders at such a pace that he seemed almost to fly through the air.

This stallion came to be known as Black Eagle, and to be thoroughly feared and hated from one end of the cattle country to the other. The Bar L ranch appeared to be the heaviest loser. Time after time were its picketed mares run off, again and again were the Bar L herds scattered by the dash of this mysterious band. Was it that Black Eagle could take revenge? Cattlemen have queer notions. They put a price on his head. It was worth six months' wages to any cowboy who might kill or capture Black Eagle.

About this time Lefty, the silent man of the Bar L outfit, disappeared. Weeks went by and still the branded stallion remained free and unhurt, for no cow horse in all the West could keep him in sight half an hour.

Black Eagle had been the outlaw king of the ranges for nearly two years when one day, as he was standing at lookout while the band cropped the rich mesa grass behind him, he saw entering the cleft end of a distant arroyo a lone cowboy mounted on a dun little pony. With quick intelligence the stallion noted that this arroyo wound about until its mouth gave upon the side of the mesa not a hundred yards from where he stood.

Promptly did Black Eagle act. Calling his band he led it at a sharp pace to a sheltered hollow on the mesa's back slope. There he left it and hurried away to take up his former position. He had not waited long before the cowboy, riding stealthily, reappeared at the arroyo's mouth. Instantly the race was on. Tossing his fine head in the air and switching haughtily his splendid tail, Black Eagle laid his course in a direction which took him away from his sheltered band. Pounding along behind came the cowboy, urging to utmost endeavor the tough little mustang which he rode.

Had this been simply a race it would have lasted but a short time. But it was more than a race. It was a conflict of strategists. Black Eagle wished to do more than merely outdistance his enemy. He meant to lead him far away and then, under cover of night, return to his band.

Also the cowboy had a purpose. Well knowing that he could neither overtake nor tire the black stallion, he intended to ride him down by circling. In circling, the pursuer rides toward the pursued from an angle, gradually forcing his quarry into a circular course whose diameter narrows with every turn.

This, however, was a trick Black Eagle had long ago learned to block. Sure of his superior speed he galloped away in a line straight as an arrow's flight, paying no heed at all to the manner in which he was followed. Before midnight he had rejoined his band, while far off on the prairie was a lone cowboy moodily frying bacon over a sage-brush fire.

But this pursuer was no faint heart. Late the next day he was sighted creeping cunningly up to windward. Again there was a race, not so long this time, for the day was far spent, but with the same result.

When for the third time there came into view this same lone cowboy, Black Eagle was thoroughly aroused to the fact that this persistent rider meant mischief. Having once more led the cowboy a long and fruitless chase the great black gathered up his band and started south. Not until noon of the next day did he halt, and then only because many of the mares were in bad shape. For a week the band was moved on. During intervals of rest a sharp lookout was kept. Watering places, where an enemy might lurk, were approached only after the most careful scouting.

Despite all caution, however, the cowboy finally appeared on the horizon. Unwilling to endanger the rest of the band, and perhaps wishing a free hand in coping with this evident Nemesis, Black Eagle cantered boldly out to meet him. Just beyond gun range the stallion turned sharply at right angles and sped off over the prairie.

There followed a curious chase. Day after day the great black led his pursuer on, stopping now and then to graze or take water, never allowing him to cross the danger line, but never leaving him wholly out of sight. It was a course of many windings which Black Eagle took, now swinging far to the west to avoid a ranch, now circling east along a watercourse, again doubling back around the base of a mesa, but in the main going steadily northward. Up past the brown Maricopas they worked, across the turgid Gila, skirting Lone Butte desert; up, up, and on until in the distance glistened the bald peaks of Silver range.

Never before did a horse play such a dangerous game, and surely none ever showed such finesse. Deliberately trailing behind him an enemy bent on taking either his life or freedom, not for a moment did Black Eagle show more than imperative caution. At the close of each day when, by a few miles of judicious galloping, he had fully winded the cowboy's mount, the sagacious black would circle to the rear of his pursuer and often, in the gloom of early night, walk recklessly near to the camp of his enemy just for the sake of sniffing curiously. But each morning, as the cowboy cooked his scant breakfast, he would see, standing a few hundred rods away, Black Eagle, patiently waiting for the chase to be resumed.

Day after day was the hunted black called upon to foil a new ruse. Sometimes it was a game of hide and seek among the buttes, and again it was an early morning sally by the cowboy.

Once during a midday stop the dun mustang was turned

out to graze. Black Eagle followed suit. A half mile to windward he could see the cow pony, and beside it, evidently sitting with his back toward his quarry, the cowboy. For a half hour, perhaps all was peace and serenity. Then, as a cougar springing from his lair, there blazed out of the bushes on the bank of a dry watercourse to leeward a rifle shot.

Black Eagle felt a shock that stretched him on the grass. There arrived a stinging at the top of his right shoulder and a numbing sensation all along his backbone. Madly he struggled to get on his feet, but he could do no more than raise his forequarters on his knees. As he did so he saw running toward him from the bushes, coatless and hatless, his relentless pursuer. Black Eagle had been tricked. The figure by the distant mustang, then, was only a dummy. He had been shot from ambush. Human strategy had won.

With one last desperate effort, which sent the red blood spurting from the bullet hole in his shoulder, Black Eagle heaved himself up until he sat on his haunches, braced by his forefeet set wide apart.

Then, just as the cowboy brought his rifle into position for the finishing shot, the stallion threw up his handsome head, his big eyes blazing like two stars, and looked defiantly at his enemy.

Slowly, steadily the cowboy took aim at the sleek black breast behind which beat the brave heart of the wild thoroughbred. With finger touching the trigger he glanced over the sights and looked into those big, bold eyes. For a full minute man and horse faced each other thus. Then the cowboy, in an uncertain, hesitating manner, lowered his rifle. Calmly Black Eagle waited. But the expected shot never came. Instead, the cowboy walked cautiously toward the wounded stallion.

No move did Black Eagle make, no fear did he show. With a splendid indifference worthy of a martyr he sat there, paying no more heed to his approaching enemy than to the red stream which trickled down his shoulder. He was helpless and knew it, but his noble courage was unshaken. Even when the man came close enough to examine the wound and pat the shining neck that for three years had known neither touch of hand nor bridle-rein, the great stallion did no more than follow with curious, steady gaze.

It is an odd fact that feral horse, although while free even wilder and fiercer than those native to the prairies, when once returned to captivity resumes almost instantly the traits and habits of domesticity. So it was with Black Eagle. With no more fuss than he would have made when he was a colt in paddock he allowed the cowboy to wash and dress his wounded shoulder and to lead him about by the halter.

By a little stream that rounded the base of a big butte, Lefty—for it was he—made camp, and every day for a week he applied to Black Eagle's shoulder a fresh poultice of pounded cactus leaves. In that time the big stallion and the silent man buried distrust and hate and enmity. No longer were they captive and captor. They came nearer to being congenial comrades than anything else, for in the calm solitudes of the vast plains such sentiments may thrive.

So, when the wound was fully healed, the black permitted himself to be bridled and saddled. With the cow pony following as best it might they rode toward Santa Fe.

With Black Eagle's return to the cramped quarters of peopled places there came experiences entirely new to him. Every morning he was saddled by Lefty and ridden around a fence-enclosed course. At first he was allowed to set his own gait, but gradually he was urged to show his speed. This was puzzling but not a little to his liking. Also he enjoyed the oats twice a day and the careful grooming after each canter. He became accustomed to stall life and to the scent and voices of men about him, although as yet he trusted none but Lefty. Ever kind and considerate he had found Lefty. There were times, of course, when Black Eagle longed to be again on the prairie at the head of his old band, but the joy of circling the track almost made up for the loss of those wild free dashes.

One day when Lefty took him out Black Eagle found many other horses on the track, while around the enclosure he saw row on row of men and women. A band was playing and flags were snapping in the breeze. There was a thrill of expectation in the air. Black Eagle felt it, and as he pranced proudly down the track there was lifted a murmur of applause and appreciation which made his nerves tingle strangely.

Just how it all came about the big stallion did not fully understand at the time. He heard a bell ring sharply, heard also the shouts of men, and suddenly found himself flying down the course in company with a dozen other horses and riders. They had finished half the circle before Black Eagle fully realized that a gaunt, long-barrelled bay was not only leading him but gaining with every leap. Tossing his black mane in the wind, opening his bright nostrils and pointing his thin, close-set ears forward he swung into the long prairie stride which he was wont to use when leading his wild band. A half dozen leaps brought him abreast the gaunt bay, and then, feeling Lefty's knees pressing his shoulders and hearing Lefty's voice whispering words of encouragement in his ears, Black Eagle dashed ahead to rush down through the lane of frantically shouting spectators, winner by a half dozen lengths.

That was the beginning of Black Eagle's racing career. How it progressed, how he won races and captured purses in a seemingly endless string of victories unmarred by a single defeat, that is part of the turf records of the South and West.

There had to be an end, of course. Owners of carefully bred running horses took no great pleasure, you may imagine, in seeing so many rich prizes captured by a half-wild branded stallion of no known pedigree, and ridden by a silent, square-jawed cowboy. So they sent East for a "ringer." He came from Chicago in a box-car with two grooms and he was entered as an unknown, although in the betting ring the odds posted were one to five on the stranger. Yet it was a grand race. This alleged unknown, with a suppressed record of victories at Sheepshead, Bennings, and The Fort, did no more than shove his long nose under the wire a bare half head in front of Black Eagle's foam-flecked muzzle.

It was sufficient. The once wild stallion knew when he was beaten. He had done his best and he had lost. His high pride had been humbled, his fierce spirit broken. No more did the course hold for him any pleasure, no more could he be thrilled by the cries of spectators or urged into his old time stride by Lefty's whispered appeals. Never again did Black Eagle win a race.

His end, however, was not wholly inglorious. Much against his will the cowboy who had so relentlessly followed Black Eagle half way across the big territory of Arizona to lay him low with a rifle bullet, who had spared his life at the last moment and who had ridden him to victory in so many glorious races—this silent, square-jawed man had given him a final caress and then, saying a husky good-by, had turned him over to the owner of a great stud farm and gone away with a thick roll of bank notes in his pocket and a guilty feeling in his breast.

Thus it happens that today throughout the Southwest there are many black-pointed fleet-footed horses in whose veins runs the blood of a noble horse. Some of them you

Race horses from Chicago—too much competition for a half-wild stallion.
BLACK EAGLE WHO ONCE RULED THE RANGES

will find in well-guarded paddocks, while some still roam the prairies in wild bands which are the menace of stockmen and the vexation of cowboys. As for their sire, he is no more.

This is the story of Black Eagle. Although some of the minor details may be open to dispute, the main points you may hear recited by any cattleman or horse-breeder west of Omaha. For Black Eagle really lived and, as perhaps you will agree, lived not in vain.

"Winner by a half dozen lengths."
BLACK EAGLE WHO ONCE RULED THE RANGES

American Indian.
Illustration by Frederic Remington

Canadian Indian.
Illustration by Frederic Remington

THE DUN HORSE
by George Grinnell

I

MANY years ago, there lived in the Pawnee tribe an old woman and her grandson, a boy about sixteen years old. These people had no relations and were very poor. They were so poor that they were despised by the rest of the tribe. They had nothing of their own; and always, after the village started to move the camp from one place to another, these two would stay behind the rest, to look over the old camp, and pick up anything that the other Indians had thrown away, as worn out or useless. In this way they would sometimes get pieces of robes, worn-out moccasins with holes in them, and bits of meat.

Now, it happened one day, after the tribe had moved away from the camp, that this old woman and her boy were following along the trail behind the rest, when they came to a miserable old worn-out dun horse, which they supposed had been abandoned by some Indians. He was thin and exhausted, was blind of one eye, had a bad sore back, and one of his forelegs was very much swollen. In fact, he was so worthless that none of the Pawnees had been willing to take the trouble to try to drive him along with them. But when the old woman and her boy came along, the boy said, "Come now, we will take this old horse, for we can make him carry our pack." So the old woman put her pack on the horse, and drove him along, but he limped and could only go very slowly.

II

The tribe moved up on the North Platte, until they came to Court House Rock. The two poor Indians followed them, and camped with the others. One day while they were here, the young men who had been sent out to look for buffalo came hurrying into camp and told the chiefs that a large herd of buffalo were near, and that among them was a spotted calf.

The Head Chief of the Pawnees had a very beautiful daughter, and when he heard about the spotted calf, he ordered his old crier to go about through the village, and call out that the man who killed the spotted calf should have his daughter for his wife. For a spotted robe is *ti-war'-uks-ti*—big medicine.

The buffalo were feeding about four miles from the village, and the chiefs decided that the charge should be made from there. In this way, the man who had the fastest horse would be the most likely to kill the calf. Then all the warriors and the young men picked out their best and fastest horses, and made ready to start. Among those who prepared for the charge was the poor boy on the old dun horse. But when they saw him, all the rich young braves on their fast horses pointed at him, and said, "Oh, see, there is the horse that is going to catch the spotted calf," and they laughed at him, so that the poor boy was ashamed, and rode off to one side of the crowd, where he could not hear their jokes and laughter.

When he had ridden off some little way, the horse stopped, and turned his head round, and spoke to the boy. He said, "Take me down to the creek, and plaster me all

over with mud. Cover my head and neck and body and
legs." When the boy heard the horse speak, he was afraid,
but he did as he was told. Then the horse said, "Now
mount, but do not ride back to the warriors, who laugh at
you because you have such a poor horse. Stay right here,
until the word is given to charge." So the boy stayed
there.

And presently all the fine horses were drawn up in line
and pranced about, and were so eager to go that their
riders could hardly hold them in; and at last the old crier
gave the word, *"Loo-ah"*—Go! Then the Pawnees all
leaned forward on their horses and yelled, and away they
went. Suddenly, away off to the right, was seen the old
dun horse. He did not seem to run. He seemed to sail along
like a bird. He passed all the fastest horses, and in a
moment he was among the buffalo. First he picked out the
spotted calf, and charging up alongside of it, *U-ra-rish!*
straight flew the arrow. The calf fell. The boy drew
another arrow, and killed a fat cow that was running by.
Then he dismounted and began to skin the calf, before any
of the other warriors had come up. But when the rider got
off the old dun horse, how changed he was! He pranced
about and would hardly stand still near the dead buffalo.
His back was all right again, his legs were well and fine,
and both his eyes were clear and bright.

The boy skinned the calf and the cow that he had killed,
and then he packed all the meat on the horse, and put the
spotted robe on top of the load, and started back to the
camp on foot, leading the dun horse. But even with this
heavy load the horse pranced all the time, and was scared
at everything he saw. On the way to camp, one of the rich
young chiefs of the tribe rode up by the boy, and offered
him twelve good horses for the spotted robe, so that he
could marry the Head Chief's beautiful daughter; but the
boy laughed at him and would not sell the robe.

Now, while the boy walked to the camp leading the dun horse, most of the warriors rode back, and one of those that came first to the village went to the old woman and said to her, "Your grandson has killed the spotted calf." And the old woman said, "Why do you come to tell me this? You ought to be ashamed to make fun of my boy, because he is poor." The warrior said, "What I have told you is true," and then he rode away. After a little while another brave rode up to the old woman and said to her, "Your grandson has killed the spotted calf." Then the old woman began to cry, she felt so badly because everyone made fun of her boy, because he was poor.

Pretty soon the boy came along, leading the horse up to the lodge where he and his grandmother lived. It was a little lodge, just big enough for two, and was made of old pieces of skin that the old woman had picked up, and was tied together with strings of rawhide and sinew. It was the meanest and worst lodge in the village. When the old woman saw her boy leading the dun horse with the load of meat and the robes on it, she was very much surprised. The boy said to her, "Here, I have brought you plenty of meat to eat, and here is a robe, that you may have for yourself. Take the meat off the horse." Then the old woman laughed, for her heart was glad. But when she went to take the meat from the horse's back, he snorted and jumped about, and acted like a wild horse. The old woman looked at him in wonder, and could hardly believe that it was the same horse. So the boy had to take off the meat, for the horse would not let the old woman come near him.

III

That night the horse spoke again to the boy and said, "*Wa-ti-hes Chah'-ra-rat wa-ta*. Tomorrow the Sioux are

"How changed he was!"

THE DUN HORSE

coming—a large war party. They will attack the village, and you will have a great battle. Now, when the Sioux are drawn up in line of battle, and are all ready to fight, you jump on to me, and ride as hard as you can, right into the middle of the Sioux, and up to their Head Chief, their greatest warrior, and count *coup* on him, and kill him, and then ride back. Do this four times, and count *coup* on four of the bravest Sioux, and kill them, but don't go again. If you go the fifth time, maybe you will be killed, or else you will lose me. *La-ku'-ta-chix*—remember." So the boy promised.

The next day it happened as the horse had said, and the Sioux came down and formed a line of battle. Then the boy took his bow and arrows, and jumped on the dun horse, and charged into the midst of them. And when the Sioux saw that he was going to strike their Head Chief, they all shot their arrows at him, and the arrows flew so thickly across each other that the sky became dark, but none of them hit the boy. And he counted *coup* on the Chief, and killed him, and then rode back. After that he charged again among the Sioux, where they were gathered thickest, and counted *coup* on their bravest warrior, and killed him. And then twice more, until he had gone four times as the horse had told him.

But the Sioux and the Pawnees kept on fighting, and the boy stood around and watched the battle. And at last he said to himself, "I have been four times and have killed four Sioux, and I am all right, I am not hurt anywhere; why may I not go again?" So he jumped on the dun horse, and charged again. But when he got among the Sioux, one Sioux warrior drew an arrow and shot. The arrow struck the dun horse behind the forelegs and pierced him through. And the horse fell down dead. But the boy jumped off, and fought his way through the Sioux, and ran away as fast as he could to the Pawnees. Now, as soon as the horse was killed, the Sioux said to each other, "This horse was like a man. He was brave. He was not like a horse." And they took their knives and hatchets, and hacked the dun horse and gashed his flesh, and cut him into small pieces.

The Pawnees and Sioux fought all day long, but toward night the Sioux broke and fled.

IV

The boy felt very bady that he had lost his horse; and, after the fight was over, he went out from the village to where it had taken place, to mourn for his horse. He went to the spot where the horse lay, and gathered up all the pieces of flesh which the Sioux had cut off, and the legs and the hoofs, and put them all together in a pile. Then he went off to the top of a hill near by, and sat down and drew his robe over his head, and began to mourn for his horse.

As he sat there, he heard a great windstorm coming up, and it passed over him with a loud rushing sound, and after the wind came a rain. The boy looked down from where he sat to the pile of flesh and bones, which was all that was left of his horse, and he could just see it through the rain. And the rain passed by, and his heart was very heavy, and he kept on mourning.

And pretty soon came another rushing wind, and after it a rain; and as he looked through the driving rain toward the spot where the pieces lay, he thought that they seemed to come together and take shape, and that the pile looked like a horse lying down, but he could not see well for the thick rain.

After this, came a third storm like the others; and now when he looked toward the horse he thought he saw its tail move from side to side two or three times, and that it lifted its head from the ground. The boy was afraid, and wanted to run away, but he stayed.

And as he waited, there came another storm. And while the rain fell, looking through the rain, the boy saw the horse raise himself up on his forelegs and look about. Then the dun horse stood up.

V

The boy left the place where he had been sitting on the hilltop, and went down to him. When the boy had come near to him, the horse spoke and said, "You have seen how it has been this day; and from this you may know how it will be after this. But *Ti-ra'-wa* has been good, and has let me come back to you. After this, do what I tell you; not any more, not any less." Then the horse said, "Now lead me off, far away from the camp, behind that big hill, and leave me there tonight, and in the morning come for me," and the boy did as he was told.

And when he went for the horse in the morning, he found with him a beautiful white gelding, much more handsome than any horse in the tribe. That night the dun horse told the boy to take him again to the place behind the big hill, and to come for him the next morning; and when the boy went for him again, he found with him a beautiful black gelding. And so for ten nights, he left the horse among the hills, and each morning he found a different colored horse, a bay, a roan, a gray, a blue, a spotted horse, and all of them finer than any horses that the Pawnees had ever had in their tribe before.

Now the boy was rich, and he married the beautiful daughter of the Head Chief, and when he became older, he was made Head Chief himself. He had many children by his beautiful wife, and one day when his oldest boy died, he wrapped him in the spotted calf robe and buried him in it. He always took good care of his old grandmother, and kept her in his own lodge until she died. The dun horse was never ridden except at feasts, and when they were going to have a doctors' dance, but he was always led about with the Chief, wherever he went. The horse lived in the village for many years, until he became very old. And at last he died.

The old Indian and his horse.
Illustration by Frederic Remington

THE FAITHFUL BRADY

by Larrey Bowman

A few springs ago a man in Arizona named Chapin became infatuated with a certain Miss Dasher, and shot a rival for the lady's favor, whereupon he was tried and condemned, and sent off to the territorial prison. But that is not the end of Chapin's story, for he left a friend behind him.

It was only a saddle horse, a little white-faced buckskin, with pretty kittenish tricks and a kind disposition, and it had no finer name than Brady.

Chapin broke the horse early in the spring, and won Brady's confidence then, for he was kind to animals. For all his overmastering temper and strange primitive ideas of justice, Chapin's ways were almost always gentle, and a horse is quick to notice that.

Brady helped his master with the luckless courting of Miss Dasher. That is, he carried Chapin into town, always prancing when the house came in sight, and swinging about so, as the lover dismounted, that you might have exclaimed, "Here's a fearless rider on a desperate steed!" But that sidling, those prances, and all, were part of an amiable game between the two. Chapin, dismounted at his divinity's door, would turn his back on the untethered Brady, and Brady, the lines pulled over his head till they rested on the ground, would roll the bit in his mouth, and stand there till he was wanted.

There are gossips in Arizona, and the Dasher girl was on their lips—before Chapin began to see her, and after.

But however that may be, Chapin went about his business, which was getting good yields off a ranch, and about his pleasure—his honest devotion—which centered around Sophy Dasher.

And, one fine day in early April, it seemed he had won the girl. Chapin came riding back to his ranch and loosed Brady, but the little pony stopped and whinnied. All about was the knee-deep alfalfa—ambrosial beds for a horse to roll in—and, back of him, from where a big mesquite in yellow blossom spread an odor like honeysuckle, you caught the tinkle of fresh, running water. Yet the friendly Brady hesitated, for all the world as if he asked a question.

"Oh, it's all right with me, little horse," said Chapin, patting a sturdy brown shoulder. "She's said yes, and we're going to be married."

The bronco snuffed his master over, horse fashion, and laid his head on Chapin's shoulder. He was not much to look at, was Brady, but his heart was right, as they say. He had never known unkind treatment, and he thought all men were his friends—but especially Chapin, big and strong and honest, who was the bravest man he knew.

"It's a grand world to live in, pony," cried Chapin, as he played with Brady's mane. Up above in the clean-swept Arizona sky there was not the trace of a cloud, and the world, as the two looked at it, was a wonderful stretch of green—trees in blossom, oleanders flaming red, and larks and blackbirds everywhere. Brady must have seen these things very dimly, and if they struck through the man's perception it was only in a nameless way. Yet they both, simple creatures, exulted to feel the warm sun on their backs, and the air was sweet to their nostrils and they felt it was good to be alive.

So much for Chapin's dream of love. Two days later there came a cousin of his, who had ridden hard to bring bad news.

The talebearer.
THE FAITHFUL BRADY

The talebearer burst in breathless. "Oh, you fool," he cried. "Didn't I tell you from the first? The girl has played with you. She's a— Take your hands off my throat. She's a— Let me loose, Ed Chapin. You don't believe me? Go and learn for yourself." The cousin laughed. "It's no secret now."

And then, as Chapin turned white and caught his breath, the other told the sordid story, and there was no doubting him: what the gossips had whispered was all true. It was not a worthy woman whose fine eyes had made a slave of Chapin. She stood openly dishonored now, through her favors to another man.

"But never mind *him*," the cousin said. "Leave him and leave her to each other. Forget you ever knew the girl—" He stopped, seeing a strange look in Chapin's face. "Ed," he urged, "you ain't thinking of *that?*" They seemed to read each other's thoughts. "What good would it do you, Ed? It wouldn't help you to kill anyone."

Chapin looked his cousin between the eyes. "No," said he, "you're right, it wouldn't." He turned away, but he came back again. "I believe—what you've told me, Harry. Now go away, I want to be alone."

Chapin fought with himself all that day, to bring himself to accept what had happened. He beat back the passionate anger that kept rising to his head. A dozen times Chapin told himself, "I will let the fellow have her. The girl is nothing to me." At length it was night, and dark outside, and then it was that that which lie fought against—the primal instinct—conquered. In a sort of daze, while the clock in the house ticked as from an immeasurable distance, and the breath caught in his throat and his ears sang, Chapin took down his revolver from the wall.

A minute later he was out in the corral, saddling Brady with trembling fingers. He set the little horse blindly at the point where the town lights made a blur against the sky, and up a dusty hill they galloped, and down the long, ill-graded slope beyond. It was the familiar way they took, but never before had Chapin used the quirt.

The man dismounted at a well-known hitching rack, and left Brady. The curious animal whinnied once or twice. He was thirsty after the rapid going, and being a rather spoiled bronco, he thought of hay in the boarding corral that Chapin patronized when in town. But Brady was obedient first of all, and he stood now, with the lines pulled over his head so that they rested on the ground, and rolled his bit and bode his time.

Pretty soon he heard a pistol shot, and was conscious of voices shouting. But the noise subsided in a little.

It was the pampered stomach in him that began to bother Brady. In his minute-long naps by the hitching rack, he dreamed of hay that was all blossom and no stalk at all; he rolled in shady places and rose to cool his hoofs in running water, where he drank till the joy of it woke him up. Waking, it vexed him that Chapin did not come—it was not like his master to forget him. After a while a real thirst came, his throat was coated and hot, and almost pained him. Towards morning the wind blew cold. Brady shifted his weight from foot to foot, letting his head drop lower and lower.

Remember, he was not tied. The reins lay on the ground before him, and they were his written instructions to stand, that was all.

The sun came up after a while. Mexican loafers, fresh from their squalid breakfast, began to line the sunny side of the street. Each found the hitching-post or yard of wall that his special back had helped to wear smooth. As the day grew hot and breathless, conversation would languish among them. But now they spoke excitedly.

With the sun and the Mexicans came flies, seeming as if they would devour Brady. But at length two men ap-

proached. "Hello," said one, "ain't that Ed Chapin's
horse?" Brady whinnied to let them know he wanted Ed.
If they could, they did not produce the master. But they
took Brady away with them, to the familiar boarding
corral.

When a man kills another, and has been tried by his
peers and sent away to some solemn keep like the Yuma
penitentiary, a public auction disposes of his goods. Brady
waited days in vain for Chapin, and then—Brady went
under the hammer.

It was a man they called a Tenderfoot that bought him,
and the first thing the Tenderfoot did was to ride Brady
forty miles through a blazing sun. Precisely, it was thirty-
nine miles, for Brady dropped with the end in sight. As he
lay he appeared to be dying, and quirt and spurs were
useless to arouse him. So the Tenderfoot hailed a passing
wagon, into which he threw his saddle and bridle, and, not
without a sense of mystification (complicated by a chas-
tened regret) he went on, leaving Brady to the buzzards.

But it happens that the buckskin color is the mark of a
sturdy stock. Brady had his awful agony, but in the end—
hours later—he found his feet. Misty-eyed and weak of
knee, with fires blazing in his chest, he wandered till he
found a canal. He was drinking there, painfully, when
along came Toppy McGune.

Now, this McGune was a vagrant and a scamp. In a city
he would have belonged to a gang, and perhaps drifted
into petty thieving. But living in Arizona, where the social
conditions are peculiar, he found "chuck-line riding" the
thing. With a horse and a blanket roll he went from ranch
to ranch (and the territory is a large one). He had a
specious adaptable story of having just come from somewhere and being eager to get somewhere else. And
because he seemed an honest wayfarer, the good folk were

glad to give him food and shelter—not in charity, by any means; for it were an impious thing, most isolated ranchers think, to turn a traveler away at nightfall.

McGune, then, was a chuck-line rider. That is, he was a mounted tramp. And being such, he admired a good horse, knowing the prestige it gives a man. From the back of his own knee-spring sorrel, he now observed Brady gulping water, and he recognized the Chapin brand on Brady's flank. He annexed Brady at once, leading him away with his lasso rope. As he did not care—quite apart from ethical reasons—to incur suspicion of horse stealing, he made some careful inquiries. And in the end he learned enough to make him think he could risk keeping Brady. The little buckskin was in a state of partial collapse. But McGune reflected, "You couldn't kill a bucksin off." Thereupon he disposed of the sorrel, and made Brady his particular steed.

And so, from being left for dead, Brady passed into the life of this vagrant. Brady had little kittenish tricks, a joy in prancing, and sometimes he liked to buck a little. McGune was not an eminently good rider, though he knew neither fear nor pity. He wanted his horse to rear and plunge while going down the street of a town, so that people would turn and look at him.

He bought a special bit for Brady that lay along Brady's tongue like a trowel and made a bone-breaking lever against the jaw. And, being long dissatisfied with his spurs, Toppy got a blacksmith to make him a pair, and the new spurs were long in the shank, with rowels that would tear the flesh.

Then McGune educated Brady in the school of fear. Mounting Brady he would draw him in till the scared little beast started back. Then, clap! and the spurs stabbed his flanks, and Brady's shoulders tingled from the flailing of the quirt.

You see, Brady was new to rough treatment. At first he thought the fault was in him. And then, driven to desperation, with bleeding mouth and his poor brains confounded, rebellion took him and he fought to shake his tyrant. He plunged and twisted while the rider yelled and beat him. But he never could quite get Toppy off.

To belong to a fellow like McGune is to work long hours and have broken rest; it is to end the day often with an empty stomach, and sometimes to begin it that way; it is to know thirst—not simple dryness, but the cruel, sharp, biting pain. And a horse's nature goes wrong, and in the end his spirit breaks.

Often Brady thought of a ranch where the sweetest alfalfa grew. Why had they taken him from it? Where was the master all this time? Of all the incomprehensible hurts he endured, this neglect of Chapin's was the hardest. And yet—Brady, on the hard road of life, was headed the way of forgetting.

McGune, as has been said, liked to clatter through a town for the edification of whoever would look. Was there a woman this side the skyline, he would display his horsemanship. In a way, you might say, it was a woman that severed Brady and McGune forever.

Horse and master were traveling some dreary road, with a little white schoolhouse ahead. It was later than three in the afternoon, and the children were gone, but there at the door of the schoolhouse stood that hand of fate, the woman. She was merely a country school mistress, adjusting the bands of her neat white sunbonnet. The sound of Brady's hoofs caused her to look up at the approaching chuck-line rider.

In the buckram soul of McGune sprang a wish to attitudinize. He "thumbed" Brady, and covertly spurred. The show that followed took place before the schoolhouse.

The rider bucked.
THE FAITHFUL BRADY
Illustration by Frederic Remington

"Oh, your cinch, your cinch!"—it was the voice of a young woman, calling.

Brady's girth had loosened and was weak; the strands had shown badly raveled that morning. But Toppy, though he noted it then, had forgotten—and now Brady was bucking.

Brady bucked with his body and his soul, as a drowning man fights for his life. He bucked in the memory of pain, and the presence of fear, and the rage of hate, feeling the frayed cinch loosen and give, and that incubus above him totter. Then—a great, supreme effort—he was free.

The lines, somehow, came over his head and touched the ground, and—strange fidelity to an older custom—he stood in his tracks as he had used to do for Chapin. Presently the unhorsed Toppy rose from the dust of the road and found his saddle which lay by itself to one side. He came over and kicked Brady in the side. Then, blinded with anger and shame, Toppy clubbed his quirt and struck out; he struck Brady on the neck and between the ears; he struck one of Brady's eyes and put it out.

For a moment, through the pain he endured, Brady staggered out against a wall of darkness. Filling the wronged, astounded soul of the horse was one desire—to regain the bright, sunshiny world. The light came back, in flaming points, in exquisite drenching showers. He saw the road, the few trees, and the sky above. But it was not the same world, somehow, nor would it ever be quite the same.

It was two years after this that a questionable company of men rode into the town of Globe. There were in the cavalcade perhaps a dozen lean men in leather trousers, booted and spurred, and sitting their mounts with ineffable swagger. A string of wicked-looking ponies, unsaddled, completed the procession.

It was Sappington's Bronco Congress, according to the premonitory handbill.

If you never heard of Sappington, know, then, that he conducts a sort of traveling circus. The members of his congress are, first, detestable, wrong-headed horses that Circe's swine would not associate with. Some graduate cowboys complete the outfit. It is for the cowboys to amuse, instruct, and elevate the daily audience by riding the horses: which, to their discredit as sane-minded gentlemen, they usually do.

And among the outlawed herd of horses was Brady, a strange fierceness in the eye which was left him. Where had Brady been these two years? It would be easier to account for Chapin that was strayed even farther from his home, and dwelt down beside the Colorado River, and was a "good man," according to his warden.

This much concerning Brady, at least. The whip and spur had done their work. He had become a "wicked" horse.

Some people, so they say, always play in hard luck. Brady, it seems, had cruel luck in his masters. And since the days of Toppy McGune he had not found a master like his present one, Pete Ovens, drunken, bragging, cowardly Ovens: Ovens whom Sappington employed but took, it must be said, little pride in.

As the bronco congress passed through Globe, a hint of rain was in the air, and later, that afternoon, the Globe audience which came together to see the show marked the gathering of a dust storm in the east. It was a weird, uncanny day—to Ovens purely notable for the fact that he was drunker than was his custom.

Of late it had been thrust upon him by his companions that he was a poltroon—had been suggested, even, that he, Ovens, rode indifferently. Today, as his turn to mount came, he swaggered into the arena, where the dust was swirling into spirals, and as the wind flattened out his leather trousers, and tore his hat awry—rushed through his unsavory teeth, even—Ovens swore he would show them all.

They fought with Brady to get the saddle on, and Brady lunged and squealed in his anger. It was delicate pleasure to the audience to see a horse nature so perverted. Ovens got a foot in the stirrup and lurched across the saddle. Then they loosed the little fighting bronco. A driving wind swept down on the flat. The shingled grandstand clattered and shook. Like a great yellow curtain, dust blotted out the arena.

When it cleared they saw a riderless horse, and Ovens lying on his face, stunned and disgraced.

Sappington discharged the man that evening. "You're no good," said the owner of the show. "Drunk or sober you're no good." Ovens muttered but made no reply: he had a score that he would settle later. The wretched Brady had shamed him, and he had a word to say to Brady.

Late that night he sneaked Brady out of the corral, and led him to a place he thought safe. Ovens had a rifle and a shovel with him, and with the latter he proceeded to dig a pit. The earth resisted him, the wind blew wildly, and as he worked he swore to himself.

At last the grave was dug, and Brady stood picketed beside it. The man stepped off a few paces and threw a cartridge into his rifle chamber.

He raised the rifle, then lowered it. Ovens was thirsty. He wrenched the cork from a flask he carried, and drank. He raised the rifle, aimed, and fired.

A startled cry from Brady as the bullet grooved along his flank. Brady plunged to escape this new terror. Into the fresh-made grave he fell, wrenching his shoulder, but he pulled his picket free. Ovens fired distractedly. The horse struggled up the embankment and cleared it.

Ovens never spoke of the affair. He was not prepared to explain it. For, though he fired shot after shot, the horse, dragging his picket-rope, got away.

It was what they call a good year in the hills, with grass in plenty, and the canyons running water. Brady, a refugee from men, ranged wild, in a sort of dull contentment.

When his belly was fairly filled, sometimes, a whiff of breeze or a trick of the sunshine sent a kind of tremor through him. All the memory he had would revert to preposterous kindness, to a world where one lived gently. So illogical is a horse that he had no bitterness for the man who broke him to the saddle, and had Chapin ever come to him he would have gone where the master led.

But another servitude awaited the horse. Through the Pinal Mountains where he was came a vagabondish trio of prospectors, who aimed to gain the level slope towards the Gila, and follow the Gila to the California line. Sighting Brady, they set after him with ropes, ran him into a blind canyon, and made him a prisoner, and they made a packhorse of him.

Maimed and broken as Brady was, he fought his captors, then and after. But, since Providence had seen fit to throw a beast of burden in their path, they did not propose to give the beast up, and they worked to slay the spirit in Brady, in ways calculated to have that effect. It naturally incensed them that a broken-down horse, a brute that no one claimed, should set himself against the primal law, which, applying to horses, seems to read, the horse is the slave of man.

But the prospectors were bungling fellows. Brady's back became raw; the burlap pad across the withers was merely salt to his wounds. With the constant pressure of a pain that every step seemed to aggravate, Brady's ribs began to show; he grew quite weak. The limp he got from the premature grave became a violent lurch. Sometimes he even fell down. This was considered in the light of an insult, for now the Gila grew wider every day; Yuma lay just beyond the horizon, and the prospectors were for straining every fiber, now the California line was so near.

For there was a Find beyond the Colorado. Other gold hunters passed them on the trail. It was: Hurry or be left, hurry or be too late, hurry or you'll curse yourselves! Yet even now the three cursed themselves; they cursed Brady, hobbling and slipping with his load.

At length it seemed they must leave the failing horse. They got them another somewhere, and they abandoned Brady in the desert. "You darned crowbait," were their parting words, "get out and rustle, and see how you like it." Brady did not attempt to follow, and the three prospectors faded in the dust that lay white along the Yuma trail.

Now, it happens that even with that trail run the tracks of a great Western railroad, and the dirt is packed hard between the rails. If you are a tramp set down in the desert and want to get to Yuma or beyond, the walking here is better than on the trail. Sometimes the time-expired felon, whom the Yuma penitentiary returns to the world with five dollars in the pocket of his prison-made denims, takes this footpath, going east, for it will bring him clear of the desert in the end, and back to the life he used to know.

Whether Brady, discarded in the desert, wandered there many days, no one can say. Simply, there in the desert one white-hot morning, he had a peculiar and strange adventure.

He felt the heat and was thirsty, and by a railroad water

tank, where the maddening drip, drip from the unattainable water merely wetted the sand, Brady stood—setting his tongue to the moistened ground. A man's footsteps upon the interspace of the rails caused him to start and arch a gaunted neck. A man was approaching Brady upon Brady's blind side, and the horse shifted curiously to bring his good eye to bear on the stranger.

It was a man of some stature—strangely bent, and seemingly deteriorated before his time. The pallid skin of his face was not the skin of those who live in the sun. It was a piece with the man's uneasy carriage, which might have been lithe and graceful once, but lacked the assurance of the outdoor world. He wore a coarse blue suit of denim, the uniform of the time-expired convict.

He came nearer, till his features showed—clean-cut, honest features of their sort: you would have picked him for a man kind and brave, though the lines of strength and weakness mingled. He was just a man, no better than you and me, and Fate might have made a hero of him. But she had dealt far otherwise.

The man's mouth quivered a little from his unused exertion in the sun, and his brows were beaded with sweat.

Suddenly, when quite near, he stopped, staring oddly at the gaunted horse. To Brady, meeting the look with his mutilated stare, the wildest flashes of things past and things dead came back. Years had passed, time had used him harshly, and yet Brady had not forgotten. He whinnied, out of his parched, dry throat. The man with the white face was Chapin.

"Good God!" cried the man, and sat him down with his face in his hands. Then, "Brady," he called doubtfully, timidly. Brady, timid himself, limped closer.

"What have they done to you, pony?" cried Chapin. "Lame, and blind, and starved, and— Good God, I won't strike you, Brady—for you're Brady, you remembered me. Don't flinch; w-won't you let me touch your mane?" His fingers closed on the yellow comb, and there, against Brady's neck, he laid his face. A rush of hot tears took him then, and he cried for the years that were past.

It was loneliness that gripped the master's heart. Well enough he knew, as the prison gates opened on his freedom, that it was not the same world he re-entered. That boyish zest in merely living was gone; he felt that nature was indifferent and cruel. The massive silence of the desert awed him. The sky looked old, and underfoot it seemed he trod on ancient ashes. Here and there a dust whirl formed and spent itself, through the power, as it seemed to him, of that iron-souled Will which creates that it may destroy.

He stood away from the horse. "Brady, Brady," he said, "don't you know what I am and where I've been? . . . I thought so much of a girl that I shot a man because he did her wrong, and I've served my time. I ain't got any ranch to go back to, and friends—why, friends forget—when you've been away."

Brady came and laid his head on Chapin's shoulder as if he, somehow, understood. Strange thing, a horse—so willing to work, satisfied with such simple pleasures, faithful, sometimes, with such a simple faith.

". . . And you've come back to me," Chapin said. "You aren't thinking—Oh, you aren't thinking, Brady, we can take up the life where we left it. Why, Brady, you're all broken, old pony, and I'm—I ain't the man I was."

The man looked out upon the old, gray desert, where nothing grew but twisted deformities, and nothing moved but the dancing sand whirls. The desolation had chilled him, and now, all at once, he knew he had read it wrong. For the voice of the Silence was not cruel. It was the voice of the unsubdued earth, saying: *I am as a woman. And*

Reunited.
THE FAITHFUL BRADY
Illustration by Frederic Remington

who conquers me I shall reward. The wind of the desert was sweet and clean, and breathed against his cheek like caresses.

"Brady," cried the man to the horse. "There's land that no man has taken, there's wealth that's never been gathered. Because a man is down he ain't beaten—while he has hands—while he has someone to work for. That's it—someone to work for. Brady, we'll begin again."

He set back to the Yuma hills, and the horse followed after him. Chapin could not read the future to know that the gound would repay his honest efforts as the ground has done. Then, merely with "someone to work for," he was stiffened to face the world. And so he went back to the world, and the faithful Brady went with him.

Broncos battling the timber wolves.
Illustration by Frederic Remington

Saddling a bronco.

Illustration by Frederic Remington

THE CHIMÆRA

from *A Wonder Book*

by Nathaniel Hawthorne

ONCE, in the old, old times (for all the strange things which I tell you about happened long before anyone can remember), a fountain gushed out of a hillside, in the marvelous land of Greece. And, for aught I know, after so many thousand years, it is still gushing out of the very selfsame spot. At any rate, there was the pleasant fountain, welling freshly forth and sparkling adown the hillside, in the golden sunset, when a handsome young man named Bellerophon drew near its margin. In his hand he held a bridle, studded with brilliant gems, and adorned with a golden bit. Seeing an old man, and another of middle age, and a little boy, near the fountain, and likewise a maiden, who was dipping up some of the water in a pitcher, he paused, and begged that he might refresh himself with a draught.

"This is very delicious water," he said to the maiden as he rinsed and filled her pitcher, after drinking out of it. "Will you be kind enough to tell me whether the fountain has any name?"

"Yes; it is called the Fountain of Pirene," answered the maiden; and then she added, "My grandmother has told me that this clear fountain was once a beautiful woman; and when her son was killed by the arrows of the huntress Diana, she melted all away into tears. And so the water, which you find so cool and sweet, is the sorrow of that poor mother's heart!"

"I should not have dreamed," observed the young stranger, "that so clear a wellspring, with its gush and gurgle, and its cheery dance out of the shade into the sunlight, had so much as one teardrop in its bosom! And this, then, is Pirene? I thank you, pretty maiden, for telling me its name. I have come from a far-away country to find this very spot."

A middle-aged country fellow (he had driven his cow to drink out of the spring) stared hard at young Bellerophon, and at the handsome bridle which he carried in his hand.

"The water-courses must be getting low, friend, in your part of the world," remarked he, "if you come so far only to find the Fountain of Pirene. But, pray, have you lost a horse? I see you carry the bridle in your hand; and a very pretty one it is with that double row of bright stones upon it. If the horse was as fine as the bridle, you are much to be pitied for losing him."

"I have lost no horse," said Bellerophon, with a smile. "But I happen to be seeking a very famous one, which, as wise people have informed me, must be found hereabouts, if anywhere. Do you know whether the winged horse Pegasus still haunts the Fountain of Pirene, as he used to do in your forefathers' days?"

But then the country fellow laughed.

Some of you, my little friends, have probably heard that this Pegasus was a snow-white steed, with beautiful silvery wings, who spent most of his time on the summit of Mount Helicon. He was as wild, and as swift, and as buoyant, in his flight through the air, as any eagle that ever soared into the clouds. There was nothing else like him in the world. He had no mate; he never had been backed or bridled by a master; and, for many a long year, he led a solitary and a happy life.

Oh, how fine a thing it is to be a winged horse! Sleeping at night, as he did, on a lofty mountaintop, and passing the greater part of the day in the air, Pegasus seemed hardly to be a creature of the earth. Whenever he was seen, up very high above people's heads, with the sunshine on his silvery wings, you would have thought that he belonged to the sky, and that, skimming a little too low, he had got astray among our mists and vapors, and was seeking his way back again. It was very pretty to behold him plunge into the fleecy bosom of a bright cloud, and be lost in it, for a moment or two, and then break forth from the other side. Or, in a sullen rainstorm, when there was a gray pavement of clouds over the whole sky, it would some-times happen that the winged horse descended right through it, and the glad light of the upper region would gleam after him. In another instant, it is true, both Pegasus and the pleasant light would be gone away. together. But anyone that was fortunate enough to see this wondrous spectacle felt cheerful the whole day after-wards, and as much longer as the storm lasted.

In the summertime, and in the beautifullest of weather, Pegasus often alighted on the solid earth, and, closing his silvery wings, would gallop over hill and dale for pastime, as fleetly as the wind. Oftener than in any other place, he had been seen near the Fountain of Pirene, drinking the delicious water, or rolling himself upon the soft grass of the margin. Sometimes, too (but Pegasus was very dainty in his food), he would crop a few of the clover blossoms that happened to be sweetest.

To the Fountain of Pirene, therefore, people's great-grandfathers had been in the habit of going (as long as they were youthful, and retained their faith in winged horses), in hopes of getting a glimpse at the beautiful Pegasus. But, of late years, he had been very seldom seen. Indeed, there were many of the country folks, dwelling within half an hour's walk of the fountain, who had never beheld Pegasus, and did not believe that there was any such creature in existence. The country fellow to whom Bellerophon was speaking chanced to be one of those incredulous persons.

And that was the reason why he laughed.

"Pegasus, indeed!" cried he, turning up his nose as high as such a flat nose could be turned up,—"Pegasus, indeed! A winged horse, truly! Why, friend, are you in your senses? Of what use would wings be to a horse? Could he drag the plough so well, think you? To be sure, there might be a little saving in the expense of shoes; but then, how would a man like to see his horse flying out of the stable window?—yes, or whisking him up above the clouds, when he only wanted to ride him to mill? No, no! I don't believe in Pegasus. There never was such a ridiculous kind of a horse-fowl made!"

"I have some reason to think otherwise," said Bellerophon quietly.

And then he turned to an old, gray man, who was leaning on a staff, and listening very attentively, with his head stretched forward, and one hand at his ear, because, for the last twenty years, he had been getting rather deaf.

"And what say you, venerable sir?" inquired he. "In your younger days, I should imagine you must frequently have seen the winged steed!"

"Ah, young stranger, my memory is very poor!" said the aged man. "When I was a lad, if I remember rightly, I used to believe there was such a horse, and so did everybody else. But, nowadays, I hardly know what to think, and very seldom think about the winged horse at all. If I ever saw the creature, it was a long, long while ago; and, to tell you the truth, I doubt whether I ever did see him. One day, to be sure, when I was quite a youth, I remember seeing some hoof tramps round about the brink of the fountain. Pegasus might have made those hoof marks; and so might some other horse."

"And have you never seen him, my fair maiden?" asked Bellerophon of the girl, who stood with the pitcher on her head, while this talk went on. "You certainly could see Pegasus, if anybody can, for your eyes are very bright."

"Once I thought I saw him," replied the maiden, with a smile and a blush. "It was either Pegasus, or a large white bird, a very great way up in the air. And one other time, as I was coming to the fountain with my pitcher, I heard a neigh. Oh, such a brisk and melodious neigh as that was! My very heart leaped with delight at the sound. But it startled me, nevertheless; so that I ran home without filling my pitcher."

"That was truly a pity!" said Bellerophon.

And he turned to the child, whom I mentioned at the beginning of the story, and who was gazing at him, as children are apt to gaze at strangers, with his rosy mouth wide open.

"Well, my little fellow," cried Bellerophon, playfully pulling one of his curls, "I suppose you have often seen the winged horse."

"That I have," answered the child, very readily. "I saw him yesterday, and many times before."

"You are a fine little man!" said Bellerophon, drawing the child closer to him. "Come, tell me all about it."

"Why," replied the child, "I often come here to sail little boats in the fountain, and to gather pretty pebbles out of its basin. And sometimes, when I look down into the water, I see the image of the winged horse, in the picture of the sky that is there. I wish he would come down, and take me on his back, and let me ride him up to the moon! But, if I so much as stir to look at him, he flies far away out of sight."

And Bellerophon put his faith in the child, who had seen the image of Pegasus in the water, and in the maiden, who had heard him neigh so melodiously, rather than in the middle-aged clown who believed only in cart horses, or in the old man who had forgotten the beautiful things of his youth.

Therefore, he haunted about the Fountain of Pirene for a great many days afterwards. He kept continually on the watch, looking upward at the sky, or else down into the water, hoping for ever that he should see either the reflected image of the winged horse or the marvelous reality. He held the bridle with its bright gems and golden bit always in his hand. The rustic people who dwelt in the neighborhood, and drove their cattle to the fountain to drink, would often laugh at poor Bellerophon, and sometimes take him pretty severely to task. They told him that an able-bodied young man, like himself, ought to have better business than to be wasting his time in such an idle pursuit. They offered to sell him a horse, if he wanted one; and when Bellerophon declined the purchase, they tried to drive a bargain with him for his fine bridle.

Even the country boys thought him so very foolish, that they used to have a great deal of sport about him, and were rude enough not to care a fig, although Bellerophon saw and heard it. One little urchin, for example, would play Pegasus, and cut the oddest imaginable capers, by way of flying; while one of his schoolfellows would scamper after him, holding forth a twist of bulrushes, which was intended to represent Bellerophon's ornamental bridle. But the gentle child, who had seen the picture of Pegasus in the water, comforted the young stranger more than all the naughty boys could torment him. The dear little fellow, in his play hours, often sat down beside him, and, without speaking a word, would look down into the fountain and up towards the sky, with so innocent a faith, that Bellerophon could not help feeling encouraged.

Now you will, perhaps, wish to be told why it was that Bellerophon had undertaken to catch the winged horse.

And we shall find no better opportunity to speak about this matter than while he is waiting for Pegasus to appear.

If I were to relate the whole of Bellerophon's previous adventures, they might easily grow into a very long story. It will be quite enough to say, that in a certain country of Asia, a terrible monster, called a Chimæra, had made its appearance, and was doing more mischief than could be talked about between now and sunset. According to the best accounts which I have been able to obtain, this Chimæra was nearly, if not quite, the ugliest and most poisonous creature, and the strangest and unaccountablest, and the hardest to fight with, and the most difficult to run away from, that ever came out of the earth's inside. It had a tail like a boa constrictor; its body was like I do not care what; and it had three separate heads, one of which was a lion's, the second a goat's, and the third an abominably great snake's. And a hot blast of fire came flaming out of each of its three mouths! Being an earthly monster, I doubt whether it had any wings; but, wings or no, it ran like a goat and a lion, and wriggled along like a serpent, and thus contrived to make about as much speed as all the three together.

Oh, the mischief, and mischief, and mischief that this naughty creature did! With its flaming breath, it could set a forest on fire, or burn up a field of grain, or, for that matter, a village, with all its fences and houses. It laid waste the whole country round about, and used to eat up people and animals alive, and cook them afterwards in the burning oven of its stomach. Mercy on us, little children, I hope neither you nor I will ever happen to meet Chimæra.

While the hateful beast (if a beast we can anywise call it) was doing all these horrible things, it so chanced that Bellerophon came to that part of the world, on a visit to the king. The king's name was Iobates, and Lycia was the country which he ruled over. Bellerophon was one of the bravest youths in the world, and desired nothing so much as to do some valiant and beneficent deed, such as would make all mankind admire and love him. In those days, the only way for a young man to distinguish himself was by fighting battles, either with the enemies of his country, or with wicked giants, or with troublesome dragons, or with wild beasts, when he could find nothing more dangerous to encounter. King Iobates, perceiving the courage of his youthful visitor, proposed to him to go and fight the Chimæra, which everybody else was afraid of, and which, unless it should be soon killed, was likely to convert Lycia into a desert. Bellerophon hesitated not a moment, but assured the king that he would either slay this dreaded Chimæra, or perish in the attempt.

But, in the first place, as the monster was so prodigiously swift, he bethought himself that he should never win the victory by fighting on foot. The wisest thing he could do, therefore, was to get the very best and fleetest horse that could anywhere be found. And what other horse, in all the world, was half so fleet as the marvelous horse Pegasus, who had wings as well as legs, and was even more active in the air than on the earth? To be sure, a great many people denied that there was any such horse with wings, and said that the stories about him were all poetry and nonsense. But, wonderful as it appeared, Bellerophon believed that Pegasus was a real steed, and hoped that he himself might be fortunate enough to find him; and, once fairly mounted on his back, he would be able to fight the Chimæra at better advantage.

And this was the purpose with which he had travelled from Lycia to Greece, and had brought the beautifully ornamented bridle in his hand. It was an enchanted bridle. If he could only succeed in putting the golden bit into the mouth of Pegasus, the winged horse would be submissive, and would own Bellerophon for his master, and fly whithersoever he might choose to turn the rein.

But, indeed, it was a weary and anxious time, while Bellerophon waited and waited for Pegasus, in hopes that he would come and drink at the Fountain of Pirene. He was afraid lest King Iobates should imagine that he had fled from the Chimæra. It pained him, too, to think how much mischief the monster was doing while he himself, instead of fighting with it, was compelled to sit idly poring over the bright waters of Pirene, as they gushed out of the sparkling sand. And as Pegasus came thither so seldom in these latter years, and scarcely alighted there more than once in a lifetime, Bellerophon feared that he might grow an old man, and have no strength left in his arms nor courage in his heart, before the winged horse would appear. Oh, how heavily passes the time, while an adventurous youth is yearning to do his part in life, and to gather in the harvest of his renown! How hard a lesson it is to wait! Our life is brief, and how much of it is spent in teaching us only this!

Well was it for Bellerophon that the gentle child had grown so fond of him, and was never weary of keeping him company. Every morning the child gave him a new hope to put in his bosom, instead of yesterday's withered one.

"Dear Bellerophon," he would cry, looking up hopefully into his face, "I think we shall see Pegasus today!"

And, at length, if it had not been for the little boy's unwavering faith, Bellerophon would have given up all hope, and would have gone back to Lycia, and have done his best to slay the Chimæra without the help of the winged horse. And in that case poor Bellerophon would at least have been terribly scorched by the creature's breath, and would most probably have been killed and devoured. Nobody should ever try to fight an earthborn Chimæra, unless he can first get upon the back of an aerial steed.

One morning the child spoke to Bellerophon even more hopefully than usual.

"Dear, dear Bellerophon," cried he. "I know not why it

is, but I feel as if we should certainly see Pegasus today!"

And all that day he would not stir a step from Bellerophon's side; so they ate a crust of bread together, and drank some of the water of the fountain. In the afternoon there they sat, and Bellerophon had thrown his arm around the child, who likewise had put one of his little hands into Bellerophon's. The latter was lost in his own thoughts, and was fixing his eyes vacantly on the trunks of the trees that overshadowed the fountain, and on the grapevines that clambered up among their branches. But the gentle child was gazing down into the water; he was grieved for Bellerophon's sake, that the hope of another day should be deceived, like so many before it; and two or three quiet teardrops fell from his eyes, and mingled with what were said to be the many tears of Pirene, when she wept for her slain children.

But, when he least thought of it, Bellerophon felt the pressure of the child's little hand, and heard a soft, almost breathless, whisper.

"See there, dear Bellerophon! There is an image in the water!"

The young man looked down into the dimpling mirror of the fountain, and saw what he took to be the reflection of a bird which seemed to be flying at a great height in the air, with a gleam of sunshine on its snowy or silvery wings.

"What a splendid bird it must be!" said he. "And how very large it looks, though it must really be flying higher than the clouds!"

"It makes me tremble!" whispered the child. "I am afraid to look up into the air! It is very beautiful, and yet I dare only look at its image in the water. Dear Bellerophon, do you not see that it is no bird? It is the winged horse Pegasus!"

Bellerophon's heart began to throb! He gazed keenly upward, but could not see the winged creature, whether bird or horse; because, just then, it had plunged into the fleecy depths of a summer cloud. It was but a moment, however, before the object reappeared, sinking lightly down out of the cloud, although still at a vast distance from the earth. Bellerophon caught the child in his arms, and shrank back with him, so that they were both hidden among the thick shrubbery which grew all around the fountain. Not that he was afraid of any harm, but he dreaded lest, if Pegasus caught a glimpse of them, he would fly far away, and alight in some inaccessible mountaintop. For it was really the winged horse. After they had expected him so long, he was coming to quench his thirst with the water of Pirene.

Nearer and nearer came the aerial wonder, flying in great circles, as you may have seen a dove when about to alight. Downward came Pegasus, in those wide, sweeping circles, which grew narrower, and narrower still, as he gradually approached the earth. The nigher the view of him, the more beautiful he was, and the more marvelous the sweep of his silvery wings. At last, with so light a pressure as hardly to bend the grass about the fountain, or imprint a hoof tramp in the sand of its margin, he alighted, and, stooping his wild head, began to drink. He drew in the water, with long and pleasant sighs, and tranquil pauses of enjoyment; and then another draught, and another, and another. For, nowhere in the world, or up among the clouds, did Pegasus love any water as he loved this of Pirene. And when his thirst was slaked, he cropped a few of the honey blossoms of the clover, delicately tasting them, but not caring to make a hearty meal, because the herbage, just beneath the clouds, on the lofty sides of Mount Helicon, suited his palate better than this ordinary grass.

After thus drinking to his heart's content, and in his dainty fashion, condescending to take a little food, the winged horse began to caper to and fro, and dance as it were, out of mere idleness and sport. There never was a more playful creature made than this very Pegasus. So there he frisked, in a way that it delights me to think about, fluttering his great wings as lightly as ever did a linnet, and running little races, half on earth, and half in air, and which I know not whether to call a flight or a gallop. When a creature is perfectly able to fly, he sometimes chooses to run, just for the pastime of the thing; and so did Pegasus, although it cost him some little trouble to keep his hoofs so near the ground. Bellerophon, meanwhile, holding the child's hand, peeped forth from the shrubbery, and thought that never was any sight so beautiful as this, nor ever a horse's eyes so wild and spirited as those of Pegasus. It seemed a sin to think of bridling him and riding on his back.

Once or twice Pegasus stopped and snuffed the air, pricking up his ears, tossing his head, and turning it on all sides, as if he partly suspected some mischief or other. Seeing nothing, however, and hearing no sound, he soon began his antics again.

At length—not that he was weary, but only idle and luxurious—Pegasus folded his wings, and lay down on the soft green turf. But, being too full of aerial life to remain quiet for many moments together, he soon rolled over on his back, with his four slender legs in the air. It was beautiful to see him, this one solitary creature, whose mate had never been created, but who needed no companion, and, living a great many hundred years, was as happy as the centuries were long. The more he did such things as mortal horses are accustomed to do, the less earthly and the more wonderful he seemed. Bellerophon and the child almost held their breath, partly from a delightful awe, but still more because they dreaded lest the slightest stir or murmur should send him up, with the speed of an arrow-flight, into the farthest blue of the sky.

Finally, when he had had enough of rolling over and over, Pegasus turned himself about, and indolently, like any other horse, put out his fore legs, in order to rise from the ground; and Bellerophon, who had guessed that he would do so, darted suddenly from the thicket, and leaped astride of his back.

Yes, there he sat, on the back of the winged horse!

But what a bound did Pegasus make, when, for the first time, he felt the weight of a mortal man upon his loins! A bound indeed! Before he had time to draw a breath, Bellerophon found himself five hundred feet aloft, and still shooting upward, while the winged horse snorted and trembled with terror and anger. Upward he went, up, up, up, until he plunged into the cold misty bosom of a cloud, at which, only a little while before, Bellerophon had been gazing, and fancying it a very pleasant spot. Then again, out of the heart of the cloud, Pegasus shot down like a thunderbolt, as if he meant to dash both himself and his rider headlong against a rock. Then he went through about a thousand of the wildest caprioles that had ever been performed either by a bird or a horse.

I cannot tell you half that he did. He skimmed straight forward, and sideways, and backward. He reared himself erect, with his fore legs on a wreath of mist, and his hind legs on nothing at all. He flung out his heels behind, and put down his head between his legs, with his wings pointing right upward. At about two miles height above the earth, he turned a somersault, so that Bellerophon's heels were where his head should have been, and he seemed to look down into the sky, instead of up. He twisted his head about, and, looking Bellerophon in the face, with fire flashing from his eyes, made a terrible attempt to bite him. He fluttered his pinions so wildly that one of the silver feathers was shaken out, and floating earthward, was picked up by the child, who kept it as long as he lived, in memory of Pegasus and Bellerophon.

But the latter (who, as you may judge, was as good a horseman as ever galloped) had been watching his opportunity, and at last clapped the golden bit of the enchanted bridle between the winged steed's jaws. No sooner was this done, than Pegasus became as manageable as if he had taken food, all his life, out of Bellerophon's hand. To speak what I really feel, it was almost a sadness to see so wild a creature grow suddenly so tame. And Pegasus seemed to feel it so, likewise. He looked round to Bellerophon, with the tears in his beautiful eyes, instead of the fire that so recently flashed from them. But when Bellerophon patted his head, and spoke a few authoritative, yet kind and soothing words, another look came into the eyes of Pegasus; for he was glad at heart, after so many lonely centuries, to have found a companion and a master.

Thus it always is with winged horses, and with all such wild and solitary creatures. If you can catch and overcome them, it is the surest way to win their love.

While Pegasus had been doing his utmost to shake Bellerophon off his back, he had flown a very long distance; and they had come within sight of a lofty mountain by the time the bit was in his mouth. Bellerophon had seen this mountain before, and knew it to be Helicon, on the summit of which was the winged horse's abode. Thither (after looking gently into his rider's face, as if to ask leave) Pegasus now flew, and, alighting, waited patiently until Bellerophon should please to dismount. The young man, accordingly, leaped from his steed's back, but still held him fast by the bridle. Meeting his eyes, however, he was so affected by the gentleness of his aspect, and by the thought of the free life which Pegasus had heretofore lived, that he could not bear to keep him a prisoner, if he really desired his liberty.

Obeying this generous impulse he slipped the enchanted bridle off the head of Pegasus, and took the bit from his mouth.

"Leave me, Pegasus!" said he. "Either leave me, or love me."

In an instant, the winged horse shot almost out of sight, soaring straight upward from the summit of Mount Helicon. Being long after sunset, it was now twilight on the mountaintop, and dusky evening over all the country round about. But Pegasus flew so high that he overtook the departed day, and was bathed in the upper radiance of the sun. Ascending higher and higher, he looked like a bright speck, and, at last, could no longer be seen in the hollow waste of the sky. And Bellerophon was afraid that he should never behold him more. But, while he was lamenting his own folly, the bright speck reappeared, and drew nearer and nearer, until it descended lower than the sunshine; and, behold, Pegasus had come back! After this trial there was no more fear of the winged horse's making his escape. He and Bellerophon were friends, and put loving faith in one another.

That night they lay down and slept together, with Bellerophon's arm about the neck of Pegasus, not as a caution, but for kindness. And they awoke at peep of day, and bade one another good morning each in his own language.

In this manner, Bellerophon and the wondrous steed spent several days, and grew better acquainted and fonder of each other all the time. They went on long aerial journeys, and sometimes ascended so high that the earth looked hardly bigger than—the moon. They visited distant countries, and amused the inhabitants, who thought that the beautiful young man, on the back of the winged horse, must have come down out of the sky. A thousand miles a day was no more than an easy space for the fleet Pegasus to pass over. Bellerophon was delighted with this kind of life, and would have liked nothing better than to live always in the same way, aloft in the clear atmosphere; for it was always sunny weather up there, however cheerless and rainy it might be in the lower region. But he could not forget the horrible Chimæra, which he had promised King Iobates to slay. So, at last, when he had become well accustomed to feats of horsemanship in the air, and could manage Pegasus with the least motion of his hand, and had taught him to obey his voice, he determined to attempt the performance of this perilous adventure.

At daybreak, therefore, as soon as he unclosed his eyes, he gently pinched the winged horse's ear, in order to arouse him. Pegasus immediately started from the ground, and pranced about a quarter of a mile aloft, and made a grand sweep around the mountaintop, by way of showing that he was wide awake, and ready for any kind of an excursion. During the whole of this little flight, he uttered a loud, brisk, and melodious neigh, and finally came down at Bellerophon's side, as lightly as ever you saw a sparrow hop upon a twig.

"Well done, dear Pegasus! Well done, my sky-skimmer!" cried Bellerophon, fondly stroking the horse's neck. "And now, my fleet and beautiful friend, we must break our fast. Today we are to fight the terrible Chimæra."

As soon as they had eaten their morning meal, and drank some sparkling water from a spring called Hippocrene, Pegasus held out his head, of his own accord, so that his master might put on the bridle. Then, with a great many playful leaps and airy caperings, he showed his impatience to be gone; while Bellerophon was girding on his sword, and hanging his shield about his neck, and preparing himself for battle. When everything was ready, the rider mounted, and (as was his custom, when going a long distance) ascended five miles perpendicularly, so as the better to see whither he was directing his course. He then turned the head of Pegasus towards the east, and set out for Lycia. In their flight they overtook an eagle, and came so nigh him, before he could get out of their way, that Bellerophon might easily have caught him by the leg. Hastening onward at this rate, it was still early in the forenoon when they beheld the lofty mountains of Lycia, with their deep and shaggy valleys. If Bellerophon had been told truly, it was in one of those dismal valleys that the hideous Chimæra had taken up its abode.

Being now so near their journey's end, the winged horse gradually descended with his rider; and they took advantage of some clouds that were floating over the mountain-tops, in order to conceal themselves. Hovering on the upper surface of a cloud, and peeping over its edge, Bellerophon had a pretty distinct view of the mountainous part of Lycia, and could look into all its shadowy vales at once. At first there appeared to be nothing remarkable. It was a wild, savage, and rocky tract of high and precipitous hills. In the more level part of the country, there were the ruins of houses that had been burnt, and, here and there, the carcasses of dead cattle, strewn about the pastures where they had been feeding.

"The Chimæra must have done this mischief," thought Bellerophon. "But where can the monster be?"

As I have already said, there was nothing remarkable to be detected, at first sight, in any of the valleys and dells that lay among the precipitous heights of the mountains. Nothing at all; unless, indeed, it were three spires of black smoke, which issued from what seemed to be the mouth of a cavern, and clambered sullenly into the atmosphere. Before reaching the mountaintop, these three black smoke wreaths mingled themselves into one. The cavern was

almost directly beneath the winged horse and his rider, at
the distance of about a thousand feet. The smoke, as it
crept heavily upward, had an ugly sulphurous, stifling
scent, which caused Pegasus to snort and Bellerophon to
sneeze. So disagreeable was it to the marvelous steed
(who was accustomed to breathe only the purest air), that
he waved his wings, and shot half a mile out of the range of
this offensive vapor.

But, on looking behind him, Bellerophon saw something
that induced him first to draw the bridle, and then to turn
Pegasus about. He made a sign, which the winged horse
understood, and sunk slowly through the air, until his
hoofs were scarcely more than a man's height above the
rocky bottom of the valley. In front, as far off as you could
throw a stone, was the cavern's mouth, with the three
smoke wreaths oozing out of it. And what else did
Bellerophon behold there?

There seemed to be a heap of strange and terrible
creatures curled up within the cavern. Their bodies lay so
close together, that Bellerophon could no distinguish them
apart; but, judging by their heads, one of these creatures
was a huge snake, the second a fierce lion, and the third an
ugly goat. The lion and the goat were asleep; the snake
was broad awake, and kept staring around him with a
great pair of fiery eyes. But—and this was the most
wonderful part of the matter—the three spires of smoke
evidently issued from the nostrils of these three heads! So
strange was the spectacle, that, though Bellerophon had
been all along expecting it, the truth did not immediately
occur to him, that here was the terrible three-headed
Chimæra. He had found out the Chimæra's cavern. The
snake, the lion, and the goat, as he supposed them to be,
were not three separate creatures, but one monster!

The wicked, hateful thing! Slumbering as two thirds of
it were, it still held, in its abominable claws, the remnant

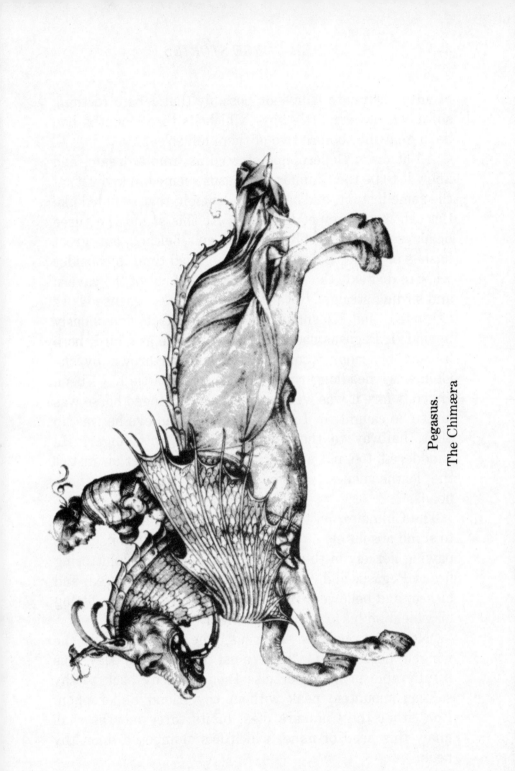

Pegasus.
The Chimæra

of an unfortunate lamb—or possibly (but I hate to think so) it was a dear little boy—which its three mouths had been gnawing, before two of them fell asleep!

All at once, Bellerophon started as from a dream, and knew it to be the Chimæra. Pegasus seemed to know it, at the same instant, and sent forth a neigh, that sounded like the call of a trumpet to battle. At this sound the three heads reared themselves erect, and belched out great flashes of flame. Before Bellerophon had time to consider what to do next, the monster flung itself out of the cavern and sprung straight towards him, with its immense claws extended, and its snaky tail twisting itself venomously behind. If Pegasus had not been as nimble as a bird, both he and his rider would have been overthrown by the Chimæra's headlong rush, and thus the battle have been ended before it was well begun. But the winged horse was not to be caught so. In the twinkling of an eye he was up aloft, halfway to the clouds, snorting with anger. He shuddered, too, not with affright, but with utter disgust at the loathsomeness of this poisonous thing with three heads.

The Chimæra, on the other hand, raised itself up so as to stand absolutely on the tip end of its tail, with its talons pawing fiercely in the air, and its three heads spluttering fire at Pegasus and his rider. My stars, how it roared, and hissed, and bellowed! Bellerophon, meanwhile, was fitting his shield on his arm and drawing his sword.

"Now, my beloved Pegasus," he whispered in the winged horse's ear, "thou must help me to slay this insufferable monster; or else thou shalt fly back to thy solitary mountain peak without thy friend Bellerophon. For either the Chimæra dies, or its three mouths shall gnaw this head of mine, which has slumbered upon thy neck!"

Pegasus whinnied, and, turning back his head, rubbed

his nose tenderly against his rider's cheek. It was his way of telling him that, though he had wings and was an immortal horse, yet he would perish, if it were possible for immortality to perish, rather than leave Bellerophon behind.

"I thank you, Pegasus," answered Bellerophon. "Now then, let us make a dash at the monster!"

Uttering these words, he shook the bridle; and Pegasus darted down aslant, as swift as the flight of an arrow, right towards the Chimæra's threefold head, which, all this time, was poking itself as high as it could into the air. As he came within arm's length, Bellerophon made a cut at the monster, but was carried onward by his steed, before he could see whether the blow had been successful. Pegasus continued his course, but soon wheeled round, at about the same distance from the Chimæra as before. Bellerophon then perceived that he had cut the goat's head of the monster almost off, so that it dangled downward by the skin, and seemed quite dead.

But, to make amends, the snake's head and the lion's head had taken all the fierceness of the dead one into themselves, and spit flame, and hissed, and roared, with a vast deal more fury than before.

"Never mind, my brave Pegasus!" cried Bellerophon. "With another stroke like that, we will stop either its hissing or its roaring."

And again he shook the bridle. Dashing aslantwise, as before, the winged horse made another arrow-flight towards the Chimæra, and Bellerophon aimed another downright stroke at one of the two remaining heads, as he shot by. By this time, neither he nor Pegasus escaped so well as at first. With one of its claws, the Chimæra had given the young man a deep scratch in his shoulder, and had slightly damaged the left wing of the flying steed with the other. On his part, Bellerophon had mortally wounded

the lion's head of the monster, insomuch that it now hung
downward, with its fire almost extinguished, and sending
out gasps of thick black smoke. The snake's head, however
(which was the only one now left), was twice as fierce and
venomous as ever before. It belched forth shoots of fire
five hundred yards long, and emitted hisses so loud, so
harsh, and so ear-piercing, that King Iobates heard them,
fifty miles off, and trembled till the throne shook under
him.

"Well-a-day!" thought the poor king; "the Chimæra is
certainly coming to devour me!"

Meanwhile Pegasus had again paused in the air, and
neighed angrily, while sparkles of a pure crystal flame
darted out of his eyes. How unlike the lurid fire of the
Chimæra! The aerial steed's spirit was all aroused, and so
was that of Bellerophon.

"Dost thou bleed, my immortal horse?" cried the young
man, caring less for his own hurt than for the anguish of
this glorious creature, that ought never to have tasted
pain. "The execrable Chimæra shall pay for this mischief
with his last head!"

Then he shook the bridle, shouted loudly, and guided
Pegasus, not aslantwise as before, but straight at the
monster's hideous front. So rapid was the onset, that it
seemed but a dazzle and a flash before Bellerophon was at
close grips with his enemy.

The Chimæra, by this time, after losing his second head,
had got into a red-hot passion of pain and rampant rage. It
so flounced about, half on earth and partly in the air, that
it was impossible to say which element it rested upon. It
opened its snake-jaws to such an abominable width, that
Pegasus might almost, I was going to say, have flown
right down its throat, wings outspread, rider and all! At
their approach it shot out a tremendous blast of its fiery
breath, and enveloped Bellerophon and his steed in a

perfect atmosphere of flame, singeing the wings of Pegasus, scorching off one whole side of the young man's golden ringlets, and making them both far hotter than was comfortable, from head to foot.

But this was nothing to what followed.

When the airy rush of the winged horse had brought him within the distance of a hundred yards, the Chimæra gave a spring, and flung its huge, awkward, venomous, and utterly detestable carcass right upon poor Pegasus, clung round him with might and main, and tied up its snaky tail into a knot! Up flew the aerial steed, higher, higher, higher, above the mountain peaks, above the clouds, and almost out of sight of the solid earth. But still the earthborn monster kept its hold, and was borne upward, along with the creature of light and air. Bellerophon, meanwhile, turning about, found himself face to face with the ugly grimness of the Chimæra's visage, and could only avoid being scorched to death, or bitten right in twain, by holding up his shield. Over the upper edge of the shield, he looked sternly into the savage eyes of the monster.

But the Chimæra was so mad and wild with pain, that it did not guard itself so well as might else have been the case. Perhaps, after all, the best way to fight a Chimæra is by getting as close to it as you can. In its efforts to stick its horrible iron claws into its enemy, the creature left its own breast quite exposed; and perceiving this, Bellerophon thrust his sword up to the hilt into its cruel heart. Immediately the snaky tail untied its knot. The monster let go its hold of Pegasus, and fell from that vast height, downward; while the fire within its bosom, instead of being put out, burned fiercer than ever, and quickly began to consume the dead carcass. Thus it fell out of the sky, all aflame, and (it being nightfall before it reached the earth) was mistaken for a shooting star or a comet. But, at early sunrise, some cottagers were going to their day's labor, and saw, to their astonishment, that several acres of ground were strewn with black ashes. In the middle of a field, there was a heap of whitened bones, a great deal higher than a haystack. Nothing else was ever seen of the dreadful Chimæra!

And when Bellerophon had won the victory, he bent forward and kissed Pegasus, while the tears stood in his eyes.

"Back now, my beloved steed!" said he. "Back to the Fountain of Pirene!"

Pegasus skimmed through the air, quicker than ever he did before, and reached the fountain in a very short time. And there he found the old man leaning on his staff, and the country fellow watering his cow, and the pretty maiden filling her pitcher.

"I remember now," quoth the old man, "I saw this winged horse once before, when I was quite a lad. But he was ten times handsomer in those days."

"I own a cart horse, worth three of him!" said the country fellow. "If this pony were mine, the first thing I should do would be to clip his wings!"

But the poor maiden said nothing, for she had always the luck to be afraid at the wrong time. So she ran away, and let her pitcher tumble down, and broke it.

"Where is the gentle child," asked Bellerophon, "who used to keep me company, and never lost his faith, and never was weary of gazing into the fountain?"

"Here am I, dear Bellerophon!" said the child softly.

For the little boy had spent day after day, on the margin of Pirene, waiting for his friend to come back; but when he perceived Bellerophon descending through the clouds, mounted on the winged horse, he had shrunk back into the shrubbery. He was a delicate and tender child, and dreaded lest the old man and the country fellow should see the tears gushing from his eyes.

"Thou hast won the victory," said he joyfully, running to the knee of Bellerophon, who still sat on the back of Pegasus. "I knew thou wouldst."

"Yes, dear child!" replied Bellerophon, alighting from the winged horse. "But if thy faith had not helped me, I should never have waited for Pegasus, and never have gone up above the clouds, and never have conquered the terrible Chimæra. Thou, my beloved little friend, hast done it all. And now let us give Pegasus his liberty."

So he slipped off the enchanted bridle from the head of the marvelous steed.

"Be free, for evermore, my Pegasus!" cried he, with a shade of sadness in his tone. "Be as free as thou art fleet!"

But Pegasus rested his head on Bellerophon's shoulder, and would not be persuaded to take flight.

"Well then," said Bellerophon, caressing the airy horse, "thou shalt be with me, as long as thou wilt; and we will go together, forthwith, and tell King Iobates that the Chimæra is destroyed."

Then Bellerophon embraced the gentle child, and promised to come to him again, and departed. But, in after years, that child took higher flights upon the aerial steed than ever did Bellerophon, and achieved more honorable deeds than his friend's victory over the Chimæra. For, gentle and tender as he was, he grew to be a mighty poet!

So this is a genuine Mexican Plug!
A GENUINE MEXICAN PLUG

A GENUINE MEXICAN PLUG

from *Roughing It*

by Mark Twain

I resolved to have a horse to ride. I had never seen such wild, free, magnificent horsemanship outside of a circus as these picturesquely-clad Mexicans, Californians and Mexicanized Americans displayed in Carson streets every day. How they rode! Leaning just gently forward out of the perpendicular, easy and nonchalant, with broad slouch-hat brim blown square up in front, and long *riata* swinging above the head, they swept through the town like the wind! The next minute they were only a sailing puff of dust on the far desert. If they trotted, they sat up gallantly and gracefully, and seemed part of the horse; did not go jiggering up and down after the silly Miss-Nancy fashion of the riding-schools. I had quickly learned to tell a horse from a cow, and was full of anxiety to learn more. I was resolved to buy a horse.

While the thought was rankling in my mind, the auctioneer came scurrying through the plaza on a black beast that had as many humps and corners on him as a dromedary, and was necessarily uncomely; but he was "going, going, at twenty-two!—horse, saddle and bridle at twenty-two dollars, gentlemen!" and I could hardly resist.

A man whom I did not know (he turned out to be the auctioneer's brother) noticed the wistful look in my eye, and observed that that was a very remarkable horse to be going at such a price; and added that the saddle alone was worth the money. It was a Spanish saddle, with ponderous *tapidaros,* and furnished with the ungainly sole-leather covering with the unspellable name. I said I had half a notion to bid. Then this keen-eyed person appeared to me to be "taking my measure"; but I dismissed the suspicion when he spoke, for his manner was full of guileless candor and truthfulness. Said he:

"I know that horse—know him well. You are a stranger, I take it, and so you might think he was an American horse, maybe, but I assure you he is not. He is nothing of the kind; but—excuse my speaking in a low voice, other people being near—he is, without the shadow of a doubt, a Genuine Mexican Plug!"

I did not know what a Genuine Mexican Plug was, but there was something about this man's way of saying it, that made me swear inwardly that I would own a Genuine Mexican Plug, or die.

"Has he any other—er—advantages?" I inquired, suppressing what eagerness I could.

He hooked his forefinger in the pocket of my army shirt, led me to one side, and breathed in my ear impressively these words:

"He can out-buck anything in America!"

"Going, going, going—at *twent—ty*-four dollars and a half, gen—"

"Twenty-seven!" I shouted in a frenzy.

"And sold!" said the auctioneer, and passed over the Genuine Mexican Plug to me.

I could scarcely contain my exultation. I paid the money, and put the animal in a neighboring livery stable to dine and rest himself.

In the afternoon I brought the creature into the plaza, and certain citizens held him by the head, and others by the tail, while I mounted him. As soon as they let go, he placed all his feet in a bunch together, lowered his back, and then suddenly arched it upward, and shot me straight

"You might think him an American horse."
A GENUINE MEXICAN PLUG

into the air a matter of three or four feet! I came as
straight down again, lit in the saddle, went instantly up
again, came down almost on the high pommel, shot up
again, and came down on the horse's neck—all in the space
of three or four seconds. Then he rose and stood almost
straight up on his hind feet, and I, clasping his lean neck
desperately, slid back into the saddle, and held on. He
came down, and immediately hoisted his heels into the air,
delivering a vicious kick at the sky, and stood on his
forefeet. And then down he came once more, and began
the original exercise of shooting me straight up again. The
third time I went up I heard a stranger say:

"Oh, *don't* he buck, though!"

While I was up, somebody struck the horse a sounding
thwack with a leathern strap, and when I arrived again
the Genuine Mexican Plug was not there. A Californian
youth chased him up and caught him, and asked if he
might have a ride. I granted him that luxury. He mounted
the Genuine, got lifted into the air once, but sent his spurs
home as he descended, and the horse darted away like a
telegram. He soared over three fences like a bird, and
disappeared down the road toward the Washoe Valley.

I sat down on a stone, with a sigh, and by a natural
impulse one of my hands sought my forehead, and the
other the base of my stomach. I believe I never appreciated, till then, the poverty of the human machinery—for I
still needed a hand or two to place elsewhere. Pen cannot
describe how I was jolted up. Imagination cannot conceive
how disjointed I was—how internally, externally and
universally I was unsettled, mixed up and ruptured. There
was a sympathetic crowd around me, though.

One elderly-looking comforter said:

"Stranger, you've been taken in. Everybody in this
camp knows that horse. Any child, any Injun, could have
told you that he'd buck; he is the very worst devil to buck

Unexpected elevation.

Universally unsettled.
A GENUINE MEXICAN PLUG

on the continent of America. You hear *me*. I'm Curry. *Old*
Curry. Old *Abe* Curry. And moreover, he is a simon-pure,
out-and-out, genuine d—d Mexican plug, and an uncommon mean one at that, too. Why, you turnip, if you had
laid low and kept dark, there's chances to buy an
American horse for mighty little more than you paid for
that bloody old foreign relic."

I gave no sign; but I made up my mind that if the
auctioneer's brother's funeral took place while I was in the
Territory I would postpone all other recreations and
attend it.

After a gallop of sixteen miles the Californian youth and
the Genuine Mexican Plug came tearing into town again,
shedding foam-flakes like the spume-spray that drives
before a typhoon, and, with one final skip over a wheelbar-
row and a Chinaman, cast anchor in front of the "ranch."

Such panting and blowing! Such spreading and con-
tracting of the red equine nostrils, and glaring of the wild
equine eye! But was the imperial beast subjugated?
Indeed he was not. His lordship the Speaker of the House
thought he was, and mounted him to go down to the
Capitol; but the first dash the creature made was over a
pile of telegraph poles half as high as a church; and his
time to the Capitol—one mile and three quarters—remains unbeaten to this day. But then he took an advantage—he left out the mile, and only did the three quarters.
That is to say, he made a straight cut across lots,
preferring fences and ditches to a crooked road; and when
the Speaker got to the Capitol he said he had been in the
air so much he felt as if he had made the trip on a comet.

In the evening the Speaker came home afoot for
exercise, and got the Genuine towed back behind a quartz
wagon. The next day I loaned the animal to the Clerk of
the House to go down to the Dana silver mine, six miles,
and *he* walked back for exercise, and got the horse towed.

Riding the Plug.

Wanted exercise.
A GENUINE MEXICAN PLUG

Everybody I loaned him to always walked back; they never could get enough exercise any other way. Still, I continued to loan him to anybody who was willing to borrow him, my idea being to get him crippled, and throw him on the borrower's hands, or killed, and make the borrower pay for him. But somehow nothing ever happened to him. He took chances that no other horse ever took and survived, but he always came out safe. It was his daily habit to try experiments that had always before been considered impossible, but he always got through. Sometimes he miscalculated a little, and did not get his rider through intact, but *he* always got through himself. Of course I had tried to sell him; but that was a stretch of simplicity which met with little sympathy. The auctioneer stormed up and down the streets on him for four days, dispersing the populace, interrupting business, and destroying children, and never got a bid—at least never any but the eighteen-dollar one he hired a notoriously substanceless bummer to make. The people only smiled pleasantly, and restrained their desire to buy, if they had any. Then the auctioneer brought in his bill, and I withdrew the horse from the market. We tried to trade him off at private vendue next, offering him at a sacrifice for second-hand tombstones, old iron, temperance tracts— any kind of property. But holders were stiff, and we retired from the market again. I never tried to ride the horse any more. Walking was good enough exercise for a man like me, that had nothing the matter with him except ruptures, internal injuries and such things. Finally I tried to *give* him away. But it was a failure. Parties said earthquakes were handy enough on the Pacific coast— they did not wish to own one. As a last resort I offered him to the Governor for the use of the "Brigade." His face lit up eagerly at first, but toned down again, and he said the thing would be too palpable.

Just then the livery stable man brought in his bill for six weeks' keeping—stall-room for the horse, fifteen dollars; hay for the horse, two hundred and fifty! The Genuine Mexican Plug had eaten a ton of the article, and the man said he would have eaten a hundred if he had let him.

I will remark here, in all seriousness, that the regular price of hay during that year and a part of the next was really two hundred and fifty dollars a ton. During a part of the previous year it had sold at five hundred a ton, in gold, and during the winter before that there was such scarcity of the article that in several instances small quantities had brought eight hundred dollars a ton in coin! The consequence might be guessed without my telling it: people turned their stock loose to starve, and before the spring arrived Carson and Eagle valleys were almost literally carpeted with their carcases! Any old settler there will verify these statements.

I managed to pay the livery bill, and that same day I gave the Genuine Mexican Plug to a passing Arkansas emigrant whom fortune delivered into my hand. If this ever meets his eye, he will doubtless remember the donation.

Now whoever has had the luck to ride a real Mexican plug will recognize the animal depicted in this chapter, and hardly consider him exaggerated—but the uninitiated will feel justified in regarding his portrait as a fancy sketch, perhaps.

A gentleman in hunt livery.

Sidesaddle.

TING-A-LING

from *Gallops II*

by David Gray

MR. and Mrs. Curtis were sitting on the balcony which distinguished the bridal suite, in the sun of the June morning. Below was the main street, animated mildly with the shopping of a dormant New England community. A few ancient carriages, reliquaries of the first families, mingled with the buggies and the delivery wagons, and at dignified intervals a horsecar jingled past and disappeared in the vista of elms.

"It's ten minutes past eleven," Mr. Curtis observed, looking at his watch. "We have five hours to wait for the four-ten train, but I believe we dine at twelve."

"Are you hungry?" Mrs. Curtis asked. "I dare say we could get something even before dinner—perhaps a pie."

They both laughed. "This is an awful place," he said, "isn't it? No more historic New England for me."

They leaned lazily upon the balcony rail, and sat with their heads together, looking down into the street. A grocer's clerk was putting things into a wagon, and they wondered who was going to have asparagus, and how big a family it might be which needed six quarts of strawberries. Presently, with the noises of the street, came the ting-a-ling of the periodic horsecar, and they turned and watched it approach.

"That is not a bad looking horse," he said judicially.

"Look!" she exclaimed. There was a note of pity and indignation in her voice. The car, as it drew near, appeared to bulge with passengers.

"It's rather a joke," he said. "Those are women delegates to the Society for the Prevention of Cruelty to Animals convention."

"It's shameful," she said.

The car stopped on the corner in front of the hotel for another passenger to worm himself into the jam on the rear platform. The horse, a big, showy chestnut, stood panting, his nostrils red and dilated. His neck was white with lather. Wet streaks extended up his ears. His body dripped, and the sweat was running down his legs.

As the two strokes of the conductor's bell gave the signal to start, he plunged forward almost before the driver had loosened the brakes. There was a clatter of hoofs on the cobblestones, and a mighty straining. The heavy car began to move, and the chestnut horse went trotting down the street, tail up and neck arched like a cavalry horse on parade.

"He's game," he said.

She put her hand on his arm. "I can't bear to see it," she whispered.

He looked down at her. Her eyes were brimming.

"Don't be a little goose," he said gently; but there was a queer feeling in his throat. He rose to his feet. "I'll be back in a few minutes," he added. "I want to go down to the office." He bent down and kissed her, and left the balcony.

She waited half an hour, and then went down to the corridor. He was not at the office. She decided to go out. As she was on the hotel steps, she met him coming in, and at the same moment a coach horn sounded, and they saw a coach-and-four come around the corner.

He looked back. "Oh, Lord!" he exclaimed, "we're caught. There's your brother, and the Appleton girls, and Frank Crewe, and Winthrop, and most of your bridesmaids. I suppose they are on their way to Lenox."

"What shall we do?" she asked.

A great uproar arose from the people on the coach.
"Hello!" said Curtis.

"Hello!" yelled the people on the coach. Mr. Crewe got
possession of the horn and produced fragments of the
"Lohengrin Wedding March." The people in the street and
the hangers-on about the hotel began to gather around.

Her brother waved his hand from the coach. "Well," he
said, "how are you getting on? Quarreled yet? I am sorry,
but we are completely out of rice."

"I don't understand," said Curtis, looking at the crowd
in dismay. "This is a beautiful country, Willie. Historic
battlefields and all that sort of thing; besides, they breed
some good horses all about here. We have been picking up
one or two."

"For the bride!" called Winthrop, and he generously
threw her an enormous bunch of wild roses which Crewe
that morning had patiently pulled from the roadside
bushes at the cost of no small suffering, and had presented
to the elder Appleton girl.

Curtis ignored the episode. His eye at that moment
caught a stableboy leading a big chestnut horse toward the
hotel. "Here's one we've just bought," he said. "I think
he's likely to make a jumper." He felt his hand, which was
behind him, squeezed surreptitiously, and he was aware of
beaming somewhat foolishly. He was glad that the people
on the coach had turned their attention to the horse.

"Where did you find that?" asked Winthrop.

Curtis hesitated a moment. "Over that way," he said
vaguely, waving his hand over an arc which extended from
east to west. "It's a great country for horses."

Her brother had been inspecting the horse in silence.
"My son," he said to the stableboy, "how did you gall that
race horse's shoulder?"

"That's a collar mark," said the boy. "Pulling a streetcar
is hard work."

Peals of laughter came from the coach.

"You needn't laugh," said the boy. "He's a horse all right."

She had moved to the horse's head. "I believe you," she said to the boy. "He's game."

"He is, ma'am," said the boy.

"Well, Ting-a-ling," said her brother, addressing the chestnut horse, "we can't stop to admire you all day. You're not a bad looking horse, but if you are a streetcar horse, as unfortunately you are, you have the nature that will jump until you get tired, and then you'll roll over things, and make my sister an attractive widow. I wouldn't have you at any price."

"Then everybody is satisfied," said Curtis.

"I am," she said. She gave him a little look that meant that she was satisfied with him, and Curtis felt that he was beaming again. He turned away.

The horse began to rub his nose against her arm and sniffed.

"He's looking for sugar," said the boy. "I give it to him sometimes."

"You are a very nice boy," she said. "What's your name?"

"Tim," said the boy.

"Let's have him take the horse down for us," she said to her husband. "We might keep him, too."

"All right," he said. "But let's get out of this crowd." They slipped away and hurried around the block.

"You were good to get him," she said in a low tone. "The way he acted made me feel that he wasn't meant for streetcar work. What shall we call him?"

"I am afraid that brother Willie has already named him," he answered.

"What?" she demanded.

"Ting-a-ling," he replied.

" 'Well, Ting-a-Ling, ... I wouldn't have you at any price.' "
TING-A-LING
Illustration by David Urquhart Wilcox

"But he ought to be called Sultan or Emperor, or something like that," she insisted.

"You and I," he said, "we know what a heart he has; but, after all, he is a streetcar horse. We'd better accept the facts."

"Well, then it's Ting-a-ling," she said.

It was November; three years had slipped away. The race for the Hunt Club cup was coming off in the afternoon, and everybody was lunching at the club. She was patiently chaperoning the elder Appleton girl and Frank Crewe at a table on the glass-enclosed veranda overlooking the polo field.

"We'll give you some lunch," she said to Winthrop, who was passing.

"I'm with Willie," he answered.

"Willie can come too," she said.

He thanked her and sat down.

"Is Ting-a-ling pretty fit?" he asked.

"I think so," she replied; "but of course he's never been steeplechased, so we don't know what he can do."

"He is certainly a good horse to hounds," said Winthrop.

"He's never been down," she said.

"Please don't say that on the day of the race," he interrupted; "it's unlucky."

Just then Willie joined them.

"Still talking steeplechase," he observed. "I suppose your husband is going to win."

"I don't know about that," she answered; "but he'll beat you."

"I'll bet he won't," he retorted. "It's a sure thing. I am not going to ride. They tell me that I am too fat, but that isn't the reason. I am afraid. Hello! here's the steeplechase jockey," he said to Curtis, who came in. "Have you provided liberally for me in your will? Haven't I always been a good brother-in-law?"

"Always," said Curtis, "and no doubt you need the money; but I am not making wills today."

"You'd better," said Willie, cheerfully. "I'd hate to have that streetcar horse roll you out and have no other consolation than the thought that you had loved me." His tone became less playful. "Bequeath me my nephew, and your widow can take the property."

"If that blessed boy of yours," Crewe said to Mrs. Curtis, "isn't ruined by the indulgence of his foolish old uncle, I shall be much surprised."

"Hush up!" retorted Willie, "and get a nephew of your own."

Winthrop turned to Curtis. "How has the horse shown in his training?" he asked.

"He rates pretty well, and I have a good deal of confidence in his jumping," Curtis answered. "He's rather a pet, you know, so that perhaps my judgment is prejudiced."

"He'll go until he gets tired," put in Willie, "and then he'll shut up and go through his fences. Those big half-breeds are all alike."

"How do you know he's a half-breed?" said Curtis.

"I don't know that he is anything," Willie retorted. "You got him out of a streetcar."

"I think we would better change the subject," said his sister; "you're becoming disagreeable. Remember," she added to the party, "you are all coming in this evening to play bridge. You can't come to dinner, because the cook is sick."

From the hill back of the clubhouse they watched the race. A horse of Winthrop's, with Crewe up, made the running for the first mile. Then Curtis took Ting-a-ling out of the bunch, and went away apparently without effort. At the two-mile flag Curtis was a hundred yards in the lead. The other horses seemed to be racing for the place.

"He seems to have things all his own way," said Winthrop to Mrs. Curtis. "My horse is done."

"He is going well," she whispered. She was very much. excited.

Toward the middle of the third mile the four horses that were running in the second flight drew up, and it became a race again. Her heart almost stopped beating. "Is he tiring?" she murmured. The five went at the board fence near the third-mile flag in a bunch. As they took off, there was crowding on the outside. Then four horses jumped clearly; one fell, and the four went on again.

A rustle of apprehension ran through the crowd.

"Who's down?" exclaimed the elder Appleton girl in a low tone.

"Is he hurt?" asked her sister.

"It's Ting-a-ling!" murmured Mrs. Curtis.

The horse got up, and galloped riderless after the leaders. A moment later the rider got up and started across the field on foot.

"He's not hurt," said Winthrop. "I'm awfully sorry. He would have won."

"That's good of you," she replied. But she suspected that he was only softening the bitterness of the disappointment. Willie was right. The horse ran himself tired and stopped. She felt that she was very white and made an effort to talk. "That's your horse ahead with Frank Crewe," she said; "he's got the race."

It was so, and the crowd was already surging down to the finish flags to congratulate the winner. Mrs. Curtis drove her cart across the meadow to meet the dismounted rider.

Their eyes met as she pulled up.

The five went at the board fence in a bunch.

TING-A-LING

Illustrated by David Urquhart Wilcox

"It's too bad," she said. "Are you hurt?"

"I think my collarbone is gone," he answered. "I'll see Tim and send the horse home, and then I'll go to the club and get bandaged."

He gave his orders to the boy.

"You was fouled, sir," said Tim. He was much excited. "I seen Mr. Crewe pull across you about two lengths from the fence."

"Not at all," said Curtis, shortly. "Walk him home at once and do him up."

"Is it so?" she asked. "Were you fouled?"

"I don't think I'd say it," he answered. "I rode very badly. It was my fault. I shouldn't have pulled him back into the crowd."

She said nothing. She saw that he was very much disappointed. But the hardest for her to bear was that her confidence in Ting-a-ling was gone.

At the clubhouse Willie was on the veranda.

"I'm awfully sorry," he said. "But, seriously, you had better shoot that horse. You'll not be so lucky another time."

Curtis looked up angrily to reply, and then turned away with his lips tightly closed.

"I'll be ready in half an hour," he said to his wife.

In rather less than that time he came from his dressing room, his arm in bandages and the hand in a sling. He sent for his carriage and found Mrs. Curtis in the tearoom.

"I think we had better go," he said. "They have just telephoned from the house, saying the baby isn't very well. I told the doctor to come along as soon as he could. Don't say anything to Willie about the little chap," he added. "He'll tag along and make a fuss and irritate me."

She rose and followed him. The carriage was at the door, and they drove away.

Earlier, the November afternoon had been flooded with

"You was fouled, sir," said Tim.

TING-A-LING

Illustration by David Urquhart Wilcox

a damp sunshine, and there had been a still and unnatural mildness in the air. Toward four, as they left the club, the sky became overcast, and out of the west a mass of blue-black cloud began to rise and stretch across the horizon. Soon it threw the western part of the plain and the hills beyond into darkness. Overhead it was still light, but the shadow drew on and began to chill the day.

Curtis looked apprehensively toward the west and touched the horse with the whip. His wife had the reins.

"It's growing colder," she said.

He bent forward and tucked the robe about her feet.

Uncertain drafts of wind rattled the brown leaves on the oaks and made the dead goldenrods along the roadside bow excitedly.

"I am afraid that we are going to get wet," he said.

The gusts became stronger. The blackness from the west had spread until it was overhead, and light clouds were moving eastwardly across the face of the sky.

"I felt a drop of rain," she observed.

He urged the horse to a gallop.

"So did I," said he a moment later.

"It will be a good night to stay home and read," he went on. "Don't you think I am getting to be quite a reader? Two books already this month; one of them had three hundred and twelve pages. But there were a good many pictures," he added conscientiously.

She smiled, but said nothing.

He watched her as they drove along. Presently he broke the silence.

"I wouldn't worry about the baby," he said. "Probably he has a little cold or a stomachache. The nurse is terrified if he sneezes."

"That's probably all," she said; "you know what a goose I am."

As they turned into the driveway the rain began to pour down. She got out of the carriage and went in while he held the horse.

Presently a man came from the stable, and Curtis too went in. He was taking off his coat when his wife came down from the nursery.

"Well?" he asked.

"He's about the same," she answered. "He seems to have a little fever. What time did the doctor say he would be here?"

"About six," said Curtis. He looked at his watch. "It will be an hour yet. It's begun to snow," he added.

They went to the library, which looked toward the west, and watched the breaking storm.

"It was too bad about Ting-a-ling," she said after a pause.

"Well," he answered, "we have to take things as they come. I should like to have shown what a horse he is. We shall next year."

"I wish you would promise never to ride him in a race again," she said.

"I don't think you ought to ask that," he answered sharply. "For the horse's sake, I want him to have a chance to redeem himself. Don't you?"

"Isn't it wrong to take unnecessary risks?" she replied.

He made no answer.

The rain had changed to sleet, and the ground was already white. The bare elms on the lawn were creaking dismally. They could see the stiff shrubs in the garden bend to the gusts. The storm beat on the windowpanes, and in the fierce blasts the house trembled. As they stood by the window, the man brought in the lighted lamps, and they realized that the night had set in.

"Suppose we have a look at him," he said. By "him" he

meant Ting-a-ling. "Won't you come? If the doctor arrives, they can send for us."

"I'd like to," she said.

On the way out, she went to the pantry and took some lumps of sugar.

The stablemen were at supper, and the stable was still except for the sound of the horses munching at their oats. As he drew the door open the grinding hushed except in the two stalls where the ponies ate stolidly on. The line of dusky heads was lifted and thrust curiously forward. From the box stall in the corner came a low whinny, and in the dim light of the wall lamp they saw a long neck stretched out and two pointed ears cocked forward. It was Ting-a-ling.

"You beggar!" said Curtis. "You know what we've got." He went into the stall and stripped off the blankets. She followed him. "Hello!" he exclaimed. His arm was nipped gently. "You have very bad manners." The horse drew back, tossed his head, and pawed.

"Look here," Mrs. Curtis said. She held out a piece of sugar. A soft muzzle touched her hand, the lips opened and scraped across her palm, and there was a crunching sound.

"You baby!" she said, and gave him a second piece. "I'm very fond of you," she added under her breath, "in spite—" She stopped.

"He seems to be feeding well," said Curtis.

He put his hand into the manger. It touched the clean, moistened boards of the bottom.

"You're a pig!" he exclaimed. "He's put away five quarts already," he said to his wife. "Doesn't he look fit?"

They drew back and looked the horse over. The legs were clean, the great muscles stood out on forearm and quarter, the flesh was hard and spare.

"He's a great type," said Curtis, "isn't he? But if he

were three-cornered I'd like him just as well. I'm ashamed to care so much for him."

"Do you remember the day we got him?" she asked.

He stepped back and put his arm around her.

"It seems yesterday, dear," he said. "How the years go by!" He put back the blankets, and stood a moment fastening the surcingle.

"Barring accidents, old horse," he muttered, "we'll have your name on the cup yet."

A swelling feeling came into his throat and he put his face against the sleek neck. He straightened up quickly as he heard the doors slide apart and somebody come in.

"Mr. Curtis," called a voice. It was Tim.

"Hello!" said Curtis.

"The doctor's come," said Tim.

"All right," answered Curtis.

He drew his wife's wraps about her, and they made their way back to the house.

The doctor met them at the door of the nursery.

"This child is sick," he said. "The temperature has gone up in a way I don't like. We've got to operate."

"Operate!" Curtis exclaimed. He put his hand upon the banister. "What do you mean?"

"Yes," said the doctor.

"When?" said Mrs. Curtis.

"Lamplight is bad," said the doctor, "but we must do the best we can. It ought to be done before ten o'clock. I should be afraid to wait longer."

Neither husband nor wife spoke. The doctor looked at his watch.

"Whom would you rather have?" he asked.

"Have?" repeated Curtis. A gust rattled the windows at the end of the hall, and as it died away he heard the tick-tick of the sleet on the pane. He looked at the doctor with a white face.

"Can't you do it?" he asked. "Suppose we couldn't get any one from town by ten o'clock?"

"We must," said the doctor, cheerfully. "I'm not a surgeon, and there is none in the village. Would you rather have Anderson, or Tate?"

"Dr. Anderson," said Mrs. Curtis.

"He must get the train that leaves town at eight o'clock," said the doctor. "There is no other until midnight."

"It's quarter past six now," said Curtis. "That gives us an hour and three quarters. I'll telephone at once." He left the room and went to the telephone.

After some delay the village operator answered.

"You can't get the city," said the girl; "the wires are down. I have been trying to get them for an hour for the telegraph people. Their line is closed, too."

"When do you expect your wires to be repaired?" he asked.

"Can't say," the operator replied. "Not tonight, though. The linemen can't work tonight."

"Thank you," said Curtis. He hung up the receiver and stood blankly before the instrument. He was about to move away when he heard a footstep. He turned, and his wife was standing beside him.

"He'll come," he answered. "I'm going to the station for him myself. I'll dine when I come back. You and the doctor get things ready." He went into the smoking room and walked the length of the room and back. "Six miles, ten, fifteen, and six more downtown," he said aloud. He looked at his watch again. It was twenty minutes past six. "Start at half past," he went on; "that's twenty-one miles in an hour and a quarter—and these roads!" He went to the wall and rang a bell. "Twenty-one miles in an hour and a quarter," he repeated. "Searchlight can't do it, nor Xerxes, nor Huron, nor the roan mare."

A servant appeared.

"Tell Hobson," he said, "to saddle Ting-a-ling at once. Tell him to hurry, and send Tim here."

Tim came, and Curtis explained.

"Can he do it?" asked Curtis.

"I don't know, sir," said the boy.

"He's got to do it," said Curtis. "Do you understand?"

"Yes, sir."

They hurried to the stable, and found Hobson buckling the throatlatch.

"All ready, sir," he said.

Tim climbed into the saddle and gathered up his reins. Then Hobson threw open the door, and the horse and boy clattered out and disappeared in the storm.

Curtis looked at his watch. It was twenty-eight minutes past six. "Have the bus and a pair of horses at the house at eight," he said, and went back to the house.

He met his wife in the hall.

"Is there any change?" he asked.

She shook her head.

"Suppose he should miss the train?" she suggested.

"He won't," said Curtis.

She sighed, and was silent for a pause. "What a wonderful thing the telephone is!" she said. "What would we have done without it?"

"That's so," said Curtis. "I'm going to the station at eight," he added.

At ten minutes of nine she was standing with her face against the windowpane, when the lights of the station bus glimmered through the storm. She went to the head of the stairway and waited breathless.

"Suppose," she thought, "he has missed the train!"

Presently there sounded the crunching of wheels on the gravel. This meant that the bus was stopping at the house. Then the door opened.

"Come along," said her husband's voice.

"Thank God!" she murmured. She sat down for a moment, and then went to the nursery, which had been made into a hospital.

There was the tramp of ascending feet on the stairs, and then the surgeon and the village doctor came in and asked her to leave the room.

It seemed a long time, but it was only half an hour, when Dr. Anderson came out.

"It's all right," he said.

"What are the chances?" she asked.

"There aren't any," he replied; "that is, perhaps only one in a million—"

She looked alarmed.

"Of anything unpleasant happening," he went on. "We got it just in time. Your son is better off than other boys who wear their appendices. His is in a bottle."

The doorbell sounded faintly from the rear of the house, and they both listened. A moment later the front door opened, and she heard voices in the lower hall.

"They're a lot of people who've come in to play bridge. I'd forgotten about them," she said. "Will you tell them I'll be down presently?"

She went into the nursery, and Dr. Anderson went downstairs.

When she came down she found them in the dining room, watching the surgeon and Curtis eating supper, and asking them questions about the operation.

Her eyes caught Willie's. He was quiet and white. He drew a chair for her, and she sat down next to him. She put her hand in his.

"It's all right," she said.

"It was an awfully close shave," he whispered.

"Yes, it was," she answered.

She turned to Dr. Anderson. "You were good to come,"

she said. "What would we have done if you hadn't been at home when Mr. Curtis telephoned?"

"Telephoned?" he repeated.

Curtis got up and went to the sideboard for a whiskey decanter.

"Yes, telephoned," she said.

The surgeon looked at Curtis.

"Mary," said Curtis, "the telephone wires were down. Tim went to town for the doctor."

She looked around in amazement.

"But we didn't know till nearly half past six," she exclaimed. She turned to Dr. Anderson. "You caught the eight o'clock train. How did Tim go?"

"On horseback," said Curtis.

"But that's twenty miles!" said Willie.

"Twenty-one," said Curtis; "he went in an hour and a quarter."

There was silence for a moment. Then she spoke.

"What horse did he ride?" she demanded.

"What horse have we that could have done it?" replied Curtis.

She looked at him for a moment in apprehension. "Is he all right?" she asked.

"I don't know," said Curtis. "Tim came back by train."

"Send for Tim," she said to the butler.

Tim came, and stood fumbling with his cap, which was soggy with melted snow.

"Weren't you frozen?" she asked.

"No, ma'am," the boy answered.

"Tell me about it," she said.

"Tell about it?" repeated the boy. "Why, ma'am—" he grew confused and stopped.

"But tell me," she hesitated, and her lip trembled, "tell me how Ting-a-ling is."

The boy made no answer, but looked toward the surgeon.

She turned to Dr. Anderson. "What is it?" she demanded.

"I was starting out to dine," said the surgeon, "when a policeman came to the door and said there was a sick horse on the corner, and a boy with him who wanted to see me. I went and found them both there."

"Well?" said Mrs. Curtis.

"Well," said the doctor, "as I reached the corner the crosstown trolley car was letting off a passenger. When the bell rang to start, the horse in the street lifted his head, scrambled to his feet, staggered a step forward, and came down again. He was dead."

There was a stillness in the room, and the crying of a sick baby sounded faintly from upstairs. Presently it ceased. For an instant the wife's eyes met those of her husband. Then resting her elbows on the table, she hid her face in her hands.

"God forgive me!" they heard Willie murmur in a queer voice. "That was a horse!"

"A streetcar horse," said Curtis, gently.

No one spoke again, but each rose and left the dining room.

Shoeing a horse.

A French Norman horse.

THE STORY OF A JOCKEY

by Richard Harding Davis

YOUNG Charley Chadwick had been brought up on his father's farm in New Jersey. The farm had been his father's before his father died, and was still called Chadwick's Meadows in his memory. It was a very small farm, and for the most part covered with clover and long, rich grass, that were good for pasturing, and nothing else. Charley was too young, and Mrs. Chadwick was too much of a housekeeper and not enough of a farmer's wife, to make the most out of the farm, and so she let the meadows to the manager of the Cloverdale Stock Farm. This farm is only half a mile back from the Monmouth Park race track at Long Branch.

The manager put a number of young colts in it to pasture, and took what grass they did not eat to the farm. Charley used to ride these colts back to the big stables at night, and soon grew to ride very well, and to know a great deal about horses and horse breeding and horse racing. Sometimes they gave him a mount at the stables, and he was permitted to ride one of the race horses around the private track, while the owner took the time from the judges' stand.

There was nothing in his life that he enjoyed like this. He had had very few pleasures, and the excitement and delight of tearing through the air on the back of a great animal was something he thought must amount to more than anything else in the world. His mother did not approve of his spending his time at the stables, but she found it very hard to refuse him, and he seemed to have a happy faculty of picking up only what was good, and letting what was evil pass by him and leave him unhurt. The good that he picked up was his love for animals, his thoughtfulness for them, and the forbearance and gentleness it taught him to use, with even the higher class of animals who walk on two legs.

He was fond of all the horses, because they were horses; but the one he liked best was Heroine, a big black mare that ran like an express train. He and Heroine were the two greatest friends in the stable. The horse loved him as a horse does love its master sometimes, and though Charley was not her owner, he was in reality her master, for Heroine would have left her stall and carried Charley off to the ends of the continent if he had asked her to run away.

When a man named Oscar Behren bought Heroine, Charley thought he would never be contented again. He cried about it all along the country road from the stables to his home, and cried about it again that night in bed. He knew Heroine would feel just as badly about it as he did, if she could know they were to be separated. Heroine went off to run in the races for which her new master had entered her, and Charley heard of her only through the newspapers. She won often, and became a great favorite, and Charley was afraid she would forget the master of her earlier days before she became so famous. And when he found that Heroine was entered to run at the Monmouth Park race track, he became as excited over the prospect of seeing his old friend again, as though he were going to meet his promised bride, or a long-lost brother who had accumulated several millions in South America.

He was at the station to meet the Behren horses, and Heroine knew him at once and he knew Heroine, although she was all blanketed up and had grown so much more

Heroine, who ran like an express train.
THE STORY OF A JOCKEY

beautiful to look at that it seemed like a second and improved edition of the horse he had known. Heroine won several races at Long Branch, and though her owner was an unpopular one, and one of whom many queer stories were told, still Heroine was always ridden to win, and win she generally did.

The race for the July Stakes was the big race of the meeting, and Heroine was the favorite. Behren was known to be backing her with thousands of dollars, and it was almost impossible to get anything but even money on her. The day before the race McCallen, the jockey who was to ride her, was taken ill, and Behren was in great anxiety and greatly disturbed as to where he could get a good substitute. Several people told him it made no difference, for the mare was as sure as sure could be, no matter who rode her. Then some one told him of Charley, who had taken out a license when the racing season began, and who had ridden a few unimportant mounts.

Behren looked for Charley and told him he would want him to ride for the July Stakes, and Charley went home to tell his mother about it, in a state of wild delight. To ride the favorite, and that favorite in such a great race, was as much to him as to own and steer the winning yacht in the transatlantic match for the cup.

He told Heroine all about it, and Heroine seemed very well pleased. But while he was standing hidden in Heroine's box stall, he heard something outside that made him wonder. It was Behren's voice, and he said in a low tone:

"Oh, McCallen's well enough, but I didn't want him for this race. He knows too much. The lad I've got now, this country boy, wouldn't know if the mare had the blind staggers."

Charley thought over this a great deal, and all that he had learned on the tracks and around the stables came to assist him in judging what it was that Behren meant; and that afternoon he found out.

The race track with the great green enclosures and the grand stand as high as a hill were as empty as a college campus in vacation time, but for a few of the stable boys and some of the owners and a waiter or two. It was interesting to think what it would be like a few hours later when the trains had arrived from New York with eleven cars each and the passengers hanging from the steps, and the carriages stretched all the way from Long Branch. Then there would not be a vacant seat on the grand stand or a blade of grass untrampled.

Charley was not nervous when he thought of this, but he was very much excited. Howland S. Maitland, who owned a stable of horses and a great many other expensive things, and who was one of those gentlemen who make the racing of horses possible, and Curtis, the secretary of the meeting, came walking towards Charley looking in at the different horses in the stalls.

"Heroine," said Mr. Maitland, as he read the name over the door. "Can we have a look at her?" he said.

Charley got up and took off his hat.

"I am sorry, Mr. Maitland," he said, "but my orders from Mr. Behren are not to allow any one inside. I am sure if Mr. Behren were here he would be very glad to show you the horse; but you see, I'm responsible, sir and—"

"Oh, that's all right!" said Mr. Maitland pleasantly, as he moved on.

"There's Mr. Behren now," Charley called after him, as Behren turned the corner. "I'll run and ask him."

"No, no, thank you," said Mr. Maitland hurriedly, and Charley heard him add to Mr. Curtis, "I don't want to know the man." It hurt Charley to find that the owner of Heroine and the man for whom he was to ride was held in such bad repute that a gentleman like Mr. Maitland would not know him, and he tried to console himself by thinking that it was better he rode Heroine than some less conscientious jockey whom Behren might order to play tricks with the horse and the public. Mr. Behren came up with a friend, a red-faced man with a white derby hat. He pointed at Charley with his cane. "My new jockey," he said. "How's the mare?" he asked.

"Very fit, sir," Charley answered.

"Had her feed yet?"

"No," Charley said.

The feed was in a trough which the stable boy had lifted outside into the sun. They were mixing it under Charley's supervision, for as a rider he did not stoop to such menial work as carrying the water and feed; but he always overlooked the others when they did it. Behren scooped up a handful and examined it carefully.

"It's not as fresh as it ought to be for the price they ask," he said to the friend with him. Then he threw the handful of feed back into the trough and ran his hand through it again, rubbing it between his thumb and fingers and tasting it critically. Then they passed on up the row.

Charley sat down again on an overturned bucket and looked at the feed trough, then he said to the stable boys, "You fellows can go now and get something to eat if you want to." They did not wait to be urged. Charley carried the trough inside the stable and took up a handful of the feed and looked and sniffed at it. It was fresh from his own barn; he had brought it over himself in a cart that morning. Then he tasted it with the end of his tongue and his face changed. He glanced around him quickly to see if any one had noticed, and then, with the feed still clenched in his hand, ran out and looked anxiously up and down the length of the stable. Mr. Maitland and Curtis were returning from the other end of the road.

"Can I speak to you a moment, sir?" said Charley anxiously; "will you come in here just a minute? It's most important, sir. I have something to show you."

The two men looked at the boy curiously, and halted in

front of the door. Charley added nothing further to what he had said, but spread a newspaper over the floor of the stable and turned the feed trough over on it. Then he stood up over the pile and said, "Would you both please taste that?"

There was something in his manner which made questions unnecessary. The two gentlemen did as he asked. Then Mr. Curtis looked into Mr. Maitland's face, which was full of doubt and perplexity, with one of angry suspicion.

"Cooked," he said.

"It does taste strangely," commented the horse owner gravely.

"Look at it; you can see if you look close enough," urged Curtis excitedly. "Do you see that green powder on my finger? Do you know what that is? An ounce of that would turn a horse's stomach as dry as a limekiln. Where did you get this feed?" he demanded of Charley.

"Out of our barn," said the boy. "And no one has touched it except myself, the stable boys, and the owner."

"Who are the stable boys?" demanded Mr. Curtis.

"Who's the owner?" asked Charley.

"Do you know what you are saying?" warned Mr. Maitland sharply. "You had better be careful."

"Careful!" said Charley indignantly. "I will be careful enough."

He went over to Heroine, and threw his arm up over her neck. He was terribly excited and trembling all over. The mare turned her head toward him and rubbed her nose against his face.

"That's all right," said Charley. "Don't you be afraid. I'll take care of *you*."

The two men were whispering together.

"I don't know anything about you," said Mr. Maitland to Charley. "I don't know what your idea was in dragging me

into this. I'm sure I wish I was out of it. But this I do
know, if Heroine isn't herself today, and doesn't run as she
has run before, and I say it though my own horses are in
against her, I'll have you and your owner before the
Racing Board, and you'll lose your license and be ruled off
every track in the country."

"One of us will," said Charley stubbornly. "All I want
you to do, Mr. Maitland, is to put some of that stuff in your
pocket. If anything is wrong they will believe what you
say, when they wouldn't listen to me. That's why I called
you in. I haven't charged anyone with anything. I only
asked you and Mr. Curtis to taste the feed that this horse
was to have eaten. That's all. And I'm not afraid of the
Racing Board, either, if the men on it are honest."

Mr. Curtis took some letters out of his pocket and filled
the envelopes with the feed, and then put them back in his
pocket, and Charley gathered up the feed in a bucket and
emptied it out of the window at the back of the stable.

"I think Behren should be told of this," said Mr.
Maitland.

Charley laughed; he was still excited and angry. "You
had better find out which way Mr. Behren is betting,
first," he said, "if you can."

"Don't mind the boy. Come away," said Mr. Curtis. "We
must look into this."

The Fourth of July holiday makers had begun to arrive;
and there were thousands of them, and they had a great
deal of money, and they wanted to bet it all on Heroine.
Everybody wanted to bet on Heroine; and the men in the
betting ring obliged them. But there were three men from
Boston who were betting on the field against the favorite.
They distributed their bets in small sums of money among
a great many different bookmakers; even the oldest of the
racing men did not know them. But Mr. Behren seemed to
know them. He met one of them openly, in front of the

Before the race.
THE STORY OF A JOCKEY

grand stand, and the stranger from Boston asked politely if he could trouble him for a light. Mr. Behren handed him his cigar, and while the man puffed at it he said:

"We've got $50,000 of it up. It's too much to risk on that powder. Something might go wrong; you mightn't have mixed it properly, or there mayn't be enough. I've known it miss before this. Minerva she won once with an ounce of it inside her. You'd better fix that jockey."

Mr. Behren's face was troubled, and he puffed quickly at his cigar as the man walked away. Then he turned and moved slowly towards the stables. A gentleman with a field glass across his shoulder stopped him and asked, "How's Heroine?" and Mr. Behren answered, "Never better; I've $10,000 on her," and passed on with a confident smile. Charley saw Mr. Behren coming, and bit his lip and tried to make his face look less conscious. He was not used to deception. He felt much more like plunging a pitchfork into Mr. Behren's legs; but he restrained that impulse, and chewed gravely on a straw. Mr. Behren looked carefully around the stable, and wiped the perspiration from his fat red face. The day was warm, and he was excited.

"Well, my boy," he said in a friendly, familiar tone as he seated himself, "it's almost time. I hope you are not rattled." Charley said "No," he felt confident enough.

"It would be a big surprise if she went back on us, wouldn't it?" suggested the owner gloomily.

"It would, indeed," said Charley.

"Still," said Mr. Behren, "such things have been. Racin' is full of surprises, and horses are full of tricks. I've known a horse, now, get pocketed behind two or three others and never show to the front at all. Though she was the best of the field, too. And I've known horses go wild and jump over the rail and run away with the jock, and, sometimes, they fall. And sometimes I've had a jockey pull a horse on me and make me drop every cent I had up. You wouldn't

do that, would you?" he asked. He looked up at Charley
with a smile that might mean anything. Charley looked at
the floor and shrugged his shoulders.

"I ride to orders, I do," he said. "I guess the owner
knows his own business best. When I ride for a man and
take his money I believe he should have his say. Some
jockeys ride to win. I ride according to orders." He did not
look up after this, and he felt thankful that Heroine could
not understand the language of human beings. Mr. Behr-
en's face rippled with smiles. This was a jockey after his
own heart. "If Heroine should lose," he said, "I say, if she
should, for no one knows what might happen, I'd have to
abuse you fearful right before all the people. I'd swear at
you and say you lost me all my money, and that you should
never ride for me again. And they might suspend you for a
month or two, which would be very hard on you," he
added reflectively. "But then," he said more cheerfully, "if
you had a little money to live on while you were suspended
it wouldn't be so hard, would it?" He took a large roll of
bank bills from his pocket and counted them, smoothing
them out on his fat knee and smiling up at the boy.

"It wouldn't be so bad, would it?" he repeated. Then he
counted aloud, "Eight hundred, nine hundred, one thousand." He rose and placed the bills under a loose plank of
the floor, and stamped it down on them. "I guess we
understand each other, eh?" he said.

"I guess we do," said Charley.

"I'll have to swear at you, you know," said Behren,
smiling.

"I can stand that," Charley answered.

* * * * * * * *

As the horses paraded past for the July Stakes, the
people rushed forward down the inclined enclosure and
crushed against the rail and cheered whichever horse they
best fancied.

"Say, you," called one of the crowd to Charley, "you

want to win, you do. I've got $5 on that horse you're a-riding." Charley ran his eyes over the crowd that were applauding and cheering him and Heroine, and calculated coolly that if every one had only $5 on Heroine there would be at least $100,000 on the horse in all.

The man from Boston stepped up beside Mr. Behren as he sat on his dogcart alone.

"The mare looks very fit," he said anxiously. "Her eyes are like diamonds. I don't believe that stuff affected her at all."

"It's all right," whispered Behren calmly. "I've fixed the boy." The man dropped back off the wheel of the cart with a sigh of relief, and disappeared in the crowd. Mr. Maitland and Mr. Curtis sat together on the top of the former's coach. Mr. Curtis had his hand over the packages of feed in his pockets. "If the mare don't win," he said, "there will be the worst scandal this track has ever known." The perspiration was rolling down his face. "It will be the death of honest racing."

"I cannot understand it," said Mr. Maitland. "The boy seemed honest, too."

The horses got off together. There were eleven of them. Heroine was amongst the last, but no one minded that because the race was a long one. And within three-quarters of a mile of home Heroine began to shake off the others and came up slowly through the crowd, and her thousands of admirers yelled. And then Maitland's Good Morning and Reilly swerved in front of her, or else Heroine fell behind them, it was hard to tell which, and Lady Betty closed in on her from the right. Her jockey seemed to be trying his best to get her out of the triangular pocket into which she had run. The great crowd simultaneously gave an anxious questioning gasp. Then two more horses pushed to the front, closing the favorite in and shutting her off altogether.

"The horse is pocketed," cried Mr. Curtis, "and not one man out of a thousand would know that it was done on purpose."

"Wait!" said Mr. Maitland.

"Bless that boy!" murmured Behren, trying his best to look anxious. "She can never pull out of that." They were within half a mile of home. The crowd was panic-stricken and jumping up and down. "Heroine!" they cried, as wildly as though they were calling for help, or the police— "Heroine!"

Charley heard them above the noise of the pounding hoofs, and smiled in spite of the mud and dirt that the great horses in front flung in his face and eyes.

"Heroine," he said, "I think we've scared that crowd about long enough. Now, punish Behren." He sank his spurs into the horse's sides and jerked her head towards a little opening between Lady Betty and Chubb. Heroine sprang at it like a tiger and came neck to neck with the leader. And then, as she saw the wide track empty before her, and no longer felt the hard backward pull on her mouth, she tossed her head with a snort, and flew down the stretch like an express, with her jockey whispering fiercely in her ear.

Heroine won with a grand rush, by three lengths, but Charley's face was filled with anxiety as he tossed up his arm in front of the judges' stand. He was covered with mud and perspiration, and panting with exertion and excitement. He distinguished Mr. Curtis' face in the middle of the wild crowd around him, that patted his legs and hugged and kissed Heroine's head, and danced up and down in the ecstasy of delight.

"Mr. Curtis," he cried, raising his voice above the tumult of the crowd, and forgetting or not caring, that they could hear, "send someone to the stable, quick. There's a thousand dollars there Behren offered me to pull the horse. It's under a plank near the back door. Get it before he does. That's evidence the Racing Board can't—"

But before he could finish, or before Mr. Curtis could push his way towards him, a dozen stable boys and betting men had sprung away with a yell towards the stable, and the mob dashed after them. It gathered in volume as a landslide does when it goes down hill; and the people in the grandstand and on the coaches stood up and asked what was the matter; and some cried, "Stop thief!" and others cried "Fight!" and others said that a bookmaker had given big odds against Heroine, and was "doing a welsh." The mob swept around the corner of the long line of stables like a charge of cavalry, and dashed at Heroine's lodgings. The door was open, and on his knees at the other end was Behren, digging at the planks with his fingernails. He had seen that the boy had intentionally deceived him; and his first thought, even before that of his great losses, was to get possession of the thousand dollars that might be used against him. He turned his fat face, now white with terror, over his shoulder, as the crowd crushed into the stable, and tried to rise from his knees; but before he could get up, the first man struck him between the eyes, and others fell on him, pummeling him and kicking him and beating him down. If they had lost their money, instead of having won, they could not have handled him more brutally. Two policemen and a couple of men with pitchforks drove them back; and one of the officers lifted up the plank, and counted the thousand dollars before the crowd.

Either Mr. Maitland felt badly at having doubted Charley, or else he admired his riding; for he bought Heroine when Behren was ruled off the race tracks and had to sell his horses, and Charley became his head jockey. And just as soon as Heroine began to lose, Mr. Maitland refused to have her suffer such a degradation,

On the homestretch.
THE STORY OF A JOCKEY

and said she should stop while she could still win. And then he presented her to Charley, who had won so much and so often with her; and Charley gave up his license and went back to the farm to take care of his mother, and Heroine played all day in the clover fields.

The Mexican horse.
Illustration by Frederic Remington

In with the herd.
Illustration by Frederic Remington

THE PACING MUSTANG

by Ernest Thompson Seton

I

JO Calone threw down his saddle on the dusty ground, turned his horses loose, and went clanking into the ranch-house.

"Nigh about chuck time?" he asked.

"Seventeen minutes," said the cook glancing at the Waterbury, with the air of a train starter, though this show of precision had never yet been justified by events.

"How's things on the Perico?" said Jo's pard.

"Hotter'n hinges," said Jo. "Cattle seem O.K.; lots of calves."

* * * * * * * *

"I seen that bunch o' mustangs that waters at Antelope Springs; couple o' colts along: one little dark one, a fair dandy, a born pacer. I run them a mile or two, and he led the bunch, an' never broke his pace. Cut loose, an' pushed them jest for fun, an' darned if I could make him break."

"You didn't have no reefreshments along?" said Scarth, incredulously.

"That's all right, Scarth. You had to crawl on our last bet, an' you'll get another chance soon as you're man enough."

"Chuck," shouted the cook, and the subject was dropped. Next day the scene of the roundup was changed, and the mustangs were forgotten.

A year later the same corner of New Mexico was
worked over by the roundup, and again the mustang
bunch was seen. The dark colt was now a black yearling,
with thin, clean legs and glossy flanks; and more than one
of the boys saw with his own eyes this oddity—the
mustang was a born pacer.

Jo was along, and the idea now struck him that the colt
was worth having. To an Easterner this thought may not
seem startling or original, but in the West, where an
unbroken horse is worth $5, and where an ordinary
saddlehorse is worth $15 or $20, the idea of a wild mustang
being desirable property does not occur to the average
cowboy, for mustangs are hard to catch, and when caught
are merely wild animal prisoners, perfectly useless and
untamable to the last. Not a few of the cattle owners make
a point of shooting all mustangs at sight, for they are not
only useless cumberers of the feeding grounds, but com-
monly lead away domestic horses, which soon take to the
wild life and are thenceforth lost.

Wild Jo Calone knew a "bronk right down to subsoil." "I
never seen a white that wasn't soft, nor a chestnut that
wasn't nervous, nor a bay that wasn't good if broke right,
nor a black that wasn't hard as nails, an' full of the old
Harry. All a black bronk wants is claws to be wus'n
Daniel's hull outfit of lions."

Since then a mustang is worthless vermin, and a black
mustang ten times worse than worthless, Jo's pard "didn't
see no sense in Jo's wantin' to corral the yearling," as he
now seemed intent on doing. But Jo got no chance to try
that year.

He was only a cowpuncher on $25 a month, and tied to
hours. Like most of the boys, he always looked forward to
having a ranch and an outfit of his own. His brand, the
hogpen, of sinister suggestion, was already registered at
Santa Fe, but of horned stock it was borne by a single old

Wild mustang colts.
THE PACING MUSTANG

cow, so as to give him a legal right to put his brand on any maverick (or unbranded animal) he might chance to find.

Yet each fall, when paid off, Jo could not resist the temptation to go to town with the boys and have a good time "while the stuff held out." So that his property consisted of little more than his saddle, his bed, and his old cow. He kept on hoping to make a strike that would leave him well fixed with a fair start, and when the thought came that the Black Mustang was his mascot, he only needed a chance to "make the try."

The roundup circled down to the Canadian River, and back in the fall by the Don Carlos Hills, and Jo saw no more of the Pacer, though he heard of him from many quarters, for the colt, now a vigorous, young horse, rising three, was beginning to be talked of.

Antelope Springs is in the middle of a great level plain. When the water is high it spreads into a small lake with a belt of sedge around it; when it is low there is a wide flat of black mud, glistening white with alkali in places and the spring a water hole in the middle. It has no flow or outlet and yet is fairly good water, the only drinking place for many miles.

This flat, or prairie as it would be called farther north, was the favorite feeding ground of the Black Stallion, but it was also the pasture of many herds of range horses and cattle. Chiefly interested was the "L cross F" outfit. Foster, the manager and part owner, was a man of enterprise. He believed it would pay to handle a better class of cattle and horses on the range, and one of his ventures was ten half-blooded mares, tall, clean-limbed, deer-eyed creatures, that made the scrub cowponies look like pitiful starvelings of some degenerate and quite different species.

One of these was kept stabled for use, but the nine, after the weaning of their colts, managed to get away and wandered off on the range.

A horse has a fine instinct for the road to the best feed, and the nine mares drifted, of course, to the prairie of Antelope Springs, twenty miles to the southward. And when, later that summer Foster went to round them up, he found the nine indeed, but with them and guarding them with an air of more than mere comradeship was a coal-black stallion, prancing around and rounding up the bunch like an expert, his jet-black coat a vivid contrast to the golden hides of his harem.

The mares were gentle, and would have been easily driven homeward but for a new and unexpected thing. The Black Stallion became greatly aroused. He seemed to inspire them too with his wildness, and flying this way and that way drove the whole band at full gallop where he would. Away they went, and the little cowponies that carried the men were easily left behind.

This was maddening, and both men at last drew their guns and sought a chance to drop that "blasted stallion." But no chance came that was not 9 to 1 of dropping one of the mares. A long day of maneuvering made no change. The Pacer, for it was he, kept his family together and disappeared among the southern sandhills. The cattlemen on their jaded ponies set out for home with the poor satisfaction of vowing vengeance for their failure on the superb cause of it.

One of the most aggravating parts of it was that one or two experiences like this would surely make the mares as wild as the Mustang, and there seemed to be no way of saving them from it.

Scientists differ on the power of beauty and prowess to attract female admiration among the lower animals, but whether it is admiration or the prowess itself, it is certain that a wild animal of uncommon gifts soon wins a large following from the harems of his rivals. And the great Black Horse, with his inky mane and tail and his green-lighted eyes, ranged through all that region and added to his following from many bands till not less than a score of mares were in his "bunch." Most were merely humble cowponies turned out to range, but the nine great mares were there, a striking group by themselves. According to all reports, this bunch was always kept rounded up and guarded with such energy and jealousy that a mare, once in it, was a lost animal so far as man was concerned, and the ranchmen realized soon that they had gotten on the range a mustang that was doing them more harm than all other sources of loss put together.

II

It was December, 1893. I was new in the country, and was setting out from the ranch-house on the Piñavetitos, to go with a wagon to the Canadian River. As I was leaving, Foster finished his remark by: "And if you get a chance to draw a bead on that accursed mustang, don't fail to drop him in his tracks."

This was the first I had heard of him, and as I rode along I gathered from Burns, my guide, the history that has been given. I was full of curiosity to see the famous three-year-old, and was not a little disappointed on the second day when we came to the prairie on Antelope Springs and saw no sign of the Pacer or his band.

But on the next day, as we crossed the Alamosa Arroyo, and were rising to the rolling prairie again, Jack Burns, who was riding on ahead, suddenly dropped flat on the neck of his horse, and swung back to me in the wagon, saying:

"Get out your rifle, here's that ——— stallion."

I seized my rifle, and hurried forward to a view over the prairie ridge. In the hollow below was a band of horses, and there at one end was the Great Black Mustang. He had heard some sound of our approach, and was not unsuspicious of danger. There he stood with head and tail erect, and nostrils wide, an image of horse perfection and beauty, as noble an animal as ever ranged the plains, and the mere notion of turning that magnificent creature into a mass of carrion was horrible. In spite of Jack's exhortation to "shoot quick," I delayed, and threw open the breach, whereupon he, always hot and hasty, swore at my slowness, growled, "Gi' me that gun," and as he seized it I turned the muzzle up, and *accidentally* the gun went off.

Instantly the herd below was all alarm, the great black leader snorted and neighed and dashed about. And the mares bunched, and away all went in a rumble of hoofs, and a cloud of dust.

The Stallion careered now on this side, now on that, and kept his eye on all and led and drove them far away. As long as I could see I watched, and never once did he break his pace.

Jack made Western remarks about me and my gun as well as that mustang, but I rejoiced in the Pacer's strength and beauty, and not for all the mares in the bunch would I have harmed his glossy hide.

III

There are several ways of capturing wild horses. One is by creasing—that is, grazing the animal's nape with a rifle-ball so that he is stunned long enough for hobbling.

"Yes! I seen about a hundred necks broke trying it, but I never seen a mustang creased yet," was Wild Jo's critical remark.

Sometimes, if the shape of the country abets it, the herd can be driven into a corral; sometimes with extra fine mounts they can be run down, but by far the commonest way, paradoxical as it may seem, is to *walk* them down.

The fame of the Stallion that never was known to gallop

was spreading. Extraordinary stories were told of his gait, his speed, and his wind, and when old Montgomery of the "triangle-bar" outfit came out plump at Well's Hotel in Clayton, and in presence of witnesses said he'd give one thousand dollars cash for him safe in a boxcar, providing the stories were true, a dozen young cowpunchers were eager to cut loose and win the purse, as soon as present engagements were up. But Wild Jo had had his eye on this very deal for quite a while; there was no time to lose, so ignoring present contracts he rustled all night to raise the necessary equipment for the game.

By straining his already overstrained credit, and taxing the already overtaxed generosity of his friends, he got together an expedition consisting of twenty good saddle horses, a mess-wagon, and a fortnight's stuff for three men—himself, his "pard," Charley, and the cook.

Then they set out from Clayton, with the avowed intention of walking down the wonderfully swift wild horse. The third day they arrived at Antelope Springs, and as it was about noon they were not surprised to see the black Pacer marching down to drink with all his band behind him. Jo kept out of sight until the wild horses each and all had drunk their fill, for a thirsty animal always travels better than one laden with water.

Jo then rode quietly forward. The Pacer took alarm at half a mile, and led his band away out of sight on the soapweed mesa to the southeast. Jo followed at a gallop till he once more sighted them, then came back and instructed the cook, who was also teamster, to make for Alamosa Arroyo in the south. Then away to the southeast he went after the mustangs. After a mile or two he once more sighted them, and walked his horse quietly till so near that they again took alarm and circled away to the south. An hour's trot, not on the trail, but cutting across to where they ought to go, brought Jo again in close sight. Again he walked quietly toward the herd, and again there was the alarm and flight. And so they passed the afternoon, but circled ever more and more to the south, so that when the sun was low they were, as Jo had expected, not far from Alamosa Arroyo. The band was again close at hand, and Jo, after starting them off, rode to the wagon, while his pard, who had been taking it easy, took up the slow chase on a fresh horse.

After supper the wagon moved on to the upper ford of the Alamosa, as arranged, and there camped for the night.

Meanwhile, Charley followed the herd. They had not run so far as at first, for their pursuer made no sign of attack, and they were getting used to his company. They were more easily found, as the shadows fell, on account of a snow-white mare that was in the bunch. A young moon in the sky now gave some help, and relying on his horse to choose the path, Charley kept him quietly walking after the herd, represented by that ghost-white mare, till they were lost in the night. He then got off, unsaddled and picketed his horse, and in his blanket quickly went to sleep.

At the first streak of dawn he was up, and within a short half-mile, thanks to the snowy mare, he found the band. At his approach, the shrill neigh of the Pacer bugled his troop into a flying squad. But on the first mesa they stopped, and faced about to see what this persistent follower was, and what he wanted. For a moment or so they stood against the sky to gaze, and then deciding that he knew him as well as he wished to, that black meteor flung his mane on the wind, and led off at his tireless, even swing, while the mares came streaming after.

Away they went, circling now to the west, and after several repetitions of this same play, flying, following, and overtaking, and flying again, they passed, near noon, the old Apache lookout, Buffalo Bluff. And here, on watch, was Jo. A long thin column of smoke told Charley to come to camp, and with a flashing pocket mirror he made response.

Jo, freshly mounted, rode across, and again took up the chase, and back came Charley to camp to eat and rest, and then move on up stream.

All that day Jo followed, and managed, when it was needed, that the herd should keep the great circle, of which the wagon cut a small chord. At sundown he came to Verde Crossing, and there was Charley with a fresh horse and food, and Jo went on in the same calm, dogged way. All the evening he followed, and far into the night, for the wild herd was now getting somewhat used to the presence of the harmless strangers, and were more easily followed; moreover, they were tiring out with perpetual travelling. They were no longer in the good grass country, they were not grain-fed like the horses on their track, and above all, the slight but continuous nervous tension was surely telling. It spoiled their appetites, but made them very thirsty. They were allowed, and as far as possible encouraged, to drink deeply at every chance. The effect of large quantities of water on a running animal is well-known; it tends to stiffen the limbs and spoil the wind. Jo carefully guarded his own horse against such excess, and both he and his horse were fresh when they camped that night on the trail of the jaded mustangs.

At dawn he found them easily close at hand, and though they ran at first they did not go far before they dropped into a walk. The battle seemed nearly won now, for the chief difficulty in the "walk-down" is to keep track of the herd the first two or three days when they are fresh.

All that morning Jo kept in sight, generally in close sight, of the band. About ten o'clock, Charley relieved him near José Peak and that day the mustangs walked only a quarter of a mile ahead with much less spirit than the day

Pursuing the stallion.
THE PACING MUSTANG
Illustration by Frederic Remington

before and circled now more north again. At night Charley
was supplied with a fresh horse and followed as before.

Next day the mustangs walked with heads held low, and
in spite of the efforts of the Black Pacer at times they were
less than a hundred yards ahead of their pursuer.

The fourth and fifth days passed the same way, and now
the herd was nearly back to Antelope Springs. So far all
had come out as expected. The chase had been in a great
circle with the wagon following a lesser circle. The wild
herd was back to its starting point, worn out; and the
hunters were back, fresh and on fresh horses. The herd
was kept from drinking till late in the afternoon and then
driven to the Springs to swell themselves with a perfect
water gorge. Now was the chance for the skilful ropers on
the grain-fed horses to close in, for the sudden heavy drink
was ruination, almost paralysis, of wind and limb, and it
would be easy to rope and hobble them one by one.

There was only one weak spot in the programme, the
Black Stallion, the cause of the hunt, seemed made of iron,
that ceaseless swinging pace seemed as swift and vigorous
now as on the morning when the chase began. Up and
down he went rounding up the herd and urging them on by
voice and example to escape. But they were played out.
The old white mare that had been such help in sighting
them at night, had dropped out hours ago, dead beat. The
half-bloods seemed to be losing all fear of the horsemen,
the band was clearly in Jo's power. But the one who was
the prize of all the hunt seemed just as far as ever out of
reach.

Here was a puzzle. Jo's comrades knew him well and
would not have been surprised to see him in a sudden rage
attempt to shoot the Stallion down. But Jo had no such
mind. During that long week of following he had watched
the horse all day at speed and never once had he seen him
gallop.

The horseman's adoration of a noble horse had grown and grown, till now he would as soon have thought of shooting his best mount as firing on that splendid beast.

Jo even asked himself whether he would take the handsome sum that was offered for the prize. Such an animal would be a fortune in himself to sire a race of pacers for the track.

But the prize was still at large—the time had come to finish up the hunt. Jo's finest mount was caught. She was a mare of Eastern blood, but raised on the plains. She never would have come into Jo's possession but for a curious weakness. The loco is a poisonous weed that grows in these regions. Most stock will not touch it; but sometimes an animal tries it and becomes addicted to it. It acts somewhat like morphine, but the animal, though sane for long intervals, has always a passion for the herb and finally dies mad. A beast with the craze is said to be locoed. And Jo's best mount had a wild gleam in her eye that to an expert told the tale.

But she was swift and strong and Jo chose her for the grand finish of the chase. It would have been an easy matter now to rope the mares, but was no longer necessary. They could be separated from their black leader and driven home to the corral. But that leader still had the look of untamed strength. Jo, rejoicing in a worthy foe, went bounding forth to try the odds. The lasso was flung on the ground and trailed to take out every kink, and gathered as he rode into neatest coils across his left palm. Then putting on the spur the first time in that chase he rode straight for the Stallion a quarter of a mile beyond. Away he went, and away went Jo, each at his best, while the fagged out mares scattered right and left and let them pass. Straight across the open plain the fresh horse went at its hardest gallop, and the Stallion, leading off, still kept his start and kept his famous swing.

It was incredible, and Jo put on more spur and shouted to his horse, which fairly flew, but shortened up the space between by not a single inch. For the Black One whirled across the flat and up and passed a soapweed mesa and down across a sandy treacherous plain, then over a grassy stretch where prairie dogs barked, then hid below, and on came Jo, but there to see, could he believe his eyes, the Stallion's start grown longer still, and Jo began to curse his luck, and urge and spur his horse until the poor uncertain brute got into such a state of nervous fright, her eyes began to roll, she wildly shook her head from side to side, no longer picked her ground—a badger hole received her foot and down she went, and Jo went flying to the earth. Though badly bruised, he gained his feet and tried to mount his crazy beast. But she, poor brute, was done for—her off fore-leg hung loose.

There was but one thing to do. Jo loosed the cinch, put Lightfoot out of pain, and carried back the saddle to the camp. While the Pacer steamed away till lost to view.

This was not quite defeat, for all the mares were manageable now, and Jo and Charley drove them carefully to the "L cross F" corral and claimed a good reward. But Jo was more than ever bound to own the Stallion. He had seen what stuff he was made of, he prized him more and more, and only sought to strike some better plan to catch him.

IV

The cook on that trip was Bates—Mr. Thomas Bates, he called himself at the post office where he regularly went for the letters and remittance which never came. Old Tom Turkeytrack, the boys called him, from his cattle brand, which he said was on record at Denver, and which, according to his story, was also borne by countless beef and saddle stock on the plains of the unknown North.

When asked to join the trip as a partner, Bates made some sarcastic remarks about horses not fetching $12 a dozen, which had been literally true within the year, and he preferred to go on a very meagre salary. But no one who once saw the Pacer going had failed to catch the craze. Turkeytrack experienced the usual change of heart. He now wanted to own that mustang. How this was to be brought about he did not clearly see till one day there called at the ranch that had "secured his services," as he put it, one, Bill Smith, more usually known as Horseshoe Billy, from his cattle brand. While the excellent fresh beef and bread and the vile coffee, dried peaches and molasses were being consumed, he of the horseshoe remarked, in tones which percolated through a huge stopgap of bread:

"Wall, I seen that thar Pacer today, nigh enough to put a plait in his tail."

"What, you didn't shoot?"

"No, but I come mighty near it."

"Don't you be led into no sich foolishness," said a "double-bar H" cowpuncher at the other end of the table. "I calc'late that maverick 'ill carry my brand before the moon changes."

"You'll have to be pretty spry or you'll find a 'triangle dot' on his weather side when you get there."

"Where did you run acrost him?"

"Wall, it was like this; I was riding the flat by Antelope Springs and I sees a lump on the dry mud inside the rush belt. I knowed I never seen that before, so rides up, thinking it might be some of our stock, an' seen it was a horse lying plumb flat. The wind was blowing like —— from him to me, so I rides up close and seen it was the Pacer, dead as a mackerel. Still, he didn't look swelled or cut, and there wa'n't no smell, an' I didn't know what to think till I seen his ear twitch off a fly and then I knowed he was sleeping. I gits down me rope and coils it, and seen it was old and pretty shaky in spots, and me saddle a single cinch, an' me pony about 700 again a 1,200 lbs. stallion, an' I sez to meself, sez I: "'Tain't no use, I'll only break me cinch and git throwed an' lose me saddle." So I hits the saddle horn a crack with the hondu, and I wish't you'd a seen that mustang. He lept six foot in the air and snorted like he was shunting cars. His eyes fairly bugged out an' he lighted out lickety split for California, and he orter be there about now if he kep' on like he started—and I swear he never made a break the hull trip."

The story was not quite so consecutive as given here. It was much punctuated by present engrossments, and from first to last was more or less infiltrated through the necessaries of life, for Bill was a healthy young man without a trace of false shame. But the account was complete and everyone believed it, for Billy was known to be reliable. Of all those who heard, old Turkeytrack talked the least and probably thought the most, for it gave him a new idea.

During his after-dinner pipe he studied it out and deciding that he could not go it alone, he took Horseshoe Billy into his council and the result was a partnership in a new venture to capture the Pacer; that is, the $5,000 that was now said to be the offer for him safe in a boxcar.

Antelope Springs was still the usual watering-place of the Pacer. The water being low left a broad belt of dry black mud between the sedge and the spring. At two places this belt was broken by a well-marked trail made by the animals coming to drink. Horses and wild animals usually kept to these trails, though the horned cattle had no hesitation in taking a short cut through the sedge.

In the most used of these trails the two men set to work with shovels and dug a pit 15 feet long, 6 feet wide and 7 feet deep. It was a hard twenty hours work for them as it had to be completed between the Mustang's drinks, and it began to be very damp work before it was finished. With poles, brush, and earth it was then cleverly covered over and concealed. And the men went to a distance and hid in pits made for the purpose.

About noon the Pacer came, alone now since the capture of his band. The trail on the opposite side of the mud belt was little used, and old Tom, by throwing some fresh rushes across it, expected to make sure that the Stallion would enter by the other, if indeed he should by any caprice try to come by the unusual path.

What sleepless angel is it watches over and cares for the wild animals? In spite of all reasons to take the usual path, the Pacer came along the other. The suspicious-looking rushes did not stop him; he walked calmly to the water and drank. There was only one way now to prevent utter failure; when he lowered his head for the second draft which horses always take, Bates and Smith quit their holes and ran swiftly toward the trail behind him, and when he raised his proud head Smith sent a revolver shot into the ground behind him.

Away went the Pacer at his famous gait straight to the trap. Another second and he would be into it. Already he is on the trail, and already they feel they have him, but the Angel of the wild things is with him, that incomprehensible warning comes, and with one mighty bound he clears the fifteen feet of treacherous ground and spurns the earth as he fades away unharmed, never again to visit Antelope Springs by either of the beaten paths.

V

Wild Jo never lacked energy. He meant to catch that Mustang, and when he learned that others were bestirring themselves for the same purpose he at once set about trying the best untried plan he knew—the plan by which the coyote catches the fleeter jackrabbit, and the mounted

Indian the far swifter antelope—the old plan of the relay chase.

The Canadian River on the south, its affluent, the Piñavetitos Arroyo, on the northeast, and the Don Carlos Hills with the Ute Creek Cañon on the west, formed a sixty-mile triangle that was the range of the Pacer. It was believed that he never went outside this, and at all times Antelope Springs was his headquarters. Jo knew this country well, all the water holes and cañon crossings as well as the ways of the Pacer.

If he could have gotten fifty good horses he could have posted them to advantage so as to cover all points, but twenty mounts and five good riders were all that proved available.

The horses, grain-fed for two weeks before, were sent on ahead; each man was instructed now to play his part and sent to his post the day before the race. On the day of the start Jo with his wagon drove to the plain of Antelope Springs and, camping far off in a little draw, waited.

At last he came, that coal-black Horse, out from the sand hills at the south, alone as always now, and walked calmly down to the Springs and circled quite around it to sniff for any hidden foe. Then he approached where there was no trail at all and drank.

Jo watched and wished he could drink a hogshead. But the moment that he turned and sought the grass Jo spurred his steed. The Pacer heard the hoofs, then saw the running horse, and did not want a nearer view but led away. Across the flat he went down to the south, and kept the famous swinging gait that made his start grow longer. Now through the sandy dunes he went, and steadying to an even pace he gained considerably and Jo's too-laden horse plunged through the sand and sinking fetlock deep, he lost at every bound. Then came a level stretch where the runner seemed to gain, and then a long decline where Jo's horse dared not run his best, so lost again at every step.

But on they went, and Jo spared neither spur nor quirt. A mile—a mile—and another mile, and the far off rock at Arriba loomed up ahead.

And there Jo knew fresh mounts were held, and on they dashed. But the night-black mane out level on the breeze ahead was gaining more and more.

Arriba Cañon reached at last, the watcher stood aside, for it was not wished to turn the race, and the Stallion passed—dashed down, across and up the slope, with that unbroken pace, the only one he knew.

And Jo came bounding on his foaming steed, and leaped on the waiting mount, then urged him down the slope and up upon the track, and on the upland once more drove in the spurs, and raced and raced, and raced, but not a single inch he gained.

Ga-lump, ga-lump, ga-lump with measured beat he went—an hour—an hour, and another hour—Arroyo Alamosa just ahead with fresh relays, and Jo yelled at his horse and pushed him on and on. Straight for the place the Black One made, but on the last two miles some strange foreboding turned him to the left, and Jo foresaw escape in this, and pushed his jaded mount at any cost to head him off, and hard as they had raced this was the hardest race of all, with gasps for breath and leather squeaks at every straining bound. Then cutting right across, Jo seemed to gain, and drawing his gun he fired shot after shot to toss the dust, and so turned the Stallion's head and forced him back to take the crossing to the right.

Down they went. The Stallion crossed and Jo sprang to the ground. His horse was done, for thirty miles had passed in the last stretch, and Jo himself was worn out.

His eyes were burnt with flying alkali dust. He was half blind so he motioned to his "pard" to "go ahead and keep him straight for Alamosa ford."

Out shot the rider on a strong, fresh, steed, and away they went—up and down on the rolling plain—the Black Horse flecked with snowy foam. His heaving ribs and noisy breath showed what he felt—but on and on he went.

And Tom on Ginger seemed to gain, then lose and lose, when in an hour the long decline of Alamosa came. And there a freshly mounted lad took up the chase and turned it west, and on they went past towns of prairie dogs, through soapweed tracts and cactus brakes by scores, and pricked and wrenched rode on. With dust and sweat the Black was now a dappled brown, but still he stepped the same. Young Carrington, who followed, had hurt his steed by pushing at the very start, and spurred and urged him now to cut across a gulch at which the Pacer shied. Just one misstep and down they went.

The boy escaped, but the pony lies there yet, and the wild Black Horse kept on.

This was close to old Gallego's ranch where Jo himself had cut across refreshed to push the chase. Within thirty minutes he was again scorching the Pacer's trail.

Far in the west the Carlos Hills were seen, and there Jo knew fresh men and mounts were waiting, and that way the indomitable rider tried to turn the race, but by a sudden whim, of the inner warning born perhaps—the Pacer turned. Sharp to the north he went, and Jo, the skilful wrangler, rode and rode and yelled and tossed the dust with shots, but down a gulch the wild black meteor streamed and Jo could only follow. Then came the hardest race of all; Jo, cruel to the Mustang, was crueller to his mount and to himself. The sun was hot, the scorching plain was dim in shimmering heat, his eyes and lips were burnt with sand and salt, and yet the chase sped on. The only

On and on he went.
THE PACING MUSTANG

chance to win would be if he could drive the Mustang back to Big Arroyo Crossing. Now almost for the first time he saw signs of weakening in the Black. His mane and tail were not just quite so high, and his short half mile of start was down by more than half, but still he stayed ahead and paced and paced and paced.

An hour and another hour, and still they went the same. But they turned again, and night was near when big Arroyo ford was reached—fully twenty miles. But Jo was game, he seized the waiting horse. The one he left went gasping to the stream and gorged himself with water till he died.

Then Jo held back in hopes the foaming Black would drink. But he was wise; he gulped a single gulp, splashed through the stream and then passed on with Jo at speed behind him. And when they last were seen the Black was on ahead just out of reach and Jo's horse bounding on.

It was morning when Jo came to camp on foot. His tale was briefly told: eight horses dead—five men worn out—the matchless Pacer safe and free.

"'Taint possible; it can't be done. Sorry I didn't bore his hellish carcass through when I had the chance," said Jo, and gave it up.

VI

Old Turkeytrack was cook on this trip. He had watched the chase with as much interest as anyone, and when it failed he grinned into the pot and said: "That mustang's mine unless I'm a darned fool." Then falling back on Scripture for a precedent, as was his habit, he still addressed the pot:

"Reckon the Philistines tried to run Samson down and they got done up, an' would a stayed done only for a nat'ral weakness on his part. An' Adam would a loafed in Eden yit ony for a leetle failing which we all onderstand. An' it ain't $5000 I'll take for him nuther."

Much persecution had made the Pacer wilder than ever. But it did not drive him away from Antelope Springs. That was the only drinking place with absolutely no shelter for a mile on every side to hide an enemy. Here he came almost every day about noon, and after thoroughly spying the land approached to drink.

His had been a lonely life all winter since the capture of his harem, and of this old Turkeytrack was fully aware. The old cook's chum had a nice little brown mare which he judged would serve his ends, and taking a pair of the strongest hobbles, a spade, a spare lasso, and a stout post he mounted the mare and rode away to the famous Springs.

A few antelope skimmed over the plain before him in the early freshness of the day. Cattle were lying about in groups, and the loud sweet song of the prairie lark was heard on every side. For the bright snowless winter of the mesas was gone and the springtime was at hand. The grass was greening and all nature seemed turning to thoughts of love.

It was in the air, and when the little brown mare was picketed out to graze she raised her nose from time to time to pour forth a long shrill whinny that surely was her song, if song she had, of love.

Old Turkeytrack studied the wind and the lay of the land. There was the pit he had labored at, now opened and filled with water that was rank with drowned prairie dogs and mice. Here was the new trail the animals were forced to make by the pit. He selected a sedgy clump near some smooth, grassy ground, and first firmly sunk the post, then dug a hole large enough to hide in, and spread his blanket in it. He shortened up the little mare's tether, till she could scarcely move; then on the ground between he

spread his open lasso, tying the long end to the post, then
covered the rope with dust and grass, and went into his
hiding-place.

About noon, after long waiting, the amorous whinny of
the mare was answered from the high ground, away to the
west, and there, black against the sky, was the famous
Mustang.

Down he came at that long swinging gait, but grown
crafty with much pursuit, he often stopped to gaze and
whinny, and got answer that surely touched his heart.
Nearer he came again to call, then took alarm, and paced
all around in a great circle to try the wind for his foes, and
seemed in doubt. The Angel whispered "Don't go." But
the brown mare called again. He circled nearer still, and
neighed once more, and got reply that seemed to quell all
fears, and set his heart aglow.

Nearer still he pranced, till he touched Solly's nose with
his own, and finding her as responsive as he well could
wish, thrust aside all thoughts of danger, and abandoned
himself to the delight of conquest, until, as he pranced
around, his hind legs for a moment stood within the evil
circle of the rope. One deft sharp twitch, the noose flew
tight, and he was caught.

A snort of terror and a bound in the air gave Tom the
chance to add the double hitch. The loop flashed up the
line, and snakelike bound those mighty hoofs.

Terror lent speed and double strength for a moment,
but the end of the rope was reached, and down he went a
captive, a hopeless prisoner at last. Old Tom's ugly, little
crooked form sprang from the pit to complete the master-
ing of the great glorious creature whose mighty strength
had proved as nothing when matched with the wits of a
little old man. With snorts and desperate bounds of awful
force the great beast dashed and struggled to be free; but
all in vain. The rope was strong.

The second lasso was deftly swung, and the forefeet caught, and then with a skilful move the feet were drawn together, and down went the raging Pacer to lie a moment later "hog-tied" and helpless on the ground. There he struggled till worn out, sobbing great convulsive sobs while tears ran down his cheeks.

Tom stood by and watched, but a strange revulsion of feeling came over the old cow-puncher. He trembled nervously from head to foot, as he had not done since he roped his first steer, and for a while could do nothing but gaze on his tremendous prisoner. But the feeling soon passed away. He saddled Delilah, and taking the second lasso, roped the great horse about the neck, and left the mare to hold the Stallion's head, while he put on the hobbles. This was soon done, and sure of him now old Bates was about to loose the ropes, but on a sudden thought he stopped. He had quite forgotten, and had come unprepared for something of importance. In Western law the Mustang was the property of the first man to mark him with his brand; how was this to be done with the nearest branding iron twenty miles away? Old Tom went to his mare, took up her hoofs one at a time, and examined each shoe. Yes! one was a little loose; he pushed and pried it with the spade, and got it off. Buffalo chips and kindred fuel were plentiful about the plain, so a fire was quickly made, and he soon had one arm of the horse-shoe red hot, then holding the other wrapped in his sock he rudely sketched on the left shoulder of the helpless mustang a turkeytrack, his brand, the first time really that it had ever been used. The Pacer shuddered as the hot iron seared his flesh, but it was quickly done, and the famous Mustang Stallion was a maverick no more.

Now all there was to do was to take him home. The ropes were loosed, the Mustang felt himself freed, thought he was free, and sprang to his feet only to fall as soon as he

tried to take a stride. His forefeet were strongly tied
together, his only possible gait a shuffling walk, or else a
desperate labored bounding with feet so unnaturally held
that within a few yards he was inevitably thrown each
time he tried to break away. Tom on the light pony headed
him off again and again, and by dint of driving, threatening, and maneuvering, contrived to force his foaming,
crazy captive northward toward the Piñavetitos Cañon.
But the wild horse would not drive, would not give in.
With snorts of terror or of rage and maddest bounds, he
tried and tried to get away. It was one long cruel fight; his
glossy sides were thick with dark foam, and the foam was
stained with blood. Countless hard falls and exhaustion
that a long day's chase was powerless to produce were
telling on him; his straining bounds first this way and then
that, were not now quite so strong, and the spray he
snorted as he gasped was half a spray of blood. But his
captor, relentless, masterful and cool, still forced him on.
Down the slope toward the cañon they had come, every
yard a fight, and now they were at the head of the draw
that took the trail down to the only crossing of the cañon,
the northmost limit of the Pacer's ancient range.

From this the first corral and ranch-house were in sight.
The man rejoiced, but the Mustang gathered his remaining strength for one more desperate dash. Up, up the
grassy slope from the trail he went, defied the swinging,
slashing rope and the gunshot fired in air, in vain attempt
to turn his frenzied course. Up, up and on, above the
sheerest cliff he dashed then sprang away into the vacant
air, down—down—two hundred downward feet to fall,
and land upon the rocks below, a lifeless wreck—but free.

Mustang with his head to the wind.

A Spanish horse.

SILVER BLAZE

from *Adventures of Sherlock Holmes*

by Arthur Conan Doyle

I am afraid, Watson, that I shall have to go," said Holmes, as we sat down together to our breakfast one morning.

"Go! Where to?"

"To Dartmoor—to King's Pyland."

I was not surprised. Indeed, my only wonder was that he had not already been mixed up in this extraordinary case, which was the one topic of conversation through the length and breadth of England. For a whole day my companion had rambled about the room with his chin upon his chest and his brows knitted, charging and recharging his pipe with the strongest black tobacco, and absolutely deaf to any of my questions or remarks. Fresh editions of every paper had been sent up by our news agent only to be glanced over and tossed down into a corner. Yet, silent as he was, I knew perfectly well what it was over which he was brooding. There was but one problem before the public which could challenge his powers of analysis, and that was the singular disappearance of the favourite for the Wessex Cup and the tragic murder of its trainer. When, therefore, he suddenly announced his intention of setting out for the scene of the drama, it was only what I had both expected and hoped for.

"I should be most happy to go down with you if I should not be in the way," said I.

"My dear Watson, you would confer a great favour upon

me by coming. And I think that your time will not be misspent, for there are points about this case which promise to make it an absolutely unique one. We have, I think, just time to catch our train at Paddington, and I will go further into the matter upon our journey. You would oblige me by bringing with you your very excellent field glass."

And so it happened that an hour or so later I found myself in the corner of a first-class carriage, flying along en route for Exeter, while Sherlock Holmes, with his sharp, eager face framed in his earflapped travelling cap, dipped rapidly into the bundle of fresh papers which he had procured at Paddington. We had left Reading far behind us before he thrust the last of them under the seat, and offered me his cigar case.

"We are going well," said he, looking out of the window, and glancing at his watch. "Our rate at present is fifty-three and a half miles an hour."

"I have not observed the quarter mile posts," said I.

"Nor have I. But the telegraph posts upon this line are sixty yards apart, and the calculation is a simple one. I presume that you have already looked into this matter of the murder of John Straker and the disappearance of Silver Blaze?"

"I have seen what the *Telegraph* and the *Chronicle* have to say."

"It is one of those cases where the art of the reasoner should be used rather for the sifting of details than for the acquiring of fresh evidence. The tragedy has been so uncommon, so complete, and of such personal importance to so many people that we are suffering from a plethora of surmise, conjecture, and hypothesis. The difficulty is to detach the framework of fact—of absolute, undeniable fact—from the embellishments of theorists and reporters. Then, having established ourselves upon this sound basis, it is our duty to see what inferences may be drawn, and which are the special points upon which the whole mystery turns. On Tuesday evening I received telegrams, both from Colonel Ross, the owner of the horse, and from Inspector Gregory, who is looking after the case, inviting my cooperation."

"Tuesday evening!" I exclaimed. "And this is Thursday morning. Why did you not go down yesterday?"

"Because I made a blunder, my dear Watson—which is, I am afraid, a more common occurrence than anyone would think who only knew me through your memoirs. The fact is that I could not believe it possible that the most remarkable horse in England could long remain concealed, especially in so sparsely inhabited a place as the north of Dartmoor. From hour to hour yesterday I expected to hear that he had been found, and that his abductor was the murderer of John Straker. When, however, another morning had come and I found that, beyond the arrest of young Fitzroy Simpson, nothing had been done, I felt that it was time for me to take action. Yet in some ways I feel that yesterday has not been wasted."

"You have formed a theory then?"

"At least I have got a grip of the essential facts of the case. I shall enumerate them to you, for nothing clears up a case so much as stating it to another person, and I can hardly expect your cooperation if I do not show you the position from which we start."

I lay back against the cushions, puffing at my cigar, while Holmes, leaning forward, with his long thin forefinger checking off the points upon the palm of his left hand, gave me a sketch of the events which had led to our journey.

"Silver Blaze," said he, "is from the Isonomy stock, and holds as brilliant a record as his famous ancestor. He is now in his fifth year, and has brought in turn each of the prizes of the turf to Colonel Ross, his fortunate owner. Up to the time of the catastrophe he was first favourite for the Wessex Cup, the betting being three to one on. He has always, however, been a prime favourite with the racing public, and has never yet disappointed them, so that even at those odds enormous sums of money have been laid upon him. It is obvious, therefore, that there were many people who had the strongest interest in preventing Silver Blaze from being there at the fall of the flag, next Tuesday.

"This fact was, of course, appreciated at King's Pyland, where the Colonel's training stable is situated. Every precaution was taken to guard the favourite. The trainer, John Straker, is a retired jockey, who rode in Colonel Ross's colours before he became too heavy for the weighing chair. He has served the Colonel for five years as jockey, and for seven as trainer, and has always shown himself to be a zealous and honest servant. Under him were three lads, for the establishment was a small one, containing only four horses in all. One of these lads sat up each night in the stable, while the others slept in the loft. All three bore excellent characters. John Straker, who is a married man, lived in a small villa about two hundred yards from the stables. He has no children, keeps one maid-servant, and is comfortably off. The country round is very lonely, but about half a mile to the north there is a small cluster of villas which have been built by a Tavistock contractor for the use of invalids and others who may wish to enjoy the pure Dartmoor air. Tavistock itself lies two miles to the west, while across the moor, also about two miles distant, is the larger training establishment of Mapleton, which belongs to Lord Backwater, and is managed by Silas Brown. In every other direction the moor is a complete wilderness, inhabited only by a few roaming gipsies. Such was the general situation last Monday night when the catastrophe occurred.

"Holmes gave me a sketch of the events."
SILVER BLAZE
Illustration by Sidney Paget

"On that evening the horses had been exercised and watered as usual, and the stables were locked up at nine o'clock. Two of the lads walked up to the trainer's house, where they had supper in the kitchen, while the third, Ned Hunter, remained on guard. At a few minutes after nine the maid, Edith Baxter, carried down to the stables his supper, which consisted of a dish of curried mutton. She took no liquid, as there was a water-tap in the stables, and it was the rule that the lad on duty should drink nothing else. The maid carried a lantern with her, as it was very dark, and the path ran across the open moor.

"Edith Baxter was within thirty yards of the stables when a man appeared out of the darkness and called to her to stop. As he stepped into the circle of yellow light thrown by the lantern she saw that he was a person of gentlemanly bearing, dressed in a grey suit of tweed with a cloth cap. He wore gaiters, and carried a heavy stick with a knob to it. She was most impressed, however, by the extreme pallor of his face and by the nervousness of his manner. His age, she thought, would be rather over thirty than under it.

"'Can you tell me where I am?' he asked. 'I had almost made up my mind to sleep on the moor when I saw the light of your lantern.'

"'You are close to the King's Pyland training stables,' she said.

"'Oh, indeed! What a stroke of luck!' he cried. 'I understand that a stable boy sleeps there alone every night. Perhaps that is his supper which you are carrying to him. Now I am sure that you would not be too proud to earn the price of a new dress, would you?' He took a piece of white paper folded up out of his waistcoat pocket. 'See that the boy has this tonight, and you shall have the prettiest frock that money can buy.'

"She was frightened by the earnestness of his manner,

"A man appeared out of the darkness."
SILVER BLAZE
Illustration by Sidney Paget

and ran past him to the window through which she was accustomed to hand the meals. It was already open, and Hunter was seated at the table inside. She had begun to tell him of what had happened, when the stranger came up again.

"'Good evening,' said he, looking through the window, 'I wanted to have a word with you.' The girl has sworn that as he spoke she noticed the corner of the little paper packet protruding from his closed hand.

"'What business have you here?' asked the lad.

"It's business that may put something into your pocket,' said the other. 'You've two horses in for the Wessex Cup—Silver Blaze and Bayard. Let me have the straight tip, and you won't be a loser. Is it a fact that at the weights Bayard could give the other a hundred yards in five furlongs, and that the stable have put their money on him?'

"'So you're one of those damned touts,' cried the lad. 'I'll show you how we serve them in King's Pyland.' He sprang up and rushed across the stable to unloose the dog. The girl fled away to the house, but as she ran she looked back, and saw that the stranger was leaning through the window. A minute later, however, when Hunter rushed out with the hound he was gone, and though the lad ran all round the buildings he failed to find any trace of him."

"One moment!" I asked. "Did the stable boy, when he ran out with the dog, leave the door unlocked behind him?"

"Excellent, Watson; excellent!" murmured my companion. "The importance of the point struck me so forcibly, that I sent a special wire to Dartmoor yesterday to clear the matter up. The boy locked the door before he left it. The window, I may add, was not large enough for a man to get through.

"Hunter waited until his fellow grooms had returned,

when he sent a message up to the trainer and told him what had occurred. Straker was excited at hearing the account, although he does not seem to have quite realized its true significance. It left him, however, vaguely uneasy, and Mrs. Straker, waking at one in the morning, found that he was dressing. In reply to her inquiries, he said that he could not sleep on account of his anxiety about the horses, and that he intended to walk down to the stables to see that all was well. She begged him to remain at home, as she could hear the rain pattering against the windows, but in spite of her entreaties he pulled on his large mackintosh and left the house.

"Mrs. Straker awoke at seven in the morning, to find that her husband had not yet returned. She dressed herself hastily, called the maid, and set off for the stables. The door was open; inside, huddled together upon a chair, Hunter was sunk in a state of absolute stupor, the favourite's stall was empty, and there were no signs of his trainer.

"The two lads who slept in the chaff-cutting loft above the harness room were quickly aroused. They had heard nothing during the night, for they are both sound sleepers. Hunter was obviously under the influence of some powerful drug; and, as no sense could be got out of him, he was left to sleep it off while the two lads and the two women ran out in search of the absentees. They still had hopes that the trainer had for some reason taken out the horse for early exercise, but on ascending the knoll near the house, from which all the neighbouring moors were visible, they not only could see no signs of the favourite, but they perceived something which warned them that they were in the presence of a tragedy.

"About a quarter of a mile from the stables, John Straker's overcoat was flapping from a furze bush. Immediately beyond there was a bowl-shaped depression in the

moor, and at the bottom of this was found the dead body of
the unfortunate trainer. His head had been shattered by a
savage blow from some heavy weapon, and he was
wounded in the thigh, where there was a long, clean cut,
inflicted evidently by some very sharp instrument. It was
clear, however, that Straker had defended himself vig-
orously against the assailants, for in his right hand he held
a small knife, which was clotted with blood up to the
handle, while in his left he grasped a red and black silk
cravat, which was recognised by the maid as having been
worn on the preceding evening by the stranger who had
visited the stables.

"Hunter, on recovering from his stupor, was also quite
positive as to the ownership of the cravat. He was equally
certain that the same stranger had, while standing at the
window, drugged his curried mutton, and so deprived the
stables of their watchman.

"As to the missing horse, there were abundant proofs in
the mud which lay at the bottom of the fatal hollow, that
he had been there at the time of the struggle. But from
that morning he has disappeared; and although a large
reward has been offered, and all the gipsies of Dartmoor
are on the alert, no news has come of him. Finally an
analysis has shown that the remains of his supper, left by
the stable lad, contain an appreciable quantity of
powdered opium, while the people of the house partook of
the same dish on the same night without any ill effect.

"Those are the main facts of the case, stripped of all
surmise and stated as baldly as possible. I shall now
recapitulate what the police have done in the matter.

"Inspector Gregory, to whom the case has been committed, is an extremely competent officer. Were he but
gifted with imagination he might rise to great heights in
his profession. On his arrival he promptly found and
arrested the man upon whom suspicion naturally rested.

"They found the dead body of the unfortunate trainer."
SILVER BLAZE
Illustration by Sidney Paget

There was little difficulty in finding him, for he inhabited one of those villas which I have mentioned. His name, it appears, was Fitzroy Simpson. He was a man of excellent birth and education, who had squandered a fortune upon the turf, and who lived now by doing a little quiet and genteel bookmaking in the sporting clubs of London. An examination of his betting-book shows that bets to the amount of five thousand pounds had been registered by him against the favourite.

"On being arrested he volunteered the statement that he had come down to Dartmoor in the hope of getting some information about the King's Pyland horses, and also about Desborough, the second favourite, which was in charge of Silas Brown, at the Mapleton stables. He did not attempt to deny that he had acted as described upon the evening before, but declared that he had no sinister designs, and had simply wished to obtain first-hand information. When confronted with his cravat he turned very pale, and was utterly unable to account for its presence in the hand of the murdered man. His wet clothing showed that he had been out in the storm of the night before, and his stick, which was a Penang lawyer, weighted with lead, was just such a weapon as might, by repeated blows, have inflicted the terrible injuries to which the trainer had succumbed.

"On the other hand, there was no wound upon his person, while the state of Straker's knife would show that one, at least, of the assailants must bear his mark upon him. There you have it all in a nutshell, Watson, and if you can give me any light I shall be infinitely obliged to you."

I had listened with the greatest interest to the statement which Holmes, with characteristic clearness, had laid before me. Though most of the facts were familiar to me, I had not sufficiently appreciated their relative importance, nor their connection to each other.

"Is it not possible," I suggested, "that the incised wound upon Straker may have been caused by his own knife in the convulsive struggles which follow any brain injury?"

"It is more than possible; it is probable," said Holmes. "In that case, one of the main points in favour of the accused disappears."

"And yet," said I, "even now I fail to understand what the theory of the police can be."

"I am afraid that whatever theory we state has very grave objections to it," returned my companion. "The police imagine, I take it, that this Fitzroy Simpson, having drugged the lad, and having in some way obtained a duplicate key, opened the stable door, and took out the horse, with the intention, apparently, of kidnapping him altogether. His bridle is missing, so that Simpson must have put this on. Then, having left the door open behind him, he was leading the horse away over the moor, when he was either met or overtaken by the trainer. A row naturally ensued, Simpson beat out the trainer's brains with his heavy stick without receiving any injury from the small knife which Straker used in self-defence, and then the thief either led the horse on to some secret hiding place, or else it may have bolted during the struggle, and be now wandering out on the moors. That is the case as it appears to the police, and improbable as it is, all other explanations are more improbable still. However, I shall very quickly test the matter when I am once upon the spot, and until then I really cannot see how we can get much further than our present position."

It was evening before we reached the little town of Tavistock, which lies, like the boss of a shield, in the middle of the huge circle of Dartmoor. Two gentlemen were awaiting us at the station; the one a tall fair man with lion-like hair and beard, and curiously penetrating light blue eyes, the other a small alert person, very neat and dapper, in a frock-coat and gaiters, with trim little side-whiskers and an eye glass. The latter was Colonel Ross, the well-known sportsman, the other Inspector Gregory, a man who was rapidly making his name in the English detective service.

"I am delighted that you have come down, Mr. Holmes," said the Colonel. "The Inspector here has done all that could possibly be suggested; but I wish to leave no stone unturned in trying to avenge poor Straker, and in recovering my horse."

"Have there been any fresh developments?" asked Holmes.

"I am sorry to say that we have made very little progress," said the Inspector. "We have an open carriage outside, and as you would no doubt like to see the place before the light fails, we might talk it over as we drive."

A minute later we were all seated in a comfortable landau and were rattling through the quaint old Devonshire town. Inspector Gregory was full of his case, and poured out a stream of remarks, while Holmes threw in an occasional question or interjection. Colonel Ross leaned back with his arms folded and his hat tilted over his eyes, while I listened with interest to the dialogue of the two detectives. Gregory was formulating his theory, which was almost exactly what Holmes had foretold in the train.

"The net is drawn pretty close round Fitzroy Simpson," he remarked, "and I believe myself that he is our man. At the same time, I recognise that the evidence is purely circumstantial, and that some new development may upset it."

"How about Straker's knife?"

"We have quite come to the conclusion that he wounded himself in his fall."

"My friend Dr. Watson made that suggestion to me as

"I am delighted that you have come down, Mr. Holmes."
SILVER BLAZE
Illustration by Sidney Paget

we came down. If so, it would tell against this man Simpson."

"Undoubtedly. He has neither a knife nor any sign of a wound. The evidence against him is certainly very strong. He had a great interest in the disappearance of the favourite, he lies under the suspicion of having poisoned the stable boy, he was undoubtedly out in the storm, he was armed with a heavy stick, and his cravat was found in the dead man's hand. I really think we have enough to go before a jury."

Holmes shook his head. "A clever counsel would tear it all to rags," said he. "Why should he take the horse out of the stable? If he wished to injure it, why could he not do it there? Has a duplicate key been found in his possession? What chemist sold him the powdered opium? Above all, where could he, a stranger to the district, hide a horse, and such a horse as this? What is his own explanation as to the paper which he wished the maid to give to the stable boy?"

"He says that it was a ten-pound note. One was found in his purse. But your other difficulties are not so formidable as they seem. He is not a stranger to the district. He has twice lodged at Tavistock in the summer. The opium was probably brought from London. The key, having served its purpose, would be hurled away. The horse may lie at the bottom of one of the pits or old mines upon the moor."

"What does he say about the cravat?"

"He acknowledges that it is his, and declares that he had lost it. But a new element has been introduced into the case which may account for his leading the horse from the stable."

Holmes pricked up his ears.

"We have found traces which show that a party of gipsies encamped on Monday night within a mile of the spot where the murder took place. On Tuesday they were gone. Now, presuming that there was some understanding between Simpson and these gipsies, might he not have been leading the horse to them when he was overtaken, and may they not have him now?"

"It is certainly possible."

"The moor is being scoured for these gipsies. I have also examined every stable and outhouse in Tavistock, and for a radius of ten miles."

"There is another training stable quite close, I understand?"

"Yes, and that is a factor which we must certainly not neglect. As Desborough, their horse, was second in the betting, they had an interest in the disappearance of the favourite. Silas Brown, the trainer, is known to have had large bets upon the event, and he was no friend to poor Straker. We have, however, examined the stables, and there is nothing to connect him with the affair."

"And nothing to connect this man Simpson with the interests of the Mapleton stables?"

"Nothing at all."

Holmes leaned back in the carriage and the conversation ceased. A few minutes later our driver pulled up at a neat little red-brick villa with overhanging eaves, which stood by the road. Some distance off, across a paddock, lay a long grey-tiled outbuilding. In every other direction the low curves of the moor, bronze-coloured from the fading ferns, stretched away to the skyline, broken only by the steeples of Tavistock, and by a cluster of houses away to the westward, which marked the Mapleton stables. We all sprang out with the exception of Holmes, who continued to lean back with his eyes fixed upon the sky in front of him, entirely absorbed in his own thoughts. It was only when I touched his arm that he roused himself with a violent start and stepped out of the carriage.

"Excuse me," said he, turning to Colonel Ross, who had

looked at him in some surprise. "I was daydreaming." There was a gleam in his eyes and a suppressed excitement in his manner which convinced me, used as I was to his ways, that his hand was upon a clue, though I could not imagine where he had found it.

"Perhaps you would prefer at once to go on to the scene of the crime, Mr. Holmes?" said Gregory.

"I think that I should prefer to stay here a little and go into one or two questions of detail. Straker was brought back here, I presume?"

"Yes, he lies upstairs. The inquest is tomorrow."

"He has been in your service some years, Colonel Ross?"

"I have always found him an excellent servant."

"I presume that you made an inventory of what he had in his pockets at the time of his death, Inspector?"

"I have the things themselves in the sitting room if you would care to see them."

"I should be very glad."

We all filed into the front room and sat round the central table, while the Inspector unlocked a square tin box and laid a small heap of things before us. There was a box of vestas, two inches of tallow candle, an A.D.P. briar root pipe, a pouch of sealskin with half an ounce of long cut Cavendish, a silver watch with a gold chain, five sovereigns in gold, an aluminium pencil case, a few papers, and an ivory-handled knife with a very delicate inflexible blade marked Weiss and Co., London.

"This is a very singular knife," said Holmes, lifting it up and examining it minutely. "I presume, as I see bloodstains upon it, that it is the one which was found in the dead man's grasp. Watson, this knife is surely in your line."

"It is what we call a cataract knife," said I.

"I thought so. A very delicate blade devised for very delicate work. A strange thing for a man to carry with him upon a rough expedition, especially as it would not shut in his pocket."

"The tip was guarded by a disc of cork which we found beside his body," said the Inspector. "His wife tells us that the knife had lain for some days upon the dressing table, and that he had picked it up as he left the room. It was a poor weapon, but perhaps the best that he could lay his hand on at the moment."

"Very possibly. How about these papers?"

"Three of them are receipted hay dealers' accounts. One of them is a letter of instructions from Colonel Ross. This other is a milliner's account for thirty-seven pounds fifteen, made out by Madame Lesurier, of Bond Street, to William Darbyshire. Mrs. Straker tells us that Darbyshire was a friend of her husband's, and that occasionally his letters were addressed here."

"Madame Darbyshire had somewhat expensive tastes," remarked Holmes, glancing down the account. "Twenty-two guineas is rather heavy for a single costume. However, there appears to be nothing more to learn, and we may now go down to the scene of the crime."

As we emerged from the sitting room a woman who had been waiting in the passage took a step forward and laid her hand upon the Inspector's sleeve. Her face was haggard, and thin, and eager; stamped with the print of a recent horror.

"Have you got them? Have you found them?" she panted.

"No, Mrs. Straker; but Mr. Holmes, here, has come from London to help us, and we shall do all that is possible."

"Surely I met you in Plymouth, at a garden party, some little time ago, Mrs. Straker," said Holmes.

"No, sir; you are mistaken."

"Dear me; why, I could have sworn to it. You wore a

costume of dove-coloured silk, with ostrich feather trimming."

"I never had such a dress, sir," answered the lady.

"Ah; that quite settles it," said Holmes; and, with an apology, he followed the Inspector outside. A short walk across the moor took us to the hollow in which the body had been found. At the brink of it was the furze bush upon which the coat had been hung.

"There was no wind that night, I understand," said Holmes.

"None, but very heavy rain."

"In that case the overcoat was not blown against the furze bushes, but placed there."

"Yes, it was laid across the bush."

"You fill me with interest. I perceive that the ground has been trampled up a good deal. No doubt many feet have been there since Monday night."

"A piece of matting has been laid here at the side, and we have all stood upon that."

"Excellent."

"In this bag I have one of the boots which Straker wore, one of Fitzroy Simpson's shoes, and a cast horseshoe of Silver Blaze."

"My dear Inspector, you surpass yourself!" Holmes took the bag, and descending into the hollow he pushed the matting into a more central position. Then stretching himself upon his face and leaning his chin upon his hands he made a careful study of the trampled mud in front of him.

"Halloa!" said he, suddenly, "what's this?"

It was a wax vesta, half burned, which was so coated with mud that it looked at first like a little chip of wood.

"I cannot think how I came to overlook it," said the Inspector, with an expression of annoyance.

"Have you found them?" she panted.
SILVER BLAZE
Illustration by Sidney Paget

"It was invisible, buried in the mud. I only saw it because I was looking for it."

"What! You expected to find it?"

"I thought it not unlikely." He took the boots from the bag and compared the impressions of each of them with marks upon the ground. Then he clambered up to the rim of the hollow and crawled about among the ferns and bushes.

"I am afraid that there are no more tracks," said the Inspector. "I have examined the ground very carefully for a hundred yards in each direction."

"Indeed!" said Holmes, rising, "I should not have the impertinence to do it again after what you say. But I should like to take a little walk over the moor before it grows dark, that I may know my ground tomorrow, and I think that I shall put this horseshoe into my pocket for luck."

Colonel Ross, who had shown some signs of impatience at my companion's quiet and systematic method of work, glanced at his watch.

"I wish you would come back with me, Inspector," said he. "There are several points on which I should like your advice, and especially as to whether we do not owe it to the public to remove our horse's name from the entries for the Cup."

"Certainly not," cried Holmes, with decision; "I should let the name stand."

The Colonel bowed. "I am very glad to have had your opinion, sir," said he. "You will find us at poor Straker's house when you have finished your walk, and we can drive together into Tavistock."

He turned back with the Inspector, while Holmes and I walked slowly across the moor. The sun was beginning to sink behind the stables of Mapleton, and the long sloping plain in front of us was tinged with gold, deepening into rich, ruddy brown where the faded ferns and brambles caught the evening light. But the glories of the landscape were all wasted upon my companion, who was sunk in the deepest thought.

"It's this way, Watson," he said at last. "We may leave the question of who killed John Straker for the instant, and confine ourselves to finding out what has become of the horse. Now, supposing that he broke away during or after the tragedy, where could he have gone to? The horse is a very gregarious creature. If left to himself his instincts would have been either to return to King's Pyland, or go over to Mapleton. Why should he run wild upon the moor? He would surely have been seen by now. And why should gipsies kidnap him? These people always clear out when they hear of trouble, for they do not wish to be pestered by the police. They could not hope to sell such a horse. They would run a great risk and gain nothing by taking him. Surely that is clear."

"Where is he, then?"

"I have already said that he must have gone to King's Pyland, or to Mapleton. He is not at King's Pyland, therefore he is at Mapleton. Let us take that as a working hypothesis and see what it leads us to. This part of the moor, as the Inspector remarked, is very hard and dry. But it falls away towards Mapleton, and you can see from here that there is a long hollow over yonder, which must have been very wet on Monday night. If our supposition is correct, then the horse must have crossed that, and there is the point where we should look for his tracks."

We had been walking briskly during this conversation, and a few more minutes brought us to the hollow in question. At Holmes' request I walked down the bank to the right and he to the left, but I had not taken fifty paces before I heard him give a shout, and saw him waving his hand to me. The track of a horse was plainly outlined in the soft earth in front of him, and the shoe which he took from his pocket exactly fitted the impression.

"See the value of imagination," said Holmes. "It is the one quality which Gregory lacks. We imagined what might have happened, acted upon the supposition, and find ourselves justified. Let us proceed."

We crossed the marshy bottom and passed over a quarter of a mile of dry, hard turf. Again the ground sloped and again we came on the tracks. Then we lost them for half a mile, but only to pick them up once more quite close to Mapleton. It was Holmes who saw them first, and he stood pointing with a look of triumph upon his face. A man's track was visible beside the horse's.

"The horse was alone before," I cried.

"Quite so. It was alone before. Halloa, what is this?"

The double track turned sharp off and took the direction of King's Pyland. Holmes whistled, and we both followed along after it. His eyes were on the trail, but I happened to look a little to one side, and saw to my surprise the same tracks coming back again in the opposite direction.

"One for you, Watson," said Holmes, when I pointed it out; "you have saved us a long walk which would have brought us back on our own traces. Let us follow the return track."

We had not to go far. It ended at the paving of asphalt which led up to the gates of the Mapleton stables. As we approached a groom ran out from them.

"We don't want any loiterers about here," said he.

"I only wished to ask a question," said Holmes, with his finger and thumb in his waistcoat pocket. "Should I be too early to see your master, Mr. Silas Brown, if I were to call at five o'clock tomorrow morning?"

"Bless you, sir, if anyone is about he will be, for he is always the first stirring. But here he is, sir, to answer your questions for himself. No, sir, no; it's as much as my place is worth to let him see me touch your money. Afterwards, if you like."

As Sherlock Holmes replaced the half-crown which he had drawn from his pocket, a fierce looking, elderly man strode out from the gate with a hunting crop swinging in his hand.

"What's this, Dawson?" he cried. "No gossiping! Go about your business! And you—what the devil do you want here?"

"Ten minutes' talk with you, my good sir," said Holmes, in the sweetest of voices.

"I've no time to talk to every gadabout. We want no strangers here. Be off, or you may find a dog at your heels."

Holmes leaned forward and whispered something in the trainer's ear. He started violently and flushed to the temples.

"It's a lie!" he shouted. "An infernal lie!"

"Very good! Shall we argue about it here in public, or talk it over in your parlour?"

"Oh, come in if you wish to."

Holmes smiled. "I shall not keep you more than a few minutes, Watson," he said. "Now, Mr. Brown, I am quite at your disposal."

It was quite twenty minutes, and the reds had all faded into greys before Holmes and the trainer reappeared. Never have I seen such a change as had been brought about in Silas Brown in that short time. His face was ashy pale, beads of perspiration shone upon his brow, and his hands shook until the hunting crop wagged like a branch in the wind. His bullying, overbearing manner was all gone too, and he cringed along at my companion's side like a dog with its master.

"Your instructions will be done. It shall be done," said he.

"There must be no mistake," said Holmes, looking round at him. The other winced as he read the menace in his eyes.

"Oh, no, there shall be no mistake. It shall be there. Should I change it first or not?"

Holmes thought a little and then burst out laughing. "No, don't," said he. "I shall write to you about it. No tricks now or—"

"Oh, you can trust me, you can trust me!"

"Yes, I think I can. Well, you shall hear from me tomorrow." He turned upon his heel, disregarding the trembling hand which the other held out to him, and we set off for King's Pyland.

"A more perfect compound of the bully, coward and sneak than Master Silas Brown I have seldom met with," remarked Holmes, as we trudged along together.

"He has the horse, then?"

"He tried to bluster out of it, but I described to him so exactly what his actions had been upon that morning, that he is convinced that I was watching him. Of course, you observed the peculiarly square toes in the impressions, and that his own boots exactly corresponded to them. Again, of course, no subordinate would have dared to have done such a thing. I described to him how when, according to his custom, he was the first down, he perceived a strange horse wandering over the moor; how he went out to it, and his astonishment at recognising from the white forehead which has given the favourite its name that chance had put in his power the only horse which could beat the one upon which he had put his money. Then I described how his first impulse had been to lead him back to King's Pyland, and how the devil had shown him how he could hide the horse until the race was over, and how he had led it back and concealed it at Mapleton. When I told

"Be off!"

SILVER BLAZE

Illustration by Sidney Paget

him every detail he gave it up, and thought only of saving his own skin."

"But his stables had been searched."

"Oh, an old horse-faker like him has many a dodge."

"But are you not afraid to leave the horse in his power now, since he has every interest in injuring it?"

"My dear fellow, he will guard it as the apple of his eye. He knows that his only hope of mercy is to produce it safe."

"Colonel Ross did not impress me as a man who would be likely to show much mercy in any case."

"The matter does not rest with Colonel Ross. I follow my own methods, and tell as much or as little as I choose. That is the advantage of being unofficial. I don't know whether you observed it, Watson, but the Colonel's manner has been just a trifle cavalier to me. I am inclined now to have a little amusement at his expense. Say nothing to him about the horse."

"Certainly not, without your permission."

"And, of course, this is all quite a minor point compared to the question of who killed John Straker."

"And you will devote yourself to that?"

"On the contrary, we both go back to London by the night train."

I was thunderstruck by my friend's words. We had only been a few hours in Devonshire, and that he should give up an investigation which he had begun so brilliantly was quite incomprehensible to me. Not a word more could I draw from him until we were back at the trainer's house. The Colonel and the Inspector were awaiting us in the parlour.

"My friend and I return to town by the midnight express," said Holmes. "We have had a charming little breath of your beautiful Dartmoor air."

The Inspector opened his eyes, and the Colonel's lip curled in a sneer.

"So you despair of arresting the murderer of poor Straker," said he.

Holmes shrugged his shoulders. "There are certainly grave difficulties in the way," said he. "I have every hope, however, that your horse will start upon Tuesday, and I beg that you will have your jockey in readiness. Might I ask for a photograph of Mr. John Straker?"

The Inspector took one from an envelope in his pocket and handed it to him.

"My dear Gregory, you anticipate all my wants. If I might ask you to wait here for an instant, I have a question which I should like to put to the maid."

"I must say that I am rather disappointed in our London consultant," said Colonel Ross, bluntly, as my friend left the room. "I do not see that we are any further than when he came."

"At least, you have his assurance that your horse will run," said I.

"Yes, I have his assurance," said the Colonel, with a shrug of his shoulders. "I should prefer to have the horse."

I was about to make some reply in defence of my friend, when he entered the room again.

"Now, gentlemen," said he, "I am quite ready for Tavistock."

As we stepped into the carriage one of the stable lads held the door open for us. A sudden idea seemed to occur to Holmes, for he leaned forward and touched the lad upon the sleeve.

"You have a few sheep in the paddock," he said. "Who attends to them?"

"I do, sir."

"Have you noticed anything amiss with them of late?"

"Well, sir, not of much account; but three of them have gone lame, sir."

I could see that Holmes was extremely pleased, for he chuckled and rubbed his hands together.

"A long shot, Watson; a very long shot!" said he, pinching my arm. "Gregory, let me recommend to your attention this singular epidemic among the sheep. Drive on, coachman!"

Colonel Ross still wore an expression which showed the poor opinion which he had formed of my companion's ability, but I saw by the Inspector's face that his attention had been keenly aroused.

"You consider that to be important?" he asked.

"Exceedingly so."

"Is there any other point to which you would wish to draw my attention?"

"To the curious incident of the dog in the nighttime."

"The dog did nothing in the nighttime."

"That was the curious incident," remarked Sherlock Holmes.

Four days later Holmes and I were again in the train bound for Winchester, to see the race for the Wessex Cup. Colonel Ross met us, by appointment, outside the station, and we drove in his drag to the course beyond the town. His face was grave and his manner was cold in the extreme.

"I have seen nothing of my horse," said he.

"I suppose that you would know him when you saw him?" asked Holmes.

The Colonel was very angry. "I have been on the turf for twenty years, and never was asked such a question as that before," said he. "A child would know Silver Blaze with his white forehead and his mottled off fore leg."

"How is the betting?"

"Holmes was extremely pleased."
SILVER BLAZE
Illustration by Sidney Paget

"Well, that is the curious part of it. You could have got fifteen to one yesterday, but the price has become shorter and shorter, until you can hardly get three to one now."

"Hum!" said Holmes. "Somebody knows something, that is clear!"

As the drag drew up in the inclosure near the grand stand, I glanced at the car to see the entries. It ran:—

Wessex Plate. 50 sovs. each, h ft, with 1,000 sovs. added, for four and five-year olds. Second £300. Third £200. New course (one mile and five furlongs).

1. Mr. Heath Newton's The Negro (red cap, cinnamon jacket).
2. Colonel Wardlaw's Pugilist (pink cap, blue and black jacket).
3. Lord Backwater's Desborough (yellow cap and sleeves).
4. Colonel Ross's Silver Blaze (black cap, red jacket).
5. Duke of Balmoral's Iris (yellow and black stripes).
6. Lord Singleford's Rasper (purple cap, black sleeves).

"We scratched our other one and put all hopes on your word," said the Colonel. "Why, what is that? Silver Blaze favourite?"

"Five to four against Silver Blaze!" roared the ring. "Five to four against Silver Blaze! Fifteen to five against Desborough! Five to four on the field!"

"There are the numbers up," I cried. "They are all six there."

"All six there! Then, my horse is running," cried the Colonel, in great agitation. "But I don't see him. My colours have not passed."

"Only five have passed. This must be he."

As I spoke a powerful bay horse swept out from the weighing inclosure and cantered past us, bearing on its back the well-known black and red of the Colonel.

"That's not my horse," cried the owner. "That beast has not a white hair upon its body. What is this that you have done, Mr. Holmes?"

"Well, well, let us see how he gets on," said my friend, imperturbably. For a few minutes he gazed through my field glass. "Capital! An excellent start!" he cried suddenly. "There they are, coming round the curve!"

From our drag we had a superb view as they came up the straight. The six horses were so close together that a carpet could have covered them, but half way up the yellow of the Mapleton stable showed to the front. Before they reached us, however, Desborough's bolt was shot, and the Colonel's horse, coming away with a rush, passed the post a good six lengths before its rival, the Duke of Balmoral's Iris making a bad third.

"It's my race anyhow," gasped the Colonel, passing his hand over his eyes. "I confess that I can make neither head nor tail of it. Don't you think that you have kept up your mystery long enough, Mr. Holmes?"

"Certainly, Colonel. You shall know everything. Let us all go round and have a look at the horse together. Here he is," he continued, as we made our way into the weighing inclosure where only owners and their friends find admittance. "You have only to wash his face and his leg in spirits of wine and you will find that he is the same old Silver Blaze as ever."

"You take my breath away!"

"I found him in the hands of a faker, and took the liberty of running him just as he was sent over."

"My dear sir, you have done wonders. The horse looks very fit and well. It never went better in its life. I owe you a thousand apologies for having doubted your ability. You have done me a great service by recovering my horse. You would do me a greater still if you could lay your hands on the murderer of John Straker."

"I have done so," said Holmes, quietly.

The Colonel and I stared at him in amazement. "You have got him! Where is he, then?"

"He is here."

"Here! Where?"

"In my company at the present moment."

The Colonel flushed angrily. "I quite recognise that I am under obligations to you, Mr. Holmes," said he, "but I must regard what you have just said as either a very bad joke or an insult."

Sherlock Holmes laughed. "I assure you that I have not associated you with the crime, Colonel," said he; "the real murderer is standing immediately behind you!"

He stepped past and laid his hand upon the glossy neck of the thoroughbred.

"The horse!" cried both the Colonel and myself.

"Yes, the horse. And it may lessen his guilt if I say that it was done in self-defence, and that John Straker was a man who was entirely unworthy of your confidence. But there goes the bell; and as I stand to win a little on his next race, I shall defer a more lengthy explanation until a more fitting time."

We had the corner of a Pullman car to ourselves that evening as we whirled back to London, and I fancy that the journey was a short one to Colonel Ross as well as to myself, as we listened to our companion's narrative of the events which had occurred at the Dartmoor training stables upon that Monday night, and the means by which he had unravelled them.

"I confess," said he, "that any theories which I had formed from the newspaper reports were entirely erroneous. And yet there were indications there, had they not been overlaid by other details which concealed their true import. I went to Devonshire with the conviction that Fitzroy Simpson was the true culprit, although, of course, I saw that the evidence against him was by no means complete.

"It was while I was in the carriage, just as we reached

"He laid his hand upon the glossy neck."
SILVER BLAZE
Illustration by Sidney Paget

the trainer's house, that the immense significance of the curried mutton occurred to me. You may remember that I was distrait, and remained sitting after you had alighted. I was marvelling in my own mind how I could possibly have overlooked so obvious a clue."

"I confess," said the Colonel, "that even now I cannot see how it helps us."

"It was the first link in my chain of reasoning. Powdered opium is by no means tasteless. The flavour is not disagreeable, but it is perceptible. Were it mixed with any ordinary dish, the eater would undoubtedly detect it, and would probably eat no more. A curry was exactly the medium which would disguise the taste. By no possible supposition could this stranger, Fitzroy Simpson, have caused curry to be served in the trainer's family that night, and it is surely too monstrous a coincidence to suppose that he happened to come along with powdered opium upon the very night when a dish happened to be served which would disguise the flavour. That is unthinkable. Therefore Simpson becomes eliminated from the case and our attention centres upon Straker and his wife, the only two people who could have chosen curried mutton for supper that night. The opium was added after the dish was set aside for the stable boy, for the others had the same for supper with no ill effects. Which of them, then, had access to that dish without the maid seeing them?

"Before deciding that question I had grasped the significance of the silence of the dog, for one true inference invariably suggests others. The Simpson incident had shown me that a dog was kept in the stables, and yet, though someone had been in and had fetched out a horse, he had not barked enough to arouse the two lads in the loft. Obviously the midnight visitor was someone whom the dog knew well.

"I was already convinced, or almost convinced, that

John Straker went down to the stables in the dead of the night and took out Silver Blaze. For what purpose? For a dishonest one, obviously, or why should he drug his own stable boy? And yet I was at a loss to know why. There have been cases before now where trainers have made sure of great sums of money by laying against their own horses, through agents, and then preventing them from winning by fraud. Sometimes it is a pulling jockey. Sometimes it is some surer and subtler means. What was it here? I hoped that the contents of his pockets might help me to form a conclusion.

"And they did so. You cannot have forgotten the singular knife which was found in the dead man's hand, a knife which certainly no sane man would choose for a weapon. It was, as Dr. Watson told us, a form of knife which is used for the most delicate operations known in surgery. And it was to be used for a delicate operation that night. You must know, with your wide experience of turf matters, Colonel Ross, that it is possible to make a slight nick upon the tendons of a horse's ham, and to do it subcutaneously so as to leave absolutely no trace. A horse so treated would develop a slight lameness which would be put down to a strain in exercise or a touch of rheumatism, but never to foul play."

"Villian! Scoundrel!" cried the Colonel.

"We have here the explanation of why John Straker wished to take the horse out on to the moor. So spirited a creature would have certainly roused the soundest of sleepers when it felt the prick of the knife. It was absolutely necessary to do it in the open air."

"I have been blind!" cried the Colonel. "Of course, that was why he needed the candle, and struck the match."

"Undoubtedly. But in examining his belongings, I was fortunate enough to discover, not only the method of the crime, but even its motives. As a man of the world,

Colonel, you know that men do not carry other people's bills about in their pockets. We have most of us quite enough to do to settle our own. I at once concluded that Straker was leading a double life, and keeping a second establishment. The nature of the bill showed that there was a lady in the case, and one who had expensive tastes. Liberal as you are with your servants, one hardly expects that they can buy twenty-guinea walking dresses for their women. I questioned Mrs. Straker as to the dress without her knowing it, and having satisfied myself that it had never reached her, I made a note of the milliner's address, and felt that by calling there with Straker's photograph, I could easily dispose of the mythical Darbyshire.

"From that time on all was plain. Straker had led out the horse to a hollow where his light would be invisible. Simpson, in his flight, had dropped his cravat, and Straker had picked it up with some idea, perhaps, that he might use it in securing the horse's leg. Once in the hollow he had got behind the horse, and had struck a light, but the creature, frightened at the sudden glare, and with the strange instinct of animals feeling that some mischief was intended, had lashed out, and the steel shoe had struck Straker full on the forehead. He had already, in spite of the rain, taken off his overcoat in order to do his delicate task, and so, as he fell, his knife gashed his thigh. Do I make it clear?"

"Wonderful!" cried the Colonel. "Wonderful! You might have been there."

"My final shot was, I confess, a very long one. It struck me that so astute a man as Straker would not undertake this delicate tendon-nicking without a little practice. What could he practise on? My eyes fell upon the sheep, and I asked a question which, rather to my surprise, showed that my surmise was correct."

"You have made it perfectly clear, Mr. Holmes."

"When I returned to London I called upon the milliner, who at once recognised Straker as an excellent customer, of the name of Darbyshire, who had a very dashing wife with a strong partiality for expensive dresses. I have no doubt that this woman had plunged him over head and ears in debt, and so led him into this miserable plot."

"You have explained all but one thing," cried the Colonel. "Where was the horse?"

"Ah, it bolted and was cared for by one of your neighbours. We must have an amnesty in that direction, I think. This is Clapham Junction, if I am not mistaken, and we shall be in Victoria in less than ten minutes. If you care to smoke a cigar in our rooms, Colonel, I shall be happy to give you any other details which might interest you."

The gentleman's favorite.

A steeplechaser.

MR. TRAVERS'S FIRST HUNT

by Richard Harding Davis

YOUNG Travers, who had been engaged to a girl down on Long Island for the last three months, only met her father and brother a few weeks before the day set for the wedding. The brother is a master of hounds near Southampton, and shared the expense of importing a pack from England with Van Bibber. The father and son talked horse all day and until one in the morning; for they owned fast thoroughbreds, and entered them at the Sheepshead Bay and other racetracks. Old Mr. Paddock, the father of the girl to whom Travers was engaged, had often said that when a young man asked him for his daughter's hand he would ask him in return, not if he had lived straight, but if he could ride straight. And on his answering this question in the affirmative depended his gaining her parent's consent. Travers had met Miss Paddock and her mother in Europe, while the men of the family were at home. He was invited to their place in the fall when the hunting season opened, and spent the evening most pleasantly and satisfactorily with his *fiancée* in a corner of the drawing room. But as soon as the women had gone, young Paddock joined him and said, "You ride, of course?" Travers had never ridden; but he had been prompted how to answer by Miss Paddock, and so said there was nothing he liked better. As he expressed it, he would rather ride than sleep.

"That's good," said Paddock. "I'll give you a mount on Satan tomorrow morning at the meet. He is a bit nasty at the start of the season; and ever since he killed Wallis, the second groom, last year, none of us care much to ride him. But you can manage him, no doubt. He'll just carry your weight."

Mr. Travers dreamed that night of taking large, desperate leaps into space on a wild horse that snorted forth flames, and that rose at solid stone walls as though they were hayricks.

He was tempted to say he was ill in the morning—which was, considering his state of mind, more or less true—but concluded that, as he would have to ride sooner or later during his visit, and that if he did break his neck it would be in a good cause, he determined to do his best. He did not want to ride at all, for two excellent reasons—first, because he wanted to live for Miss Paddock's sake, and, second, because he wanted to live for his own.

The next morning was a most forbidding and doleful-looking morning, and young Travers had great hopes that the meet would be declared off; but, just as he lay in doubt, the servant knocked at his door with his riding things and his hot water.

He came downstairs looking very miserable indeed. Satan had been taken to the place where they were to meet, and Travers viewed him on his arrival there with a sickening sense of fear as he saw him pulling three grooms off their feet.

Travers decided that he would stay with his feet on solid earth just as long as he could, and when the hounds were thrown off and the rest had started at a gallop he waited, under the pretence of adjusting his gaiters, until they were all well away. Then he clenched his teeth, crammed his hat down over his ears, and scrambled up on to the saddle. His feet fell quite by accident into the stirrups, and the next instant he was off after the others, with an indistinct feeling that he was on a locomotive that was

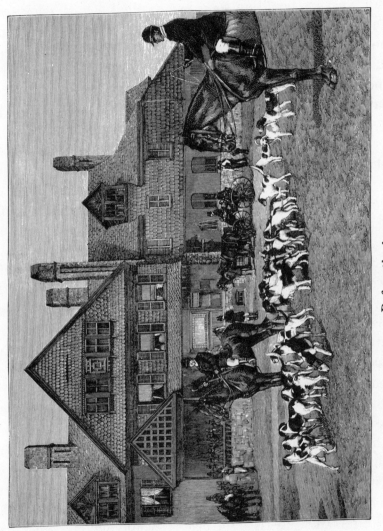

Before the hunt.
MR. TRAVERS'S FIRST HUNT

jumping the ties. Satan was in among and had passed the other horses in less than five minutes, and was so close on the hounds that the whippers-in gave a cry of warning. But Travers could as soon have pulled a boat back from going over the Niagara Falls as Satan, and it was only because the hounds were well ahead that saved them from having Satan ride them down. Travers had taken hold of the saddle with his left hand to keep himself down, and sawed and swayed on the reins with his right. He shut his eyes whenever Satan jumped, and never knew how he happened to stick on; but he did stick on, and was so far ahead that no one could see in the misty morning just how badly he rode. As it was, for daring and speed he led the field, and not even young Paddock was near him from the start. There was a broad stream in front of him, and a hill just on its other side. No one had ever tried to take this at a jump. It was considered more of a swim than anything else, and the hunters always crossed it by the bridge, towards the left. Travers saw the bridge and tried to jerk Satan's head in that direction; but Satan kept right on as straight as an express train over the prairie. Fences and trees and furrows passed by and under Travers like a panorama run by electricity, and he only breathed by accident. They went on at the stream and the hill beyond as though they were riding at a stretch of turf, and, though the whole field set up a shout of warning and dismay, Travers could only gasp and shut his eyes. He remembered the fate of the second groom and shivered. Then the horse rose like a rocket, lifting Travers so high in the air that he thought Satan would never come down again; but he did come down, with his feet bunched, on the opposite side of the stream. The next instant he was up and over the hill, and had stopped panting in the very center of the pack that were snarling and snapping around the fox. And then Travers showed that he was a thoroughbred, even though he could not ride, for he hastily fumbled for his cigar-case, and when the field came pounding up over the bridge and around the hill, they saw him seated nonchalantly on his saddle, puffing critically at a cigar and giving Satan patronizing pats on the head.

"My dear girl," said old Mr. Paddock to his daughter as they rode back, "if you love that young man of yours and want to keep him, make him promise to give up riding. A more reckless and more brilliant horseman I have never seen. He took that double jump at the gate and that stream like a centaur. But he will break his neck sooner or later, and he ought to be stopped." Young Paddock was so delighted with his prospective brother-in-law's great riding that that night in the smoking-room he made him a present of Satan before all the men.

"No," said Travers, gloomily, "I can't take him. Your sister has asked me to give up what is dearer to me than anything next to herself, and that is my riding. You see, she is absurdly anxious for my safety, and she has asked me to promise never to ride again, and I have given my word."

A chorus of sympathetic remonstrance rose from the men.

"Yes, I know," said Travers to her brother, "it is rough, but it just shows what sacrifices a man will make for the woman he loves."

RAKUSH AND HIS MASTER

by James Baldwin

"A horse whereon the governor doth ride."

—Measure for Measure

RUSTEM was eight years old when his grandfather, the mightiest of all the princes of Iran, came up out of Seistan to see him. For the old man had heard that the boy excelled all others in stature and beauty, and the fame of his strength was known throughout the whole of Persia. At the head therefore of a splendid retinue of warriors, the aged prince set out for Zaboulistan, the home of Rustem and his noble father, the white-headed Zal. When he was yet a day's journey from the city, the young boy, mounted on an elephant of war and accompanied by a cavalcade of lords and nobles, went out to meet him.

As the long line of riders wound through the defiles of the mountains or passed in orderly array across the plains, it presented a picture of splendor and beauty which even in the gorgeous East has seldom been surpassed. The young prince's bodyguard, mounted on coal-black steeds, rode in advance. They were armed with golden maces and with battle-axes that gleamed like silver, and they carried the red banner of the house of Zal. Then followed the elephants, upon whose backs were the nobility of Zaboulistan seated in howdahs decked with curtains of embroidered silk and ornamented with flags and waving plumes. After these came a thousand young men, the flower of the land of Iran, riding on horseback, with swords at their sides and long spears resting upon their saddlebows. The march, however, was enlivened with music and song, and nothing was left undone that would give pleasure to the boy or add to the sincerity of the welcome which was to be accorded to the ruler of Seistan.

When at length Rustem saw his grandfather's caravan a long way off he bade his own retinue stand still, while he, dismounting from his elephant, went forward on foot. And when he drew near and could look into the face of the old prince he bowed his head to the ground, and cried out, "O mighty ruler of Seistan, and prince of princes in Iran, I am Rustem, thy grandchild! Give me, I pray thee, thy blessing, ere I return to my father's house."

The aged man was astonished, for he saw that not the half had been told him concerning the boy's stature and grace. He commanded his elephant to kneel while he descended and lifted him up, and blessed him, and placed him in the howdah beside him; and the two rode side by side into Zaboulistan.

"For more than a hundred years," said the grandfather, "have I been the chief of the princes of Iran, and at no time has any one arisen to dispute my will. Yet never have my eyes been gladdened as now. I am an old, old man, and you are only a child; but you shall soon sit on my throne, and enjoy the pleasures which have been mine, and wield the power both in your father's kingdom and in my own."

"I am glad," answered Rustem, "that I can call you my grandfather. But I care nothing at all for pleasure, and I never think of play, or rest, or sleep. What I want most of all things is a horse of my own, and a hard saddle such as the Turanian riders use, and a coat of mail and a helmet like those your warriors have. Then with my lance and my arrows, which I already can use quite well, I will vanquish the enemies of Iran, and my courage shall be like yours and my father's."

This speech pleased the old prince very much, and he blessed Rustem again and promised him that as soon as he should reach the ordinary stature of a man he should have his wish. During the whole of his stay in Zaboulistan he wanted the boy to be always with him, nor did he care to see any one else. And when at the end of the month messengers came from Seistan with news which obliged him to return, he said to his son, the white-headed Zal: "Remember that when this child's stature is equal to thine he shall have a horse of his own choosing, a hard saddle like that of a Turanian rider, and a coat of mail and a helmet such as we ourselves wear into battle. And forget not this my last command."

"And see, father," said Rustem, "am I not now almost as tall as you?"

Zal smiled and promised that he would remember.

But before Rustem reached the stature of his father, the good prince of Seistan had passed from the earth, and Zal, himself an old man, had succeeded to his throne. Then news was brought that a vast army of Turanians, the hereditary foes of Iran, had come down from the north and were threatening to cross the Oxus into Persia. They had even cut in pieces an army which the Shah had sent out against them, and messengers had arrived in Zaboulistan beseeching aid from Zal. Then Rustem begged of his father that he might lead a band of young men against the invaders.

"It is true," said he, "that I am only a child in years. But, although I am not quite so tall as you, my stature is now equal to that of ordinary men; and I am skilled in the use of all kinds of weapons. Give me therefore the steed that was promised me, and the mace of my grandfather, and let me go to the succor of Iran."

These words pleased Zal not a little, and he answered: "O my son, thou art still very young, and thy lips smell of milk, and thy days should be given to play. But the times are full of danger, and Iran must look to thee for help."

Then he at once sent out a proclamation into all the Persian provinces, commanding that on the first day of the approaching Festival of Roses all the choicest horses, of whatsoever breed, should be brought to Zaboulistan in order that Rustem might select from among them his steed of battle. For the one that was chosen, its owner should receive mountains of gold in exchange; but should any man conceal a steed of value, or fail to bring it for the prince's inspection, he should be made to feel the displeasure of the Shah.

On the day appointed, the finest horses in all Persia were assembled at Zaboulistan. The most famous breeders from Cabul and the Afghan pasture lands were there with their choicest stock, and the hill slopes to the south of the city were white with tents. A caravan of low-browed men from the shores of the Caspian had just arrived, weary with their journey, but proud of their horsemanship and of the clean-limbed, swiftly-moving animals which they had brought fresh from the freedom of the steppes, and which they were accustomed to ride at full speed, while standing erect on their saddles. A company of half-wild Tatars, wearing black sheep-skin caps and carrying long spears, were tending a few heavy-built, dark-maned steeds which they had tethered on the plain a mile from the gates. Near them were the tents of a patriarchal sheik who had come from the distant valley of the Euphrates, bringing his numerous family and his large following of servants and herdsmen, and four matchless Arab coursers for which he had already refused more than one princely offer. But the greater number of horses had been brought in by the men of Seistan and the more central districts of Iran, some of whom were encamped outside of the walls while others lodged with friends and acquaintances in the city. Most of

"Fresh from the freedom of the steppes."
RAKUSH AND HIS MASTER

these last had brought only a single animal each, and they had done this not so much for the hope of reward as for the fear of punishment. Every one had brought the best that he had, and I doubt if the world has ever seen a nobler or more wonderful collection of steeds.

At an early hour in the morning the whole city was astir. Everybody both within and without the walls was moving toward the western gate, just outside of which Prince Zal and young Rustem had already taken their stand in order to inspect the animals that would be presented. A troop of armed men was drawn up in such a way as to form a passage through which the competing horses were to be led directly in front of Rustem. On the top of the wall was a covered pavilion from which the ladies of Zaboulistan, without being seen, could look down upon the concourse below. All other available points of view were crowded with a motley rabble of spectators, nearly every one of whom was in some manner directly interested in the choice that was about to be made.

At a given signal, the horses, which had already been brought together at a convenient spot, were led one by one before the prince. The first were those of the Zaboulistan herds, strong, beautiful steeds, many of which had been bred and cared for with the sole thought of their being chosen for the use of Rustem.

"Do you desire swiftness?" asked the keeper of the foremost. "Here is a steed that can outstrip the wind."

"Not swiftness only, but strength," answered Rustem. Then he placed his hand upon the horse to see if it could stand that test; and the animal shuddered beneath his grasp and sank upon its haunches from the strength of the pressure. Thus it fared with all the steeds that were brought forward—with those from Seistan as well as those from the steppes of the Caspian; with those from the plains of the Oxus, as well as those from the mountain valleys of Kandahar.

"Do you want a perfect steed?" asked the long-bearded sheik from the west. "If so, here are beauty, and strength, and swiftness, and intelligence, all combined in one." And he led forward the largest of his magnificent Arabs.

There was a murmur of admiration from all the lookers-on, for seldom, in that land of beautiful horses, had an animal been seen which was in every way so perfect. Rustem said nothing, but quietly subjected the steed to the same test that he had applied to the others. Lastly, the traders from Cabul brought forward a herd of ten which they had carefully selected as the strongest from among all that had been bred in the Afghan pastures. But every one of them quailed beneath Rustem's iron hand.

"Whose is that mare that feeds on the plain beyond your tents?" asked Rustem. "And whose is the colt that follows after her? I see no marks on its flanks."

"We do not know," answered the men from Cabul. "But they have followed us all the way from the Afghan valleys, and we have been unable either to drive them back or to capture them. We have heard it said, however, that men call the colt Rakush, or Lightning, and that although it has now been three years ready for the saddle, its mother defends it and will let no one touch it."

The colt was a beautiful animal. Its color was that of rose leaves scattered upon a saffron ground, its chest and shoulders were like those of a lion, and its eyes beamed with the fire of intelligence. Snatching a lariat from the hands of a herdsman, Rustem ran quickly forward and threw the noose over the animal's head. Then followed a terrible battle, not so much with the colt as with its mother. But in the end Rustem was the winner, and the mare retired crestfallen from the field. With a great bound the young prince leaped upon Rakush's back, and the rose-colored steed bore him over the plains with the speed of the wind. But when the animal had become thoroughly tired, he turned at a word from his master and went quietly back to the city gate.

"This is the horse that I choose," said Rustem to his father. "Let us give to the Afghan herdsmen the prize that is due."

"Nay," answered the herdsmen; "if thou be Rustem, take him and save Iran from its foes. For his price is the land of Iran, and, seated upon him, no enemy can stand before thee."

And that is the way in which Rustem won his war steed.

To relate all the adventures of Rakush and his master—how they led the men of Iran against the Turanians, how they alone put whole armies to flight, how they vanquished the Deevs in their mountain fastnesses, and how they extended the dominions of the Shah from the sea to the great salt plains—would alone fill a volume. Their names were known throughout the length and breadth of Iran, and so inseparable were they that one was never mentioned save in connection with the other. It will be enough if I relate a single one of their adventures.

It chanced upon a time that the great Shah conceived the foolish plan of conquering Mazinderan and obliging the king of that country to pay him tribute. But the small army which he led was utterly defeated by the forces of Mazinderan, and he himself, being taken prisoner, was thrown into a dungeon where the light of day was never seen. Nevertheless, with the aid of one of his keepers, he contrived to write and send a letter to Prince Zal of Zaboulistan. After narrating all his misfortunes he said:

"I have sought what the foolish seek, and I have found what the foolish find. And if thou wilt not speedily send me help I shall surely perish."

When Zal received this letter he was much troubled, and he gnawed his very fingertips for vexation. For the Shah's expedition had been undertaken contrary to his advice. Yet he called to Rustem and said: "See how our lord the Shah has been vanquished by his enemies. It has happened just as I told him, and yet it behooves us to send him aid. Saddle Rakush, therefore, and cast your leopard skin about you, and hasten by the nearest route to the deliverance of Iran's ruler."

"It is well, my father," said Rustem. "My sword is ready, and I will ride alone into Mazinderan. And if fortune favor me I will retrieve the losses that have been suffered there."

The he mounted Rakush and set out by the shortest road across the Great Salt Desert that lies toward Mazinderan; and such was the speed of the good horse that in twelve hours they accomplished a journey of more than two days. Late in the evening Rustem dismounted, and having taken the saddle from the horse's back, he turned him loose to graze upon the scant herbage. Then he built a fire of dry brush and lay down beside it to rest for the night.

A fierce lion, who had his lair in a cluster of reeds close by, saw the tall man and the rose-colored steed, and crept forward to attack them. Rakush heard him coming and hastened to meet him; and before the lion could make a spring, the horse leaped upon him and beat him down with his hoofs and stamped upon him till he died. Rustem, awakened by the great noise, sprang to his feet only in time to see the dead lion upon the ground, and the horse still trampling upon him. He was angry that Rakush instead of himself had slain the beast, and instead of praising the faithful animal he scolded him unmercifully.

"O rash and foolish steed!" he cried, "who told you to fight with lions? You should have awakened me at the first, for had you been killed in your folly, who would have carried me into Mazinderan?"

Then he lay down again to sleep; but the horse was much grieved by his unkind words.

At the first peep of dawn Rustem was again in the saddle. All day long he rode over the barren wastes where there was no green thing nor anywhere a drop of water. The hot sun beat pitilessly down upon man and horse, and the sand beneath them was like a burning oven. At length Rustem was so overcome by the heat and with thirst that he lost all hope, and alighting from his steed lay down in the sand to die. But while he was commending his soul to God and expecting that every moment would be the last, he chanced to see a fine sheep running at no great distance.

"Surely," thought he, "there must be water not far away, or this animal could not be here."

The hope gave him new courage, and remounting Rakush, he urged him forward in pursuit of the sheep. Nor did they have to follow it far, for it led them into a narrow green valley, through the middle of which ran a little brook. And man and beast drank their fill, and while Rustem gave thanks to Ormuzd for their deliverance, Rakush nipped the fresh herbage that grew along the banks of the stream. When at length the sun had set and the stars had risen, Rustem lay down to sleep. But first he charged his steed that he should not fight with any wild beasts.

"If any danger come," said he, "you must waken me at once, and I will defend both myself and you."

Rakush listened to his master's words, and then returned quietly to his grazing. All went well until near midnight, when a fierce dragon which lived in that valley, coming out of his den, was astonished to see the horse feeding and a man asleep not far away. Angry that any one should intrude upon his domain, he was just ready to rush upon them and destroy them with his poisonous breath, when Rakush, seeing the danger, hastened to awaken his master. At the sound of the horse's shrill neighing Rustem sprang up quickly and seized his sword, expecting to meet an enemy. But the wily dragon had hastened back into his den, and no cause of fear could be seen in all the valley.

"Unkind steed that you are," cried Rustem, angrily, "why do you thus needlessly disturb my sleep?"

Then he lay down again to rest. Soon the dragon came out a second time, fiercer than before, and a second time did Rakush awaken his master in vain. A third time did this happen, and a fourth, and then Rustem could no longer restrain his anger. He heaped reproaches upon the horse and abused him with vile epithets, and declared that if his slumbers were again disturbed thus uselessly, he would kill him and make his way on foot into Mazinderan. Rakush was in great distress, and yet he was as watchful as before. When the dragon came out the fifth time he hastened quickly to waken his master. Rustem, filled with rage, sprang up and seized his sword, intending to slay his best friend. But this time he saw the dragon ere it could return to its den, and there followed such a battle as had never been seen before. The dragon leaped upon Rustem and wrapped itself about him, and would surely have crushed him to death had not Rakush come to the rescue. With his teeth the horse seized the reptile from behind, and as it turned to defend itself, Rustem's arm was freed so that he could use his sword. With one mighty stroke he cut off the dragon's head; and the vile pest of the desert was no more. Then Rustem praised Rakush for his valor, and washed him in the stream, and fondled him until the break of day; and the horse forgot the unkind words which had been spoken to him. And when the sun arose they set out on another day's journey across the burning sands.

But, I need not follow them farther on their perilous way, nor relate what befell them in the land of the magicians and in the country of darkness, where there was no light of sun or stars, and where they were guided by Rakush's instinct alone. Neither will I tell of their adventures after they had come into Mazinderan, nor how, after meeting innumerable dangers, they delivered the Shah from his dungeon, and rallied his scattered army and led it to victory. These things are narrated in the songs of Firdusi, the Persian poet.

Never in all the East was there a hero that could be likened unto Rustem, and never a horse that could in any way be compared with Rakush. Many years passed by— years of peace and years of war—and many Shahs sat upon the throne of Iran; but the real power was in the hands of Rustem of Zaboulistan. And although he lived to a great age, and Rakush was so very, very old that he was no longer of the color of rose leaves, but white as the snow of winter, yet both of them retained their strength and their wisdom to the end. And the end came in this way:

The king of Cabul had become tired of paying tribute to Rustem, and he resolved, if possible, to bring about the old hero's death, and thus free himself from that burden. Hence, by the advice of his nobles, he invited Rustem to visit him in his country palace, where they could spend the summer months in hunting and in other amusements of which both of them were fond. Rustem suspected no guile, for he had enjoyed the king's hospitality many times before. He therefore accepted the invitation, and with Rakush and a retinue of his noblest men arrived in due time at the king's summer home. The king had prepared a royal welcome for him, and for several days they feasted together and made merry in the palace. Then a great hunt in the forest was proposed, and to this Rustem gladly

Rakush.
RAKUSH AND HIS MASTER

consented, because, next to feats of courage in battle, he loved the excitement of the chase.

It was known that there were many wild animals in the mountain valleys, and the company set out from the palace with high expectations—for but few of the guests suspected the dark designs of the king. All went well until the afternoon, and much game of all kinds was taken. At length a deer was started from its covert, and all the party gave chase. But Rustem, through the king's designing, followed a different pathway from that taken by the others—a pathway across which deep pits had been dug and then carefully concealed with leaves and sod. Huntsmen had been stationed here and there to direct Rustem into the snare, and he rode fearlessly onward, looking for nothing except traces of the fleeing deer. When they came to the first pit, Rakush smelled the newly turned soil and stopped suddenly. Rustem urged him to go forward, but the horse, for the first time in his long life, refused to obey. Then Rustem, growing impatient, urged him still harder, but he reared upon his hind feet and tried to turn back. This aroused Rustem's anger, and raising his whip he struck the faithful beast—a thing that until this sad day had never been done. So grieved and terrified was Rakush that he sprang forward and fell into the pit, and both horse and rider were pierced with the sharp spears which projected, points upward, from the bottom.

As they lay weltering in their blood and dying, the King of Cabul came up, and seeing their plight, pretended to be overcome with grief.

"O matchless hero," he cried to Rustem, "what mishap is this which has befallen thee? I will run and call my physicians to come to thy aid."

But Rustem answered: "Thou traitor, this is thy doing. The time for physicians is past, and there is for me no healing save that of death, which comes once to all men! I pray thee, however, to place beside me my bow and two arrows, and deny not this my last request. For I would not that while thou art calling a physician a lion should come upon me and devour me."

Without taking thought, the king did as Rustem desired; but he had no sooner placed the bow within the hero's reach than, filled with fear, he ran and hid himself in a hollow tree which stood close by. Rustem in great agony raised the bow, and with his last strength shot an arrow with such force that it transfixed the king where he stood and pinned him to the tree. Then the hero gave thanks to Ormuzd the Good, that he had been permitted thus to take vengeance upon the traitor. And when he had spoken he fell back upon his horse, and Rakush and his master, in the same moment, passed from the world.

Yearlings at play.
EARLY RECOLLECTIONS

EARLY RECOLLECTIONS

from *Memoirs of a Cow Pony*

by John H. Burns

I am just a common yellow cow pony. Since I was four years old I have been a saddler on the ranges of Texas, and the trails over which the vast herds of long-horned Texas and Mexican cattle are moved to the ranges of the Dakotas, Montana and Wyoming. I am now owned by the TU brand; at least that is the last brand which has been burned on my hide.

My present master—and I want to say here that a kinder one I have never had—tells me that I have earned my retirement. By that, I guess he means I am not to be called upon to do much more hard work.

Many times my master has told me that if I would just give to the public my experiences in life, and my observations of ponies and men, it would be of great interest, and might be of benefit to ponykind, but I would answer to him that I had neither seen nor done anything worth recording.

"Just tell, Buck," he said, "from your pony viewpoint, what a cow pony and a cowboy should be, and how the former should be broken to work, also how he should be treated thereafter. Thus you may do to ponykind a great service."

I hesitated. There are incidents—one at least—in my life which I shrank from even thinking of, and to relate it to the world, I had not the courage.

Finally, one black night when I was carrying my master

out of the Hay Creek brakes, he asked me again, and I yielded.

The moaning of the wind in the tops of the ragged, stunted pines told that a storm was coming, and we hurried to reach level ground, but the double darkness of a stormy night smote us full in the face.

While we were still in the brakes, the trail, none too plain at the best, wound around the heads of yawning canyons, down dangerously steep declivities, over and across obstructions, all requiring the utmost care on my part to avoid accident. Strange shapes of beasts, obscure and ghostly, scurried across our way, seeking the shelter of remoter regions. Whether these were the shapes of harmless or of those stronger and more savage animals which at times dragged down the strongest cattle on the range, we could not tell.

The snow swirled up out of the canyons in strangling gusts. It struck and froze on the eye lashes and choked the nostrils.

Nose to the ground, mainly by the smell of the light trail, and its feel under my feet, I slowly worked out the problem, and when at length the ranchhouse light flared in our faces, it was warmly welcomed by two thoroughly tired and chilled people, master and I.

Master was grateful to me for bringing him safely home. His wet right hand sought my cold neck and stroked it.

"Buck, old faithful," he said and there was a quiver in his voice, "you must tell me your life story, I will write it out, and we'll be partners in the deal."

I stopped stock still there in the storm and the night. Master let me stand, for he knew I was thinking. The past with all its lights and shadows unrolled itself before me in a flash, and I thought: "A pony who has lived through what I have should have the courage to look the world in the face and tell the truth, and I will relate a true story of a common cow pony, a life such as many thousands have lived and are living today, and no incident will be set forth which has not actually occurred, for it must be a true record.

My earliest recollection is of blinding light and a gasping for breath. I was cold and shivery. My mother was standing over me. She fondled, petted and helped me to get upon my feet. When I had done this I was weak and trembly, and I think I was not very pretty to look at then. After mother had given me my first dinner I felt better, and the warm, caressing Texas sun beat down upon and warmed me. Weak and wobbly as I was, I wanted to run and play, but when I tried to do this my mother ran with me and kept me off the rough and dangerous places, and coaxed me and led me up a hill onto a wide sweep of tableland.

I was nothing but a little filmy-eyed baby pony; my legs too long for my body, and I would follow another as readily as I would my own mother. She had to watch me all the time to keep me from getting into trouble. Of course, I was too young to appreciate the extreme beauty of the landscape, but from the standpoint of a pony, it was a paradise. As far as my eyes could reach was the billowy expanse of upland, with the grass shimmering and waving in the sunlight.

The whole landscape was dotted with ponies, idlers all. Some lay stretched out groaning in an excess of comfort and contentment, others grazed, some played, all were having the good time of their lives.

When I was four days old I felt that I was quite a horse, and I joined the other colts in their mild races and sports. Mother told me that now I could run as fast as I would be able to at four years of age. It is many a wild race I ran at four years old, and it is a fact that my little soft yellow hoofs as a four-day-old could clip off a short quarter as fast as I have even been able to do since.

Our range was the Staked plains of Texas. Over this we wandered as we would, with no care, nothing to do but eat, drink and frolic. That was a sweet summer; the responsibilities of life, its labors and sufferings were undreamed of by us youngsters.

Occasionally an old broken-down cow pony would come among us and we would laugh at and josh him shamefully. If I had my life to live over again, I would be kinder to those old fellows.

We had our little tragedies, it is true, during that first summer. Sometimes the great gray wolves would sweep the range. They came in packs, vicious, snarling, poisonous, hunting for us colts. Then there would be a mad rush of colts to a common center. We grew crazy with fear and crowded in behind and among our mothers, who fought for us and charged into the midst of the pack, biting and kicking, and protecting us at the risk of their own lives, until the dawn drove the coward brutes to cover. One strange thing I noticed was that if any colt was bitten, ever so slightly, the colt died, but a grown horse or a cow would recover from severe wounds.

That precious first summer passed, winter came; the grass dried up and blew away: icy cold winds beat upon us; snow storms swept the Mesa, and life became one continuous struggle for existence. We sought such natural shelter as we could find and there we would huddle together in piteous misery until the storm had passed. We grew thinner and thinner; many of my playmates and friends died. I, too, would have died but for the devotion of my mother.

Grass came again and I fattened. The memory of a pony colt is not a long memory, and soon I forgot the dangers and sufferings of the past winter and romped again with my fellows. Up to this time I had seen no animals save the wild beasts of the plains, long horned cattle and my own kind. If I thought at all at this time, it was to think that the "Mesa" on which we ranged was all there was of the world, that where the waving grass tops touched the sky was the end and that we ponies owned it. We suffered the cattle to stay about there and scorned them all the time, simply because it was too much trouble to chase them away. As for the wild beasts, we tolerated them because we couldn't help it.

Finally, there came to me and my young friends a sudden and stern awakening to the fact that we did not own the world. One bright morning I was running a few races with some young friends, when we saw a most amazing sight. A dozen or more ponies, at a long easy canter were coming over the brow of the "Mesa," and on the back of each was a big, strange looking and homely thing. In wild affright we ran into the thickest of the herd. I hunted up mother and asked her what these things were.

"My son, those are cowboys," she answered.

"And what are cowboys, mother?"

"My son, cowboys are our masters. They are the masters of all things, and you must learn to like them."

The other and older ponies laughed at me, and said that I would soon find out.

The "cowboys," as mother called them, circled around us and gradually moved us toward a great round corral into which we were driven; then they made a great fire into which they put a lot of irons. Of course I did not know what all this meant, but I was soon to find out.

I hugged close to mother's side, scared and in fear that I was to be hurt. I was!

Soon the cowboys rode into the corral, swinging long ropes. I started to run across the corral, but one of them threw his rope, and although I jumped as high as I could to keep out of the way, he caught me by the forelegs and threw me to the ground. Then another jumped off his pony and ran up and sat down on my head. Still another ran in with one of the hot irons and burned upon my hide my first brand, which was the letters BXB. I thought they were burning my whole hip off, but they were not, and the pain was as nothing to what came after. The man who sat on my head kept me from seeing, holding me so tight that I could scarcely move. Then someone cut and mutilated me dreadfully. When they let me go I sprang to my feet, dizzy and blind from pain; I staggered and fell, but they only laughed at me and struck me with a rope and said:

"Get out, Buck!"

This was the first time I had heard my name spoken. It was many weeks before I was well, and for a long time after this I thought that men were fiends who lived only to make life a burden, an agony and a shame to ponies, but as I grew older, I found that there were a few men who are not so cruel.

My present master is all that a just, generous and considerate master should be.